Stephen Watson Fullom

The Life of General Sir Howard Douglas, Bart.

From His Notes, Conversations, and Correspondence

Stephen Watson Fullom

The Life of General Sir Howard Douglas, Bart.
From His Notes, Conversations, and Correspondence

ISBN/EAN: 9783337094591

Printed in Europe, USA, Canada, Australia, Japan

Cover: Foto ©Raphael Reischuk / pixelio.de

More available books at **www.hansebooks.com**

THE LIFE

OF

GENERAL SIR HOWARD DOUGLAS,

BART.,

G.C.B., G.C.M.G., F.R.S., D.C.L.

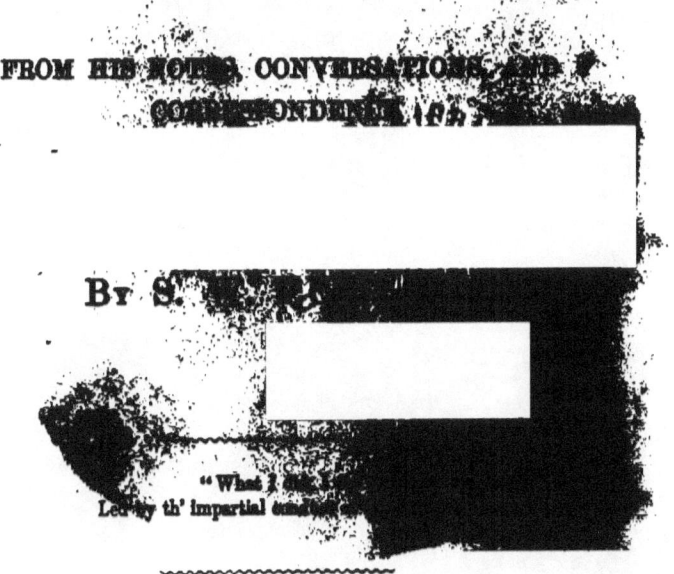

FROM HIS NOTES, CONVERSATIONS, AND CORRESPONDENCE.

By S

" What I ...
Le... ty th' impartial ...

LONDON:

JOHN MURRAY, ALBEMARLE STREET.

1863.

PREFACE.

THE materials for the Life of Sir Howard Douglas consist of his despatches, letter-books, and corre-spondence, with some notes of his early career, some detached minutes, and two pocket-books referring to his services in Spain. The last have supplied links in the narrative of his proceedings given in his despatches and letters, and made it very clear to one acquainted with the incidents of his life from his own lips. Every facility has been afforded for the work by Major-General Sir R. Percy Douglas, Bart., Captain Douglas, R.N., the Rev. W. F. Douglas, and the ladies of the family, but no responsibility attaches to them for its mode of execution or expressions of opinion, which are chargeable to the author alone.

The author has been honoured with Her Majesty's permission to include in the work a letter addressed to Sir Howard Douglas by His Royal Highness Prince Alfred, and one of many he received from His Royal Highness the Duke of Kent.

Liberty of publication has also been given to him by the Duke of Wellington, K.G., the Earl of Derby, K.G., Lord Raglan, and other personages concerned

b

in Sir Howard's correspondence.   This licence has n ot
been sought where the letters are not of a private
character, or in cases where the writers are dead.

The author has to express thanks for obliging com-
munications to Generals Sir William Gomm, Sir
Robert Gardiner, Sir Hew Ross, Sir James Simpson ,
and General Forbes ; to Lieut.-General Sir Frederick
Smith, M.P., the Chaplain General, Colonel Basil
Jackson, Colonel Fitzmayer, R.A., the Rev. Jonathan
Cape, F.R.S., the Rev. Edwin Jacob, D.D., of Maple-
down, New Brunswick, Quartermaster Connolly, R.E.,
W. Bateman, Esq., of Folkestone, Walter F reeth
Esq., and Rowland Richardson, Esq.

Tudor Villa, Surbiton,
        January 14, 1863.

CONTENTS.

b 2

viii

APPENDIX.

LIFE

OF

SIR HOWARD DOUGLAS.

CHAPTER I.

THE name of Douglas is familiar to English ears, and none is more famous in Scotland. It has figured in tale and history there from the days of tradition, when we are told of its being won by the "black-grey man" who came to the rescue of the King's lieutenant in a battle with a pirate chief. Our own great poet has celebrated the

> " Renowned Douglas, whose high deeds,
> Whose hot incursions, and great name in arms,
> Holds from all soldiers chief majority,
> And military title capital,
> Through all the kingdoms that acknowledge Christ."

And there is hardly one of Scotland's bards who has not touched on the same theme.

The family became allied to the Scottish crown by the marriage of the Lord of Dalkeith with the Lady Mary, fifth daughter of James I., and sister of James II. ; and the latter monarch created his brother-in-law Earl of Morton. The title descended from father to son through three generations, when King James V. seized James, the third Earl, and imprisoned him in Inverness Castle until he consented to

B

entail it on Robert Douglas of Lochlevin, whom the King wished to console for having a little disturbed his wedding by carrying off the bride. But nothing was gained by the motion, as he died before the Earl, and no sooner lay in his grave than Morton abjured the arrangement, and executed a new deed, entailing the title on the husband of his second daughter—James Douglas, brother of David Earl of Angus, and Lord Chancellor and Regent of Scotland during the minority of James VI.—who became fourth Earl of Morton. This nobleman was succeeded by his nephew, Archibald Douglas Earl of Angus, from whom the title of Morton passed by the entail to William Douglas of Lochlevin, who was descended from the first Earl, and made the sixth inheritor of his honours.

Another sixth generation threatened the earldom with a new diversion, as it was now borne by an old man, apparently determined on dying a bachelor. But the twelfth hour brought him to better thoughts, and he fell in love with a beauty who enabled him to leave his title to a son. This shut out the next branch of the family, represented by young Charles Douglas, who had come almost within reach of the coronet, being the lineal descendant of Sir George Douglas of Kirkness, second son of Earl William of Lochlevin, and hence presumptive heir. But Fortune made up for the slip by designing him to win honours of his own; and these lost none of their lustre on descending to his son HOWARD DOUGLAS, whose career forms the subject of this volume.

Charles Douglas ran his course in the navy, which he entered as a child, passing through the successive grades of rank until he appears in command of a frigate—at one time taking part in the naval operations on the coast of America during the War of Independence, and afterwards capturing prizes in the Channel. Subsequently he was employed in organizing the navy of Russia, on the recommendation of the British Government; and he succeeded in placing it on a good footing, when he returned to England. His reputation now stood so high that the Admiralty selected him to command a squadron for the relief of Quebec, which the Americans had besieged, and were exerting every means to reduce. Its capture would entail the loss of Canada if not of our whole dominion in America, and the public were in the greatest alarm at the danger, as the closing of the St. Lawrence seemed to cut off assistance. But the panic abated on the announcement that the succours to be sent out were intrusted to Captain Douglas, who was known to be familiar with the American waters, and had established a character for energy and action which inspired confidence. The general feeling is reflected in a letter addressed to him on the occasion by Lord Townshend.

"The day before I left town to bring my family out of the country," writes his Lordship, "I asked either Lord George Germain or Lord Sandwich (I think it was the former) who went up the river with the relief? and was told it was you. I replied, 'I am glad you have fixed on so good a man. You cannot inquire better upon all occasions after the river St. Lawrence than from him. He will tell you as much as Mr. Cooke [1] or any one else.'"

---

[1] Probably the celebrated Captain Cook.

Captain Douglas worked day and night to hasten the equipment of the ships, and the Admiralty urged him to even greater exertion. "For God's sake, get the 'Isis' down to Blackstakes the next spring-tide," writes Lord Sandwich, the First Lord. "Your being ready to leave early in February is of the utmost importance to the public service. I think the fate of Quebec depends upon it."

The squadron sailed at the appointed time, and the beginning of April found it on the coast of Newfoundland, waiting for the break up of the ice to make for the St. Lawrence. But Captain Douglas was not content to wait long. There seemed no prospect of the navigation opening, and he knew that Quebec must be in the last extremity, as it had now been invested some months, and subjected to repeated assaults. It occurred to him that he might drive his ship through the ice, and he took advantage of a rising gale to put her before the wind, and run against a block twelve feet thick as an experiment. The shock had a greater effect than he expected, crumbling the ice in pieces. "We now," he says in his despatch to Mr. Stephens, "thought it an enterprise worthy of an English ship of the line in our King and country's sacred cause, and an effort due to the gallant defence of Quebec, to make the attempt of pressing her by force of sail through the thick, broad, and closely-connected fields of ice (as formidable as the Gulf of St. Lawrence ever exhibited), to which we saw no bounds." The frozen tract was found to extend for sixty leagues; but he persevered in his design, unde-terred by gales and snow-storms and innumerable perils and accidents, and nine days of unwearied labour brought the ship to open water. Here she was joined by the 'Surprise' and 'Martin,' which had followed in her track; and the little squadron entered the St. Lawrence under a heavy fall of snow. On the 3rd of May it ran into the basin of Quebec, and was received with acclamations; the ships lowered their boats and landed the reinforcements under cover of their guns, while General Carleton made a sortie with the garrison, and drove the besiegers from their works. The siege was raised in an instant; the British flag waved over the heights, and Canada was saved.

The Americans still held Lake Champlain, where they kept a flotilla, which gave them command of the shore. But Captain Douglas considered his work but half done while they retained this advantage. He had brought from England the framework of a sloop prepared at his suggestion, and he put her together at St. John's, and launched her on the lake. She was armed with eighteen guns, and he provided her a consort in a schooner, carrying fourteen, and remarkable for her speed. Both vessels were completed within six weeks; and his exertions were so unremitting that the same time sufficed to equip a flotilla equal to the enemy's, comprising thirty vessels mounting cannon, as many flat-bottomed boats, and a gondola of thirty tons, with four hundred bâteaux. These he caused to be transported overland, then had them dragged up the rapids of Theresa and St. John's, and assembled them on the lake, under the command of Captain Pringle, who hoisted a commodore's pendant in the 'Maria,' and advanced on the enemy.

The anxiety and harass of the undertaking were repaid by success. The American flotilla was brought to bay after a chace of several days, and every vessel destroyed, the few that escaped sinking being driven ashore. This victory cleared the lakes, and completed the liberation of Canada, which obtained for Captain Douglas the approbation of the King, who rewarded his services by the gift of a baronetcy.

The experience he acquired in the preparation of the flotilla developed a mechanical turn, and this led to his suggesting improvements in ships of war, both in equipment and construction. He originated the principle of a false keel, the use of locks, and the allotment of heavier guns to the quarter-deck of three-deckers, —all of which were adopted by the Admiralty.[1]

His activity excited the wonder of his Russian friends, as they were aware that the death of a relative had brought him an independence, and he had refused the most tempting offers to remain in Russia. Admiral Greig writes to him from St. Petersburg in 1777: "I have just been dining with Count Panim, who inquired after you with professions of great esteem and regard. He said he was surprised to find that you still served at home, after having declined service here, from the easy and affluent fortune bequeathed to you. I told him I did not imagine any change of fortune or circumstances would make you decline the service of your native country, whenever your services were required."

His friend had justly estimated his character, for the sequel proved that he was now only in the middle of his career. On the 23rd of July, 1778, he commanded the 'Stirling Castle' in Admiral Keppel's

---

[1] The facts are shown in a series of letters in the 'Douglas Papers,' addressed to him by Sir Charles Middleton.

engagement with the French fleet under Count
d'Orvilliers, and went into action with the van.   But
that engagement opened no way to distinction, and it
was not till he was appointed Captain of the Fleet to
Sir George Rodney that he found an opportunity of
displaying his genius.   The fleet of Count de Grasse
came in sight on the 8th of April, 1782, and kept the
British Admiral to leeward for three days, though he
exerted all his seamanship to bring on an action.
Maintaining the chace, his fast sailers drew so near,
that they compelled De Grasse to relinquish the
weather-gauge; but hardly had he done so, when a
change of wind gave it to him again, and Rodney
perceived that he must either engage him to leeward
or allow him to escape.   There could be no doubt as
to the course for a British Admiral in such a situation, and a signal from the 'Formidable' directed
the 'Marlborough' to lead along the lee of the French
line, with the view of bringing on a general action.
The 'Marlborough' was followed by the van of the
British squadron, until it became apparent that the
course of the 'Formidable' pointed directly through
an opening in the centre of the French fleet.   This
suggested to Sir Charles Douglas one of the boldest
manœuvres ever practised in naval warfare, and he
urged the Admiral to cut the enemy's line in two by
piercing his centre.   The incident is related in a letter
from Admiral Sir Charles Dashwood in the 'Douglas
Papers :' [1]—

   " I shall simply relate facts, to which I was an eye-
witness, and can vouch for their truth.   Being one of

---

[1] The letter has been printed in Sir Howard Douglas's 'Naval Evolutions.'

the aides-de-camp to the Commander-in-Chief on that
memorable day, it was my duty to attend both on
him and the Captain of the Fleet, as occasion might
require.   It so happened that some time after the
battle had commenced, and whilst we were warmly
engaged, I was standing near Sir Charles Douglas,
who was leaning on the hammocks (which in those
days were stowed across the fore part of the quarter-
deck), his head resting on one hand, and his eye
occasionally glancing on the enemy's line, and apparently in deep meditation as if some great event
was crossing his mind. Suddenly raising his head,
and turning quickly round, [he] said, 'Dash! where's
Sir George?'   'In the after-cabin, sir,' I replied.
He immediately went aft; I followed, and, on meeting
Sir George coming from the cabin close to the wheel,
he took off his cocked-hat with his right hand, holding
his long spy-glass in his left, making a low and profound bow, said, 'Sir George, I give you joy of the
victory.'   'Poh!' said the chief, as if half-angry,
'the day is not half won yet.'   'Break the line, Sir
George,' said Sir Charles; 'the day is your own, and I
will insure you the victory.'   'No,' said the Admiral,
'I will not break any line.'   After another request,
and another refusal, Sir Charles desired the helm to
be put a-port: Sir George ordered it to starboard.
On Sir Charles ordering it again to port, the Admiral
sternly said, 'Remember, Sir Charles, that I am
Commander-in-Chief; starboard, sir,' addressing the
Master, who, during the controversy, had placed the
helm amidships.   The Admiral and the Captain then
separated; the former going aft, and the latter forward.   In the course of a couple of minutes or so,

each turned and again met on the same spot, when
Sir Charles quietly and coolly again addressed the
chief,—'Only break the line, Sir George, and the day
is your own!'   The Admiral then said in a quick and
hurried way, 'Well, well—do as you like,' and immediately turned round and walked into the after-cabin.
The words 'Port the helm' were scarcely uttered
when Sir Charles ordered me down with directions to
commence firing on the larboard side.   On my return
to the quarter-deck I found the 'Formidable' passing
between two French ships, each nearly touching us.
We were followed by the 'Namur' and the rest of
the ships astern; and from that moment the victory
was decided in our favour." [1]

---

[1] The occurrence is thus narrated by Admiral Count Bouet Willaumez,
in 'Batailles de Terre et de Mer :'—

"C'est le 12 Avril, 1782, que les deux flottes se rencontrent par une
brise variable de l'est au sud-sud-est ; la flotte Française court babord
amures, mais mal formée, et présente des lacunes dans sa ligne ; la flotte
Anglaise l'atteint par sous le vent, à contre-bord, et son avant-garde pro-
longe les vaisseaux Français à distance ; mais, au moment où le vaisseau
'le Formidable,' monté par Rodney, atteint la flotte Française pour la pro-
longer à son tour comme a fait l'avant-garde Anglaise, le vent fraîchit un peu
et adonne de deux quarts : 'Serrez le vent,' dit le Capitaine Douglas, *flag-cap-
tain* de Rodney, au *master*, qui tenait la barre du gouvernail : Rodney veut
d'abord contrarier cet ordre ; mais reconnaissant ensuite qu'il va lui permettre
de couper la ligne Française et de la mettre en désordre, peut-être même
entre deux feux, il s'écrie, au dire de l'historien Anglais Ekins, ' *Then do
it as you please!* ' (Faites donc comme il vous plaira !) Et cependant, dans
ce hasard du vent, dans ces trois mots du Capitaine Douglas, mots incom-
pris d'abord de Rodney, il y avait tout un nouveau système de combats
de mer ; bientôt, en effet, les vaisseaux Anglais 'le Formidable,' 'l'Aga-
memnon,' 'le Duke,' &c., coupent la ligne Française et se répandent, les
uns au large, les autres le long des vaisseaux Français, qu'ils mettent entre
deux feux ; le contre-amiral commandant l'arrière-garde Anglaise, imitant
la manœuvre de Rodney, vient, toujours à contre-bord, couper de nouveau
notre ligne après le dernier vaisseau de notre avant-garde : en vain De
Grasse multiplie ses signaux pour masser au combat sa ligne désemparée
et coupée en trois tronçons ; il est trop tard, la fumée empêche de voir les
signaux."

Little is known of Sir Charles Douglas's domestic life during this period, except that he married a foreign lady, who died about 1770, after she had borne him two sons and a daughter. He subsequently married Miss Wood, the daughter of an old Yorkshire family, and this union brought him another son, born at Gosport on the 23rd of January, 1776, and who received the baptismal name of Howard.

Howard Douglas had reached his third year when he sustained the greatest bereavement that can befall a child, in the death of his mother, though the loss was alleviated by the care of his aunt Helena, wife of James Baillie, Esq., of Olive Bank, near Musselburg. To her care he was now confided, together with his sister and half-brother Charles, and she became the centre of his early recollections. Such a character might leave an impression on natures of the sternest mould, and it is not surprising that one so warm-hearted remembered her fondly, describing her as a gentle, loving, simple, yet shrewd Scottish matron, such as Sir Walter Scott has taught us to venerate. Nor must the fact be omitted that she stood on Sir Walter's list of friends, and was one of his recognised favourites. He always made his way to her in Edinburgh society, if she happened to be present, and nothing could draw him from her side when she opened her " auld world" stories, of which she had no end. The charm may have been the greater from the link of connexion with his own associations, which carried him back to the Regent Morton and the Lady of Lochlevin, whom she lineally represented. " She was a true Helen Douglas," we learn from her nephew, and her worth receives further testimony in his own character, which she helped to form, and so inspired with the chivalrous spirit of his race. And it may have been from her that he derived some of his minor traits, his playful humour, his happy art in story-telling, and his love of music and flowers. The only drawback to Mrs. Baillie's lessons seems to have been the pure Doric in which they were imparted, so clearly marking her nationality that it could not be disguised by her best English. Of this she had proof on one occasion, when she entered a confectioner's shop in London, and addressed herself to the man at the counter, inquiring, "Have you got any sweetmeats for the children?" "Oh, ay, a' got sweeties for the bairns," was the reply, in a somewhat resentful tone. " I did not say sweeties for the bairns," rejoined Mrs. Baillie. "Ay, but ye *suld* have said it," retorted the confectioner, who it is needless to say came from the right side of the Tweed.

Little Howard repaid the love of his aunt with a tender affection which sprang up at once and never declined. An incident of his childhood evinces the existence both of this attachment and of the manliness that marked his character even at that time.

One day his aunt received a visit from a lady who had not seen him before, and she asked Mrs. Baillie who he was, and why he was staying at Musselburg, when he ran forward and answered for himself. " My name is Howard Douglas: my mamma is dead, my papa's at sea, and that's why I am here with my own dear auntie." No one could have better told his history, and his words and air so charmed the lady that she regarded him afterwards with maternal interest.

Much might have been learnt of this period of his life from the correspondence of Mrs. Baillie with her brother, but unfortunately only three of her letters can be found, and but one makes reference to the children in her charge. This was written on the 1st of January, 1782, and Sir Charles sailed from Plymouth on the 2nd, so that it may not have reached his hands till after the great battle of the 12th of April.

"I received yours of the 18th ultimo, from Plymouth, Saturday last. Well do you conceive my anxiety about you at present. Our lovely three [his children] have been to us all this day—all happy and well. Gracious God, grant that their father and protector may be soon and happily restored to them and me again. How happy should I be to see that your only employment was attending to the rearing and educating of those sweet sensible lambs. . . . . Says Howard, 'I will pray for papa,' and Miss in this, as in everything else, 'So will I too.' . . . .

"Mr. Baillie's best compliments of the season, and prays that you may be successful in humbling the pride of the enemies of Great Britain. I send best wishes to my dear William [his eldest son, who accompanied him to sea].

"Remember, my dear Charles, that Lieutenant Congelton of the 'Yarmouth' is cousin to our own beloved now angel mother. Let him know that I have wrote to you about him. Praying for your health and preservation,

"I remain, in haste, my dear Charles,

"Your very indebted and attached sister,

"Helena Baillie."

The tidings of the victory reached Musselburg in the autumn, and were read aloud by Mrs. Baillie to the children, making such an impression on little Howard that he never forgot the scene. From this moment all his aspirations were inspired by the exploits of his father and the thought of himself becoming a sailor. Though not yet emancipated from his nursery governess, he found a never-failing attraction in a pond in the garden, where he could launch and manœuvre his toy ships, which received constant additions from Mrs. Baillie, who knew that his father destined him for the sea, and so encouraged his nautical tastes. Sir Charles paid a visit to his sister during a stay on shore, and was entreated by Howard to go to the pond and review his fleet. He playfully consented, expecting a child's show, and was surprised to find the little vessels set in squadrons with professional skill. The display touched a chord near his heart, and he broke into an exclamation of pleasure, as he recognised his boy as a born tar.

Howard ascended from the governess to a tutor, and subsequently entered the grammar-school, but his chief study was still the same, and he spent every leisure hour on the lake at Fisher Row, where he formed intimacies with fisher-lads, and afterwards with youths belonging to the vessels that frequented the port. Hence he became so initiated in seamanship that he could manage a fishing-boat or a ship's yawl, and often made his escape to sea in one of these craft, to the great alarm of his aunt and dominie.

But an event shortly happened that changed the course of his life, disappointing the aspirations he had formed, and placing him in a new position. In the spring of 1789 Sir Charles Douglas was appointed Commander-in-Chief on a foreign station and hoisted his flag at Portsmouth, when he paid a hasty visit to Scotland, to bring away Howard, and take him on board his own ship to sea.   He arrived at Musselburg in the midst of the excitement caused by the recovery of George III. from his first illness, and intended to take part in the rejoicings, but a sudden attack of illness confined him to his room.   This was not allowed to interfere with the enjoyment of his children, and they went to a juvenile ball at a neighbour's, given in honour of the occasion.   It is indicative of the thoughtful kindness inherent in Howard that he ran over from the dance to see his father several times during the evening.   He found him complaining of pain in the head, and saw that he was disturbed by the glare of the illumination, which he proposed to shut out by darkening the window.   " God forbid that my window should be the first darkened on such a night as this!" said the old Admiral, showing his ruling passion of loyalty strong in death: for these were his last words.   He was seized with apoplexy during the night, and the morning found him dead.

CHAPTER II.

Young Days.

The destiny of Howard Douglas was now in the hands of his guardians, and they judged it inexpedient to carry out his father's design of placing him in the navy, considering that he might interfere with the prospects of his two half-brothers, who were already in the service. Hence they applied to have him nominated for admission into the Royal Academy at Woolwich, without deeming it necessary to consult himself; and he first heard of their plans on being ordered to proceed to Woolwich for examination, in the summer of 1790. He thus began life with the surrender of his ambition; and his sense of disappointment must have been bitter indeed, for he spoke of it to the last. But he yielded without a murmur : it was his first lesson in duty, and he was to prove that duty weighed with him above every other feeling.

There is nothing to show whether his attainments underwent polishing before he left Musselburg as a preparation for the approaching examination; but a voyage to London in a Scotch smack was too fruitful of interest to a spoiled sailor not to efface such instruction if received. He was now actually in a ship at sea, and could help to haul the ropes, and even mount the rigging, while he charmed the sailors by his familiarity with the tackle, and the sublimest nautical phrases.   In fact, he spent those happy days in learning navigation instead of poring over Euclid, and arrived at Woolwich in first-rate order for the midshipman's berth, but not so qualified for the Academy.

Time had been when the gate of the establishment stood wide, and admission was an easy affair.   But in 1773 the Inspector of Instruction came in contact with a young gentleman unacquainted with the alphabet; and it was thought prudent to insist that every candidate should " not only understand reading and writing,"[1] but even the Rule of Three.   From this simple beginning the standard of qualification had advanced until it embraced a certain proficiency in mathematics, and Howard Douglas went up on this test, and was plucked.

The anguish of that moment he never forgot.   He turned away from the examiners with drooping head and a look of despair, conscious only of rejection. But the power which the song declares to sit up aloft watched over the little sailor.   Though turned back, he had displayed the ability opening in his mind; and the mathematical professor told him he was sure to do, and bade him take courage and try again.   It had flashed across him that he might avoid the humiliation of returning disgraced to his friends by running to sea, changing his name, and leaving no clue by which he might be traced.   But those kind words brought him to a clearer perception of his duty, and a belief in his power to succeed.   The courage they

---

[1] Records of the Royal Military Academy.

told him to cherish he had never lost; and the un-
guided boy of thirteen now walked through Woolwich
looking for a competent teacher. His little stock of
money forbade his applying to the expensive grinders
of the town; but it would seem that he already possessed the germ of that insight into character which
marked his maturer years, and he found a skilled
mathematician in the master of an obscure day-school,
whose abilities he was the first to discover. Within
three weeks he again presented himself at the Academy,
and passed the examination in triumph. Six weeks
more found him at the head of the mathematical class;
and he attained such proficiency, that Dr. Hutton
always told any boy in a difficulty to "go to Douglas."
The pupil reciprocated the appreciation of his master,
and ever spoke of him with gratitude; nor can there
be a doubt that he remembered him to the last; for
his biographer found a medallion of Dr. Hutton in the
box containing his latest papers.

The cadets of those days were left great liberty in
their movements, though regulations existed for maintaining discipline, and attempts were continually
made at improvement. It had been found necessary
to ordain that no one should "presume to go out after
tattoo, either *over* the wall or any other way;" but
there would seem to have been no other way, as the
porter locked the gates at tattoo. Another injunction
forbade any cadet to carve his name on the desks, or
to break open the desks or drawers of the Inspectors,
Professors, and Masters; and the regulations went so
far as to add—"or even to attempt to take anything
out of them under the name of smouching;" though
the prefatory "even" seemed to admit this was

C

rather arbitrary. The cadets were cautioned against employing school-hours in reading light works under cover of studying their tasks; and also against throwing stones at the masters, which the regulations declared a capital offence, though they thought it capital fun. The masters themselves came in for admonition; and a manifesto from the Lieutenant-Governor complains that the cadets "are frequently left without either professor or master for the space of half an hour, and sometimes for much longer time, by which neglect they remain totally unoccupied in any study, and are besides, by the absence of the controlling power, led into very disorderly and improper behaviour."[1]

The cadets' barrack stood in the Warren, on a spot since occupied by the buildings of the Royal Arsenal; and Colonel Wilmot has engraved a representation of it as it appeared about 1790. This shows a row of trees in the front, overshadowing a lawn, where a couple of cadets are seen reclining, while they receive the greetings of a third, got up as the beau of the company. He wears a scarlet coat, frilled shirt, and top-boots, arranged to expose striped silk stockings, and has given his arm to another character of the time, a lackadaisical-looking youth, known as the "ladies' man." This group pays no heed to a knot of cadets at the barrack door, standing by a four-horse coach, on which the attendants are stowing their luggage, and which is to carry them home for the summer holidays. Two others are settling accounts with Mother Montagu, the cake-woman; and

---

[1] Records of the Royal Military Academy, Woolwich, 1851.

a third is seen at a window above, waiting to efface his score in another way, by sluicing her with water.

Such was the little world in which Howard Douglas suddenly found himself a notable. Having been only six weeks in the Academy, he must have become chief of his class while he was a neux, the title borne by the junior of a room. As such, he was expected to discharge those offices which could not be imposed on the small complement of servants; such as bringing in the water to wash for dinner, making the tea, and toasting the bread. Indeed, custom bound him to obey every command of the head of the room, though the neux is never required to do anything degrading, like the fags of other schools; and it is certain that Howard's yoke was not heavy, as he never made it a subject of complaint. Nor would many have thus ventured to put him on his mettle, for his bold and fearless nature made itself felt in a manner that precluded oppression; and he was soon as much a leader in the playground as the school-room. If he ever knew fear, he took every occasion to show that he held it in contempt; for none of the cadets approached him in feats of daring. One of his gambols was to run close to the line of fire when the Company was exercised with artillery, and this gained him something more than schoolboy plaudits, though only done in bravado, for his alert eye caught points in the practice which he afterwards turned to account. Sir Hew Ross describes him as more prudent during the latter part of his stay at the Academy, as he would then have been the first to prevent any one running into danger, and he had acquired such influence in the Company that few would pursue what he opposed.

The vicinity of the Thames afforded him opportunities of nautical practice, which he did not neglect, though they could only be pursued under restrictions; for the authorities of the Academy kept a jealous eye on the river, and the regulations ordained that "the first cadet that is found swimming in the Thames shall be taken out *naked* and put in the guard-room." But he managed to be enough on the water to keep in his hand, and he always spread a sail in blowing weather, which brought out his points, while he paid more than one visit to Deptford Dockyard in search of higher knowledge. The holidays secured him a larger experience, for then he had the range of the Berwick and Leith smacks, in which he took his passage to and from Scotland, where he spent the interval. On board these craft he learned the mysteries of knotting and splicing, of plaiting points and gaskets, and of making grammets, and became expert in heaving the lead. We hear nothing from him of his reputation at the Academy at this period, and the good opinions he won from all around; but a memorandum of the time betrays his predilections by referring to his sailorcraft. "I will venture to say," he notes, "I know as much of cutter-sailing as any middy or mate in His Majesty's navy."

His enthusiasm for the sea had been sustained by the reverence he cherished for his father, which was of the deepest kind; for he observed the anniversary of his death as a sacred day through a period of seventy-two years. A packet among his papers attracted his biographer by a label in his own hand which revealed this veneration in the inscription—"Relating to the services of my honoured father." The old name was now to be signalized by his own services in a career as brilliant.

CHAPTER III.

IN COMMISSION.

THE events passing at this time occupied every mind. The heart thrills at the incidents of the French Revolution even in the present day, and how must they have been felt when the Reign of Terror was in progress, and society looked on! It constantly seemed that human wickedness had reached its limit, when the newspapers reported atrocities which out-horrored what had gone before. War heightened the excitement, and strained every nerve of England, obliging her to maintain the forces of her allies as well as her own, and guard all her possessions, while she stood in fear for her own soil. The English people fired at this danger, and all classes caught the fervour. The most enterprising flocked to the army or navy; the agricultural population recruited the militia; the towns swarmed with volunteers; and the combined services numbered as many as 800,000 men at one period of the struggle. The island might then have been likened to a fortress, and the nation to its garrison.

Young Douglas felt all the influence of such surroundings. He had begun to note public events in his childhood, when his perceptions were quickened by the exploits of his father in the war with the American colonies, and this gave him a political bias even at that time. The impression deepened as he grew up, and stood a witness of the French Revolution, and the ruin it spread through Europe. His patriotism was inborn, but it expanded under the pressure of the time, till the danger of invasion made love of country his dominant feeling. Thus his life was a testimony of devotion to England, showing him ever zealous to promote her greatness, and shield her from misfortune; nor can the most factious complain that he sought these objects by a Conservative course, since he had seen the country reel before the popular movements of his youth, one of which stripped her of half her dominions, while the other imperilled her existence. The same faith animated his old age, after an experience of eighty years, and was reflected in devotion to the State, loyalty to the Crown, and a deep sense of religion. The vulgar notion of a Tory found no warrant in such a character, who withstood innovation, but advocated progress, and always invited discussion. It might be well if vaunted Liberals would allow the same freedom, and show the same respect for opponents. "I never heard him speak ill, or even unkindly, of any one," writes one who knew him well.[1] "If he disapproved of the conduct or opinions of others, he would say so; but always with apparent regret. His mind was too full of higher things to have space for envy or bitterness."

Sir Hew Ross mentions that he bore the same character in 1795, when he received his first commission,

---

[1] The Chaplain-General, in a letter to the author.

and left the Academy for the Royal Artillery. He
was now seventeen, and might be satisfied with the
position he had attained, though not in the profession
he would have chosen. He had stepped in advance of
older lads, competing for the same prize, which was
awaited with such impatience that some were even
tempted to don the Artillery uniform before their
appointment.[1] The uniform is still a fascination, and
exercises such a spell over newly-appointed officers
that they are said to sleep in it the first week.

Exclusion from the vocation of our choice is often
made an excuse for failure, but the power of election
is given to few, and industry will make way in any
pursuit, however uncongenial. Lieutenant Douglas
indulged in no regrets over lost prospects, but threw
himself into the profession he had adopted, though his
preference for the navy remained unchanged, and
though he seized every opportunity of mixing with
sailors. Nor was he satisfied with discharging only
such duties as he could not avoid. He took his profession in hand, and sought to extend its bounds, so
mastering the incidence of artillery that he could seize
any opening for bringing it into play. He wished to
be a good officer, and hence perfected himself in drill
and manœuvring, and qualified himself to act in any
capacity, by observing and sketching country, and
practising reconnaissance. His turn for mechanics
attracted him to the workshop, but he did not neglect
the laboratory, and took care to keep up his proficiency
in mathematics.

---

[1] Records of the Royal Military Academy.

His merit was recognised immediately, and he had
been in the corps but a few months when he was despatched to Tynemouth Castle, to take command of the
Artillery in the northern district.   The expulsion of
the Duke of York from Holland had increased the
danger of invasion, since it left that country to the
enemy, whose armies were thus placed on our flank as
well as our front, while they possessed a port of aggression in Antwerp.   Yet parts of our coasts were
left unprotected, and Lieutenant Douglas found such a
gap in his command in the north.   The detachment
consisted of only two sergeants, four corporals, and
thirty gunners at Tynemouth ; a non-commissioned
officer and three gunners at Sunderland; the same
number at Hartlepool; and a small body of invalid
artillery at Berwick.   The day after his arrival he
represented the insufficiency of the force to General
Nesbit Balfour, the officer in command of the district,
and the General forwarded his report to the higher
authorities, backing it with a demand for reinforcement.   But he asked for what did not exist, and learnt
that he must make the most of his numbers, as they
could receive no addition.   The answer brought the
General to the end of his devices.   He saw the artillerymen at Tynemouth were too few to man the guns,
but he had made the fact known in the proper quarter,
and there was nothing more to be done.   Lieutenant
Douglas suggested that they might find a resource.
He proposed that a detachment of thirty men should
be sent to Tynemouth Castle from every regiment in
the district, together with a subaltern, and that he
should train them in the service of two field-guns,

which would enable them to act as Artillery. The
scheme was approved by the General, who ordered
down two detachments at once, and these were succeeded by others, till the required number were
trained. But the young officer required something
more, and success urged him to further effort. He
could only be satisfied with efficiency, and he was still
without force to man sixty heavy guns in battery at
the fort intended to rake the mouth of the Tyne. His
intercourse with the town assured him of the patriotic
spirit of the merchants and shipowners, and he suggested to the General to call them together, and
recommend the formation of a corps of gunners from
the men in their employment. General Balfour seems
to have had a faculty for appreciating his conceptions,
though they came from a subordinate, and the project
was set on foot. It met a warm response, bringing to
his aid five hundred young men, whom he enrolled in
companies, and trained in the service of the guns—
first with blank cartridge, and afterwards with shot at
floating targets.[1] Thus he placed Tynemouth in a
good posture of defence.

Such occupation left him little leisure, but he found
time to indulge his passion for sailoring, and made
himself master of a sea-boat which he delighted to
take out in squally weather. It was his practice to
board vessels trading to the port, and accompany
them into harbour, whence he contracted friendships
with the captains and mates, and obtained from them
valuable instruction. Sometimes he took a party of

[1] 'The Defence of England,' by General Sir Howard Douglas.

friends for a sail, and remained afloat for the day,
when he regaled them with sailor's fare a little improved.   One summer morning he was cruising about
with a brother-officer, when they espied two young
ladies of their acquaintance sufficiently near to claim
recognition.   Lieutenant Douglas thought he could
do nothing less than run the boat in, and invite them
to a sail round the harbour, and his companion took
the same view.   The invitation was kindly received,
though the ladies felt obliged to decline from motives
of propriety : but they could not resist a little chat,
and this drew them nearer the boat, in which two
captivating lieutenants were waiting to renew the
temptation.   It then met a fainter refusal, and one
young lady thought there could be no harm in going
halfway across the harbour, to which the other was
persuaded to accede.   But this tied young ladies
and captivating lieutenants to impossible conditions.
Who could remember such a compact when the breeze
on the water was so refreshing, the morning so fine,
the company so good, and the conversation so engross-
ing?   Instead of turning back in the middle of the
harbour, the boat stood out to sea ; wine and eatables
were produced, and it was not till the day wore on
that the fair cruisers remembered the account they
must render on their return home.   They then became
alarmed, and the two officers pushed for the shore,
anxious to cover their trespass.   For some days they
were impatient to learn the issue ; but the ladies did
not appear at their usual resorts, and they remained in
a state of uncertainty.   Three weeks elapsed, and it
is to be feared that they had forgotten both the oc-

currence and the young ladies, when the younger one was seen by Lieutenant Douglas at an attic-window, looking inconsolable—Patience on a monument, without her smile. Afterwards they met at a ball, and it transpired that both ladies had been kept prisoners, and now were only at large under guard.

The North was full of uniforms—regulars, militia, and volunteers—so that there was no end of revelry and good fellowship. One of the militia regiments had for its colonel the Duke of Norfolk, who fitted up his quarters as a wine-cellar, and there gave sumptuous entertainments. But few quarters at Tynemouth could be adapted to such uses, as the town was so packed with military, that officers could only be stowed in holes and corners. Lieutenant Douglas occupied a room barely habitable, and had to contest the tenancy with rats, which asserted their claim with such tenacity, that he went to sleep at the risk of being devoured. Their incursions compelled him to furnish himself with loaded pistols and a tinder-box, and he kept watch one night, remaining quiet till there was an irruption, when he started up and struck a light. But his vigilance proved of no avail, for the clink of the flint and steel caused a stampede, and not a rat remained by the time he had kindled the tinder. Their flight suggested to him another device. He looked out all the holes, and covered them with slides, connected with each other by wires, and these he fastened to a string, which enabled him to draw them all with one pull, and thus close the outlets. The contrivance claims to be mentioned as his first success in mechanics, fore-

shadowing his future expertness. It came into use
the same night: he pulled the string without rising
from bed, then struck a light, while the rats flew
off to the holes to find them blocked, and he shot
them at leisure.   Two or three such massacres
cleared off the intruders, and left him undisturbed in
his quarters.

CHAPTER IV.

ADVENTURES AT SEA.

EARLY in August, 1795, Lieutenant Douglas was
ordered to take charge of a detachment of troops with
women and children, and proceed to Quebec in the
'Phillis' transport. He joined the ship at Gravesend,
and found himself the senior officer on board, in command of six subalterns. But he was not so elated by
his position as by the prospect of a voyage across the
Atlantic, which afforded scope for the exercise of his
seamanship, and whatever time could be spared from
his duties was given to this object.

There is an impression of awe in our first experience of the ocean, when we lose sight of the shore
which enchains us by so many ties, and from which
we cannot part without a pang, even in boyhood.
Who can say we shall ever rejoin the friends we leave
behind, or at what time we shall return, if ever?
Change and uncertainty are suggested by every object
—by the rolling ship, the toppling waves, the vast
expanse bounded by clouds, and the sky hanging from
immensity. They strike the mind of youth like an
allegory, stirring thought to its depths, and one moment imparts a burst of character that might else be
the work of years. It cannot be known that such
an inspiration swayed Lieutenant Douglas; but the

voyage showed this development in his faculties, and gave the lad of nineteen a lead among men.

We now describe the Atlantic passage as a trip; but it was a serious undertaking in those days, when the fastest ships were heavy sailers, and comfort at sea unknown. The 'Phillis' went her own pace, and week after week advanced her but little on the voyage, though Lieutenant Douglas saw no ground for complaint, for they were favoured with very bad weather, and this afforded fine opportunities of turning out at night and going aloft in a gale of wind. None of the crew excelled him in reefing, and he often appeared at the weather-earring, and sometimes at the lee, in heavy lurches. Such a pleasure could not be enjoyed at ease for any length of time; and the pinch came in an appreciable shape, when the steward announced the failure of the fresh provisions. Nothing could be made of salt pork and biscuit in a musty state, and there was slender prospect of improvement; for the vessel had been nine weeks out before they sighted the island of St. Peter's, about forty leagues to the east of the southern entrance of the Gulf of St. Lawrence. Here they met a tempest which placed them in great danger, a mountainous wave striking the ship, and tearing both her boats from their lashings. The boats were thrown on the deck and with difficulty secured, as the sea had swept off their chocks, and they could only be lashed bottom upwards. This caused little concern at the time, but proved of consequence when their services were required.

The gale subsided next day, and then fell to a calm, which was succeeded by a light breeze. There seemed a promise of better weather, and this brought

up the women and children, who had rarely been able
to appear on deck, and now enjoyed the fresh air. But
danger arose in the midst of congratulation, and again
drove them below. The military officers were spend-
ing the evening in the cabin, and the captain had
joined the party, when he was called out by the mate,
and they hastened on deck together. Something in
their manner alarmed Lieutenant Douglas, and he
followed them unobserved, reaching the deck at the
same moment. He had no need to inquire their situation ; for his ear caught the roar of breakers, and
their proximity was attested by the sound, though
they could not be seen in the darkness. The clouds
overhead seemed to meet the waves, as they rose up
at the side—a wall of water, and the yard-arm almost
dipped, as the gale burst in gusts through the rigging,
heeling the vessel on her beam. The scene appalled
the crew, of whom only two were English, and they
stood helpless, though their lives depended on action.
The Captain applied to Lieutenant Douglas for the
assistance of the soldiers, who were turned up, and
all hands set to bend the cables and let go the best
bower-anchor. It fell in about twenty-five fathoms
water, and seemed to check the ship, though a strong
current was running towards the breakers, and nautical eyes discovered land on both quarters like a
bank of cloud, bringing the dreadful conviction that
they were embayed.

Wreck was even nearer than it appeared, for they
presently found there was no hold in the anchor, and
nothing remained but to take to the boats. But it
was first necessary to weather a reef on the lee bow,
which could only be accomplished by making more

sail, and the crew were ordered aloft to shake out a
reef. To attempt such a task seemed death, when the
gale broke in thunder-claps, the darkness hid the
spars, the masts bent like twigs, and the ship floundered
in foam. The sailors shrank back, and none would
obey the order. Their defection confounded the
Captain, but he knew there were brave men in the
ship, and called for volunteers. One sprang into the
shrouds on the instant, it was Lieutenant Douglas;
and his example drew out the two cabin-boys, who
were English, and followed him aloft, one helping
to shake out a reef of the close-reefed main-topsail,
while the other loosed the main-topgallant-sail. The
next few moments were passed in an agony of suspense.
The ship laboured as for life, plunging and rocking,
her canvas strained to splitting, and bearing her
nearer and nearer the reef, which was marked by the
raging breakers, riveting the gaze of men, women, and
children. Happily she cleared the point; for otherwise all must have perished, as it shut off the land,
and left them no approach.

Lieutenant Douglas now rushed below to secure his
valuables, but had mislaid the key of his desk. There
was no time for a search, and he broke it open, taking
out his father's watch, the only thing he saved, and
fastening it in his belt. He threw off his redundant
clothes, to be prepared for swimming—which proved
a happy thought—and then caught up a child from the
waist, and flew back to the deck. He was attended
by a faithful companion, a Newfoundland dog, which
followed him wherever he went, though never im-
peding his movements. But the child was past rescue,

D

and only clung to his breast an instant, when it died
without a moan.

He found the sailors bringing up some fowling-
pieces and powder, with a quantity of clothes and
provisions, and stowing them in the boats, which
were fitted with yard and stay tackle, and hoisted
away.   But the manner in which they had been
secured on drifting made them unhandy, and a surge
of the sea caught the bottom of the long-boat as it
swung in the weather roll, and dashed it to pieces.
The next wave grappled the ship, shook her from
stem to stern, and flung her on a sunken rock.   The
terror of the crash was heightened by the conduct of
the crew, who lost all self-control, " behaving like
cowards," [1] and by the frantic cries of the women
and children, the roar of the storm and the sea, the
quivering of the ship, and the spectacle of the foaming
waters, almost lighting up the darkness.   " That
horrible scene," writes Lieutenant Douglas, " baffles
all description, nor can the most lively imagination
conceive half its horrors." [2]   Again and again the ship
struck the rock, each time with the same violence and
the same terrible effect.   But she still drifted towards
the shore, and this was not more than a quarter of a
mile distant ; so there were hopes that it might be
reached in the remaining boat.   It had hitherto been
in shadow, but the moon now appeared, and showed
a black iron coast, rising perpendicularly from the
breakers.   There could be no doubt that it was uninhabited, and every heart quailed at its bare wild

[1] Copy of letter from Lieutenant Douglas to Captain Frazer, in the
'Douglas Papers.'   [2] Ibid.

aspect, hardly less frightful than the gulf between. The Captain called on the crew to man the tackle and lower the boat, but only the two mates and the carpenter responded. These were joined by Lieutenant Douglas and two of his comrades, Lieutenants Caddy and Forbes ;[1] but their united efforts could hardly get the boat over the side. It then seemed that she would stave the ship, and Douglas jumped in to keep her off, followed by Forbes and Caddy. But the boat was already half full of water, and they were obliged to spring back, in doing which Douglas missed his footing and fell into the sea. The boat dashed against the ship the same moment, breaking in pieces, but he kept afloat by swimming till a wave lifted him up and Forbes seized his collar and dragged him on deck. This did not place him in safety, for the vessel was found to be sinking and every one expected instant destruction. A few awaited their fate with composure, some broke into a frenzy of terror, others threw themselves on their knees in prayer, and those who could swim stripped themselves for a last struggle with the waves. But the ship drifted on for a quarter of an hour and then settled on the slope of a bank, which kept her deck above water, and it became possible that she might hold together till daylight. "We stood during the remainder of that long, long night," says the letter of Lieutenant Douglas, " wet through with the continual dashing of the breakers, eagerly wishing for day." And day took away their last hope—the hope that had buoyed them through the night; for it showed them the impossibility

---

[1] Now General Forbes, Colonel Commandant of the Royal Artillery.

of reaching the shore without assistance, the space
between being studded with rocks, through which the
high waves surged in floods, forming a caldron of
foam ; and they saw themselves cut off from escape
within fifteen yards of the land.   The situation nerved
one of the crew with the courage of despair, and he
suddenly jumped overboard and struck boldly out,
rising on a high sea and wrestling with the waves.
He disappeared in the surging foam, but rose again,
lifted himself over the breakers, and gained the beach.
Here he was caught by a rushing surf, which dashed
him against the rocks, and he was seen no more.

His progress had been watched from the ship as if
every life depended on his—with strained eyes and
bated breath.   They were so absorbed by the sight
that they heeded neither the drenching spray from
above nor the quivering of the ship under their
feet, and they burst into a cry as they saw him
perish.   But he had gained the beach before he was
swamped, and this brought forward one of the artillery officers, who undertook to make fast a hawser
to the shore, and thus rescue all.   The name of this
brave lad was Barclay, and his good nature had won
the esteem of every one on board ; but he could not be
dissuaded from the step he proposed, though eyes filled
with tears as he threw off his clothes.   He took an
affecting leave of his brother officers, gave one look
round, and plunged into the sea.   They watched for
his reappearance, but only to see him throw up his
arms and sink for ever.

The horror of the incident was scarcely felt in the
danger of the moment, for a mountainous wave struck
the ship, and threatened all with the same fate.   Lieu-

tenant Barnes was washed out of the forechains, where
he had posted himself to watch Barclay, and engulfed
in the sea. Another wave broke over the deck and
tore Mrs. D'Ellmonville from the arms of her husband,
sweeping her overboard in the same way, and a soldier's
wife was seen holding her two children above the wave
till they sunk together. Sea upon sea struck the ship,
and successive breaches carried off half a dozen others,
Lieutenant Barclay's servant following his master and
bearing with him one of the boys who had accompanied
Lieutenant Douglas aloft.

All were drenched to the skin and almost frozen
with exposure, while they had now been many hours
without food, but the motion prevented them going
below for supplies, and they famished with abundance at hand. In this extremity the mate secured
a piece of raw pork and a cheese which he saw floating
in the scuppers, and these were cut up and distributed amongst the company, every one receiving a
share. It formed the only meal of the day, and
again night closed around, while the storm raged
unabated.

The prospect of another night on the wreck appalled
the bravest, and the women became stupified with
terror, crouching over their children, whose cries they
could not still. The wind howled through the rigging;
the sea washed the deck, or burst against the bulwarks,
throwing over torrents of spray; the masts threatened
to snap or go by the board; and the roar of the
breakers was deafening. The after part of the ship
began to settle, and every lurch shook the cabin bell,
which rang dismally, and blended with the whine of
Douglas's dog, seeming to knell their doom. A sailor

made a push at the dog, and shoved it overboard to
see if it would reach the shore; and soon it was heard
from the nearest point, where it remained all night
whining and howling. Such were the sights and sounds
for hour on hour.

The women lost their hold of the ropes and were
washed overboard, with one exception: nor did the
strongest men expect to see morning. Four of the
crew determined to seek refuge below, and contrived
to descend the main hatchway, where they obtained
a light, and broke into the store-room. Here they
found a cask of rum, and their draughts were deep
and long, till they became mad drunk; and the gale
brought up their shouts of laughter, mingled with
curses and snatches of song. It was like the revelry
of demons, exulting in the darkness and tempest, and
heightening their horrors. But these orgies hushed
as the night advanced; nothing was heard but the
raging of the storm, and the hatchway gave out the
silence of death. The drunkards had sunk into sleep,
and two of them never awoke.

The weather moderated towards morning, and it
became possible to move about the deck, which suggested immediate action; and Lieutenant Douglas
proposed the construction of a raft capable of bearing
two or three men, who might aid the rescue of the
rest. His counsel was adopted, and two of the crew
succeeded in landing. But they wandered off inland,
without carrying out their orders, and regardless of
shouts from the wreck and the Captain's signals, which
they showed no intention of obeying. Their desertion
caused the more dismay, as the wreck was found to
be sinking, and the chance of escape lessened with

every moment.   Not a heart but throbbed while the
carpenter prepared another raft; no one ventured to
speak; and the ear thrilled with the ring of the
hammers and clatter of spars.   Then came the splash
of the launch; it floated and lived; and the second
mate, carpenter, and two seamen pushed for the shore.
There they established a bridge to the wreck by
making fast a hawser from the bowsprit, and all on
board were brought safe to land.

CHAPTER V.

Cast Away.

They had hardly assembled on the cliff when the wreck began to part, and the channel between became strewn with broken plank and drifts from the cargo. But there was nothing around to make their escape seem fortunate. The country imaged desolation, rising from the sea in masses of rock capped with snow, and spreading back in rugged tracts seamed with hollows and gullies. On every side rose mountains clothed with forests, which looked impenetrable, and had never been entered by man, while not a trace appeared of bird or beast. The snow lay deep on the ground, and the blast swept up from the sea, driving them for shelter to a thicket of spruce-trees, where it was decided to pass the night. Fortunately some bales of cloth were washed ashore, and these were torn in pieces and equally distributed, supplying every one with a wrapper. Thus the day closed, and the shivering company huddled together, quailing under the gathering clouds, which grew blacker and blacker; and night had hardly begun when rain fell in floods. Yet the two nights on the wreck had caused such exhaustion that it prevailed over wet and cold, and all fell asleep. A frost set in, and they must have been frozen to death, only that Lieutenant Douglas was aroused by a scream. This broke from

his servant's wife, who had been brought ashore insensible—the only woman who survived—and now
started from a disturbed sleep. He awoke her husband and gave her into his charge, while he dragged
himself through the party and made them all get up,
his own paralysed limbs assuring him that they would
perish otherwise. They were all stiffening, and ascribed their preservation to his forethought, though
they lay down again after stirring a little, being quite
worn out. But they were now kept awake by the cries
of the suffering woman, to whom the scene had given
another shock, and she started up mad. Her husband
and his master drew her back and held her down,
while they tried to soothe ; but persuasion fell void
on her ear, and she raved and shrieked for hours.
Her voice blended with the rain and wind—now in
wail, now with a piercing cry, a torrent of fierce
words, or exclamations of despair. But nature
snapped under the strain ; the voice spoke no longer ;
and the storm resounded alone : the last woman was
dead.

Lieutenant Douglas seemed to have but closed his
eyes after this horror when he was awakened by day,
which cleared away the clouds, and brought warmth
and sunshine. He mentions that " the sun shone forth
with great power—the greatest blessing the Almighty
could send us."[1] It enabled them to dry their tinder,
soaked through on its way ashore, and they kindled a
fire, the drifts from the wreck supplying fuel. The cold
and rain had caused great suffering during the night,
rendering several helpless, and Lieutenant Bennett and
Ensign Truscott were found insensible. They were

[1] Letter to Captain Frazer.

brought to the fire and their limbs warmed by rub-
bing, when Douglas moistened their lips with wine,
a cask having broken from the wreck and washed
ashore.   They rallied after a time, but remained
powerless, and their limbs proved to be frost-bitten.
Wine was needed by others, but the crew seized the
cask and carried it to the cliff, where they shared
the contents, and were soon rolling about drunk, or
fighting over the dregs.   Lieutenant Douglas preserved his authority over the soldiers, and they behaved well, with two exceptions, remaining together,
and obeying his orders.   He employed them in col-
lecting the drift from the wreck, and thus secured the
broken timber, and a quantity of smoked pork which
had formed the cargo, so that they had now no lack
of supplies, and the whole company gathered round
the fire and made a common meal.   They afterwards
deliberated as to the course they should follow, and
Douglas pronounced for remaining on the spot, and
erecting a beacon, which they might expect to attract
the notice of any passing ship.   But it was objected
that no vessel was likely to come within sight there, the
shore being out of the track of navigation, and known
as dangerous ; nor would they have approached it
themselves but for their run before the tempest.
Hence they could only be delivered by making their
way to a settlement, and one could hardly fail to be
reached if they penetrated to the interior.   Such reasoning convinced nearly all, but it was agreed to wait
two days for Truscott and Bennett, as Douglas protested against their being abandoned, though he
admitted that every one must depend on his own
exertions.

Little hope could be entertained that the two
officers would recover; but they sank so rapidly that
the time granted seemed the verge of their lives. He
remained with them till the last moment, when both
were delirious, while their pulse was scarcely perceptible, and their feet were like stone. Assured they
were beyond help, he joined the party on the cliff,
and they moved away through the frozen rain and
snow, each man wrapped in his cloak, and bearing as
much provision as he could carry.

"In solemn silence," he writes,[1] "we continued our
day's journey over almost inaccessible mountains and
through almost impenetrable woods, till about two
o'clock, when we took up our quarters for the night
in a wood on the side of a hill." Here they made a
fire; water was procured from a stream in the forest,
and every one received a ration of pork. But food
and rest came too late for two of the party, who sank
from fatigue, and the survivors laid their bodies
outside the wood, as they had no means of dig-
ging a grave. In vain they sought to forget their
misery in sleep; for those who yielded to drow-
siness awoke benumbed, and passed the remainder
of the night in suffering. But this did not prevent
them limping off with the others at sunrise, for to
remain behind was death. And the sun now gave no
warmth, but gleamed through clouds heavy with rain,
while they dragged their way through the snow in the
teeth of a cutting wind. A man dropped from the
ranks, then a second, and a third, perishing where
they fell, and the hardiest began to admit the obstacles
to success. Nor had they power to go further; for

[1] Letter to Captain Frazer.

they stood in a valley blocked with trees and walled
in by mountains, which poured down swollen torrents,
forming an impassable river in their front. The
prospect brought all to a stand, and it was agreed to
abandon the enterprise, and return to the bay.

Imagination could add nothing to the long agony
of their march back, which broke down some of the
strongest; but youth and vigour sustained Lieutenant
Douglas, and he led the party in. Only one thought
possessed his mind on reaching the cliffs—a thought
so absorbing that it raised a hope, and he dragged
himself into the wood in search of Truscott and Bennett. He was so spent that he could hardly proceed,
though he now saw their bodies stretched on the ground
on the spot where they were left. But he hardly believed his eyes as he advanced; for the sound of his
steps spread through the thicket, and the two officers
looked round—they were alive!

It appeared that they had regained consciousness
almost at the same time, and cheered each other
in their misery, sustaining themselves with the food
placed within reach. Their looks presented sad evidence of suffering; but they had youth on their
side, and their tenacity of life induced hopes that
they might recover, procuring them every attention that circumstances permitted, as the company
straggled to the spot, marvelling to find them
alive. The weariness of the scene was broken by
a fire kindled by the soldiers, and round this they
all grouped, remaining quiet for the night, and
obtaining what rest they could. The next morning
they exerted themselves to carry out the plan of
Lieutenant Douglas, erecting a beacon on the cliffs,

formed of the mainmast of the ship; and this they
furnished with a flag of black cloth stitched to a
piece of canvas, an object visible at a great distance.
Others were employed in building a hut, for which he
cleared a space in the middle of the thicket, sparing
such trees as were in a right line as supports for the
sides.   These consisted of planks from the wreck
raised to a height of three feet and a half, and bound
to the trees by lashings, strengthened outside by
stakes in the ground.   The side most exposed to the
sea received a further defence in a wall of stones
raised to the same height, and faced with a thick coat
of sods to keep out the wind and spray.   Rafters were
laid above, supporting the roof, which was formed of
planks, also covered in with sods, but with a small
hole in the centre for a chimney.   They had nearly
completed the hut by night, and next day gave them
a refuge which would not have been scorned by Robin-
son Crusoe.

But this afforded little defence against the climate;
and they saw another terror in their slender stock of
provisions, which would not long supply their dole of
food.   Mutiny added a new element to their misery.
The sailors found some casks of wine and a quantity
of pork and cheeses, which had drifted to the beach
at some distance, and refused to give them up, carrying them to another thicket, where they formed a
bivouac of their own.   The wine attracted a few of the
soldiers, and they were leaving the hut for the wood
when Lieutenant Douglas called them back. "No
more of your orders," answered their ringleader, de-
fiantly. "We're all equal now." Douglas flew at
his throat with a knife. "We are equals in misfor-

tune," he said, "and your officers are willing to bear
equally all your privations; but you shall discharge
your duty, and we will be obeyed. You are under
my command, and I shall act as if we were in the
field. Obey my order, or, by Heaven, I'll kill you
on the spot." The man instantly submitted; and this
decided the others, who were waiting the issue. Nor
did they waver afterwards, though their sufferings
increased every hour, and they lost their powers of
endurance in proportion as they were most needed,
men inured to hardship sinking under the cold and
privation, and resigning themselves to death. The
carpenter and first-mate became disabled, and a feeling of despair seized every breast, as days and nights
succeeded each other and brought no prospect of relief.
Starvation might be said to have begun, when a shout
broke from the look-out on the cliff, and twenty voices
echoed the cry—" A sail! a sail!"

CHAPTER VI.

Before the Mast.

It was three in the afternoon when the look-out descried the ship—a small schooner—just visible on the horizon; and already the sky lowered with a shade of night, which might prevent the beacon being seen. They felt all the misgivings of despairing men combating with hopes, and now doubted whether the signal would be understood, even if discerned. Who can imagine their feelings as they gazed on the distant sail, now thinking that she receded, now that she drew nearer, and straining their eyes for some token of recognition! The minutes seemed hours under this suspense. But soon they made out her hull and rig, and saw a streamer fly to her top. She was coming!

Such a cry rang out as she entered the bay and anchored, while her skipper waved his hat from the stern, and her crew gave a cheer, rushing aft to lower a boat. It came off with two men, but they were afraid to land as they saw the number of the castaways, who now all crowded to the water. Thus they kept an oar's length, and seemed indisposed to take them off, when Lieutenant Douglas made a spring, and jumped into the boat, tumbling over them both. He then threw the painter to the others, who drew the boat ashore, and a load started for the schooner.

The skipper admitted them on board, though he hesitated about receiving so many, but finally yielded, as Douglas would not leave a man behind. He even sent for the mutineers, who had not seen the arrival, and took them off with the rest.

It appeared that the skipper had guessed the object of their beacon from being familiar with the coast, as he had visited it in his voyages to Great Jervis, where he traded for fish, and knew it to be uninhabited. To that settlement he was now bound, and he told them they must be content to remain there through the winter, as there would be no opportunity of leaving till the fishing-season expired. They had hoped that he might take them to Halifax, but were not in a position to make terms, and closed with his offer, all hurrying on board, and rejoicing together as the vessel bore them away.

They duly arrived at Great Jervis, and received the utmost kindness from the fishermen, who lived here amidst ice and snow, cut off from the world, and pursuing their calling amidst perpetual storms. There was some difficulty in providing them lodging, but the result verified the proverb that hinges the way on the will, and a roof was found for all. Lieutenant Douglas shared his cabin with Lieutenant Forbes, and they made room for the first mate and carpenter, whose crippled state excited their pity. Lieutenant Truscott and Ensign Bennett were carried some miles inland, in order to be placed under the care of a woman who was the physician of the settlement, and who ultimately restored them to health, either by her skill or nursing.

The party were almost naked on landing, having

no clothes but those in which they escaped from the wreck, and which were in tatters from wear and exposure. But the settlement contained a store, where they found an assortment of slops, and Douglas rigged himself out as a sailor, donning the jacket and tarpaulin with as much pride as he had ever assumed his uniform. The place afforded scope for indulging his nautical tastes, and he spent the day in mingling with the fishermen, and sometimes sharing their pursuits. The long nights were heavy work, as they could obtain no books, and devise no amusements; but the convalescence of his guests improved his resources in this respect, as he could then practise navigation with the mate, and talk over mechanical problems with the carpenter. But all grew weary of their detention at the settlement, and this put him on considering whether they might not try to reach Placentia, whence it would be easy to make their way to Quebec. He kept the project to himself for some time, fearing that it would be deemed chimerical, and thought it over and over again, as he paced to and fro on the cliff before his hut, looking down on the rocks and broken ice of Fortune Bay. The more he turned it in his mind, the more he felt disposed to put it in practice, and he determined to see what means existed for making the attempt.

The settlement maintained no communication with Canada, or any part of British America, but was visited in the spring by vessels from England, which came to exchange supplies for fish, and then sailed to different regions, chiefly the West Indies, Spain, Portugal, and the Mediterranean. They there bartered the fish for the productions of the soil, and carried these

E

to England, where they found a ready market. The nearest point to America that he could hope to reach by such a channel was the West Indies, and he might be detained there an indefinite time, as no vessel would leave until the despatch of a convoy, and one so adventurous deemed it worth any risk to endeavour to make a direct passage.

He reminded his three messmates of these facts, and they talked them over together, when he broached his project of a dash, and they hailed it with rapture. He next enlisted a St. Lawrence pilot, brought off in a gale of wind the year before, and left at Fortune Bay, and he completed his number with a seaman from Newfoundland, who was anxious to leave the settlement, and whose knowledge of the coast would be of service.

It proved easier to obtain a crew than a vessel, but this was not beyond reach, and he met with a good fishing-boat, which the owner agreed to sell. The carpenter pronounced her adaptable, engaging to make her equal to the voyage, and Lieutenant Douglas became the purchaser; for he had no lack of means, as his bills on the authorities passed as money. They decided to rig the boat as a schooner, and set about her equipment, which furnished them with occupation during the short winter days, in that latitude so gloomy and depressing. Its progress afforded Douglas the greatest pleasure, as he was fired by the prospect of carrying off his detachment in a vessel under his own command, and landing in triumph at St. John's. This banished from his mind all thought of the danger, and he longed for the moment when the weather would moderate, and permit of their setting out. So early did he cherish his passion for distinction in the manner revealed in his maturer life, by seeking to excel in the performance of his duty rather than by bootless daring, though few found the same attraction in dangerous adventures.

The days that were not given to the schooner he spent in wandering round the coast or exploring the interior, sometimes in company with Lieutenant Forbes, but often alone; for his power of enduring cold and fatigue carried him where few could follow. And he felt that solitude heightened the sublimity of this wild outskirt of Nature, where rock upon rock started from the sea in fantastic shapes or prodigious boulders—Ossa on Pelion—and mountains rose to the clouds, or stood mantled in snow, frowning over precipices and chasms which gaped on valleys of granite, sending ravines into gloomy woods never pierced by the light of day. His mind had a poetic temper, though its habit was so practical, and such scenes left on it an impression that never faded.

The boat was completed for sea by April, but then came a succession of gales, which obliged them to defer setting out, and Douglas and Forbes spent the interval in a tour of the island. An incident happened in their absence that frustrated their whole plan. A storm drove into the harbour of St. Pierre a Newfoundland schooner, bound from Halifax to St. John's, and there the Captain heard that a party of shipwrecked soldiers were detained at the fishing-station. He decided to go round to Fortune Bay and take them off, a lull in the weather permitting—for the shore was usually inaccessible at that season, and even now was approached with danger. His appearance

*

brought out the whole population, who met him as he
landed, and he made known his object, announcing
that all must be on board within half an hour, as the
sky and rising wind foretokened a tempest. This
caused such excitement that no one thought but of
himself, and some jumped into the boat at once, having
nothing to carry away, and fearing to be left behind.
It was not till the schooner was starting that the party
.missed Douglas and Forbes, and then they gathered
round the Captain, and entreated him to wait till a
messenger could go to the hut and see if they had
returned. With difficulty they brought him to consent, and the schooner hove to, while a boat pulled
ashore, and one of the artillerymen started up the cliff,
disappearing in an instant. But he returned alone;
nothing could be heard of the two officers; and the
schooner got under way.

This cruel necessity damped the joy of rescue; and
eyes still watched the shore, as they moved through
the water, unwilling to surrender the last hope. And
now a gun flashed from the beach, as a signal that the
absentees had appeared. They were seen to spring
into a boat, which spread all sail, and came bounding
through the waves, while the Captain brought up and
awaited her approach, cordially welcoming the two
officers as they alighted on the deck.

The schooner hardly escaped from the shore before
the gale broke; but the Captain had no cause to
regret his delay, since it secured him such a hand as
Lieutenant Douglas. Nor had it involved much risk;
for the weather improved towards morning, and then
became fine, promising a swift passage. But it did not
terminate without adventure; for they fell in with His

Majesty's ship 'Shark,' off Placentia, and were ordered
to bring to and send a boat on board, as the crowd on
deck excited suspicion. The yawl was hoisted up, and
Lieutenant Douglas formed one of her crew, pulling
the after-oar, the helm being taken by the Captain.
The sea ran high, but they laid the boat alongside the
frigate in dashing style, and the skipper ascended to
the deck, while Douglas dropped astern to await his
reappearance. He came within hail of the seamen
in passing the main deck ports, and they called to him
to leave a hand in the boat and jump up with the
others to "have a jaw." He readily assented, and
clambered in at a porthole, after securing the con-
nivance of his companions by a wink, understood as
implying that he was to appear as one of themselves.
He met a kind welcome, and a shower of questions
which naturally brought on the shipwreck, and those
who have heard the story from his lips may imagine
the fascination it exercised on the rough fellows
gathered round. The recital so absorbed eyes and
ears that no one heeded a call from the Captain's
cabin for "Mr. Douglas," until the word passed to
send aft the artillery officer who had come in the
yawl, and Lieutenant Douglas now stepped out to
obey, to the bewilderment of the circle, who fell back
with exclamations of surprise, which merged in a
general roar before he reached the cabin. He received a cordial greeting from Captain O'Brien, who
commanded the frigate, and whom he found discussing
a decanter of wine with his First Lieutenant and the
Captain of the schooner. The glass went round, and
he heightened its enjoyment by explaining how he
had come on board, and relating his adventure for'ard.

F

This elicited a compliment to his appearance from Captain O'Brien, who said, " Your Captain declares you are an excellent sailor, and you bear out his report." They spent a pleasant half-hour, and then bade each other good-bye, Lieutenant Douglas and the skipper returning in the yawl to the schooner, and the ships parting company.

The next day the schooner sighted St. John's, and stood into the harbour, where the crowded appearance of her deck attracted the notice of another man-of-war, which was lying at anchor, and she sent a boat to board her on her passage up. Thus the Captain found himself confronted by a Lieutenant from His Majesty's ship ' Pluto ' before he scented the danger.

" Hilloa ! what a number of hands you've got in this small vessel ! " cried the Lieutenant.

" Yes," was the reply.

" Where the —— did you find them ? "

" I picked up the survivors of a shipwreck."

" Whew ! " cried the Lieutenant, in ecstasy ; " what a glorious chance for us ! We're short of hands, and can take them all. Just separate them from your crew ; they couldn't have a better opening ; for we're off to the West Indies to-morrow, and there'll be a swarm of prizes."

" But some of them are soldiers," interposed the skipper.

The Lieutenant made a gesture intimating that such tales were not for his book. " Here's a sailor, at any rate," he said, slapping the shoulder of Lieutenant Douglas. " How long have you been at sea, my lad ? "

" This is my first voyage on the ocean."

" Oh, bred in the coasting trade, eh ? "

" Well, I know something of the coasting trade."

" I thought so.   What craft ? "

" The Berwick and Leith smacks."

" That will do—nothing better. Stand aside here ! "

The young officer obeyed, with unmoved features,
and was soon joined by others, who had been subjected
to like inquiries. At length the Lieutenant considered
that he had made a good haul, and ordered the party
to jump into the boat.

" I tell you there are soldiers in that lot," cried the
skipper, thinking the joke had gone far enough ; " and
a soldier-officer, too."

" An officer ! "

" Yes ; that's him "—pointing to Lieutenant Douglas—" he's in the artillery."

The Lieutenant laughed out, and referred the skipper to the marines, giving him to understand that he
was a sailor, and knew a sailor, and that it would take
a clever fellow to make him see an artillery officer in
a lad rigged in sailor's slops, with figure to match.
The skipper repeated his assertion, and he demanded
to see the young man's commission, which obviously
could not be produced, having gone to the bottom,
and he now felt persuaded that the Captain wished
to cheat him out of his best man. He declared that
he should carry off his party, and any claim to exemp-
tion must be made on the quarter-deck of the ' Pluto,'
where it could be fully investigated. But he now
met an unexpected check ; for the skipper called his
attention to the schooner's pendant, denoting that she
sailed under a Government charter, and this obliged

him to sheer off disappointed, as he could not deny
that it protected all on board.

His narrow escape from impressment did not deter
Lieutenant Douglas from going ashore, and he and his
friend Forbes landed together, after they had brushed
their blue jackets and made a nautical toilet.   Nor
was this preparation without an object, as they had
determined to pay their respects at Government
House, and thither they repaired at once, and met
the kindest reception from the Governor, General
Skinner.

They accepted an invitation to dinner, on the understanding that deficiencies should be excused, and made
their appearance at the appointed hour in forecastle
costume.   The company included the Captain of the
'Pluto' and his smart Lieutenant, who opened his
eyes on seeing Douglas.   But a knowing look set him
at ease.   The morning's adventure was not mentioned,
and nothing interrupted the harmony of the evening.
The 'Pluto's' boat put the two artillerymen on board
at a late hour, and the schooner sailed for Halifax at
daybreak.

CHAPTER VII.

Commanding a Cruiser.

THE commanding officer of the artillery at Quebec
had been informed of the departure of the ' Phillis '
from Gravesend, and began to feel alarmed for her
safety, as the time passed when she should have
arrived. Hopes were entertained up to the close of
the navigation, when her non-appearance was reported
to Lord Dorchester, the Governor of Canada, and he
requested the Admiral commanding the squadron to
ascertain if she had taken refuge in one of the sea-
ports on the coast of Newfoundland, Cape Breton, or
Nova Scotia; or whether there were any traces of
her being wrecked on the Sable Bank.   The search
proved fruitless, and · it was concluded that the
' Phillis ' had gone down at sea with all hands.

Such a disaster threw a gloom over the military
community in British America, as many mourned the
loss of comrades, not to mention nearer connexions;
while their fate brought home to the mind the dangers
of the passage, which each might himself be required
to face at any moment.   But soldiers forswear melancholy, and six months had almost effaced the impression, when a report spread of the arrival of a schooner
with the survivors.   This caused the greatest excitement, and the news was carried to His Royal Highness Prince Edward, who commanded the forces in
Nova Scotia, and who instantly sent his aide-de-camp

to bring up to his quarters any of the wrecked officers who might be in a state of health to attend. Captain Wetherall returned with Douglas and Forbes, who were presented to His Royal Highness and received with the most gracious sympathy. The Prince almost immediately inquired for Lieutenant Barnes, and learnt his fate with the deepest pain, knowing that he was an only son, and that the blow would be irreparable to his father, Colonel Barnes, to whom His Royal Highness was much attached. He asked Lieutenant Douglas to relate the whole story of the shipwreck, and listened with breathless interest, not concealing his emotion; and his kindness and sympathy made such an impression on the narrator, that he mentioned it to the author of this work sixty years after the occurrence. His Royal Highness commanded both officers to dine with him in the evening, at the Lodge, an honour they fully appreciated, but from which they seemed to be precluded by their limited wardrobe. "Sir," said Lieutenant Douglas, after a moment's hesitation, "we have no clothes but what we stand in." His Royal Highness could not repress a smile at the disclosure. "If all the tailors in Bond Street were here, I would receive you in no other dress," he said. "Come as you are." Such a command was not to be disobeyed, and they only infringed it so far as to appear in clean check shirts, which they purchased for the occasion. His Royal Highness distinguished them by the kindest attention, though a large company was present, and requested Lieutenant Douglas to repeat his account of the shipwreck, after dinner, as he knew it would interest everybody. The Prince sent his secretary on board the schooner next morning, to offer them and their companions surgical attendance, and whatever money, clothes, or other necessaries they might require ; but they gratefully declined his bounty, having now drawn six months' pay, and being well supplied. The duty of recording these acts of the Prince is most gratifying to the author of this work, who owes a personal debt to his memory, from the distinguished notice His Royal Highness took of his father, whom he selected from the whole army for the adjutancy of his own regiment, though the wear of hard service prevented his accepting the appointment.

Lieutenant Douglas and his companions left Halifax in a West India vessel carrying produce to Canada, and passed between Nova Scotia and the island of Cape Breton to the Gulf of St. Lawrence. Here they met a squall which sprung the fore-topmast, and compelled them to enter the bay to refit; affording the young officer an opportunity of visiting Douglas Town, erected to commemorate his father's relief of Quebec. The rescued party did not reach the capital till July. Here the name of Douglas was as familiar as at the town below, and would have insured the son of the great Admiral a cordial reception at any time ; but obtained him a heartier welcome now that he came as from the grave, seven months after his supposed loss. What gratified him most was the recognition of his meritorious conduct by his superiors— conveyed to him in the following letter from Lieut.- General Pattison, Commandant of the 4th Battalion of the Royal Artillery, and intended to acknowledge a narrative of the shipwreck he had addressed to Captain Frazer :—

To Lieutenant Douglas, 4th Battalion Royal Artillery.

" Dear Sir,   "[London], Hill-street, 22nd April, 1796.

    "Your letter to Captain Frazer, reciting all the circumstances of your shipwreck, is a tale of such deep woe and distress as must necessarily make a forcible impression on the feelings of every one who has read it. I am sure it had a full effect upon mine. It only remains for me to offer you my sincere congratulations on the providential escape which you and your surviving companions most fortunately met with; and whilst I gratefully admire the ways of Providence in preserving your lives, I must at the same time pay *a just tribute to your cool, firm, and undaunted behaviour* during the scenes of horror you underwent. *I am convinced that the prudent steps you took after getting on shore proved the happy means of your preservation.* After the arrival of your letter I lost no time in laying it before the Master-General, and, since that, I made the strongest application to the Board of Ordnance, requesting that they would be pleased to grant you and all the sufferers an indemnification for the losses sustained by that melancholy event, to which I yesterday received an answer, and which I transmit enclosed; although you will probably receive one directly from the Board, requiring the affidavit therein specified. Unluckily I had not received this letter from the Board when Lieutenant Kiggell called upon me yesterday, previous to his departure from London; but I hope this will reach him at Portsmouth before he sails; and that he may have the pleasure of giving it to you at Quebec.

    "I desire you will remember me with my good

wishes to your young companions in the hour of distress, and accept the same yourself from, dear Sir,

"Your very faithful humble servant,

"JAMES PATTISON."

It will be seen that General Pattison ascribes the
preservation of the survivors to the steps taken by
Lieutenant Douglas, and the account of the occurrence
must suggest the same conviction to every mind. At
the age of nineteen he had shown an aptitude for
grappling with difficulties, a degree of fortitude amidst
privation and danger, and a power of influencing
others, worthy of an experienced commander; and the
manner in which his future life developed kindred
qualities induces a regret that he had no opportunity
of bringing them into play on the widest field.

The tribute paid to his conduct by General Pattison
had an effect upon him similar to the recognition of
his talents by Dr. Hutton in earlier years, encouraging
his self-reliance without raising his self-esteem; and
he used to say that the pleasure it afforded surpassed
any he experienced from future appreciation. Nothing
could show more the elevation of his character than
this feeling, for he was to receive approval from the
lips of kings; but he felt greater pride that the first
trial had proved him worthy of his name, in a region
connected with his father, and where it became him to
sustain his father's exploits.

The reputation he had acquired now obtained for
him an employment of the very kind he could have
wished. News reached Quebec that a French squadron
was scouring the coast of Newfoundland, and had been
seen bearing towards St. John's, sweeping before it the

colonial traders and the vessels fishing on the great bank. Then came reports that it had not ventured to force the harbour of St. John's, but ran into the Bay of Bulls, where it destroyed the fishing stages, but made only a short stay, hurrying off to the northern entrance of the Gulf of St. Lawrence. Here Admiral Richey hoisted the French flag on the island of St. Pierre, which had surrendered to a force from Halifax the year before, but had been left without a garrison, though a number of British fishermen had taken possession, and built a little town. This the French destroyed, as well as the fishing establishment and all the stages, leaving the island a desert. The squadron then divided, and a portion sailed for the coast of Labrador, to intercept the homeward-bound fleet from Quebec, while Admiral Richey remained near Cape Breton with four sail of the line and a frigate. The British naval force on the station consisted only of a 50-gun ship of an obsolete type, and four frigates, not one of which was in the St. Lawrence. Hence the French Admiral's vicinity excited great alarm at Quebec, and it became important to know what he was doing in the Gulf, particularly as the outward-bound fleet from England was due, and it appeared certain that it would be cut off. The situation of affairs determined the Canadian Government to send out a vessel for intelligence, and a schooner was equipped and got ready for the service, but so completely had the maritime class been absorbed by the war, that no competent person could be found to take her to sea.

In this emergency eyes began to be cast at a little sailing-boat which cruised about the bay in all weathers, but never more than when it blew fresh;

and it transpired that she belonged to young Douglas, the hero of the shipwreck and the son of the Admiral who relieved Quebec. A rumour spread that he had been in the navy, and this set the authorities to think that he was the very man they wanted and would make an excellent captain for their cruiser.

The subject came before the Governor, General Prescott, and he sent the Deputy Adjutant-General to confer with Douglas, and ascertain his inclination, at the same time that he represented the importance of the service, and that it must be abandoned if not accomplished at once. It was too much to the taste of the young officer to be declined, but he set a modest appreciation on his own capacity, and only agreed to command the schooner if "no better man could be found." The Governor declared that he wished for no better, and placed the vessel in his charge.

He might now feel rewarded for the self-denial he had practised in resigning the profession of his choice at the bidding of his guardians; for what more could he have achieved as a sailor than to be selected for such a post on the spot where he would most desire— this recognition—in the basin of Quebec. Indeed the navy would not have afforded such an opening at an age when he might still be a midshipman; and his success taught him that he could be in no better way to distinction if he made use of his opportunities.

The schooner was from 220 to 250 tons burthen, deep waisted in build, and reputed a swift sailer. Her armament consisted of eight 12-pounder carronades, and two long guns, in charge of artillerymen, and she carried a good crew with a first and second mate, and a pilot for the passage down the river. She set sail about the middle of September, proceeding to the island of Bic, where her commander took measures to prevent pilots boarding strange vessels, and arranged for the transmission of intelligence to the seat of Government. He vividly remembered the incidents of the expedition to his latest years, taking pride in relating them to the few whom he entertained with his adventures, and no one who had been much at sea could resist the animation with which he described his mode of handling the schooner. It was necessary that he should make himself acquainted with her best points, in order that he might bring them out in the event of being chased by the French fleet, and he tried her on every tack, whence he found that she carried a tight weather helm, coming to the wind readily, and making a long short directly to windward, with the helm amidships, when not impeded by her square topsails. Then she easily paid off with the fore-staysail sheet close hauled to windward, and helped a little with the jib, and never fell off after tacking. He avoided using the topsails when close hauled on turning to windward, except in very light winds, always working the vessel under her fore and aft sails.   The experience he acquired of her weatherly qualities determined him to approach the French fleet from the windward, should it fall in his way, for he was satisfied that no square-rigged ship could give him chase on that course, whatever the direction of the wind, and he cared little about receiving a shot or two if he could get sufficiently near to ascertain whether the ships carried troops. Hence he denied himself the gratification of hoisting a pendant, as this might put them on the alert, and the schooner sailed under the usual merchant ensign displayed at the main peak.

They passed the first night of her voyage above Crane Island, where they came to anchor, and Lieutenant Douglas turned in, after giving orders that he should be called at high water. This brought him on deck before daylight, and he immediately loosed sail, and set to heaving up anchor. But here he met a difficulty of an unexpected kind, as if to put him on trial, for the ordinary purchase had no effect in moving the anchor. The handspikes were double manned with the same result, and the mate recommended cutting it adrift. But he could not be reconciled to this sacrifice, the vessel having no spare bower-anchor, and he had been in danger enough to learn the value of such a provision; so he determined to persevere, and ordered a tackle to be fixed round the cable, and taken to the windlass, on which the men again heaved up, and the anchor came away. But there was still a strain, and the cause plainly appeared on catting, as the fluke was found to have hooked in the ring of another and larger anchor, which it brought up from the bottom, in a condition that showed it had been lying there many years. The incident exhibited the character of Douglas in one of its strong points, his tenacity of purpose, and had an inspiring effect on the crew, who were now ready to follow him wherever he led.

A light wind accompanied the schooner for a time, but left her off Gruse Island, where it fell calm, and Douglas perceived a change in the colour of the water, as if it had shallowed. The pilot declared it was of great depth, but he retained his opinion, and ordered soundings, which reported only twenty-six fathoms. The chart was now produced, and corroborated the pilot, showing no bank, so he laid one down on the spot, marking it by the bearings of two headlands which stood pretty distant, and it proved a valuable discovery. He tested its worth himself, for he instantly threw out a span of hooks baited with pork, and hauled up two splendid cod. The line was sent down again and again, and upwards of a hundred fish were caught while they drifted over. A number were split and salted, and afterwards distributed by Lieutenant Douglas among the merchants and fishmongers of Quebec, who established a fishery near the bank in the following year, and it may be in operation to the present time.

Off Ante Costi Island the schooner sighted a large square-rigged vessel, coming up under a press of sail, and the pilot declared her to be the 'Caroline,' a well-known craft in the Quebec trade. This emboldened Lieutenant Douglas to carry on after the usual signals, and he then hoisted his pendant and fired a gun. The stranger shortened sail, but apparently with some confusion, and eyes in the schooner began to peer at her more narrowly. But the pilot insisted that she was the 'Caroline,' and spoke so positively that Douglas launched the jolly-boat, determined to go on board, and see if he could obtain intelligence of the fleet. Strange appearances came out as the boat advanced, and he ordered the men to lay on their oars till he took a better look. All the officers of the ship were standing abaft, the deck was crowded for'ard, and some heads in the waist showed the red cap of the French Revolutionists. But any

misgivings these excited were dispelled by the Captain,
who presented himself at the side of the ship, and
requested Douglas to come alongside, declaring that
all was right, that the vessel was the 'Caroline,' and
that he was the bearer of important intelligence. The
rowers gave way, a rope was thrown, and Douglas
jumped on board.

He almost started back as he looked round and saw
a strong barricade of timber across the deck, and a
carronade pointed for'ard through a porthole in each
waist. But these mysterious appearances were now
explained, and he learned that the 'Caroline' had been
chartered to bring out three hundred French prisoners,
who volunteered for the second battalion of the 60th,
in garrison at Quebec; and the party had conspired
to rise on the crew during the voyage, and carry her
into a French port. The scheme was discovered, and
the Captain took precautions against surprise by erecting the barricade, which gave him the control of the
Frenchmen, whom he compelled to work the sails
for'ard on pain of being shot down, while they were
only permitted to appear on deck in certain numbers.
Thus the ship crossed the Atlantic; and her preservation seemed the more wonderful as she had
fallen in with the homeward-bound Quebec fleet on
the coast of Labrador, and they had been attacked by
the French squadron, when she alone escaped. The
Captain heard from fishermen that he would meet another French squadron in the Gulf of St. Lawrence, but
afterwards discovered that it had gone north and joined
the sister force off the Banks of Newfoundland, where
they had been seen bearing away together; and this
was the intelligence he wished to forward to Quebec.

Douglas lost no time in carrying it on, and it spread through the city, dispelling the apprehension of an attack on Canada, as it established the fact that a fleet of seven sail of the line and three frigates had been sent out for no other object than a raid. He received the thanks of the Canadian Government for having undertaken so difficult a service, and performed it so successfully, while his praises were repeated on every side, and he found himself a popular hero before he was twenty.

The winter of 1796 passed very gaily, and every house was open to the young officer who had so well sustained his father's fame. In the spring he was invited to a public banquet given by the Volunteers who had taken up arms for the defence of the city in the campaign of 1776, and intended to celebrate the anniversary of its relief by Sir Charles. He met an enthusiastic reception, and his name was coupled with the toast of the day, eliciting his first speech. No fragment of this oration has survived; but he used to recite a stanza of a poem composed for the occasion by a Presbyterian minister who had been chaplain to the Scottish corps during the siege, and which acclaimed the exploit of his father. The lines will not be out of place here :—

> " With freedom, peace, and plenty blest,
>   Protected by Britannia's sway,
> Secure we sing of dangers past,
>   And hail the sixth of May,
>   The glorious sixth of May :
> Brave DOUGLAS, wafted on the gale,
>   Did anchor in the bay."

CHAPTER VIII.

Among the Indians.

In May, 1797, Lieutenant Douglas was ordered to
Upper Canada, in command of a detachment of artillery
consisting of two officers and a considerable number
of men, who were to relieve a like force at Kingston.
The movements of the troops were then all effected by
water; but there was no chain of canals, as at present,
the only one in existence being higher up, at the Falls;
and the boats had to be rowed up the river from
Quebec, a service for which the troops were regularly
trained, and at which they were very expert.

The detachment embarked in Canadian bâteaux,
each provided with two voyageurs, a headsman and
sternman; for the steering was conducted at both
ends, being carried on with paddles in deep water,
and long poles in shallow, or by dragging the boat
by tow-lines where there was a path. The party
landed at night and bivouacked on the banks—a mode
of travelling very agreeable to its commander, as it
afforded him leisure to contemplate the scenery. This
was of a character to strike an imagination so attracted
by adventure, for the mighty stream bore him through
forest and prairie, morasses and savannas, such as
he had never conceived; while behind rose towering
heights, sometimes backing a settler's clearing, but
oftener the wigwams of Indians, almost the only
tenants of these solitudes. The voyage occupied a

G

month, but he never found it irksome, and felt no
elation at the sight of Kingston, where they arrived
towards the end of June.

He had reason to be satisfied with the situation of
the town, breasting Lake Ontario, which gave a scope
to his nautical habits; and the facilities it afforded
were not neglected. During the summer he was constantly afloat, crossing the lakes in sailing vessels, or
coasting along in boats, often going a distance in his
Indian canoe spearing salmon by torchlight, or led by
his adventurous spirit into the woods. Here he roamed
about with Indians, living in their wigwams, and
joining them in deer-stalking, shooting, fishing, and
other pursuits. His adventures carried him where
few white men had penetrated, and were sometimes
attended with danger. On one occasion he was fishing in a stream, when he felt something cold strike
his leg, and found his foot on the neck of a rattlesnake, which had coiled itself above his ankle. It
might be imagined that his first idea would be how
to effect his escape; but how to prevent the escape
of the rattlesnake was all his care. Izaak Walton
never played more dexterously with a trout than
he set to work on this object. He wished to
"catch him alive;" and this required instant action
as well as adroitness, while he seemed without any
means of proceeding. But he had learnt the arts of
the Indians, and now put them in practice, applying
them with the same facility. Keeping his foot still,
he broke a branch from a tree within reach, tore down
the bark, and made it into a string, one end of which
was left fast to the branch, while the other formed a
noose, which he slipped round the rattlesnake as he

sprang aside, and caught it up dangling from the stick, carrying it home uninjured.

The bite of the rattlesnake is usually considered fatal; but he heard from the Indians that the plantain-leaf is an antidote, and once saw its efficacy proved. He was out hunting rattlesnakes with an Indian, when his companion was bitten, and looked very disturbed for a moment, but then caught sight of a plantain, and this set him at rest. To apply the remedy was the work of an instant. He drew out his knife, scarified the bite, and then covered it with plantain-leaves, which he had first chewed into a pulp, swallowing the juice. A few days healed the wound, and it gave no further trouble. Douglas remarked that the plantain grew profusely where rattlesnakes were most common.

It seems a contradiction that one so addicted to the wildest adventures should find attraction in the gentle art of angling. Yet Walton himself was not a more ardent fisherman; and he was ready to start with his rod at any hour whether of the day or night. Nor does his passion for the quiet sport appear incongruous if we remember that it exacts alertness; for this ministered to his activity, though not employing it, while it left him free to meditate. Thus it remained his diversion in later years; and some of the old chiefs of our army recall their instructor by the side of the little stream at Sandhurst more familiarly than in any other situation.

His roving habits could not escape notice in so small a community, and now brought him again before the Canadian authorities, who were looking for a person to head a mission to the Cherokees, a tribe of

Indians expelled from the United States for its British
sympathies, and which they had located on Lake Erie.
They learnt that Lieutenant Douglas possessed just
the experience needed, and hastened to place the mission under his charge, remembering his good service
in their cruiser. The party consisted of two or three
other officers, an interpreter, and a few Canadian
woodsmen; and the object in view was to induce the
Cherokees to forego some obnoxious customs which
gave occasion for scandal. The matter required to
be handled with delicacy, and the way was to be
smoothed by presents, as the chief of the Cherokees
stood upon his dignity, and guarded it with a
tomahawk reputed to take off scalps with artistic
precision. But he received the mission with great
courtesy, and pledged himself to every demand as
soon as he understood that they brought him a supply
of rum. This was one of the presents that Lieutenant
Douglas intended to hold back till his departure; but
the Indians baffled his vigilance, and seized it by
stealth, carrying it off to the chief's wigwam, where
they immediately began a carouse. Later in the day
they paid a visit of ceremony to the mission in a very
unceremonious way, and a state unsuited both to ceremony and business. Hence they were not invited
to partake of refreshment, which they considered an
insult, and seemed disposed to resent, going away
very sulky. Their manner caused the white men an
uneasy feeling; but it gradually wore off, and they
sat down to dinner after a scout had gone down the
village, and brought back a report that it appeared
quiet. But his intelligence proved delusive; for they
had hardly begun their meal when the blanket in the

doorway was dragged aside, and the Indians reappeared, now all armed, and looking ferocious, but
stalking in without speaking in their usual single file.
The chief displayed his famous tomahawk; but how
it took off scalps with such nicety seemed to puzzle
some of the Canadians, for they eyed it dubiously, as
if they would prefer their scalps left on till he produced a more efficient instrument. He was not in a
mood to respect such scruples, but drew his men
round the table in a threatening manner, and as
steady a line as their topweight of rum would permit
—all being done so quickly that no opposition could
be organised, and every one kept his seat, feeling
that a movement might provoke attack. The silence
was broken by the chief, who harangued his men; and
Douglas noticed that the Canadian interpreter looked
graver as he proceeded, which led him to inquire the
cause, and he learnt that the chief was dwelling on the
affront of the morning, and claiming vengeance. The
Indians needed little incitement; for they now broke
into a low chant, and moved slowly round the table,
waving their tomahawks above their heads, and leaving
no doubt of their intentions. Douglas gave a hint to
his companions, and they all snatched their knives
from the table, and sprang into the clear side of the
hut, where they planted their backs to the wall and
awaited attack. But their manœuvre disconcerted
the Indians, who also came to a stand, and looked
over at the white men with an air of bewilderment.
Then the chief demanded the meaning of this display
—protested that he meant nothing uncivil himself—and
led his warriors out of the hut, leaving the Canadians

with their scalps untouched, but not much disposed to finish their dinner.

They deemed it prudent to keep quiet for the rest of the day, and no one ventured forth; but Douglas felt reassured as the day closed and they saw nothing of the Indians. It is difficult to remain in-doors in America in the early nights of Fall, when the fresh air comes sweeping through the forest or over the mountain-side, and the sky is radiant with stars. The young officer slipped out, and turned up a path towards the wood, looking now at the spangled heavens, now at the darkened landscape, only visible in its outlines. He was so free from fear that he had come out unarmed, and wandered carelessly on, thinking of anything but danger. But his ear had become so quickened by training that it caught the slightest sound, and now attracted him to a tree close by, where he saw a dark object, which he made out to be an Indian. The man started out and stood right in his path, laying his hand on his shoulder as he came up, and uttering a cry like a horse's neigh, but more shrill and piercing. This is the Indian mode of giving a challenge, and Douglas responded with a blow, which caught the savage between the eyes, and rolled him in the dust, where he sprawled a moment and then crawled off in a manner that the victor used to describe as "going away like a snake." He saw him no more, and returned to the hut without further adventure.

A few days of his management brought the Indians to a better disposition, and the chief of the mission and the chief of the Cherokees became such fast friends that they afterwards travelled together into the backwoods. and visited some of the distant tribes. Douglas represented to the Canadian Government that his friend should be rewarded for the services he had rendered to England, and this obtained for him a pension,[1] which had such an effect on his habits that the famous tomahawk went out of practice, and the settlers had no better neighbour than Joseph Brandt, the chief of the Cherokees.

One of the distant tribes introduced Douglas to a young white girl, who had been living amongst Indians from her infancy, when a party of warriors ravaged a settlement and carried her off. He describes her as being " beautiful as possible," and a great favourite with the Indians, all the tribe paying her deference. But the example she offers of the influence of beauty over savages is not surprising, and we may wonder more at what he records of the influence of savage life on herself; for a strange chance discovered her to her brother, and he entreated her to return home, but she refused, declaring that she was perfectly happy, and could not support a different existence. " Feelings and happiness being unknown, a kind of contented apathy succeeds," remarks Lieutenant Douglas, in the old note-book which preserves this anecdote.

These adventures might seem unproductive for future use. But such an impression would be erroneous, for they formed an admirable training for a soldier—inuring him to privation and fatigue, exercising his self-reliance, and quickening and deve-

[1] This anecdote was related to the author by General Sir Hew Ross, G.C.B.

loping his invention by the constant demand for stratagem and contrivance. These were qualities in which he came to excel, and his wanderings taught him other lessons of value in his profession. He surveyed the country with a military eye, learnt how its features were used in desultory warfare, and thus convinced himself that undisciplined men might carry on a struggle against regular troops if they were properly handled. We shall see that this knowledge proved serviceable at a later period of his life.

His activity knew no limit, and he practised athletic feats on the ice when winter shut him out from the water. His power of enduring fatigue was marvellous. On one occasion he wished to be present at a ball at Quebec, and skated the whole way from Montreal, in company with a brother officer. The achievement cost his companion his life, but it made no impression on himself, and he attended the ball, and returned to Montreal as hale as he set out.[1]

[1] For this anecdote the author is indebted to Colonel Basil Jackson.

CHAPTER IX.

Roughing it Home.

The death of his half-brother Charles called Lieutenant Douglas to England in the autumn of 1798, and
he obtained leave of absence, hoping to reach Quebec
for a passage by the Fall fleet.   But he arrived
too late, and had determined to make his way home
by Boston or New York, when he heard of an opportunity of proceeding by a little brig which had failed
to complete her crew and cargo in time to accompany
the fleet, and was now on the point of sailing.   He
hurried on board, and found a rough north-country
skipper, who agreed to give him a berth if he would
put up with the accommodation ; and the beginning
of November saw him running down the St. Lawrence
on his way home.

The brig was laden with timber, and mustered a
running crew—so called from a practice during the
war of engaging hands to carry a vessel to port—and
the young officer might think that a winter-passage
did not promise well under such auspices, particularly
after his adventures in the voyage out.   But he enjoyed a little roughing, took things in a cheerful way,
and made himself as useful as agreeable, so that the
Captain discovered he was both a valuable help and a
pleasant companion.   He felt all the animation of
high spirits in the flush of youth, and could spin a
yarn of a quality to make the forecastle stare, while

he sang all Dibdin's songs, and danced a hornpipe. His qualifications in sailorcraft would have rated him A.B. in any ship afloat; for he could haul, reef, and steer, heave the log and cast the lead, make points and gaskets, form grummets, splice the main brace, mend ropes of the running rigging with the long splice, and the standing rigging with the short; make all kinds of knots, whether reef or single and double bend, close hitch or bowling knots; and point ropes with unequalled neatness. His friends well remember how he gloried in these accomplishments when his literary and scientific attainments received no allusion, and he said nothing of the productions which had been translated into every language of Europe. His nautical knowledge was all needed for the voyage now in progress, and proved of the greatest service.

The third morning out brought an increase of wind, but no appearance of bad weather, and the Captain and his passenger went to their berths at night, leaving the brig in charge of the mate. Lieutenant Douglas soon fell asleep, but was awoke by a violent lurch, and found the vessel pitching about in a way that he could not account for, though allowing for a gale of wind which could be heard roaring above. He felt so uneasy that he threw on his clothes and rushed to the deck, where his first glance made him call out for the mate, and the helmsman answered that he had gone below. The brig was in a trough of the sea, staggering under single-reefed topsails, with the maintop-gallant sail set, and the jib and fore and aft mainsail, while the wind blew nearly abeam. Douglas saw that they could only be saved from foundering by instant action, and he snatched a marline-spike from the windlass, ran to the fore-hatch, and gave the well-known taps which call up all hands. He then shouted to the watch to stand by the top-gallant braces and haulyards, and ease off the weather-haul upon the lee-brace. The company now came tumbling up, and he ordered them to let go the haulyards and sheets as the sail shook and clew up the top-gallant sail. Two boys started aloft, and the sailors instinctively obeyed his orders, without considering how he came to be in command. As swiftly as he spoke, the top-gallant sail was handed, the jib hauled down, the tacks of the mainsail hauled up, the top-sail braces manned, the weather fore-topsail brace rounded to, and the lee eased off, and the weather main topsail brace eased off, and the lee rounded to. The uproar roused the Captain, and he came on deck in time to hear the final order—" Lower away the top-sail; haul up the reef-tackle; watch, away up; reef the main topsail!" The brig was safe!

The Captain had stood speechless in this crisis, but now seized his passenger's arm, and asked for the mate. Douglas replied by describing how he had come on deck, and the position in which he had discovered the ship, but the mate he knew nothing about. His name was called in vain, and Douglas thought that one of the heavy lurches of the ship might have pitched him overboard; but the Captain had other misgivings, and ordered a search. It turned out as he suspected, and the mate was found stretched between his chest and the bilge of the ship's side, helplessly drunk. The Captain paced the deck for a moment after this discovery, and then suddenly brought the ship to the wind on the other tack.

" I am sorry for your disappointment," he said to
Douglas, " but I must return to Quebec, and lay the
brig up for the winter."

" On what account?" asked the young officer with
surprise.

" You see I can't trust the mate; and how can I
undertake a winter's voyage across the Atlantic without one?"

" Well, you have complimented me on my activity
and seamanship. Stand on your voyage, and I'll take
charge of the mate's watch, if you'll accept of my
services. I assure you, you may trust me far beyond
what you have seen. At least I shall never get
drunk; nor will I ever leave the deck while you are
below; and I promise to do nothing important during
my watch without consulting you, until you have more
experience of my abilities."

No proof of his efficiency could be needed after such
a trial, and the skipper closed with the offer on the
spot without disguising his satisfaction. The brig was
put on her old course, and the new mate took up his
duties by remaining on deck till the next watch.

The situation met both his tastes and wants. It
enabled him to indulge his love of sailoring and gather
fresh experience, while it opened to him a field for
exertion which he had begun to miss. He now found
an object for the energy he had expended on boatings
and skatings, in wanderings in the backwoods and
adventures with the Indians, and derived more pleasure from its exercise. Nor was it immaterial that he
came into closer relations with men of humble stamp,
for this taught him to appreciate merit in whatever
rank it might appear. Indeed, all the early part of

his life tended to expand his perceptions in this
respect, and raised him above any prejudice of caste,
so that no one could be less influenced by pride of
birth or station.   Indeed, his pride was to feel that
he had made his own position, and it was his ambition
to be valued for himself, not to shine by his lineage
or title, nor by the honours on his breast.   " I don't
belong to the aristocracy," he once said to his biographer, " and am satisfied to be one of the people."
Nor did the author suspect his descent from the great
Douglas, till he came to write his biography.

Daylight brought an improvement in the weather,
and a severe cold knocked up the Captain, keeping
him below, and increasing the responsibilities of his
deputy.   These were the more onerous, as he had to
navigate the ship by dead reckoning, the gloom rendering it impossible to take an observation.   Thus he
pursued a course for three days in anxiety and doubt,
hardly venturing to leave the deck.   At last the sun
gave a promise of peering out.   He ran down for the
Captain's sextant, caught a momentary gleam, and
ascertained the position of the ship.   Soon afterwards
the weather cleared up ; the Captain became convales-
cent, and his troubles ceased, leaving him at ease for
the rest of the voyage.

A fair wind carried the brig to Greenock, and they
reached the anchorage in the twilight of a winter's
morning, which threw a dimness over the shore, as its
outlines rose to view.   They had now to shorten sail,
and Douglas called out the order, when he missed five
of the best hands, rendering it difficult to work the ship.
He complained to the Captain, who was standing by,
but received a signal to be silent, and presently heard

a boat grate alongside ; a boathook grappled the gangway, and a pressgang scrambled on deck.

"Hilloa! you're short-handed here," said their chief.

"It seems we are," answered the Captain, looking
round.

"Oh! you don't know? Well, let's see the pay-
roll of your crew."

The book was produced, and overhauled.

"One—two—four; you're five short! Below, eh ?"

"I wish you may find 'em," replied the Captain.
"The rascals have left us to do the work; and I
doubt have got off in some of the shore boats, for
we've had several board us, as we came up."

The pressgang replied to this speech in strong
language, intimating a low opinion of the Captain's
veracity, and spread over the brig, searching hole and
corner. But no skulkers turned up, and they were
obliged to go off balked. Douglas rubbed his eyes
as they vanished in the distance, for the five missing
men had reappeared on deck, and were composedly
chewing their quids. His bewilderment amused the
Captain, who took him below and disclosed a recess
between the after-cabin and his own berth, formed by
a bulkhead, and so contrived that the door of the
berth could not be opened without covering the entrance. It just afforded room for half-a-dozen men to
stand shoulder to shoulder, and here the absentees had
taken refuge.

The time was now come for parting. Lieutenant
Douglas had more than satisfied the Captain, and
brought the rough sailor to appreciate his character
as well as his seamanship. They bade each other an
affectionate farewell, and the young officer hastened to

join his family. But the separation pressed heavily
on the sailor, and he thought that one with such a
leaning to the sea might be tempted to give up the
military profession and return to the cabin; so he
wrote to him in this strain, making him a most liberal
offer, little short of putting him in his own place. At
the same time, he dwelt on the dangers they had met
together, and the pleasant hours they had passed,
while he pointed out that the sea was the natural field
for the son of a great Admiral, and his own favourite
element. Such a proposal might have seemed ridicu-
lous to a young man of family, in the situation of
Lieutenant Douglas, already a noted officer and likely
to win high rank. But the heart it addressed never
denied a response to good feeling, however displayed,
and he saw only the pathos of the Captain's offer, not
its absurdity. He studied how to decline it in a way
that would give no wound; and this led him to reply
in a poetic epistle, which paid a tribute to the sailor's
calling, declaring that it would have been his choice
if duty had not made him a soldier—that he must now
return to his profession, but should never forget either
the dangers they had shared, or their convivial hours
—and that he wished nothing but prosperous gales to
the 'Favourite!' There is no copy of the effusion
amongst his papers; but he once recited it to his
biographer, and it struck him as breathing the very
spirit of Dibdin.

CHAPTER X.

Training Generals.

Lieutenant Douglas had not been long in England before he fell under the yoke of matrimony, and became the husband of Miss Anne Dundas, daughter of James Dundas, Esq., of Edinburgh, a lady in her nineteenth year, and who was to prove that beauty is not always ephemeral, for in her it seemed unfading. But the personal attractions of Mrs. Douglas were her least merit; it was in her amiable qualities that she excelled; and these made her loved in the social circle, while she was venerated in that of her family. It may certainly be affirmed that no one ever fulfilled more tenderly the duties of wife and mother.

The young officer obtained his company in October, 1799, and was transferred to the 5th battalion, in which he became Adjutant. Hence he passed to the Horse Artillery, and was placed in command of the Mortar Brigade. Both positions afforded him opportunities of extending his professional experience: the one by accustoming him to manœuvre a larger body of artillery than is often brought into action; the other by opening up a different range of evolutions and practice, consequent on the force being mounted. Meanwhile he strengthened his practical knowledge by study, and spent some years in thus perfecting himself in his profession, till he obtained the reputa-

tion of being one of the most scientific officers in the
army.

The British service did not stand high for science
at this time. A great minister had said that an
English General meant an old woman in a red riband ;
while a story was current of an English soldier who
told his French captors they had nearly made a
prisoner of his commander, and elicited the reply—
" Ah! we know better than that: he does us more
good at the head of your army." Such jibes effected
what could not be accomplished by disasters, and the
discovery was made that an officer would be all the
more efficient for a professional education. Hence
arose the Royal Military College, established at High
Wycombe, and placed under the supervision of General
Jamy, who had been aide-de-camp to Frederic the
Great. The post of Superintendent of the Senior
Department was offered to Captain Douglas.

The field presented to his talents in the Artillery
opened to him such prospects that he did not respond
to the overture, however he might be gratified by
the selection. But the mischief caused by ignorant
staff officers had been so apparent in Holland that the
Duke of York determined to secure his co-operation
in the movement, as the best instructor the army
could supply, and he tempted him with contingent
advantages. He first proposed to give him a brevet
majority in the Artillery, but this was thought likely
to create " uneasiness," and met an opponent in the
Master-General, Lord Chatham, though he declared
himself willing to recommend " His Majesty to prevail
on Captain Douglas to retire from the Artillery," with

H

the rank of Major in the line.[1] His Majesty intimated
his wishes accordingly; and Captain Douglas received
notice of his appointment from General Harcourt, the
Governor, on the 4th January, 1804.[2]

Major Douglas did not leave Woolwich without an
adventure, which displayed his ingenuity and adroitness, no less than his courage. The severe weather
had frozen over Bowater's Pond, on Woolwich
Common, and a party of officers were skating and
sliding round the sides, when Lieutenant W. M. Smith
ventured over the bound, and the ice gave way, pre-
cipitating him into the water. He came to the surface
two or three times, and caught at the ice round the
hole, but it broke in his clutch, and its thinness
prevented any one going to his assistance. Major
Douglas heard an outcry, and hastened to the spot.
Instantly he ordered the soldiers standing round to
pick up some wattles that were lying on the banks,
and push them over towards the hole, thus forming a
sort of gangway; and on this he extended himself,
caught Lieutenant Smith as he was sinking, and
dragged him out of the water. The wattle bore their
weight, and he succeeded in drawing him to the bank,
amidst the congratulations of the spectators.[3]

Another day he was attracted by a crowd in the
street, and found a drunken man lying on the ground,
crying out, and moving his arms and legs as if swimming. He saw that he was one of the party who had

---

[1] Letter from the Earl of Chatham to the Duke of York, in the 'Douglas
Papers.'
[2] Letter from General Harcourt, in the 'Douglas Papers.'
[3] This anecdote has reached the author from Lieut.-General Sir Frederic
Smith, M.P., the nephew of the rescued officer, who was present.

been with him in the shipwreck, and touched his arm,
when the man looked up, giving him a vacant stare.
"Where were you on that night?" asked Major
Douglas. The man sobered in a moment. "I was
by your side, sir, hanging on by the shrouds," he
answered. "Well, it's all over," returned Major
Douglas; "you must be quiet now." He sent him
to a lodging, and tried to place him in comfort, paying
for his maintenance, but nothing could keep the poor
fellow from drink, and it drove him mad. He lingered
in this state for a time, and then died.

The army dates an era from Major Douglas's
appointment to the Military College; for he supplied
it with a new class of officers, who made it able to
"go anywhere and do anything." The training hand
was unseen, but its work was apparent everywhere,
and nowhere more than in the staff of Wellington.
Our commanders have borne the same impress down
to our own time, and it has been signalised by
Hardinge, Gomm, Simpson, and Brown in our latest
struggles on the fields of India and the Crimea.

Rugby has canonized Dr. Arnold, who cast the
slough from the teacher's office, and raised it to a
ministry. Major Douglas achieved the same result on
a rougher field, cultivating the minds of grown men
who were versed in the uses of the world and the camp.
He brought knowledge down to the humblest ability,
and advanced it to a point that satisfied the highest, at
the same time raising the moral tone of the students by
keeping before them the example of his own conduct.
No part of the task of preparing this volume has been
so interesting to its author as the perusal of the letters
addressed to him by the officers thus moulded, writing

H 2

from every clime, and often from the very scene of battle, and whose names are among the proudest in our military annals. Fond glances are here thrown back at the circle at Wycombe from the midst of the big wars, the pleasant hours spent there are remembered on the bed of suffering, and the presence of the teacher is felt a thousand miles away; for more than one of the writers obtains the approval of his superiors through carrying out his suggestions; others write to remind him that they owe their position to his good offices; and others accidentally discover that he was their friend, when they have long held their appointments. One incident of this kind is touchingly brought out. A Mr. Deane writes to inform him of the death of his son, who had passed through the College and then obtained an appointment under the Duke of Gloucester, and he relates that the Duke had surprised him with the information that the post had been given to his son on the recommendation of Major Douglas. He pathetically adds, " You will easily imagine the feelings which agitated the mind of an afflicted father." Then he begs him to accept some of his son's books, " in remembrance of one who cherished the greatest respect and esteem for you." Another letter is from a Lieutenant Thorne, who asks him for a certificate of his conduct while at the College, and what he thinks of the possibility of his obtaining a company without purchase. The reply of Major Douglas enclosed a letter from Colonel Gordon, acknowledging the receipt of his " particular recommendation of Lieutenant Thorne of the Buffs," and stating that it had been laid before the Commander-in-Chief, who had ordered Lieutenant Thorne to be noted for promotion.

Captain, afterwards General Sir Philip Bainbrigge, writes to inform him of his being placed on the Quarter-master-General's Staff, which he learns at the Horse Guards is " in consequence of the favourable report you were kind enough to make of me." Another of the officers who thus thanks him for his first employment on the Staff is Captain, afterwards Lord Hardinge.

He was as alert to check vice as to promote merit, and gave a reality to the phrase of " officer and gentleman," which became characteristic with all under his command. His consistency on this point is instanced in a draft of a letter to an officer at the College, amongst his papers, and it would be hard to adduce a case in which authority tempered firmness with more kindness and delicacy. The letter disclaims any right to interfere in the defaulter's private affairs, but warns him that he cannot be allowed to bring discredit on the College, and insists on his paying the debts he had incurred while there, and conforming to all the rules. He upheld the same standard on every occasion. An officer under his command might be sure of never being watched, but he was called up at once if he obtruded irregularities, and learnt that military liberty did not extend to licence, and never forgot honour.

Such was Howard Douglas, in the flower of his life—the guardian of virtue, the kind fosterer of merit, and above anything mean or little. Few can rejoice at the promotion of others, when kept in the background themselves, or even when themselves advancing; but here was one who took a pleasure in helping others forward, and often did it by stealth, while he seemed destined to toil unknown, charged with the part of effecting a great work, which would never reveal the workman. But this engaged all his energies, though it did not satisfy his ambition. He panted for action, but his withers were unwrung. To repeat the words of the Chaplain-General, "his mind was too full of higher things to have space for envy or bitterness." He was content to drudge on, not living only for himself, but for his country and age, though conscious of his own military genius, requiring but an opening to win distinction. His feelings are apparent in the interest he evinces in his pupils after they have left his charge; and they write to him in a strain that recognises the tie, and seeks its continuance. Nothing could mark the impression he made upon them more, except the pride they show in each other, for these men of war seem imbued with his spirit, when we see them glorying in every success of a " Wycombite," and preserving the friendships they formed under his eyes through a hundred battles.

It must not be supposed that he found his work at the College all smooth, or pursued it without opposition. New ideas are distrusted by military authorities, and the notion in favour at the moment was to fight by manœuvres, in imitation of Frederic of Prussia, the idol of his old aide-de-camp, Jamy. But Major Douglas looked for instruction to passing operations, and from these learnt a different lesson. He had seen the Duke of York and the Austrian commanders carry on war by rule, and always unsuccessful, while the French generals had won victories against rule, and brought the finest manœuvres to grief. This led him to perceive that the art of war rested on the simplest principles, and that success resulted from their application. His theory was what Napoleon afterwards bruited, when declaring that victory remained with the strongest battalions; and he taught that strategy consisted in massing the greatest force at the vital point, and striking before it could be succoured. We shall see him venturing to give this counsel to the Great Captain, and hear Wellington exclaim " Douglas was right," when a different course forced him to retreat.

The mode he adopted of teaching military sketching, reconnoitring, and surveying, was an improvement so obvious that it could not be resisted; but he only succeeded in introducing other changes after long delays. The following extract from a letter which he received in 1806 from General Harcourt, shows what obstacles he had to surmount, and how they cramped his usefulness :—

" I shall be very anxious to know whether you have made a convert of General Jamy to your ideas for the improvement of your model, though, however desirable it may be to have the approbation of so scientific a person, I confess I am so strongly impressed with the utility of the plan proposed, that, if necessary, it shall have my full support towards carrying it into execution.

" Your proposal for instructing the students in the principle and construction of military bridges, and the general uses of artillery, deserves every encouragement; and although you may occasionally suffer mortification from the illiberality of one individual and the prejudices of another, I am persuaded your zeal will not be diminished in a matter where the improvement of the establishment is so much concerned."

No doubt it was cheering to possess the confidence of the Governor, and encouraging to have his support, but he detested contention, and must have been under constant harass. His temper could bear the strain, but a check in the performance of his duty was felt; for he had no interest in view but the public service, and liked this to be acknowledged. His open nature let his feelings be seen, and General Harcourt knew the chord to touch in order to sustain him in his efforts. "I am persuaded your zeal will not be diminished in a matter where the improvement of the establishment is so much concerned." Such an assurance gave the support he most coveted, for it recognised his disinterestedness as well as his judgment; and failure brought no humiliation. It cannot be denied that he attached too much importance to hostile criticism, for he never perceived his own weight; but the appreciation of his superiors reconciled him to any annoyance.

General Harcourt's letter marks the time when he began to give his attention to the construction of military bridges, on which he afterwards wrote an important work, remarkable for having furnished Rennie and Telford with their first notion of a suspension bridge, as they both avowed. He also designed a pontoon, which was tested by the authorities and reported on favourably, but not brought into use till the following year.

General Jamy retired from the College in December, 1806, and his duties fell on Major Douglas, who soon received the appointment of ˙Commandant, with the rank of Lieutenant-Colonel in the army. He remained at his post through the year, by which time the scientific vein of the army seems to have been exhausted; for in February, 1808, he reports to the Quartermaster-General that so few officers remain in the Senior Department, that he can be spared for active service, and earnestly begs to be employed in an expedition then known to be fitting out. He refers to the manner in which he has been shut out from service, when it opened the road to honour, and hopes that he may not be compelled to show his desire for it by "a great sacrifice,"—the resignation of his post at the College. General Brownrigg's answer was all he could wish:—" If I should be so fortunate as to succeed in an earnest request I have made to be employed in my present staff situation [in the expedition on foot], I shall consider myself proud to have the advantage of your talents and experience. I have not failed to communicate your wishes to the Commander-in-Chief, who expressed much satisfaction at the perusal of your letter."

He was now to have a respite from study in the dangers of the field, but not before he had turned out the men who were to be the lieutenants of Wellington, and who won for him the testimony which the Duke so characteristically expressed—" Douglas is a d——d clever fellow !"

CHAPTER XI.

With Sir John Moore.

Colonel Douglas had been deeply interested by the conflict raging in Spain, and his feelings were those of every Englishman in every grade of society. The national sympathy could not be withheld from a people struggling for their country trepanned by a foreign despot, and overrun by his armies; but something more seemed claimed when the invader was the common enemy. The same power had threatened England with the same ruin, and the wounds of Spain might to-morrow be our own, whence a desire arose to support the Spaniards with a military force. This led to the despatch of an expedition under Lieutenant-General Sir John Moore, a host in himself, but who could do little execution with a handful of soldiers.

Colonel Douglas was appointed Assistant Quarter-master-General to the expedition in the autumn of 1808, and ordered to set out with despatches for Sir John Moore. The telegraph directed the Admiral commanding at Plymouth to hold a vessel ready for the service, and he hired and equipped a small cutter, being unable to spare a man-of-war. Colonel Douglas arrived the next day, and proceeded to sea as soon as they obtained a wind, though it blew hard, and the sky threatened bad weather. A strong easterly gale swept the Bay of Biscay, and the cutter rolled along under close-reefed trysail, with the main boom lodged and bowsprit run in, waves bursting over the deck, and keeping it almost under water during the whole voyage, though the Captain managed the little craft very cleverly. Colonel Douglas bore the tossing for a week, when he began to think they must be near Vigo, and found the distance had been run by log, though there was no appearance of a port. It now transpired that the Captain's navigation was less perfect than his seamanship; for he had set out for Spain without a chart of the coast, though he had never been there, and nothing remained but to stay at sea till they could inquire their way. The weather was thick, the rolling what it always is in that quarter, and their position only guessed. Colonel Douglas recommended that they should heave to, and the Captain agreed, but had not time to carry out his intention, for a cry rose of "A sail to starboard," and another and another followed till they sighted a whole fleet. This proved to be British transports in charge of a frigate, and came on under all sail. The cutter bore away for the man-of-war, making a signal which brought her to, and the skipper revealed his difficulty in coming round, asking for information. His inquiry infuriated the Captain of His Majesty's ship 'Diana,' thus pulled up to tell a cutter the way to Vigo, and he answered wide, referring him to a region of objectionable repute. But the announcement that the cutter had an officer on board with despatches for Sir John Moore made all right, and he directed the cutter to fall in with the fleet, as they were bound for Vigo, and she had only to follow the frigate's lead. They all anchored in Vigo Bay the same evening.

The French had scattered the Spanish armies, but

this had not deterred Sir John Moore from pushing forward, though the enemy mustered three hundred thousand men, and the English numbered only twenty-five thousand. A cavalry action was fought on the 15th of December, when the English Hussars defeated a greatly superior force, though sometimes obliged to dismount and lead their horses, in consequence of the ice and snow on the ground.

Sir John Moore continued his operations, and made arrangements for a general attack; but Napoleon hastened up with an overwhelming force, which compelled him to retire.

Colonel Douglas met the retreating army at Benevente, at the moment held by the English cavalry, with parties guarding the fords of the Esla, which the infantry had crossed. But six hundred sabres of the French Imperial Guard succeeded in dashing over the river, and drove back the videttes, when they encountered Lieutenant-General Lord Paget, who held them in check till reinforced by a detachment of the 10th Hussars. The combat then became furious, and seemed doubtful for a time, but ended in the repulse of the French, who fled across the river, after a heavy loss of killed, wounded, and prisoners.

Colonel Douglas could have been in no position more fruitful of experience than the one he now held; for his duties connected him with every arrangement, and all his energies were called out by the destitution of the army. The retreat was one of the severest ever imposed on British soldiers, and is only surpassed by the flight of the French from Moscow. Officers and men endured the same privations, hurrying through a ravaged country without food and in ragged clothing, exposed to the most rigorous weather, and incessant attacks from the enemy. The roads were deep with snow, which continued to fall, and many sunk to their knees in the ruts, where their boots were torn off, leaving them to march on barefoot. Colonel Douglas exerted himself to alleviate these privations, and with such success that the Quartermaster-General's department issued new blankets and a hundred and fifty pairs of shoes to every regiment two days after he joined the army, in the midst of the retreat.

It would be out of the province of this book to follow the steps of the troops, but it may be mentioned that they kept Colonel Douglas in the saddle day and night, while his duties brought him to every threatened point, so that he witnessed the charges of the French cavalry, the drunken scene at Bembibia, and the entanglement with the broken army of Romana. The French held the rearguard in a constant skirmish, and it was thus engaged when the bullocks drawing the treasure fell down, blocking the road with the waggons, and he now saw the adroitness with which Sir John Moore met difficulties. The road could only be cleared by emptying the waggons, and leaving their load behind; but this might lead to a scramble and endanger the safety of the rearguard. The General avoided such a catastrophe by having the casks of dollars rolled to the side of the road, and there tumbled over a precipice. The light company of the 28th stood by with orders to shoot any one who left the ranks, but not a man stirred. No restraint was placed on the camp-followers, and they could not resist the attraction of the coin, which burst from the casks as they split against the rocks, and invited them to risk knee and neck in the pursuit. A few waifs on the road detained the French when they came up, securing a little breathing-time to the English rearguard. But Soult continued to press on, and thus forced the battle of Corunna, which taught him the superiority of English troops, though at the cost of their General's life.

Colonel Douglas was in another part of the field at the moment that Sir John Moore thus fell, shattered by a cannon-ball; and his duties prevented him joining the little train which carried the body to the ramparts, though he saw it borne away as the dirge narrates. A later incident of his life connects him with the story, and forms its sequel, now related for the first time. After recording the hero's death, Napier says, "the guns of the enemy paid him funeral honours, and Soult, with a noble feeling of respect for his valour, raised a monument to his memory."[1] Sir Howard Douglas has left a note disproving this statement. The monument was not erected by Soult, but by the Marquis de Romana, who returned to Corunna at the head of a Spanish army on its evacuation by the French, when they advanced into Portugal. The gallant Spaniard saw the unmarked grave, and placed over it a memorial of timber, painted to imitate stone, and representing the broken shaft of a column, rising from a pediment, with trophies formed of real guns and shells. He repaired to the spot in state on the completion of the structure, attended by his Staff, the civil authorities of the town, and the garrison, while the whole population lined the way, and the solemnity was heightened by the mournful strains of bands of music. The

[1] 'Peninsular War,' vol. i.

Marquis uncovered the monument in presence of this assembly, and wrote on it the following inscription in black chalk, with his own hand :—

'A la gloria del Excellentissimo Señor
Don Juan Moore,
General en gefe del Exercitos Britannicos,
Y a la de sus valientes soldados.
La Espagnia Agradecida
Battaglia de Elvina : Januario 16 de 1809.'

Spain has been reproached with ingratitude to England, but gratitude never looked nobler than in this incident.

A description of the memorial was forwarded to the Prince Regent by Major-General Sir Robert Walker, and Colonel Douglas was ordered by the Minister for War to convert it into a permanent structure, on his being employed in Spain a second time. He was to carry out the work by fitting the compartments with slabs of marble, which were to bear a Latin inscription furnished by Dr. Parr. But the proposed change of inscription struck him as injudicious, and he suggested that nothing could equal what had been written on the monument by Romana, and urged that it should be retained. Government adopted his counsel, and he had the satisfaction of completing the work, thus paying the last duty to his commander.[1]

Errors have also crept into the reports of the embarkation, and not unaccountably, for it was chiefly effected at night. The baggage had been embarked on the 13th, under the superintendence of Colonel

---

[1] The author has no doubt these facts ultimately became known to his lamented friend Sir William Napier, who must have heard them from Sir Howard's own lips.

Douglas and his department; and their excellent arrangements now prevented confusion as the troops, artillery, and ambulances poured in a stream through the streets, lit by the fire of the picquets. The movement was covered by the rearguard, which held the land-fronts of the fortifications across the isthmus, facing the enemy, who watched for the moment when these should be evacuated, leaving the rearguard at his mercy. Colonel Douglas saw the danger, and resolved to make an effort to ward it off. His duties brought him in contact with the Spanish authorities, and he made them see that Corunna would be treated as captured by assault if the enemy found the works undefended on the retirement of the English, while they might now be taken over by the relics of Romana's army, and held long enough to cover the embarkation of the rearguard and command terms for themselves, though they were not equal to standing a regular siege. His suggestions were communicated to the Spanish General, and that officer despatched a message to General Hill, requesting possession of the works, and pledging his honour to hold them till all the English had embarked. The arrangement was carried out, but not unnoted by the French, who brought up their field-guns and opened fire on the transports. The terrors of the scene were heightened by night. The Admiral signalled for the transports to make off, and more than a hundred slipped their cables, running before the wind out of the bay, and heaving to in the offing, while the rearguard mustered on the beach within the citadel. A number of the transports ran foul of each other, entangling their rigging; and several were wrecked, but their crews

got off in boats, after setting the ships on fire.   A
naval officer called from a boat to Colonel Douglas,
and said he was told by the Admiral to look out for
him and take him on board the 'Barfleur.'   But he
waited to watch the embarkation of the rearguard,
as it threatened to be hazardous—the transports
being only accessible by a long pull to seaward; and
casualties might have occurred if Sir Samuel Hood
had not sent all his boats to bring the troops to the
'Barfleur' and 'Resolution,' lying near the shore, and
which he turned into receiving-ships. Colonel Douglas
ascribes their preservation to this arrangement, claiming no credit for himself; though he must have felt
conscious of some share in the achievement when he
thus summed it up in his notes: "All being taken
off, those two ships got under way, and with great
coolness and no hurry moved majestically down to
the fleet to leeward."

CHAPTER XII.

At Walcheren.

THE dockyards and arsenals of England again rang with preparation ; pressgangs were busy ; vessels were taken up as transports ; and regiments ordered to hold themselves in readiness for embarkation. It became known that Government was equipping an armament for another little blow at the enemy ; and the Horse Guards was flooded with applications for employment. Repeated disasters had not checked the expectations of statesmen or the confidence of the public, and they once more dreamt of success, blind to the fact that petty expeditions are a waste of power, and can never achieve an object worth a war.

The death of his half-brother, Sir William, raised Colonel Douglas to the baronetcy, as he was afforded this opening for further service. He had now every inducement to remain at home, if his ambition could be satisfied with hereditary rank, a lucrative post, and an honourable position, not to mention his sympathies as a husband and father, whose life was invaluable to a young family. Nor could he expect that the expedition on foot would prove equal to the object in view, for it sought nothing less than the forcing of the Western Scheldt, and the destruction of the enemy's resources at Antwerp ; and these results could not be achieved by a few thousand soldiers. But such considerations failed to shake his purpose, and he again applied for employment. General Brownrigg invited him to join the assembling force as Assistant Quartermaster-General, his old post; and he readily agreed. Lady Douglas gave her consent with tears. "I was old-fashioned enough to ask it," he writes to General Harcourt; but the mention of her tears is all that he betrays of her objections.

The expedition mustered in the Downs on the 27th of July. Great attention had been paid to its equipment, which included six of the military bridges invented by Sir Howard and constructed at Woolwich.[1] Sir Howard embarked with Lord Chatham, the General Commanding-in-Chief, and his staff, in the 'Venerable' line-of-battle ship, bearing the flag of the Admiral, Sir Richard Strachan. Sail was made next morning at five o'clock, and the ship came to anchor in the Stone Deep, off Walcheren, at seven in the evening. Here she was joined by other ships of the fleet bringing the left wing of the army under Lieutenant-General Sir John Hope, while a squadron under Commodore Owen proceeded to Weeling Passage with the division of Lieutenant-General the Marquis of Huntley.

It had originally been intended to make a rush at Antwerp from the coast of Flanders; but such an enterprise would cut the army off from the fleet, and naval co-operation was considered indispensable:

---

[1] " We received orders last night to construct six of your military bridges, and one or two carts to carry them. We are, however, making three [carts]. There has nothing in the way of alteration occurred to me worth telling.' —Letter from Lieut.-Colonel Millar, R.A., to Sir Howard Douglas, in the 'Douglas Papers.'

so Government diverted the attack to a point where ships could act, and the troops were accompanied by a squadron and flotilla, which promised a support, while it secured transport for the equipment. The break-down in this service foiled every operation on shore.

After vacillating between several projects, Lord Chatham decided on a plan of attack combining three operations—namely : a disembarkation on the island of Walcheren ; the occupation of the islands of North and South Beveland ; and the reduction of some strong batteries commanding the entrance to the West Scheldt on the island of Cadsand, which was to be carried out by the division of Lieutenant-General the Marquis of Huntley. The left wing effected a landing on Walcheren the same evening, and the reserve occupied the Bevelands early on the following day, the 1st of August ; but the troops could not be disembarked at Cadsand, owing to the tempestuous weather. Thus the miscarriages of the expedition began at the beginning.

Sir Howard Douglas was charged with the departmental arrangements of the first brigade, which landed under the command of Lieutenant-General Sir Eyre Coote ; but was accompanied by the whole head-quarter staff, as well as Lord Chatham. They got ashore without damage, though the enemy fired from Den Haak fort at the covering vessels, and made an attempt to dispute a small wood which the light troops advanced to secure. But they then abandoned Den Haak fort, and Lord Chatham fixed his head-quarters there, while Colonel Pack hurried forward to seize the town of Terr Verr. Heavy firing came from this direction in the evening, exciting fears for the safety of his small force; and Sir Howard Douglas was despatched to ascertain its position. He reached the spot about eleven at night, and discovered Colonel Pack close to Verr, with four companies of the 71st. The little band had advanced in face of a strong corps, but met such a hot reception that they fell back, leaving a number of dead. Sir Howard galloped back to Den Haak fort, after he had seen them re-inforced by Major-General Clinton, with the 50th Regiment; and there found Rear-Admiral Sir Home Popham, who heard his report, and settled with the Commander-in-Chief to take up the gunboats. These made their way to the town by the Veer Gat, under the command of Sir Home himself, while Sir Howard returned to the land force, which had been strength-ened in the mean time, and concerted measures for a combined attack. The gunboats opened fire at seven in the morning, and the troops completed the investment by eight; but the garrison made a stout resistance, inflicting heavy loss before they surren-dered : nor could the gunboats prevent more than two hundred getting off by water, and entering Flushing.

Sir Howard now joined the force detailed to attack Ramakins, and was present at the surrender of that post, which left the gunboats free to complete the investment of Flushing. Lord Chatham had been struck by his acquaintance with naval movements, and now selected him as his medium of communi-cation with the Admiral—a delicate trust, owing to the jealousy with which the two Commanders regarded each other. Nor could all his tact impart animation

to Sir Richard Strachan, who held back the flotilla
and thus delayed the investment.   Precious days were
lost when moments told, and the town retained its
communications by water, which admitted succours
and supplies.   Nothing could be more fatal to the
object of the expedition, which was only attainable by
a dash; for the pause enabled the French to advance
their forces, and place Antwerp out of danger.   Nor
did its evils end here; for the baneful air of the
swamps engendered fever—more destructive than the
sword—and the English fell before it in files.

Sir Howard retained his fortitude through this
misery, and never suffered his misgivings to appear.
His duties kept him employed, and made his talent
apparent to every one, whence he was pronounced
one of the ablest officers of the army by Sir John
Macleod, who commanded the Artillery at the siege.[1]
His kindness to the sick and wounded is remembered
after half a century, and cost him some sacrifice; for
he denied himself indulgences that he might minister
to their wants.   He obtained the confidence of both
the General and Admiral, who agreed here, when
every other point found them differ; and this led to
his being named in orders as the staff officer appointed to decide the moment when the fleet should
open fire on the final assault of the town.

The post assigned him was the Nolle battery,
directed against the sea-line of the enemy's works,
which commanded the entrance to the West Scheldt,
and could only be passed safely under cover.   Hence
his orders left him a discretionary power as to

---

[1] This is stated on the authority of General Sir Robert Gardiner, G.C.B.,
the son-in-law of Sir John Macleod.

the time when he should call for the fire of the
squadron; but he signalled the Admiral that all
was ready as soon as the officer in charge of
the siege-batteries made his report.   The ships instantly weighed, and seven sail-of-the-line had come
within the enemy's range, where shot were beginning
to strike their hulls and rigging, before he gave the
signal to fire.   This was the discharge of the second
gun from the Nolle battery, on which the fleet poured
forth its broadsides, and the other guns of the battery
opened on the sea-line works at the same moment,
firing with such precision as to disable the guns commanding the passage.   Thus he covered the advance
of the fleet by carrying out his own principle of
massing an overpowering force on the vital point.
He remained so cool amidst the action, that he employed himself in watching the ricochetting of the
enemy's shot along the surface of the sea, and his
notes describe it as "an admirable opportunity of
observing the great value and importance of that
description of practice in naval warfare."

Sea and land joined in the bombardment, encircling
Flushing with fire, while shells and rockets tore
through the air; and the kind soldier was touched
with pity as he saw a town in flames.   He joyfully
obeyed an order from Lord Chatham to suspend firing.
The Commander-in-Chief had resolved to demand a
surrender, and an officer was despatched to General
Monnet, requiring the French to give up the town
and yield themselves prisoners of war.   But an hour
and a half elapsed without bringing a definite answer,
and the English resumed the bombardment; nor did
the enemy accept the invitation to capitulate till the

afternoon of the next day. The firing then ceased, and the garrison surrendered.

Sir Howard improved the "admirable opportunity" of the bombardment to mark its results in every particular. The pressure of his departmental duties left him no unoccupied time, but he rose an hour earlier in the morning, that he might go round the sea-wall at low water, and examine the effect produced by the fire of the line-of-battle ships. The wall had been penetrated by some of the shot, and others were sticking in the face, but there was no breach, and the greatest number of shot were lying on the beach. The embrasures had received a battering, as had the crests of the parapets, and shot had dismounted guns and broken their carriages, while those which passed over had riddled the neighbouring houses and knocked down a little brickwork. But he found that it was the land batteries, and the rockets and shells, which had produced the greatest impression on the town, setting it on fire at several points, and reducing one quarter to a ruin. This led him to conclusions which we shall see him urging when fleets were used in bombardments during the late war with Russia, and his notes express a conviction that Flushing could not have been taken without the operations on land.

The capture proved of no importance, for the time had gone by for an attack on Antwerp, which now possessed a garrison of 20,000 men, while the fortifications had been strengthened, and the passage of the river barred by twelve line-of-battle ships. Approach by land was cut off by the breaching of the dykes, which inundated the surrounding country, and every assailable point had its fort and garrison. But the

British squadron was not commanded by Nelson, and no defences were necessary against an army smitten by pestilence, and perishing where it stood. General Brownrigg reports the sick at 3000 on Saturday the 26th of August; the Monday found it 4000; and a few days raised it to 7000. Then a Council of War decided on returning to England, while there were still troops to re-embark.

So disastrous a failure excited a general outcry. It seemed a repetition of the blunders in Holland on a larger scale, and parties united against a system which employed such Commanders. The bitterest harangues were directed against the Government; Parliament ordered an inquiry into the conduct of the expedition; and newspapers mingled satire with invective in criticising the operations. The friends of the two Commanders heightened the agitation by their bitter recriminations: one side maintained that the General had behaved with skill, but was foiled by the inaction of the Admiral; while the party of Sir Richard Strachan contended that he would have captured Antwerp, had he not been held back by Lord Chatham. Hence arose the well-known epigram:—

> "The Earl of Chatham, with his sword drawn,
> Stood waiting for Sir Richard Strachan:
> Sir Richard, longing to be at 'em,
> Stood waiting for the Earl of Chatham."

Sir Howard returned to his duties at the Military College, and took no part in the controversy, but Lord Chatham and General Brownrigg claimed his assistance in their defence. A memorandum in the 'Douglas Papers' shows that he gave his testimony to the authorities in favour of Lord Chatham, ascribing the detention at Walcheren to the imperfect co-operation of the naval force, though he expresses doubts whether any combination of the two Commanders would have achieved the design on Antwerp. The methodical way in which he had jotted down the points of the campaign now proved of service, by showing the occasions on which naval co-operation failed; and the following letters attest the importance attached to the journal prepared from these notes for the vindication of Lord Chatham.

" My dear Sir Howard,

" Horse Guards,
20th September, 1809.

" I had hoped for the pleasure of hearing of, or seeing something of you before this time, and trust I shall not be much longer disappointed. The clamour that has been raised against Lord Chatham, and the extraordinary state in which the government of the country is, make it more than ever necessary that the most comprehensive and satisfactory statement of the transactions of the army he commanded should be made, and that with the least possible loss of time. As you have commenced this work, I hope to have your able assistance in completing it. I think this might be done if you could spare a week or ten days in town; and if Lady Douglas will accompany you, it will afford my daughter and myself the greatest pleasure to endeavour to make your time pass pleasantly, and we would try to get you lodgings near us. Pray let me hear from you on this subject, and believe me

" Truly and faithfully yours,

" Robert Brownrigg."

"Horse Guards,
28th September, 1809.

" My dear Sir Howard,

" On coming to the office I found a note from
Colonel Taylor, expressing the King's anxiety to
receive Lord Chatham's report as early as possible.
This I shall communicate to Lord C. in the morning,
and I have no doubt that his Lordship will press for
the Journal. I only mention this to request your
attention to the completion of it; and to suggest that
possibly you may postpone your journey to Lord
Harcourt until this business is finished, that you may
devote your undivided time to it. I shall certainly
hope to meet you here on Monday.

" Ever truly yours,

" Robert Brownrigg."

The 'Journal' was ordered to be printed and laid
before Parliament. It details the operations day by
day, and mentions the officers employed in a prominent manner, with the exception of Sir Howard
himself, whom we can only trace under the modest
designation of " an officer of the Quartermaster-
General's Department."

CHAPTER XIII.

In Gallicia.

Sir Howard's experience of war had not cooled his military ardour. In his quiet sphere at the College he gave his thoughts to the conflicts waged abroad, where glory waited on danger. From every camp he received letters from his pupils, relating what passed, as well as what was in prospect; and their plain unvarnished narratives made him impatient of inaction. But it was the struggle in Spain that he watched most earnestly: his Spanish campaign had interested him in its people, and excited a desire to serve under Lord Wellington, an object he would gladly have purchased by the sacrifice of his position at home. Unknown to himself events were working to bring about his wishes, though in a way he could never have conceived, and which left his position untouched. The Minister of the day had heard of the officer who came to the rescue of his superiors on the Walcheren inquiry, and now thought of him for another delicate service, calling for the same tact. The first hint came to Sir Howard in the following note from Colonel Torrens, the Military Secretary:—

" My dear Douglas,　　　" Horse Guards,
　　　　　　　　　　　　　　July 24th, 1811.

　"Immediately on the receipt of this, the Duke [of York] requests that you will come to town. In order that you and Lady Douglas may be prepared for what is to happen, I beg to apprise you that it is intended to send you upon a confidential and important mission to Spain.

" Yours ever sincerely,

" H. TORRENS."

Six days later he heard from the Minister for War, in an official communication from Downing Street, and learnt that, " it being judged expedient, under present circumstances, that an officer of the British army should be appointed to reside in the province of Gallicia, for the purpose of communicating with the Commanders of the Spanish armies in that and the adjoining provinces of Spain, and of distributing such arms and stores as may be sent from this country, His Royal Highness the Prince Regent has directed that you should be selected for this service." The letter enjoined him " to lose no time in repairing to the head-quarters of Lieutenant-General Lord Wellington, Commander-in-Chief of the British Forces in the Peninsula," and placing himself under his orders; while he received instructions to keep in communication with Lord Liverpool, and forward him copies of all his letters to Lord Wellington for the information of the Prince Regent.

Sir Howard did not neglect the admonition to "lose no time;" for he set out for Plymouth the next day, after a long interview with Lord Wellesley. His coming was awaited by a man-of-war schooner, appropriately named the ' Active,' and she started on her voyage directly he stepped on board. For once he got a fair wind, and the ' Active ' reached the Tagus

on the 12th of August, ten days after she had left
England.

The voyager nowhere meets a pleasanter surprise
than in this river, where he passes from a bay of
storms into smooth water, almost in a breath, changing
the cliffs for green slopes flanked by vineyards and
windmills. But the scene now excited a feeling of
sadness, for Sir Howard could not forget the presence of war, which had made the rest of the country a
desert, and he reflected that all might have been as
fair and smiling but for this irruption. He became
impatient to join Lord Wellington, and the Admiral's
boat met them near the bar, which enabled him to go
rapidly up the river, and he reached Lisbon before the
evening.

Here there was nothing to mark the situation but
swarms of beggars, infesting the streets, and betraying
the ruin of the population; for the Tagus caught an
air of bustle from the squadron in the basin and a
crowd of transports, and the city wore its best dress
in honour of the Regent's birthday. The houses
streamed with flags, and the great square offered the
attraction of a parade of Portuguese troops, who were
firing a salute as Sir Howard arrived. Night brought
an illumination, which he found of great use in picking
his steps through the city, a pit of darkness, and noted
for its abominations. "Edinburgh is nothing to it,"
he writes to Lady Douglas. He had wished to set
off for the quarters of the army, but this he was
obliged to forego, having important business with the
Quartermaster-General, who could not be seen till
next day; and he would have experienced difficulty in
escaping from a party of roysterers, who caught him

up as he was looking about, and carried him off to
dinner. The names of these choice spirits are not
revealed, but a suspicion arises that the dinner must
have been at the expense of the Regent, as they
evinced an exuberant appreciation of His Royal Highness, first drinking his health in sherry, then in cham-
pagne, and then in claret, finishing with what Sir
Howard marks by *et cetera*. But potations pottle-deep
offered no seduction to one habitually temperate, and
it is a proof of his sobriety on the occasion that he
went from the dinner to the theatre, and brought away
a notion of the performance for Lady Douglas.

His business in Lisbon was despatched next morning, and he started post for head-quarters, which the
retreat of Soult and Marmont had advanced to the
frontier. His arrival found Lord Wellington absent;
but he saw him on his return, and Sir Howard drew
a favourable augury from his simple manners. The
Great Captain read the instructions from Lord Liverpool, "made some short, clear, and striking observations on the state of the war as regarded Gallicia,"[1]
and described his present position, which he had taken
up to protect that province, while he threatened Ciudad
Rodrigo. He threw off his reserve as he penetrated
Sir Howard's character, and condescended to explain
his objects, instead of simply giving orders. He declared his intention of besieging Ciudad Rodrigo as
soon as the enemy's movements should leave him
to carry on the operation without interruption; but
he remarked that even the fall of that place would
not free the army for other service until the Spanish
authorities could undertake the defence of Gallicia.

---

[1] Letter from Sir Howard to Lady Douglas.

Hence it was of the utmost importance that Sir
Howard should exert himself to place them in this
position, which could only be done by reorganizing the
broken Gallician army, and employing it to draw
attention from the British Commander. Sir Howard
dined with Lord Wellington in the evening, and learnt
that an appointment on the general staff had been
given to his cousin, Captain Charles Douglas, in order
that he might accompany him as aide-de-camp, the
rank held by Sir Howard not entitling him to such an
attendant.

With the morning's light the two kinsmen were
mounted, and galloped off to the cantonments of the
Horse Artillery, where they stopped to breakfast with
an old comrade. They made another halt at Fuentes
d'Onores, and Sir Howard received an account of the
fight, as Charles Douglas led him from point to point
of the fields, showing the positions in which he had
been engaged for three days with the enemy. Relics
of the battle still littered the ground, and they passed
mournfully by the graves of the dead, buried where
they fell, friend and foe in the same pit. Another
day's journey brought them to Almeida, where they
were surprised with a good dinner, to which they were
invited by George Macleod, of the Engineers; and the
same friend gave them breakfast in the morning, starting them on their way. They would have fared badly
but for this hospitality, as the town was in ruins, and
the surrounding district had been left by the French
as if swept by Attila. Everywhere they met the same
devastation, compelling them to carry necessaries for
themselves; and they were obliged to keep a constant
watch against the peasants, who eased them of little

traps at every stage. This made the journey more
harassing, and it was a great relief to embark on the
Douro, where a boat had been provided for their reception. They rapidly descended the river, and might
forget the misery they had witnessed amidst the scenery
on either side, blending rock and mountain and forest
with castle and monastery, perched where foot could
scarcely climb. But it is difficult to enjoy the pic-
turesque in a dirty boat which is half full of water,
and smells not the sweetest, so that they felt little
disposition to loiter. An autumn evening induced
them to land at a rural mansion, which looked a
paradise from the river, and raised a hope of comfortable quarters. But appearances proved decep-
tive; for its master had fled on the advance of the
French, and left behind a garrison of fleas, which held
possession against all comers. They exceeded the
audacity of the rats at Tynemouth Castle, and Sir
Howard spent the night in striking lights and making
charges, while his cousin and servant were employed
in the same manner. Nor were their miseries confined
to discomfort; for the servant went to bed leaving his
door unlocked, and arose in the morning to find himself bereft of everything but the equipment in which
he had lain down. He rubbed his eyes as he looked
round for his coat, breeches, and other invaluables, and
could hardly believe that they were missing, till it
flashed across him that the fleas had carried them off.
" Poor fellow!" writes Sir Howard to Lady Douglas,
" his look when he came to tell me of it set me screaming with laughter. I must refit him entirely."

A couple of hours in the morning brought them to
Oporto, and Sir Howard was occupied for the remain-

K

der of the day with the authorities, though he found
time to inspect the bridge and fortifications. Indeed,
he observed the military features of the country all
through his journey, marking and sketching the positions, ascertaining the capabilities of the defensive
works of the various towns, and noting where rivers
could be forded, and roads commanded by boats. Nor
did he forget the loved circle of his home, turning
to it in this ride of nine hundred miles, so taken up
with the duties of his mission and his studies as a
soldier. "Let my boys read this," he writes to Lady
Douglas, "and be aware how much I depend on their
giving you no cause for uneasiness, but, on the contrary, that they conduct themselves in a manner to be
your comfort. Remember, my boys, I depend on
this." So simple and open was his nature, yet so
formed to sway others; for what could touch his children like this appeal! His character shows a consistency in these traits when they seem to present
a diversity; for they are all truthful and natural. He
is the same when "screaming with laughter" at the
rueful face of his servant, as when he addresses his
children, and draws out their better qualities by his
reliance. The good humour is as genial as the good
sense, and both are inspired from his heart.

He needed to go but a short distance to learn the
condition of Gallicia. His first visit to Spain had
shown him the noble qualities of its people, and he
now came among them more eager for their deliverance. As a race they may repel us at first, but
their cold manners disappear on acquaintance, as if
they were but a veil over their nature, which is
cordial and generous. They soon bring us to abjure

the doctrine that Cervantes lashed chivalry out of
Spain.   Sir Howard's faith in them was not shaken by
their present wretchedness, which had destroyed it in
themselves; for Gallicia was suffering the horrors
of anarchy and military licence combined.   The
authorities were divided and distracted; the people
terror-struck; the army almost naked; the enemy in
force on the border, and his way open to Corunna.
Hence arose continual panics, rendering the Junta
powerless; and the city had now reached the last
point of misery.   Yet the population were brave and
loyal, animated by the noblest spirit, and ready to face
the enemy, if they could procure arms and a leader.
Such was the posture of affairs when English ships
landed a large supply of arms and clothing, which was
stored in the town, and rumour announced the arrival
of an English officer charged with its distribution
and with the organization of resistance.   The news
brought a crowd to Sir Howard's quarters; guerilla
chiefs forced their way to his door; the civil authorities
came to pay him their respects; and a feeling grew up
that there was yet hope for Gallicia.

CHAPTER XIV.

Doubling up the Enemy.

Lord Wellington had warned Sir Howard that his mission would prove full of difficulty. But probably even he was not aware of the obstacles in the way, or the number of interests requiring to be reconciled. The destitution of the Gallician army had compelled it to prey on the country, while it could do nothing for its defence; and hence it became as oppressive as the enemy, and almost as odious. This bad feeling it returned, but more towards the guerillas than the people, as they had increased its discredit by maintaining the resistance it had abandoned. Nor was there less discord among the authorities. No two generals would act in concert; the guerilla chiefs followed their own impulses; the Supreme Junta received no obedience from the local ones, and its measures failed to obtain the public confidence. The disunion was increased by newspapers in French pay, which laboured to excite distrust of England, ascribing her intervention in Spain to a selfish policy, and representing her object to be the acquisition of the Spanish colonies in America, which she sustained in revolt while engaging the Spanish people at home. Such assertions made a deep impression on a nation jealous of foreigners, and this became so apparent that Lord Wellington advised Mr. Wellesley to hire one or two newspapers to rebut the attacks. "This is a matter, however," he wrote, "to be managed with great secrecy and discretion, and whatever you should think proper to publish should be confined to a simple statement of facts and dates, in plain language, with the obvious reasoning resulting from them."[1]

The course taken by Sir Howard accorded with this counsel—all his dealings with the Gallician authorities and people being frank and truthful. It came to be known that he meant what he said, that he spoke only the truth, and that he would never waver from what he had stated. They saw that he persisted in following out his objects through every difficulty, and could neither be turned aside by opposition, nor misled by deception; for he succeeded through his energy on the one hand, and established such a system of intelligence that he was rarely matched on the other. At the same time, his character inspired respect as well as confidence—for the one fell to his talent and activity, the other to his address and zeal, his kind and winning manners, and his appreciation of the national capabilities, so soothing to the proud spirits with which he came in contact. Thus a few weeks raised him to authority, and his influence spread so far that messengers came from the Pyrenees for his counsel and assistance.

One of his first acts was to visit the hospitals, where he found the sick without blankets, and he issued a supply the same day from the stores at his disposal. Soon afterwards he heard of a wounded Frenchman, in a hospital out of the town, and went to pay him a visit, when he discovered that the

[1] Wellington Despatches.

Spanish officials had neglected to give out the blankets, and he made arrangements for their distribution on the spot. He also sent a convoy of clothing to the Spanish army, and furnished the guerilla bands of Longa and Minas with 300 carbines and 1200 muskets.[1]

He remained some weeks at Corunna to carry out his measures, and then proceeded to join the army of General Abadia, who had fixed his head-quarters at Ponperada. Manifestations of goodwill met him at every step, and attested the impression he had made. Passengers raised their hats as he passed, the postmasters refused payment for their horses, and the Marquis Porlasga rode out to invite him to a banquet, on hearing that he was near his mansion. A report of his approach reached the camp, and General Abadia and the chief of his Staff hastened to pay him their respects. The following day he arrived at head-quarters, and received visits from General Castaños and the chiefs of corps and departments, who all showed him the utmost respect and consideration.

Next morning he reviewed the army, and found it in a worse condition than he had expected, half the soldiers being without trowsers, and wearing only capots, while the clothing of the rest showed great room for improvement. But they were a fine body of men, standing well, though deeply marked by privation, and as badly trained as equipped. The best corps only manœuvred singly, not attempting movements of the line, and a Toledo battalion broke down in trying to change front in échellon. The

---

[1] Despatch to General Lord Wellington.

cavalry were on a level with the infantry, and moved with wide gaps between the squadrons, nor could they go accurately through the sword exercise.   Their horses might all be thought to have come from La Mancha, each being a Rosinante; and the artillery was as wretchedly manned as horsed.

The muster did not correspond with the reported numbers, which led Sir Howard to make inquiries, and he learnt that nearly half the army was employed by the officers as cooks and servants.   It became his duty to urge General Abadia both to correct this abuse and to raise the quality of the troops by having them drilled.   This was touching points very irritating to a jealous commander, but he contrived to avoid offence, though he did not attain his object —General Abadia pleading the sanction of custom for the number of servants.   Sir Howard represented that the country now called for every man in the field, and entreated him to allow no custom to stand in the way; and he then consented to open the subject to General Castaños.   The drill was more easily settled, as his strictures could not be denied, and the General pledged himself to give it attention.   His suggestions were not taken so kindly by the officers of the army, and the good feeling he had elicited disappeared when they became aware that he had attacked their privileges.   They showed their resentment on the first opportunity, which arose on an order from General Abadia to send round the order-book to the English Commissioner, according to the custom of regular armies; and the Chief of the Staff announced that the Staff would make a remonstrance if the order were not withdrawn.   Such was the notion entertained of the relations of officers to their commander! General Abadia yielded the point, but warded off the affront by arranging that Sir Howard should receive his private order-book.

Sir Howard made allowance for the irritation of a defeated army, suspicious of interference, and took no umbrage—not being obliged to see what had occurred, and thinking it a moment to evince good-will. He wished to raise the pride of the troops, believing that proper training would endue them with high qualities; and he seized every occasion of expressing this opinion, and acquiring their confidence. He made way from the first, and gradually the feeling against him subsided, as all recognised his zeal and diligence, his interest in the soldiers, attention to the sick, and unfailing suavity and courtesy.

Yet he worked on delicate ground; for General Abadia failed in his promise to improve the drill of the troops, and they were still untrained in line movements, so that he felt obliged to renew the pressure. It required continued efforts to set the General in motion, and the absence of energy affected the soldiers, who made little progress, though a change appeared after a few weeks, and gave them the look of an army. He also succeeded in reducing the number of servants, which increased the effective force by four thousand men.

The object he had first in view was now attained. The troops were in a condition to march, and he reported the fact to Lord Wellington, though apprehending difficulty with General Abadia. And the result transcended his fears, for the General proved

immovable. Sir Howard represented the importance
of an advance, both as a support to the operations of
Lord Wellington, and a means of gaining the public confidence, while he affirmed that it would have the best
effect on the army itself. But the General maintained
that there was no cohesion in the army, and no subsistence in its front—alleging one excuse upon another
as the Commissioner parried his objections.   Nor
could it be denied that the march would be attended
with difficulty, but Sir Howard asserted that obstacles
would always exist, while an advance could not often
be made with the same effect ; and he pointed out to
the General the honour he would acquire by embracing the opportunity. The General broke in with
an exclamation, assigning the task to his successor,
and drew forth a letter he had prepared for the
Supreme Junta, in which he accused them of having
rendered him powerless by leaving him without resources, and declared that he had resolved to strip off
his uniform if they did not sanction his retirement,
and leave the army where it stood, as he could not
retain the command with honour, and honour was
dearer to him than life. This disclosure stunned Sir
Howard, as it dashed his hopes of a movement at
the moment that he looked for their fulfilment,
bringing all his projects to the ground. " What
could I say to the chief who intended to desert his
country's cause ?" he writes in a memorandum-book
which he seems to have carried about. It was
nothing that the General was incompetent for his
position ; his retirement would create a panic, and
he must be persuaded to remain at all hazards.

Sir Howard begged him to consider whether the Government had not failed him through want of means—not of will; and stated his conviction that honour bound him to his post, be the conduct of the Government what it might, nor would he stand acquitted before the country if he took any other course.

This brief note gives but a glimpse of the interview, for he remarks that it did not call for record, as the impression it made upon him could never be effaced. And we may understand his agitation if we picture to ourselves the Spaniard detailing his grievances in a burst of frenzy, and remember the gravity of the crisis, the point in debate, and the consequences hinging on the issue. He must have weighed every word as he interposed, from a fear of using some argument which might have the opposite effect from what he intended; and he may then have thought it well to leave him to reflection, for he retired without asking his decision.

They met again in a day or two, when the Spanish Commander was still out of humour, but did not refer to their conference, and Sir Howard renewed his proposal that the army should make a movement. He received an evasive reply, but found the General had no intention of advancing, and had actually sent off his best regiments to join an expedition fitting out at Cadiz for the reconquest of the colonies. It seems incredible that a government should attempt such an enterprise when unable to defend its own soil; but the finest battalions of Spain were now swept off for this service, and it absorbed munitions that would have

delivered a blow at home. Sir Howard heard of
the expedition just as he received an application for
supplies, and declared that he would give nothing
more, except for the equipment of troops brought
immediately into the field. But General Abadia no
longer concealed his design of remaining inactive,
and informed him that he had apprised General Castaños of his intention to retreat to Lugo, as he could
not hold his present ground for want of provisions.
His letter reached Sir Howard simultaneously with
one from Lord Wellington,[1] stating that he had opened
his trenches before Ciudad Rodrigo, and that the
French would probably muster their whole force to
interrupt his operations, whence he begged that they
might be kept employed in Gallicia by the Spanish
army. Sir Howard determined not to leave his chief
without support in such a conjuncture, and he addressed
a formal letter to General Abadia, representing Lord
Wellington's situation, and begging to know what aid
he might expect from the Spanish forces. The answer
allowed of no misconception; for General Abadia

[1] The following is Earl Wellington's despatch to Sir Howard on this
occasion :—

"DEAR SIR,   "Gallegos, Jan. 10th, 1812.

"I request you to inform General Abadia that I am now engaged in
the siege of Ciudad Rodrigo, which we are carrying on with the greatest
activity. We broke ground before the place on the 8th at night, within
600 yards, having carried a redoubt by storm on that evening at that distance. We shall open our fire, I hope, on the 13th, from the first parallel.

"It would be very desirable if General Abadia would endeavour to make
some movement to draw the attention of the enemy from us, as I think it
probable that they will collect their whole force to endeavour to interrupt
our operations.

"Ever, dear Sir, yours most faithfully,

"WELLINGTON.

"Lieut.-Colonel Sir Howard Douglas, Bart."

threw the responsibility of his inaction on Sir Howard, since he had refused him supplies.

Such were some of the obstacles which met the Commissioner at every step, and so often did he see his efforts frustrated and his plans overthrown. But he was not one to give up his object; and his fertile mind now conceived a measure quite out of his instructions, but which promised the support required. He determined to arm the people.

The law committed the defence of the kingdom to a levy of the masses in the event of invasion, and each district mustered its own band, under the name of an " Alarm." Sir Howard pointed out to the Supreme Junta the capabilities of this force, and engaged to equip it from the English supplies, if the Junta would put it on foot. This offer was accepted; arrangements were made for an immediate muster, and the proclamation for a levy appeared within a few days.

The effect surpassed expectation; a patriotic fervour seized all classes, and every one hastened to the nearest station to enroll himself for service. " Having witnessed with deep regret," writes Sir Howard, " the apathy into which the Spanish people had been sinking, on account, among other reasons, of the inefficiency and discomfiture of all their armies, I now beheld with inexpressible satisfaction a fresh outbreak of that popular enthusiasm with which the Gallicians first rose on the invaders; and I felt, and still enjoy, the consciousness that I could not be wrong in pursuing a course which rekindled it and inspired them with fresh confidence, calling into new life and vigour that pure national spirit of the

Spanish people, to which Great Britain had by acclamation allied herself in their first noble struggle against
the French."[1]

The proclamation raised the whole country. Sir
Howard received the thanks of the Junta for his co-
operation, and was requested to make a tour of the
stations, and inspect the different musters. He set
out accordingly, accompanied by the Secretary of the
Junta, and attended by Captain Douglas. Everywhere he met the most touching reception, evincing
the gratitude of men, women, and children, who
flocked round him in crowds, and hailed him as their
deliverer. A brave nation felt itself free, when arms
were in every hand.

The muster of the Alarms emboldened the guerillas,
whose numbers greatly increased; and the bands of
Longa and Minas continually harassed the enemy.
Sir Howard had brought the gallantry of these two
chiefs to the notice of Lord Liverpool, with a suggestion that it claimed some recognition; and he
opportunely received a case of arms, to be presented to them in the name of the British Government. The compliment gratified their pride, and
aroused emulation in others; so that hardly a day
passed without its conflict, and the enemy could not
leave his entrenchments except in force. Hence he
could detach no succour to Ciudad Rodrigo without
abandoning Asturia; and this required time, though
General Bonnet began the operation as soon as he
discerned the necessity.

Such a state of affairs infuriated General Abadia,

---

[1] Memorandum in the 'Douglas Papers,' endorsed "Memo. by Sir Howard
on vol. ix. of the Wellington Despatches."

who saw his consequence lessened by the change, and
the helm of command taken from his hands. But Sir
Howard did not intend to throw him in the background, and now visited his quarters on his old errand,
persuaded that a forward movement would defeat the
project of Bonnet. General Abadia burst out in
exclamations as they met in the presence of his staff,
and complained of the proclamation of the Junta, as
well as the gifts to Longa and Minas. But he justified
both, contending that neither the Junta nor himself could
have acted differently, as Lord Wellington pressed for
support, and that the presents to the guerilla chiefs
attested the good feeling of the English Government.
He then produced a despatch he had just received
from Lord Wellington, again requesting a movement
of the army, and convinced him that an advance
would retrieve all his credit.

The General agreed to march, but proposed to confine the operation to pushing one line on the Asturias,
and another against Astorga, which Sir Howard contended would fail to divert a force from joining Marmont; and he urged a forward movement, as certain
to attain this result. Their deliberations were interrupted by the entry of General Mendizabal, and he
sided with his chief, maintaining that the Gallician
army could not appear in the plain for want of cavalry.
The dispute lasted several days, for Sir Howard would
not give way, attaching no value to a flank movement,
and caring only to employ the army to drive back
General Bonnet. He now obtained intelligence that
Bonnet was in motion, while he received from Lord
Wellington a more urgent appeal for support, and he
prevailed on General Abadia to yield. The Gallician

army marched out of its cantonments under a heavy fall of snow, and made its way over execrable roads across the mountains, through streams, in the teeth of a cutting wind, and often knee-deep in drift. The people heard of its advance with joy, the French with wonder, and they fell back as it approached, without venturing a blow. Four days later Sir Howard received the news that Ciudad Rodrigo had fallen.

CHAPTER XV.

In Spanish Society.

BONNET now concentrated a force at Astorga, and General Abadia determined to fall back on the great road; to which Sir Howard raised no objection, the purpose of the forward movement being attained. Its success excited joy throughout Gallicia, and the English Commissioner was hailed with enthusiasm wherever he appeared—for to him the credit was ascribed. None showed him more attention than the clergy and religious orders. He stopped to rest at a convent on his way back from the army, and expressed a wish to pay his respects to the lady abbess, when he was invited to her parlour, and received with the utmost kindness, the abbess insisting on his waiting for a repast. She then conducted him over the convent, and took him to visit the principal sisters in their cells, a favour that had never been granted to a layman before. She gave him her benediction on his departure, and went as far with him towards the door as the rules of her order permitted.

A rumour of his approach reached Santiago, and the Archbishop of Toledo met him outside the city, in a state carriage, and conveyed him to his palace, the population awaiting him in the streets and cheering him to the gates. The Archbishop placed the palace at his disposal, and entreated him to consider it his own as long as he remained at Santiago,

declaring that he would regard his compliance as an
obligation. A chamberlain attended at the door, and
marshalled him and his cousin to a noble room,
furnished with princely splendour. Here he asked for
their orders, and Sir Howard begged for a little tea;
for the presence of luxury had no effect on his frugal
habits. He thought the chamberlain seemed a little
embarrassed by his wish, but imagined that he must
be mistaken, when he retired bowing, and a chat
with his cousin drove the incident from his mind.
But such an interval passed that the conversation
flagged, and they began to think the tea was a long
time coming. Their patience met its reward at last;
for the chamberlain threw open the great doors of the
room, disclosing a saloon beyond; and they saw a
table loaded with plate, and attended by servants in
livery, while the chamberlain looked the image of
triumph. Sir Howard was dismayed to cause so
much trouble, and explained that he did not want
dinner, but merely a little tea. The chamberlain
bowed to the earth, then stepped forward, and lifted a
massive silver cover from a dish on the table, exposing
to the amazed Englishmen what seemed to be a pile
of spinach swimming in butter, but which proved to
be stewed tea. He apologised for the delay in serving
it up, which had been caused by the difficulty of
obtaining it, only one packet having been found in the
whole city. The two officers looked at the dish and
at each other, and managed to keep from laughing, but
politeness could not bring them to eat such a mess,
and they knew not how to escape. A happy thought
struck Sir Howard, and he hinted that they did not
want the tea itself, but the water in which it had been

L

boiled. Alas! the precious liquid had been thrown away; and nothing remained but to disappoint the chamberlain and go to bed tealess.

Next day the Archbishop paid Sir Howard a visit of ceremony, as if he had been living in his own house; and he received visits from the nobility and magistrates of the neighbourhood, and the heads of the religious orders. The Archbishop invited him to dinner, and he was met by a large company, including several grandees, who treated him with marked consideration. The banquet was served on plate, and presented everything that could tempt the palate, with Spanish fruit and flowers to lure the eye, while the saloon was thronged with servants and blazed with light. From the dinner the guests passed to a concert, embracing some excellent music, and the entertainment closed with a display of fireworks.

Next morning the chamberlain informed Sir Howard that he must now give a banquet to the Archbishop, and invite the same company; but everything was to be done at the Archbishop's expense. To this part of the proposal Sir Howard objected; but found that he could not pay the cost himself under the prelate's roof, and that his host would be wounded by any breach of the arrangements; so he gave way, and the banquet was ordered, and the invitations sent out. All passed off as could be wished, eclipsing the success of the previous night, and the display of fireworks lit up the city.

The nobility vied with the Archbishop in their attention to the Commissioner, and the Count Mauda entertained him at a banquet followed by a concert, at which the band played a piece of music composed in his honour, while the company remained standing. Nor was he less appreciated by the religious orders. The friars of the San Martini monastery gave him a repast in their refectory, and a concert of sacred music, performed on two organs played together. But the most singular attention he received was an invitation to a convent of Benedictine nuns, where he was served with a repast on plate, and admitted to a ball got up by the young ladies under education in the building. These belles invited him to join the dance as he looked on with admiring, and perhaps aspiring eyes, and overruled his plea that he was ignorant of the Spanish waltz by offering to become his teachers. He writes to Lady Douglas that he could not resist such an opportunity, and it is hardly necessary to add that a few lessons made him perfect.

The priesthood regarded him with such favour, that they threw open to him the palace of the Inquisition on his wishing to pay it a visit. Happily its functionaries had been suppressed, and he might think that the calamities of the French invasion were not too great a price for such a deliverance; for he passed the threshold reflecting how many had entered in terror, though dust now told that the pavement was seldom crossed. The empty chambers threw back his steps; the groined roofs echoed his voice: and he might think of the words of the prophet—"The stone shall cry out of the wall, and the beam out of the timber shall answer it." Surely the second Philip would have looked for such a manifestation, if he thought of an heretic thus visiting the judgment hall, standing before the vacant tribunal, and having for his conductor a Spanish archbishop. Sir Howard gave a sigh to the victims of the institution as he looked on the gloomy pillars, and raised his eyes to the ceiling which had frowned back their appealing looks. He threaded the passages below, and explored the dungeons, reading the inscriptions on the walls, and he evinced such interest in these sad memorials, that the Archbishop ordered them to be copied for him. They then visited the library, and he examined the forbidden books, amongst which he noted the French ' Encyclopædia,' the works of Voltaire and Frederick the Great, and a ' History of the French Revolution.'

They proceeded from the Inquisition to the convent of Mosquiver, and were received by the whole sisterhood, who presented Sir Howard with a token of their handiwork, but what shape it took he does not mention. Nor did this visit conclude the day's engagements, as he spent the evening at the Countess of Poiega's, who held a grand tertullia in his honour.

The public institutions of Santiago included a college, divided between the army and civil service, one wing being assigned to civilians, and the other to cadets. Such an establishment naturally interested Sir Howard, who attached such importance to education ; and he paid it an early visit. He found the military wing in decay, though it still supported masters, and offered the attraction of a good system. The cadets were few in number, but well trained, and went through their drill in a manner that elicited his praise. He determined to make an effort for the preservation of the establishment, and wrote to the Supreme Junta the same day, reminding it of the want of trained officers in their armies, and pointing to the College as their proper source, which would

be cut off, if not liberally endowed.   Nor did he trust
solely to his own representations, but obtained the
co-operation of the Archbishop and Mr. Ballusteros,
the Secretary of the Junta, whom he invited to accompany him to the College, and they proceeded there the
next morning.   He paraded the cadets in their presence, and put them through their drill and such line
movements as their small number permitted, both
to show their proficiency and the advantage of such
training.   He afterwards marched them into the
school-room, where they underwent an examination by
the masters, followed by questions from himself; and
this impressed the Archbishop and Mr. Ballusteros
with such an opinion of the institution, that they became its advocates with the Government.   Their
intercession proved successful, and Sir Howard had
the satisfaction of knowing that he had saved the
College.

Such attention to the public interests extended his
authority and spread his influence everywhere, for it
was seen that he acted in the noblest spirit.   But he
understood the Spanish character, and knew the point
beyond which it might be unsafe to step; so he declined the command of the Alarms, which the Supreme
Junta wished him to assume, and pointed out that a
foreigner would be considered an intruder in such a
position.   But he undertook to organise the force, and
laboured at this task incessantly, riding from one
station to another, and assembling and reviewing the
musters.   Such acts showed his singleness of purpose
and won him universal respect, adding to the weight of
the English name, and making a watchword of his own.

Sir Howard did not leave Santiago without thank-

ing the Archbishop for his hospitality, and recognising
the attention of his household, amongst whom he
distributed a sum equal to what would have been his
outlay at an inn. Their intercourse acquainted the
Archbishop with our national character in one of its
best types, and this proved not unnecessary; for he was
now to see it in another form. The strain came first on
Sir Howard himself in the Spanish cantonments. Here
he was visited by an English midshipman and boat's
crew who had been wrecked on the coast, and fell into
the hands of the French; but contrived to effect their
escape, and arrived at the cantonments in company
with an officer of Hussars, much out at elbows. The
stranger had joined them on the way, and announced
himself as Captain Charles Allen, of the 5th Hussars
of the King's German Legion. He stated that he had
been taken prisoner in action, and sent to the frontier,
where he eluded the guard, and found shelter with a
guerilla chief in Navarre; passing from him to a chief
below, and so on till he met the midshipman. Such
adventures as he had encountered!—and he told them
in such a manner, so like what became Captain Allen,
who was noted for his dash and vivacity. General
Abadia invited him to dinner, and the Spanish officers
were charmed by his bearing and stories, not knowing which to admire most. Sir Howard asked for
his passport, and he produced it directly, calling
attention to the signature of the guerilla chiefs, which
confirmed his statements, though these spoke for themselves: and he gave Sir Howard such particulars about
his own friends in the Legion, that he could have
vouched for everything he said. He might have enjoyed
free quarters with the Spanish army, but professed

impatience to rejoin his corps; and Sir Howard advanced him forty pounds to cover his expenses. The hussar showed a proper sense of his kindness, but no more; and they parted the best of friends, and mutually pleased—Sir Howard with his new acquaintance, and the hussar with his forty pounds. But news came that he had made a raid on Santiago, and told the same story to the Archbishop, from whom he extracted a sum equal to a hundred; and this raised a hue and cry. Sir Howard started a pursuit, but it was always behind the hussar, whom it just missed at Oporto, and again at Almeida, losing all trace of him at Lisbon. Of course it was found that Captain Allen had not been absent from his regiment, and it remained uncertain whether his personator was a French spy or an English sharper.

Any mortification the incident caused must have been effaced from Sir Howard's mind on his arrival at Corunna, where he met the kindest reception, every one seeking to do him honour. He was invited almost daily to entertainments, and received the most flattering tributes, which we may regret he has noted so briefly; for the details would have introduced us to Spanish society at an absorbing crisis. But what relates to himself is skimmed over, and we catch but a glimpse of his triumph in little billets to Lady Douglas. " I have been absolutely oppressed with honours and attentions," he writes. Yet it is plain that he enjoyed the outbreak, and Spanish gallantry knew how to make it acceptable. " At a most magnificent entertainment given me yesterday," he writes again, "a friend of mine, who has often heard me speak of you and our children, whispered the host; and your health was drunk in the English manner, and the toast was honoured with a discharge of fireworks and some excellent music. I will leave you to guess how I felt it." Another letter tells her of a ball given by himself, and he takes credit for its success, though he appears to have fully shared the pleasure of his guests. "I gave a dance to the principal families, which I assure you went off very well. They danced till five o'clock, and I was obliged, of course, to see the last of it. The dances were waltzes and waltz-country-dances, which are very pretty, but which I hope never to see in England. Charles begins to waltz a little. I am no proficient, and kicked the ladies' feet." Ladies will be shocked to hear that he had so soon forgotten his lessons at Santiago.

CHAPTER XVI.

Working the Guerillas.

Sir Howard left the cantonments to visit the hospitals, now packed with sick, and obliged to turn numbers away. Only the kindest and bravest nature would have sought these sinks of misery, where suffering rotted in neglect—ear and eye were alike shocked—and the atmosphere reeked with infection. But he knew that his supervision was nowhere more required, and could be nowhere more beneficial; for he went to enforce cleanliness, and administer relief furnished by the English Government on his requisition. His judicious arrangements were most successful, and reduced the number of the sick in a surprising manner, while the supplies he distributed kept the remnant of the army in health. "I will not shock your tender nature by any recital of the scenes I have witnessed," he writes to Lady Douglas. "The timely arrival of supplies from England put it in my power to administer the only remedy; for nearly one-half the army was in the hospitals (if they can be called such), and the British Government may be assured that the succours I have distributed have saved at least 6000 men."

This reference to his duties indicates their compass, but shows us nothing of their drudgery, which

involved an amount of labour hardly credible. The
pen was constantly in his hand, and he scarcely
passed an hour without writing—now to Lord Well-
ington and Lord Liverpool; now to the Supreme
Junta; and incessantly to General Abadia, the
Guerilla chiefs, and the Captains of the Alarms.
He maintained a correspondence with the Count of
Amaranthe and General Bucella, commanding the
Portuguese armies,—with Generals Castaños and
Mendizabal, and the Honourable Mr. Wellesley, the
British Minister in Spain. His instructions required
him to send Lord Wellington copies of all his letters
and despatches, to whomsoever addressed, and to
furnish duplicates to the Minister for War; while he
had to keep a record of the disposal of every article
of clothing in his charge, and every musket and cartridge issued to the Spanish levies. He employed a
number of spies, whose reports he forwarded to Lord
Wellington, and thus supplied him with intelligence
from every part of the country; but we see nothing
of the labour this imposed but the result. It is true
he had the assistance of a secretary, but much of the
work was of a character that could only be executed
by himself, and how little assistance he received is
apparent when we find despatches copied in his letter-
books in his own hand.

Nor was he one to think that he had done enough
in discharging this routine; for he found time for
further work, undertaking tasks that others would
never have conceived. He made it one of his first
duties to ascertain the amount of subsistence in the
province, and the sources of the national revenue, as

well as the manner in which it was expended. Such information could neither be sought without caution, nor obtained without difficulty; but he persevered in his inquiries, and succeeded in forming estimates that proved of the greatest service.

One of his devices against the French was a proclamation to their foreign soldiers, reminding them that England was fighting for the liberties of the world, and inviting them to come into the Spanish lines, and enroll themselves in her service, when they would receive a bounty according to their rank. This he printed in three languages—German, Italian, and French—and his spies dispersed it so effectually, that it brought over a number of Germans and Italians, who were despatched to England for employment in other regions. His success recommended the measure to General Abadia, who began to form a similar corps for the Spanish service, and it numbered four hundred before Sir Howard heard of the proceeding. He instantly applied to the Supreme Junta to have it suppressed, representing that Spain could have no defenders like her own sons, and that the formation of such a body would produce the worst impression on the people. The Junta admitted his objection, and ordered the enrolment to be discontinued.

The measures he had taken to arm the population received the approval of the English Government,[1]

---

[1] Among other gratifying testimonies, Sir Howard received a letter from Colonel, afterwards Lord Bloomfield, informing him of the approbation of the Prince Regent:—"You seem to have conducted the objects of your mission with great adroitness and success," writes Colonel Bloomfield, "and I have much satisfaction in assuring you that the Prince speaks of you with great respect. No doubt your task is full of difficulties, but I know no one more likely to rise out of them than yourself."

and Lord Liverpool engaged to furnish the Spanish authorities with arms and uniforms for 100,000 men, to be forwarded as fast as they could be obtained. Vessels constantly arrived at Corunna with these supplies, and Sir Howard received them in store, and regulated their issue.   He had suggested the fabrication of some small guns to be carried up mountains on the backs of mules, and used by the guerilla chiefs to dislodge the enemy from farm-buildings, where they were in the habit of taking refuge from their attacks; and these light pieces came out, and proved very serviceable in later operations.

He never lost sight of the work of organising the Alarms, and had now brought that force into good training, though he confined the drill to the simplest movements, and left the men to their own intelligence, after he had taught them to act in concert and support each other.   He received a despatch from Lord Wellington in the midst of this work, begging to know whether General Abadia was in a position to move forward again, or whether he could undertake the defence of Gallicia during the months of March and April, as this would relieve the English army for other operations.[1]   Sir Howard had no hope of animating General Abadia; but he proceeded to the Spanish quarters, and acquainted him with Lord

---

[1] Lord Wellington's despatch is dated Gallegos, Jan. 22nd, 1812, and is marked by Sir Howard as received on Feb. 2nd.   The following is the passage relating to General Abadia :—" Having taken Ciudad Rodrigo, it is very desirable that I should move from this quarter.   If General Abadia cannot move forward, so as to divert the attention of the enemy from me, or from other quarters, can he in the months of March and April, when all the streams will be full, defend Gallicia ?   Pray let me hear from you

Wellington's wishes. General Abadia made an evasive reply, and threw the responsibility of deciding on Sir Howard. "I do not shrink from this, my Lord," wrote the Commissioner to Lord Wellington, "but it would have been satisfactory to me, as well as to your Lordship, to have had a more explicit answer from him." He then gives a view of the condition of the army, from which he drew the conclusion that it could effect nothing; at the same time he expressed the greatest reliance on the peasantry and the efforts of the guerillas; and "from these considerations," he concludes, "together with the impracticable nature of the country at this season, and the scarcity of grain, more than from dependence on the army, I should not feel uneasy about Gallicia during the months of March and April."[1]

But he was not disposed to leave the issue to chance, and he set to work to place it beyond doubt, aiming at such an organisation as would prevent the French operating in Gallicia, except with more powerful means than they possessed, and also disable them from moving reinforcements against Lord Wellington. He concerted measures of co-operation with the Count of Amaranthe, commanding the Portuguese army, and combined these movements with those of Generals Mendizabal, Porlier, and Poll,

in answer to this question soon. The French are talking of moving in this direction, but they had not heard of the fall of Ciudad Rodrigo. If they move this way I hope to give a good account of them.

"Ever yours most sincerely,

"WELLINGTON."

[1] Despatch to Lord Wellington, dated Feb. 4th, 1812.

commanding in the Asturias, and with the operations of the guerilla chiefs Minas, Longa, Palto, Campilza, Sarazar, Sabzeda, and others, supporting all by the attitude of the Alarms. He was everywhere seconded by the popular enthusiam, which rose to such a height that it could hardly be restrained, and the people clamoured to be led against the enemy. Such a movement of the irregular forces again aroused the jealousy of General Abadia ; and he complained of Sir Howard's supervision of the Alarms, though undertaken at the request of the Supreme Junta,[1] declaring that it was a slight to the army. Sir Howard would not allow such an impression to prevail, and ceased his personal interference, but continued to give counsel to the chiefs, and they carried out his orders with the greatest cheerfulness.

Lord Wellington was reassured by his promise for Gallicia, and felt himself at liberty to undertake the siege of Badajos, on which he moved forthwith, sending him some general instructions, in connexion with the plan of operations he had conceived himself. This was at once put in train. General Mendizabal made a rapid movement towards the Douro, with the view of occupying the enemy in that part of the north of Spain, and the other regular corps assumed a menacing attitude at various points, while the enemy was everywhere harassed by the guerillas and Alarms.

---

[1] Mr. Ballusteros thus addressed him on the 1st of March :—" The Supreme Junta has determined to request of you that, while visiting the Alarms of those provinces through which you intend passing, you will condescend to propose the best method for regulating and superintending those bodies."

His columns were pounced upon when they most reckoned on security, in the middle of the night and the broad day, in the mountain pass and the open plain, the Spaniards being invisible till a discharge of carbines announced their presence, or till they galloped through the French ranks. Many of these achievements were of an heroic character, and retrieved for the nation the renown lost by its generals. Longa, Minas, and Cruchaja united the Navarrese division of Alarms in an attack on General Abbe, which ended in his flying from the field, leaving behind two pieces of cannon and 600 dead. "They were pursued for two leagues," writes Longa to Sir Howard, "and only owed their safety to the darkness."[1] Maceda headed the guerillas at Porto San Payo, and joined an English frigate in an attack on the corps of Marshal Ney, which they drove from its position, after inflicting a severe loss. Salazar led his band against the town of Sasamon, which he captured, and put the enemy to the sword.[2] Duran took three towns by assault without an open breach. The town of Tudela was garrisoned by 1000 men, supported by a division of 3000 foot and 600 horse under the orders of Generals Avi and Panatier. It was defended by two forts, and contained a train of artillery, brought from Saragossa, comprising fifteen heavy guns, 16, 18, and 24-pounders, a 9-inch mortar, six 7-inch howitzers, and two royal howitzers. By adroit movements and

[1] Despatch of Don Francisco Longa to Sir Howard Douglas, in the 'Douglas Papers.'

[2] Despatch of Don Francisco Salazar to Sir Howard Douglas, in the 'Douglas Papers.'

countermarches Duran succeeded in deceiving Generals
Avi and Panatier, as well as the garrisons of Logrono
and Lodon, and cut off the communications of the town.
At nine in the evening Colonel Tahiena led the
battalion of Rioji and the light regiment of Soria
under the walls of the garden of the barefooted
Carmelites, and there planted the scaling ladders,
which he was the first to mount. He reached the
garden unobserved, and formed the troops into companies, when they seem to have been discovered; for
the enemy sounded the attack as he dashed into the
town. The Place de los Toros was defended by
artillery, but such was the impetuosity of the Spaniards
that a quarter of an hour sufficed to capture the guns,
and put the French to the rout. Lieutenant Tabaenca
rushed at the Gate of Vitella at the same moment,
with forty men, and made prisoners of the guard,
throwing open the gate and thus admitting the remainder of the Spanish force. The French were
obliged to take refuge in the fortified barrack of
Santa Clara, and the Spaniards retired from the town,
after they had burnt the military stores and spiked
the guns, though they carried off the mortars and
howitzers.[1]

A dashing movement by Minas on the Aragon was
witnessed by Sir Howard, who had the satisfaction of
seeing the French turn their backs, with a heavy loss
in killed and wounded. Minas followed at the double,
obliging them to seek the shelter of the town of
Losada, where they held fortified houses, while the

---

[1] Despatch of Don Josef Duran to Sir Howard Douglas, in the 'Douglas
Papers.'

Spaniards ravaged the country up to Pampeluna.
Minas then crossed the mountains in search of Soulier,
though worn out with fatigue and almost famishing.
The march was conducted with such secrecy that the
French General was in bed when a heavy fire of
musketry announced his presence.   Soulier's force
consisted of 1600 infantry and 170 cavalry, posted in
the town of Sangrassa; "and he formed his infantry
with his usual coolness and valour," writes the Spanish
chief to Sir Howard, "notwithstanding the surprise,
and the loss he had sustained."   The Spaniards had
seized the bridge, and his first object was to drive
them from this point, which he attempted directly,
leading the attack himself.   Minas allowed him to
advance within pistol-shot, and then opened on him
with his field-gun and a volley of musketry, by which
his column was almost destroyed.   But he retained
his coolness, threw himself into the broken ranks, and
maintained a running fight for five hours, effecting a
retreat to Sos, and wresting the highest praise from
his brave enemy.[1]   The loss of the French was 900
killed and wounded, Soulier himself being hit; while
that of the Spaniards was only 200 wounded and 30
killed, including four officers.

Minas again left his fastness in the mountains at
the beginning of April, and accomplished a march of
fifteen leagues in one day, with the intention of inter-
cepting a French convoy, escorted by 150 cavalry and
2000 infantry composed of Poles and the Imperial
Guard.   He showed himself near Victoria, and caused
letters to be dispersed in the town intimating that
he was on his way to the Pyrenees, but he had no

---

[1] Despatch of General Minas to Sir Howard Douglas, in the 'Douglas
Papers.'

thought of such a movement, and made a forced march to Artaban, where he took post unobserved. His force was so placed as to form a circle, which would surround the convoy on its coming up, as well as the escort, but he gave an order that no man should molest the convoy till the escort was defeated. The French were seen approaching in a careless way, without suspecting an ambush, the high rocks concealing the Spaniards, who did not present themselves till a shower of balls had thrown the escort in confusion. They tried to rally, but the Spaniards now poured over the rocks and charged them with the bayonet, completing their rout. " The haughty Poles and Imperial Guard, being completely dismayed," writes Minas to Sir Howard, " threw away their arms and fell victims on our bayonets."

The carnage in this action was dreadful, and Minas informed Sir Howard that not one of the French would have escaped only for the vicinity of the castle of Artaban. To this fortress about 800 made good their retreat, after a loss of nearly 600 killed, 500 wounded, and 150 prisoners. Among the killed was Deslandes, Cabinet Secretary to King Joseph; and the captives included his wife, Donna Carlotta Ariana, who was wounded, and two other ladies, with five children. The spoil embraced 100 waggons, two standards, the military chest of the Polish regiment of infantry, the correspondence of King Joseph, which Deslandes was conveying to France, the carriage and valuables of Deslandes, and eight drums.[1]

---

[1] Despatch of General Minas to Sir Howard Douglas, in the 'Douglas Papers.'

Such were some of the achievements of the irregular forces during the time that Sir Howard undertook to hold Gallicia, and occupy the French in the north of Spain. They had the effect desired, in keeping Lord Wellington from being embarrassed at a critical period; and Sir Howard received a despatch from Lord Fitzroy Somerset towards the end of April, announcing the capture of Badajoz.

The guerilla successes exasperated the French, who resorted to the severest reprisals, and the peasants returned from their forays to find their homes devastated and their wives and daughters dishonoured and sometimes butchered. These atrocities were so common that they are mentioned as things of course by the guerilla chiefs in their despatches to Sir Howard. But he relates one enormity that drove them to madness, and excites a shudder even at this distance of time. The French desired to occupy a monastery commanding a strong pass, but admission was denied by the monks, who made a stout resistance. They were overcome, and the French punished their temerity by roasting several of them, and putting the rest to the sword. A party of the French afterwards fell into the hands of the guerillas, who obtained possession of an immense oven constructed for the use of a regiment, and baked them alive. Such are the horrors of invasion!

CHAPTER XVII.

SERVING WITH THE SPANISH ARMY.

THE enthusiasm of the Alarms and guerillas at these successes was damped by the absence of Sir Howard, who no longer superintended their musters and drills. He continued to furnish them with arms, and to correspond with their chiefs, directing the movement with the same zeal, but he was not seen at their posts. They had become so used to his presence that the change excited remark; and a rumour spread that the Government had forbidden him to attend. The sensation produced showed the popularity he had attained, and how completely he had won their confidence. Addresses poured in upon him from all parts;[1] exasperated crowds paraded the streets of the towns; and the Alarms broke up from their musters with threatening cries. The military became frightened at these demonstrations, and proposed that the bands should be disarmed; effecting this measure in several villages, though at such risk that it was carried no further. Indeed the Supreme Junta ordered it to be discontinued, and the arms to be restored, at the same time censuring the Generals; and they begged Sir Howard to resume his inspections of the Alarms, of the interruption of which

---

[1] A translation of one of these addresses is given in the Appendix.

they now first heard. But he felt that such a course would confirm, the popular impression, and widen the breach with the army, which he desired to heal; and he convinced the Junta that it would be better to give out that he was kept away from the musters by his other duties, which might be said with truth. He was always ready to renounce himself, and never more so than now; for it was important to avoid offending General Abadia, whom he wished to join in some operations on the Esla. He had put the army in a serviceable condition, supplying it with arms and clothing; and the influence he thus acquired had been exerted to push forward its training. His withdrawal from the supervision of the Alarms gratified General Abadia, and the reason he pleaded for the step screened him from blame, and soothed the people; so that he preserved his influence with both, while he calmed the jealousies a foreigner naturally provoked. This appeared on his next visit to the camp, when General Abadia received him with compliments; and he might feel proud that one so prejudiced acknowledged his services, and expressed appreciation of what he had done for Spain. He paid the General a tribute in return, crediting him with the improved efficiency of the army, and then unfolded the plan of Lord Wellington, which contemplated the advance of the division of General Castaños, to co-operate with the Gallician army on the Orbigo and Esla, and keep the French in that quarter employed. He entreated Abadia to act at once, and the General replied that he had but one objection, his want of artillery, which

Sir Howard could not deny justified inaction. He determined to see if some equipment could not be obtained, and hastened back to Corunna; but his hopes fell as he entered the arsenal, and beheld the lately-deserted foundries ringing with the sound of the anvil, and sending up volumes of smoke; for his knowledge of the ruling powers made him look for disappointment in what others might have thought encouraging. He dreaded another expedition to America; and inquiry confirmed his fears, eliciting that this was the destination of a battery of artillery there, comprising just the pieces wanted by the Gallician army. It stood ready for shipment, and an order came to prepare a number of gun-carriages for the same service while he was questioning the artificers.

He considered whether it might be possible to avert the shipment, and secure the artillery for General Abadia; but his functions did not extend to political transactions, and he could only approach the Regency by a report to Sir Henry Wellesley, who resided at Cadiz, and would receive it too late for use. It suddenly occurred to him to make an application for the guns without appearing to know their destination. He instantly acquainted the Junta and General Castaños with the wants of the Gallician army, and represented that here was the very equipment required,[1] begging that it might be issued for service. General Castaños had now entered Gallicia, and announced that he was crippled by the same deficiency, which

---

[1] Despatch of Sir Howard Douglas to the Earl of Liverpool.

he entreated him to correct by securing the battery in question.[1]   Sir Howard rode off with his letter to Mr. Ballusteros, the Secretary of the Supreme Junta, and learnt that the Junta had made inquiries about the guns, and were incensed to find that they were to be despatched to the colonies, although paid for out of the Gallician revenue. The battery was embarked the same day for Ferrol, where a Spanish frigate waited to convoy it to America; and the Regency added to its folly by again diverting the best troops of General Abadia to the same service. These regiments had been armed with muskets and carbines furnished by England, and were partly clothed from the English supplies.[2]

The people could hardly be kept from insurrection when this proceeding became known; and it created a division in the Government itself, for the Bishop of Reufe seceded from the Regency to mark his disapproval of the step; and the Supreme Junta made a protest against the continuance of the American struggle while the French remained on Spanish soil. Sir Howard failed to stop the enterprise, but had aroused opposition, and the part he took increased his popularity and influence. On the other hand, every day gave proof of the madness of the Go-

---

[1] "Since artillery of the competent calibre in proportion to the object is indispensable, I have great satisfaction in learning that through your means I can reckon upon a train which till now I had been in want of, and not to lose time I have advised the Commandant of the artillery of the army to repair to Corunna, to dispose its immediate departure for Lugo, trusting that you, who know the necessity of this arm, will contribute to lessen the difficulties that may retard its leaving that place."—Despatch of General Castaños to Sir Howard Douglas, in the ' Douglas Papers.'

[2] Despatch of Sir Howard Douglas to Sir Henry Wellesley.

vernment, for their armies were perishing of hunger[1]
at the moment that they despatched this expedition; and its cost left them without means to pay
for a cargo of flour which arrived at Corunna for
their use.

The arrival of General Castaños in Gallicia inspired
hopes that he would render material support to Lord
Wellington in the campaign about to open, and Sir
Howard hastened to secure his co-operation as soon
as he could leave Corunna. The object he thought of
greatest consequence was the reduction of Astorga,
which would deprive the French of a most important
post; and he urged this with such force that General
Castaños assembled a council of war to consider the
project.   Reference was made to the commanding
officer of the Artillery, and he reported that the army
possessed no means of undertaking such an operation, which the council found to be perfectly true, and
declared that it could not be entertained. Sir Howard
knew the inadequacy of the artillery, but felt persuaded that means of attack did exist, though in a
small way, and he considered how he should proceed
to get them applied to the purpose. Could he expect
that the statement of his views would have any result
but to excite professional resentment, when it set his
opinion against the verdict of a council of war? He
saw the difficulty of moving, but he also saw the great
importance, and he determined to open the subject
privately to his friend General Giron, the Chief of the
Staff.   The General met it in the best spirit, with a

---

[1] "Their daily existence may be considered a miracle."—Despatch of
General Castaños to Sir Howard Douglas.

sincere desire to promote the credit of the army, and
see it efficiently employed. Sir Howard quickly convinced him of the advantages to be gained; and
he acknowledged that the town would add to the
security of Gallicia, and must even oblige the French
to evacuate the Asturias. But Astorga had made
a long stand against Junot at the head of a French
army, which gave it a repute for capabilities of
defence, and he pronounced the want of artillery a
fatal bar. Sir Howard stated that this might be
remedied, and adverted to his recent visit to the
arsenal, where he had seen six brass 16-pounders, with
carriages, which were available for service, though
not in the best condition; and he engaged to supply
a brigade of five-and-a-half howitzers from the English
stores as a further equipment. The arsenal contained
abundant materials for the construction of waggons
and trucks, and he entreated the General to go to
Corunna, and form his own judgment of what could
be obtained, giving him directions where to look
for everything he had mentioned, and even drawings of the places where they were stowed. General
Giron secretly left the cantonments the same evening, went to Corunna by post, and returned satisfied.
Sir Howard now told him that he had served in the
Artillery, and his experience enabled him to say that
the means available for the siege were adequate, which
he begged him to impress on General Castaños, and
get the question re-considered. The General acted on
his advice, and gained over General Castaños, who
carried the point with the council of war. Orders
were given for the necessary preparations, and they
were pushed on with vigour, though some delay arose

from want of money—as important a sinew as artillery.   But energy overcame all difficulties, and 16,000 men marched on Astorga.

Sir Howard announced the expedition to the Count of Amaranthe, as well as to General Bucella, and warned them to guard the country left open; but Lord Wellington made a movement that relieved them of this duty, just as their advance obliged the French to retire.[1]   The same intelligence set in motion the guerilla parties and Alarms; and Merino took advantage of the diversion to sweep across the track of a French column engaged in levying a contribution of meat in the district of Penaranda. He planted his infantry on some heights cutting the line of march, and surrounded the French as they came up, first riddling their ranks with a volley of musketry. His cavalry seized the only gap for retreat, leaving them no resource but to surrender, and they laid down their

---

[1] Lord Wellington informed Sir Howard of this arrangement in the following despatch :—

"Sir,   "Guinaldo, May 25, 1812.

"I received yesterday your letter of the 18th instant, and I had at the same time one of the 20th from the Conde d'Amaranthe, from which I learnt that the enemy, after plundering the villages on the frontier of Gallicia, had retired to Benevente.

"There is no chance of their attacking Gallicia as long as this army shall be on this frontier; and entertaining this opinion and feeling an anxious desire that the Portuguese Government should be saved the expense of the militia in arms, when not necessary to be incurred, and that the individuals composing the militia should have the advantage of returning to their homes when their services shall not be required, I desired that the militia should be disbanded as soon as I brought back the army to this quarter, with the exception of those corps necessary to observe the enemy's movements.   They are, however, ready to turn out again at a moment's notice.

"I have the honour to be, &c.,

"Wellington.

"Lieut.-Col. Sir Howard Douglas, Bart."

arms amidst a heap of dead and wounded. Merino sullied the victory by a massacre, which the atrocities perpetrated by the French provoked, but do not excuse. He singled out 110 of his captives to be shot on the field, and carried out their execution in the most solemn manner, prefacing it with this speech:—" I inflict this chastisement for the horrible sacrifice of the three members of the Royal Supreme Junta of the province of Burgos, whom the French surprised on the 20th at Grando, and put to an infamous death at Soria and Aranda, hanging them afterwards to a gallows, where they still remain, for no other crime than that of having taken an active part in defence of their country, so unjustly invaded, pillaged, and insulted by these monsters." [1]

The French sent out a column to intercept the victors and rescue the prisoners, but their design came to Merino's knowledge, and a lonely cross-road enabled him to plant an ambuscade. The usual volley of musketry too late revealed the danger, and they fled in confusion, throwing away their arms, and leaving an addition of 200 to Merino's captives, instead of recovering those in his possession. [2]

This was the moment chosen by the Spanish Regency to order another detachment of troops to be embarked for South America. It transpired that a larger body would have been sent before, only for the obstacles raised by Sir Howard, and he endeavoured to induce General Castaños to suspend the embarkation of the present force until the measure could be

---

[1] Despatch of Don Geronimo Merino to Sir Howard Douglas.
[2] Despatches of Sir Howard Douglas to the Earl of Wellington and Sir Henry Wellesley.

reconsidered. The General convinced him that he could not delay, as his orders were imperative, and the troops were sent off to Vigo the same day. But Sir Howard prevented their embarkation,[1] and his interference obtained the approbation of the English Minister in Spain: "Your endeavours to defeat a measure so injurious to the interests of Gallicia," wrote Sir Henry Wellesley, "cannot fail to be approved by the Government of His Royal Highness the Prince Regent, and you will do right to use every exertion to defeat any project of the kind in future."[2]

But the party of the Regency did not regard his proceedings with the same favour, and an incident happened at the time which enabled its adherents to show their bad feeling. A convoy of reinforcements for Lord Wellington was met by a storm on its way to Lisbon, damaging one of its transports, which took refuge in Corunna Bay; and Sir Howard's thoughtful kindness prompted him to apply to the Governor of Corunna for permission to bring the soldiers ashore. He made the request as a matter of form, not dreaming of objection; but faction easily raises difficulties,

---

[1] "Nevertheless, so strange a people are the Spaniards, that a second expedition against the colonies, having with it all the field artillery just supplied by England, would have sailed from Vigo but for the prompt interference of Sir Howard Douglas."—Peninsular War, vol. v. 23.

[2] Despatch of the Hon. Sir Henry Wellesley, K.B., to Sir Howard Douglas.

Lord Liverpool was equally satisfied with his proceedings. His secretary writes to Sir Howard from the War Department on the 15th of May:— "His Lordship has learned with great regret that the Spanish authorities have persisted in the very impolitic measure of sending troops from Gallicia to their American colonies, and he desires me to convey to you his full approbation of the conduct you have held upon this delicate occasion."

and General Taboada replied that it would be a breach of his orders to permit the landing of foreign troops. Sir Howard reminded him that these troops must be regarded as allies and defenders, and begged him to refer the question to General Abadia, whose sentiments the Governor knew to be his own, and accepted him as arbiter. The General decided that the soldiers might be put ashore in the daytime, on the other side of the bay, but that they must land without their arms. Such a proposal seemed an insult, and Sir Howard received it in a manner becoming a British officer—declining the favour, and assuring the Governor that the terms prescribed should never be divulged to the soldiers who had come to the succour of Spain.

The same feelings met Sir Howard at other points. Lord Wellington's plan for the campaign embraced operations to the north by the Spanish forces, based on a depôt of stores to be established on the coast; and he directed him to report on the fitness of the Bayonne Islands for this service. He went to fulfil this duty, notifying his object to the Governor of the district, and apprising him of Lord Wellington's orders. But the projects of the English General carried no weight with that officer, and he declined to permit the survey, alleging that it might be used to the disadvantage of Spain in the event of a war with England. Such an objection seemed monstrous at a moment when the two nations were so closely allied, and could only have been started by faction. Happily it was disavowed by General Castaños, who removed all obstructions, and Sir Howard made an inspection of the whole coast. His examination led him to the

conclusion that the spot marked by Lord Wellington
was not suited for a base of operations, and he suggested that the depôt should be established at the
island of Arosa, which afforded the requisite facilities.
"I concur with you in your opinion of the advantages
of the island of Arosa over the Bayonne Islands,"[1]
wrote Lord Wellington, in reply. But it became
necessary to refer the point to Lord Liverpool, as the
occupation of the island involved an outlay of 10,000*l.*
for the construction of works of defence. Sir Howard
had before recommended Lord Liverpool to send out
a squadron to operate in this quarter in conjunction
with English marines, which would enable him to
furnish supplies to the guerillas in Navarre and
Biscay by a direct channel, at the same time that it
cut off the water communications of the French, and
opened a way for turning their positions if they resorted to a line of defence between the Ebro. He
now received intelligence that Lord Liverpool had
adopted his views, having fitted out a squadron with
great secrecy and despatched it to the Spanish waters,
with a battalion of marines and a company of artillery, and Commodore Sir Home Popham arrived at
Corunna to consult him on its movements. The
Commodore's letter reached him at the cantonments,
and he instantly sought General Castaños, as little
could be effected without his concurrence, while
it was desirable that he should understand the
objects in view. The General promised to join him
and the Commodore on the following day, and Sir
Howard took post for Corunna to prepare—visiting

[1] Despatch of the Earl of Wellington to Sir Howard Douglas, April 29,
1812.

Sir Home as soon as he arrived. He found him on board his own old ship, the 'Venerable,' and learnt that he had left the rest of the squadron at sea, to prevent any warning reaching the French. He had discovered Sir Howard's value in the Walcheren expedition, and now declared that he could not act with effect unless he accompanied the squadron, as nothing but his authority would draw around it the guerillas and peasantry. Such a service held out great attractions to Sir Howard, and he also wished to give the Commodore his support, but did not feel at liberty to move without the orders of Lord Wellington. They referred the point to General Castaños on his arrival, and he recommended him to go, adverting to the effect his appearance would produce on the guerillas, and promising to keep the French employed in his absence. His arguments removed Sir Howard's objections, for they had already occurred to himself, and he had only hesitated from a fear that his judgment might be swayed by his wishes. But he did not shrink from the responsibility now that he felt satisfied as to his duty, and it was settled that he should accompany Sir Home.[1]

Arrangements were made to prevent inconvenience from his absence. He gave over the stores to Com-

---

[1] Sir Howard's conception of the expedition is thus mentioned by Napier :—"Sir Howard Douglas, observing the success of the enemy in cutting off the Partidos from the coast, and the advantage they derived from the water communication—considering also that, if Lord Wellington should make any progress in the coming campaign, new lines of communication with the sea would be desirable—proposed that a powerful squadron, with a battalion of marines and a battery of artillery, should be secretly prepared for a littoral warfare on the Biscay coast. This suggestion was approved of, and Sir Home Popham was sent from England in May."—Peninsular War, vol. v. 27.

missary-General White, directing him to continue
their issue, and obey the requisitions of General
Castaños, and he empowered the General to apply for
whatever he needed.   Proper communications were
addressed to other authorities, and to the principal
guerilla chiefs; and Sir Howard received a note from
General Castaños enjoining all the functionaries of the
Government to afford him every assistance.   He embarked with great privacy, and a fair wind carried the
' Venerable ' out of the harbour on her errand of
succour and deliverance.

CHAPTER XVIII.

Takes the Field.

The French obtained information of the arrival of a British squadron, in spite of the endeavours to keep it secret, and the appearance of the 'Venerable' on the coast was the signal for their abandoning several posts. Sir Howard proposed to take advantage of the westerly wind to reach Beruca de Lecitia, and open communication with Don Gaspar, a guerilla chief,[1] as his support might enable them to attack a strong post at Le Cintio Rey. On the 17th of June they came up with the other vessels of the squadron, in a stiff breeze, off Cape Mechichaco, and all pushed out to sea to avoid the swell near the shore. Two days passed before this subsided, when they stood in under the Cape, and boats were sent into the bay in the evening to cut out all craft that could be useful in landing troops. The operation was effected with great gallantry, under a fire from the French, though they evacuated the place when the boats regained the ships, retiring in the direction of Le Cintio Rey. The squadron shaped its course for the same place, while the seizure of the shore boats spread the fact of its presence over the country without the aid of messengers.

Such a result had been anticipated on board, and

---

[1] Sir Howard's despatches do not mention the chief's surname, but always speak of him as Don Gaspar.

Sir Howard and the Commodore felt no surprise next morning to see a boat put off from under an abutting cliff and come alongside, bringing a guerilla officer. He announced himself as Don Gaspar's second in command, and reported that the chief had conjectured that the squadron would attack Le Cintio, and was ready to give his co-operation, but thought it well to point out that they were close to the French frontier, and that the Commodore must be prepared to afford him and his men a refuge on board the ships, if the enemy came upon them from the rear. Sir Howard reassured him on this point, and arranged that Don Gaspar should appear before the place on the following day, when the squadron would be present to share the attack. He recommended that a party should be stationed near the beach with draught oxen, in case of its being found desirable to land guns; and the officer promised compliance, hastening off to prepare his chief.

The day opened unpromisingly; for the vicinity of the squadron alarmed the French, and they sent off for reinforcements, while Don Gaspar had to march from a distance, and the roads were almost impassable. Hours elapsed without any sign of his appearance, and the weather was growing bad, making it dangerous for the ships to approach the shore, when the guerillas were seen crowning the heights about four in the afternoon. Sir Howard feared the effect of any failure to back them at the outset, particularly after placing them in so perilous a situation; for the French might be expected to hasten up a flying column from the rear to cut them off, and hence he would have fulfilled the compact at almost any risk. Fortunately the Com-

modore shared his sentiments, and stood in for the
shore as soon as a lull of the breeze lessened the
swell.

The works consisted of a fortified convent and a
redoubt, and the guerillas effected the investment on
the land side, while the 'Venerable' was brought into
position for bombarding the convent, and Sir Howard
took post on her lower deck to watch the play of her
guns.   Some of the other ships came up, and they
opened a cannonade; but the convent stood on a hill,
and it was impossible to afford the guns the necessary
elevation.   Sir Howard felt more scandalized at the
bad gunnery, which made him tremble for the laurels
of the navy; and he now conceived his scheme for
introducing improvements and leavening the service
with trained gunners.   He looked over the guns to see
how the lines were laid, and what approach was made
to accuracy in allowing for the rolling of the ship, and
then ascertained the different points in the disturbing
effects of the motion, gathering the conclusions which
formed the basis of his famous treatise.   So quick were
his conceptions, that the idea of writing it flashed upon
him at the same time, but did not divert him from the
claims of the moment, and he went on deck to recommend a change in the mode of attack.   This had been
suggesting itself to Sir Home Popham, and they decided that a force from the 'Surveillante' should take
possession of an island facing the town with a carronade and mortar, and that a hundred seamen from
the 'Venerable' should land on the beach with a
24-pounder, for the purpose of breaching the redoubt.
The gun might be dragged up a hill opposite the
work, as the guerillas were at hand with the oxen, and

Sir Howard's forethought in suggesting this provision now struck all. The hill was of about the same elevation as the one occupied by the redoubt, and the 24-pounder could open here, while the pieces on the island engaged the convent.

The guerillas received orders to protect the spot with a breastwork, which they promptly threw up, though opposed by a fire from the redoubt and convent, as well as from advanced parties of the enemy, posted in enclosures and the skirts of the town. A hawser was attached to the trunnions of the gun on reaching the beach, and the seamen drew it through the surf, and looped it to the horns of the oxen, when the guerillas lent their aid, the sailors again gave their strong arms, and the united force ran it up the hill. Here the seamen placed it in position, in spite of the enemy's fire, and made good practice on firm ground, silencing the French 18-pounders, and effecting a breach before sunset. The guerillas rushed to the assault, but the French met them with the same valour, and they reeled a little, borne back by the clash. But they quickly rallied, and dashed on with cheers, disappearing in the dense smoke, which rose in clouds, and enveloped the breach. An instant more decided the struggle, and the air rang with cries as they put the defenders to the sword.

The 24-pounder turned its fire on the convent from this time, and was supported by the guns on the island, while the enemy's advanced parties were driven in by a party of English marines firing from an eminence there, and by the guerillas. The French held out till next day, but then surrendered at discretion, just as a party told off for storming. Sir

Howard recommended the convent to be destroyed, to prevent its re-occupation, and the seamen carried out the operation under his orders, placing barrels of gunpowder under the strongest parts and blowing them into the air.   The explosion announced the event to a French column of eleven hundred men, hurrying up from Bilboa as a reinforcement, and which had arrived within two leagues.   From a neighbouring height they saw the squadron sail away with the captured garrison, while the guerillas vanished, leaving them uncertain where they would appear next.

The ships came to anchor off Bermi at six o'clock in the evening of the 23rd, and Sir Howard and the Commodore landed with a party of marines, and prepared to attack the fortified convent and batteries. But the French evacuated the works without firing a shot, leaving behind their ammunition and numerous pieces of artillery, with a large quantity of provisions. The food was distributed among the poor, the guns disabled, and the convent blown up.   A force from the 'Sparrow' and 'Rhine' landed at the same time, and captured the neighbouring post of Plencia, where they also spiked the guns and destroyed the battery and guard-houses.

Two intercepted letters informed Sir Howard that the operations of the squadron caused the greatest alarm to the enemy up to the frontier of France, while they gave corresponding encouragement to the guerillas and Generals Benevales, Mendizabal, and Porlier, commanding the Spanish troops.   Communications were established with the Generals, and Sir Howard issued a circular to the guerilla chiefs, urging them to increased action and vigilance.   This was dispersed

over the country,[1] from the Pyrenees to the gates of
Madrid, and united all the guerilla bands in the efforts
about to be made.[2]

The squadron stood into Porto Bay, and a party
landed from the 'Lyra' to destroy the batteries at the
entrance of Bilboa Bar, under the guns of the 'Rover'

---

[1] The circular is given here to show the manner in which Sir Howard
brought the irregular troops to act in concert :—

" On board H.B.M.S. 'Venerable,' North Coast of Spain,
25th June, 1812.

" SIR,

" Circumstances very important to the common cause, and which
cannot be trusted to a letter, oblige me to call your attention to the following
operations. I am not only invested with the authority of your Government
to execute them, but I am also the Commissioner of Great Britain, by whose
hands quantities of arms and ammunition have been liberally distributed to
assist you in combating the common enemy. I therefore have no doubt that
you will consent to obey these recommendations.

" First. It is of the highest importance that a strict watch be kept over
Burgos, Victoria, and Torrelavega, and speedy advices of whatever move-
ments the enemy's forces may make in those quarters despatched to General
Mendizabal and to Brigadiers Porlier and Longa.

" Secondly. The small garrisons are to be equally watched and threatened in a way to oblige them to remain within their quarters, which, if they
attempt to abandon, must be immediately destroyed.

" In case the enemy should make any movement towards the coast, the
partidas must follow them closely, harass their rearguards, cut off their
provisions, intercept their correspondence and communications, and in all
manner possible work their ruin.

" I have no doubt that your well-known patriotism, bravery, and activity
will now be exercised in a surpassing manner, and I venture to promise
you with the greatest confidence the most happy results.

" In consequence I have resolved that you should, with the troops under
your command, keep yourself in readiness from the 7th July till the 20th
of the same month, or till new advice.

" I have the honour to be, Sir,
" Your most obedient humble servant,
" HOWARD DOUGLAS."

[2] In a return in the 'Douglas Papers' the guerilla force thus put in
motion is estimated at 28,000 infantry and 8000 cavalry. It fell off after
Sir Howard's departure for England, and was very weak in the next campaign, when the allied army had gained possession of a great part of the
country.

and 'Sparrow,' supported by the frigate 'Medusa.'
The 'Venerable' bore up with the 'Surveillante' and
'Rhine' at seven in the evening, and put ashore the
marines of the three ships, with Sir Howard, the Commodore, and Brigadier-General Carrol. The enemy
did not wait for their attack, but hastily abandoned
the batteries, which the sailors and marines destroyed,
as well as the castles of Gulea and Begma, and rendered the guns useless by knocking off their trunnions.
Another party laid barrels of powder under the barracks and guard-houses, and blew them into the air.
This dashing enterprise was accomplished in an hour
and a half, and the marines and sailors regained the
ships without the smallest casualty.

Spies reported that a strong force had moved on
Argolta, and next morning brought off the Alcalde
with a message from the French General. The poor
magistrate was in great terror, and the message excused his trepidation, for it informed the Commodore
and the English Commissioner that he was to be
hanged and the town burnt if the squadron molested
the French. Sir Howard told him that nothing would
be done to compromise the town, unless the French
broke its neutrality by firing the first shot, when they
must acknowledge that they draw the attack on themselves, and hold him blameless. The French had
arrived in the last stage of fatigue, and sank down
exhausted in the batteries, but sprang to their guns on
the approach of the 'Lyra' brig, and opened a cannonade. They had now violated the understanding,
and the ships replied by a bombardment which
obliged them to fly from the town, and left them no
time to execute their threats. Yet the Alcalde may

have partly owed his escape to his own prudence; for
he took care to keep out of the way of the General,
who went off mad with rage, and not indisposed to
hang a few Spaniards.

It is a proof of the organization established at this
time through Spain that Sir Howard's circular reached
Longa, many leagues in the interior, and brought an
answer by his second in command within a few days.
This officer was Colonel Alvarez, himself a noted
leader, and he described their force as consisting of
four thousand infantry and two hundred cavalry, which
he engaged to present on the heights behind Castro
Diobiale on the afternoon of the 6th of July. The
squadron was to make its appearance at the same
time, and lend its aid in an attack on the place, reputed
of great strength and suitably garrisoned. Bad weather kept the ships from the coast for the next few
days, but the 'Lyra' contrived to land some arms
and artillery which Sir Howard had engaged to send
General Benivales, and to arrange that he and the
other Spanish Generals should meet him at Camillas
on the 2nd. The Commodore stood in close to Lan-
tino, that Sir Howard might reconnoitre the position,
and they were unmolested from the shore, though a
sloop ran under the batteries on their approach, and
hoisted her colours, at the same time firing a gun. He
had drawn a plan of the works from information, and
now finished it correctly, ascertaining that the batteries
were of a very formidable character, particularly to
the westward of a promontory commanding the sandy
beach, where attacking troops must land.

They sheered off on the completion of the reconnaissance, and he went to hold a conference with the

Spanish Generals at Camillas, according to his arrangement, by the 'Lyra.' It had leaked out that he was
to come, and a crowd waited on the beach, and saluted
him with acclamations. They formed his escort to the
house of the principal resident, who met him at the
door, and received him with the greatest cordiality.
He became his guide round the town, and took him
to a spot from which he could reconnoitre the neighbourhood, still under the command of the French,
though not occupied. Evening drew on without
bringing the Generals, and he proposed to stay
with his host for the night, not doubting that they
would arrive next day. His words reached the ear
of a French spy loitering in the adjoining room, and
he stole out of the house, mounted a horse, and
carried the news to the French. The opportunity
of capturing such a prisoner threw the commanding officer into ecstasies, and he concerted his measures at once, waiting impatiently for night. Then
he silently mustered his corps and made a swoop on
the town. They found all still; not a soul appeared
in the streets, and they came unobserved to the house
under the guidance of the spy. But their caution
proved of no avail; for the host had represented the
danger to Sir Howard, who had abandoned his intention, and was now comfortably asleep in the
' Venerable.'

It appeared that the Generals had been prevented
attending by the vigilance of the French, and a messenger informed them that Sir Howard would proceed
to St. Vincente de la Barquera, where they could
meet without risk. But he was to have another
narrow miss before he reached St. Vincente, and the

incident may be mentioned as an instance of his presence of mind, while it shows how he retained his youthful activity. Two seamen had been posted in a boat attached to the stern for steerage, and the 'Venerable' was wearing ship in a squall, when the rope broke, and it became very difficult to pick up the boat and men. A creaking noise attracted Sir Howard as he watched the proceedings, and he turned to see a large brass gun break loose, and tilt in a manner that seemed to leave him no escape from destruction. There was not time for a second thought, and he instantly made a spring and leaped over the gun, which dashed to the lee quarter, and would have jammed him into a mummy there but for his prompt movement.

The Governor and his staff came down to meet him at St. Vincente, and they were joined by Generals Mendizabal and Porlier, with the chief of his staff; and he had now the satisfaction of learning that they had received all his communications and agreed in his suggestions, so that every precaution had been taken to insure the objects of the expedition. Such was the footing on which he had established himself with the Spanish officers, who originally regarded him with jealousy, and mistrusted his counsels. The success of his measures had won their confidence, and gave weight to whatever he proposed, while his kind and unassuming manner disarmed ill-will, and made everybody his friend.

He recommended General Mendizabal to leave General Porlier in observation of Torre la Viga, and muster all his force against Andrea, passing on to attack Viga as soon as Andrea fell. Everything promised well for the operations; he had brought the Generals in communication with Sir Home Popham, and given the fullest instructions to the guerilla chiefs; and he considered that the time had come for his return to Corunna. He took leave of the Commodore the same evening, and sailed in the 'Sparrow' brig, which was proceeding to Corunna for supplies.

A few days brought him to his destination, and he received a sort of public welcome on his arrival, all the authorities hastening to pay him visits. But his activity could not be arrested by ceremony, and he was at work the moment he landed, sending off 300,000 musket-cartridges and 10,000 flints to Sir Home Popham, and starting couriers to Lord Wellington and General Castaños.[1] The Spanish corps before Astorga was at a stand for ammunition, and he forwarded a supply, and then went to see what progress had been made with the siege. He found that the troops had surmounted extraordinary difficulties, and were animated by the best spirit. The

---

[1] Sir Howard now received from the Captain-General Castaños a letter of congratulation, a part of which is here given, translated from the original in the 'Douglas Papers:'—

"My esteemed Friend,   "Santiago, 8th July, 1812.

"In addition to what I officially communicate, I congratulate you upon the beginning of the campaign in Cantabria, in the direction of which your presence has been of great importance. It would also be of much use here, as we are in a miserable state; but without attending to obstacles we are obliged to act, in order not to lose any advantage. Providence has disposed that all our undertakings shall be attended with a happy result, which ought to augment the confidence Lord Wellington should have in his good fortune. He writes to me very contented from Medina del Campo on the 3rd. . . . .

"I beg you for God's sake to assist us with clothing; and trusting very soon to have the pleasure of seeing you,

"I am your friend and servant,

"Castaños."

obstinacy of the defence had not diminished their
ardour, and he was a spectator of an 'exploit by the
regiment of Rivera, which would have reflected honour
on any troops.   It became necessary to dislodge the
enemy from a small rising ground where they harassed
the men employed in the prolongation of the right
trench, and the Rivera regiment dashed at them with
the bayonet under a galling fire, and compelled them
to fly.   He felt proud that his anticipations had been
so verified ; for everything bid fair for success, as
the approach was already curtained, the trenches
advanced, and the guns mounted in the breaching
batteries.   He saw that he could be of no use for the
moment, and accepted an invitation to accompany
General Santocildes to Leon, to witness the proclamation of the new constitution.

The ceremony was one of grave import, and lacked
no accessary that could render it imposing.   Flags
decorated the public buildings, and waved over the
churches ; the tradesmen closed their shops, and
dressed them with evergreens and flowers ; and loyal
mottoes glittered on banners, and emblazoned the
walls.   Holiday crowds paraded the streets, and the
windows of the houses were thronged with ladies,
attended by nobles and cavaliers.   The Grand Plaza
was lined with troops, and rolling drums and the bray
of trumpets notified the approach of the General, who
rode at the head of a brilliant train, composed of his
staff and the functionaries of the province.   He was
warmly received by the people, but they burst into
acclamations at sight of Sir Howard in the British
uniform, and his horse could hardly make its way
through the crowd, which pressed round him on all

sides, mingling his name with shouts for Wellington
and England.   Hats were raised aloft, and ladies
waved their handkerchiefs and threw flowers from the
windows.   So kind a nature could not receive such
greetings without emotion; but he was affected less
by the people's enthusiasm than by the tokens of
their affection and gratitude, not a few shedding tears
as they called out the name of Wellington.   On the
other hand, the proclamation of the constitution
occasioned little excitement, so completely were the
sympathies of the nation absorbed by the war.

He returned with the General to Astorga, and
charmed the soldiers by going into the trenches,
exposing himself to the heavy fire for several days
in succession.   A despatch from Lord Wellington
called him away from the siege by informing him that
King Joseph had left Madrid at the head of 12,000
men, which made it desirable that General Santocildes should draw nearer the English army; and he
arranged with the General to advance on the Douro
with 8000 men, leaving a similar force to prosecute
the siege.   The late successes had given the people
hope, as well as gratified their pride, and the troops
met a joyous welcome as they pushed forward; while
Sir Howard received a perfect triumph.   The moment
was at hand when he was to reap the reward of his
efforts, in seeing their object fulfilled.   His scheme for
occupying the French in the north by the expedition
under Sir Home Popham, and for covering the allied
army by the operations of the several Spanish corps and
of the guerillas and Alarms, was acknowledged to have
contributed to the victory of Salamanca, by keeping
off Lord Wellington two divisions of infantry and one

of cavalry, except about fifteen hundred sabres which were pushed forward, and joined Marmont the night before the battle.[1] The armies engaged were so nearly equal,[2] that fortune might have inclined to the French if they had obtained this reinforcement, and the fruits of the campaign would have been endangered. The Spanish army was entering Carvajales when news came of the victory, and it excited the wildest joy among the troops and the population of the surrounding country. "It caused me the greatest delight," writes Sir Howard, who had just received a letter from the Minister for War, recalling him to England. The objects for which he had laboured were attained, and his mission was at an end.

---

[1] The succours thus diverted are mentioned by Napier:—"Forty-nine thousand men, of which thirty-eight thousand were with the eagles, composed the army of the north, under Caffarelli, and were distributed on the grand line of communication from St. Sebastian to Burgos; but of this army *two divisions of infantry and one of cavalry, with artillery, were destined to reinforce Marmont.*"—Peninsular War, vol. v. 111.

[2] The allied army numbered 46,000; the French 42,000.—Peninsular War, vol. v. 209.

CHAPTER XIX.

Foils the French Generals.

No one but Lord Wellington understood the position of the French in the Peninsula so well as Sir Howard, and it was from him that the Great Captain drew most of his information.   He could thus appreciate the victory of Salamanca, and see what consequences it opened.   The time has come when it may be stated that he took a different view of the situation from his chief.   He was of opinion that Lord Wellington should have followed up the defeat of Marmont by a vigorous pursuit, which would drive his army beyond the Ebro—involving the fall of Burgos before it could be succoured by the French force in the south—and giving such support to the squadron and guerillas in the north by this advance that the enemy's line of communications with France on that side would be cut off, and Soult and King Joseph compelled to move towards the other line, and form a junction with Suchet.   Indeed, the first line was already broken, for intelligence had arrived of the fall of Castro, the siege of which we have seen Sir Howard arrange with Sir Home Popham and Longa ; and he had settled with the Commodore and General Mendizabal to proceed from there to Santona and Laredo.   They had strictly followed his plans, and brought Santona to great extremities, so that it must

fall on Lord Wellington's appearance, and the possession of St. Andrea would insure him every supply by
sea.   This movement seemed to result so plainly
from Marmont's defeat, that Sir Howard felt sure it
was what the Commander-in-Chief designed.   But he
had written to him to say that he would take advantage of the approach of General Santocildes to repair
to head-quarters while the Spanish troops invested
Zamora, and he resolved to avail himself of any
opening to refer to the position of the different armies,
and deliver his opinion.

He was obliged to make a halt at Valladolid, and
here he learnt how his name had spread through
Spain, the notables of the town coming to pay their
respects as soon as they heard of his arrival.   He was
most affected by a visit from the Bishop, who had
originally been a partisan of the French, and been
rewarded by the Grand Cross ; but lost their favour on
refusing to issue an address in their interest.   General
Kellermann even seized him by the throat, and flung
him out of the room, without respecting either his
office or years, and the old man of eighty thought it
prudent to fly, having received a hint of danger.   The
incident taught him that he could not halt between
two opinions, and he returned to the city a changed
man, avowing devotion to the Royal cause, and caring
for neither threats nor cajoleries.   He talked cheer-
fully to Sir Howard, spoke of his exertions and
achievements, and eulogised Lord Wellington, whose
recent victory filled every mouth.   Sir Howard expressed a wish to see the works of art in the city, and
he gave him an order to visit the religious houses,
describing him by name, which obtained him un-

expected attentions. He was in the chapel of the
Bernardine convent, when the nuns heard of his
presence, and went to do the honours themselves,
which they did in the most complete manner, showing him all the statues and pictures, and relating
their history. The curiosities included the body of
their benefactor, Don Garcia, son of the great Duke,
the tutor of the unfortunate Don Carlos; and he asked
for a memento, expecting to receive a clip of his
garment. But the nuns carried their complaisance
further, and one of the party broke off the Don's
great toe, and presented it to him in a silk purse,
the work of her own hands. Yet these women felt
kindly impulses—only they had so familiarised themselves with death, that they looked on inanimate
forms as but clay. They introduced him to a nun
who had entered the convent in her girlhood, and
unexpectedly succeeded to a vast inheritance, which
led to her being taken from her noviciate, and brought
out at court. There she attracted a host of suitors,
and every effort was made to reconcile her to the
world. But she persisted in her first intention,
and was finally allowed to take the veil, leaving
her property to the next heir. Her story reminded
Sir Howard of the English girl whom he found
amongst the Indians, and he attributed her decision
to the same cause—a lethargy of feeling induced by
habit.

He met as kind a reception at the Franciscan
convent, devoted to noble ladies, who were obliged to
prove descent from a remote period. The Abbess
had been celebrated for her beauty, and preserved its

o

remains, being only in middle life ; and he was fasci-
nated by the manners of the nuns, who retained the
polish of the court.   They entertained him with a
little concert, one playing the organ while the others
sang, and then showed him round the convent.   It
now appeared that they possessed as great a treasure
as the nuns of St. Bernard — a dead benefactor ;
and Sir Howard duly examined the body of the
Marquis of Sule Yghsa, secretary to the Duke of
Lerma, but whether the same secretary who figures
in *Gil Blas* he does not mention, his thoughts
being bent on obtaining another relic.   It is amusing
to find the nuns presenting him with a finger,
which one wrenched off the mummy, perhaps to pair
with his toe.   To such ends do secretaries and Cæsars
come !

The nuns were not so out of the world as to be
ignorant of what passed, and told Sir Howard they
had heard of his services to their country, and what
they effected.   "They all begged me to visit them
again," he writes in his note-book, "most particularly
at Posta Cela, where they actually embraced me, and
wept for joy."

He noticed a diverting result of the French occupation of Valladolid, in the games of the boys, who
were all playing at soldiers, and fought battles in
every street.   They had begun the practice in the
French time ; but one day fired off toy-cannons and
pistols with charges of powder, and this raised an
alarm, when a guard beat to arms, and the garrison
turned out before they discovered the cause.   Playing at soldiers was then found to be incompatible

with soldiering in earnest, and was placed under an interdict.

Sir Howard met Lord Wellington near the city, and had cause to be pleased with his reception.   But he saw there was no intention of taking the course he had surmised, as the pursuit of Marmont had been given up, and Lord Wellington merely ordered him to call upon Santocildes to occupy Valladolid, in communication with the other Spanish corps and the 6th Division at Queguar.   He concluded that something had arisen to divert the Commander-in-Chief from the forward movement, and did not regard the occasion as one on which he could speak, though his suggestions always received consideration.[1]

The pursuit of Clausel to Valladolid presented no obstacle to the advance of King Joseph, who might have formed a junction with the defeated army, and made it the superior force.   He could then have prevented Lord Wellington from moving on Madrid, as well as from advancing into the north, and forced him back to the line of the Douro, if he did not compel him to retire into Portugal.   But the French lost the favourable moment through the negligence

---

[1] The march on Madrid is thus adverted to by Sir Howard in a minute on the battle of Salamanca :—" I felt convinced that some unexpected and imminent necessity elsewhere, in directions of which I knew nothing, rendered this indispensable, and it would not have been prudent—scarcely respectful—in an officer to have ventured unsolicited an opinion to the illustrious General upon matters of such high import.   Many attempts were made to draw me out upon the subject ; but I most carefully reserved my opinions at the time, only imparting them confidentially to one or two friends.   The manner in which Marmont was brought to battle by Lord Wellington was masterly in the extreme."

of the King, and Lord Wellington's movement was unopposed.[1]

The Commander-in-Chief invited Sir Howard to dinner, and spoke in a gratifying manner of his services, mentioning the large force kept off his hands by the operations on the coast, and requesting him to state this to Sir Home Popham. Sir Howard had also a long conversation with Colonel Burgoyne of the Royal Engineers, and they arranged to suspend the siege of Zamora, which he had left in progress, and only carry on that of Astorga, as Lord Wellington directed him to set off in the morning, and bring the Gallician army to Medina del Campo.

They had another conference on the morrow, when they rode away at the same time, Lord Wellington proceeding to Cuillar, where he had stationed a division of the army, and Sir Howard making for the heights of San Roman. To this place General Santocildes had advanced, and he again put his army in motion on the arrival of Sir Howard, who accompanied him to his assigned post.

Even Sir Howard's frame bent under so much fatigue, and the strain brought on an attack of fever, which confined him to bed for two days, a most untoward event, for it prevented his being present at the interview of General Santocildes with Lord Wellington. This led to embarrassment in their future intercourse, for the General treated him with reserve on perceiving that he was ignorant of his instructions, though they would doubtless have been communicated by Lord Wellington, if he had not thought that the

---

[1] Minute by Sir Howard Douglas on the battle of Salamanca.

General would report what passed, as he knew
Sir Howard was to have attended the meeting.   Sir
Howard felt the more annoyed as he was certain the
French would retrace their steps directly they heard
of the advance on Madrid, and it became important to
know whether such a contingency had been estimated.
He stated his apprehensions to Santocildes, and requested information, but to no purpose, and he went
to make inquiries about the enemy on the road.   An
orderly dragoon met him at Torre de Cilhas, with
despatches, and he found his misgivings verified, for
the French had crossed the Duenos, and were marching
in force on Valladolid.   A despatch overtook him
from General Santocildes at the same time, informing
him of this movement, and requesting a meeting at
Villa de Fraydes to devise new arrangements.   Sir
Howard reached the spot at five in the afternoon, the
time appointed, but the General did not make his
appearance, and he waited for him through the night
in great anxiety.   This was relieved about four in the
morning by an aide-de-camp from General Cabrera,
who announced that the Gallician army was retiring
on Castro Nuovo.   The night's harass left him
very exhausted, but he rode off directly, and found
General Santocildes was suffering from fever, which
rendered an interview impossible.   The army was
in retreat, but he could elicit no information from
General Cabrera, and only gathered its destination
from conjecture.   One of his spiès came in during the
night and reported that the troops pushed forward by
the enemy were commanded by General Foy, one of
the most enterprising of the French Generals, whence

it struck him that they would aim at nothing less than
the disruption of the communications of the allies, and
the relief of Astorga, if they did not try to recover
Salamanca.   Both the Gallician army and the Portuguese force under the Count of Amaranthe were thus
placed in a critical position, as General Santocildes
had retreated on a line which left the communications
exposed, and brought him into a country open to
cavalry, in which the enemy was very strong, while
the Spaniards numbered but 300 sabres.   Hence they
had no way of escape but by making for the mountains, and he went to impart his views to the General
as soon as he saw the danger.   The hour might seem
unseasonable for disturbing a sick man, as it was but
four in the morning, but the case did not admit of
delay, and he proved behind time, for Santocildes had
set out for the rear an hour before, leaving the troops
without a commander.

   Such was the position of the retreating army!   Sir
Howard spurred off to the Count of Belvidere, the
officer next in rank, and begged him to assume the
command, for all must be lost if there were any hesitation.   His notes describe the Count as "really a
very fine fellow," and the character seems deserved;
but he shrank from the command under such circumstances, and urged his infirm health and ignorance
of Lord Wellington's instructions, without which he
should feel paralysed.   Thus the army was without
instructions or a chief, and the enemy advancing.
Sir Howard tried what could be done with General
Cabrera, but found him equally unwilling; and he
justly said that the command devolved on the Count,

and that he could not assume it over his head.
Ultimately Sir Howard persuaded the Count to act
until orders should be received from General Castaños,
and induced him to march in a direction to take up a
position behind the Esla, where he would be in communication with the Count of Amaranthe and the
Portuguese corps, and whence both might retreat into
Portugal, if necessary.

Sir Howard informed Castaños of his conviction
that the first object of the French would be the relief
of Astorga; and he is proved to have been right
by a minute from General Foy in later years,
which states that "l'Empereur Napoléon attachait
la plus haute importance à la conservation d'Astorga."[1]   The French advance would compel the
withdrawal of the division before the town, so that
the Spaniards must raise the siege or capture the
place by a dash, and he exhorted General Castaños
to adopt the latter course.   Only a few hours remained for the work, as General Foy had reached
Toro, and was approaching by forced marches; but he
possessed no means of forewarning the garrison, and
they had lost hope of relief.   General Castaños took
advantage of their want of information, and threatened to spring a mine if they did not surrender, and
they laid down their arms to find that the Spaniards
had withdrawn their battering train, and formed to
retreat.   Thus fell Astorga, after a two months'
siege, which provokes a sneer from Napier, but
unmarked by his usual judgment; for it is no

---

[1] Minute by General Count Foy, in reply to Sir Howard Douglas.—See
Appendix.

reflection on the Gallician army to have been detained for this period before a town which had stood
out against Junot for six weeks, resisting a powerful French army, supplied with every equipment.
Sir Howard affirms that they behaved with spirit,
and that the achievement shed honour on the Spanish
arms.

He left the retreating columns to visit the Count of
Amaranthe, and give him the benefit of his counsel.
His only companion on the journey was his secretary, and they rode through a lonely country,
where he incurred some danger; for the French
would pay for his capture, and were said to have
adherents in this quarter. But he deemed himself
safe amongst Spaniards, and felt no misgiving as
he spurred along, surveying the wild scenery which
there meets the eye. They stopped to dine at a
roadside inn, and their nostrils caught a savoury
odour as they entered, promising unexceptionable
cheer. Such indications are very pleasant on the
table, but tantalize in the distance, and the secretary could not bear the delay that ensued with the
same patience as the Commissioner, but cast looks
at the door, as steps again and again approached,
and again passed by. But relief came at last, for
the steps paused at the threshold, the hostess appeared, and a stew steamed on the board. Can
we marvel that he fell to amain? Who would wish
Sancho Panza's physician to have stood by, and
laid an interdict on the dish? Yet some such
caution had been well, for his knife and fork plied
quick, and he was only pulled up by a qualm

which took away his breath. He began to feel giddy,
and started from the table, making a rush for the
door. But he fell short, and rolled on the floor in
convulsions.

His discomposure escaped Sir Howard till he
rose up, but he now sprang to his assistance, and
called for the servants of the inn. He sank himself as they arrived, seized with the same symp-
toms, followed by vomiting. The secretary also
became sick, and the hostess and servants looked
on bewildered, neither knowing what to make of the
occurrence, nor what to do. Their terror acquitted them of foul play, though this could hardly be
suspected, as they were Spaniards, and Sir Howard's
uniform insured good will. But they had traversed
an infected district, and it was possible that some
French spy had followed them to the inn, and
drugged their dinner. Sir Howard learnt that a
Portuguese doctor was staying in the village, and he
requested the hostess to call him in, while the servants carried them to bed. The doctor promptly appeared, heard their report, and came to the same
conclusion as themselves.

"They have been poisoned," he said to the hostess.
The poor woman stood speechless. He turned to
the servants, and repeated the words, with angry
gesticulations. But they burst out in chorus, with
gesticulations surpassing his own, and declared that
it could not be, invoking the saints to bear them
witness, and mentioning a totally different person-
age in connexion with the doctor. Then the hostess
found words, and protested her innocence, which

Sir Howard never doubted, although she did protest too much. The clatter lasted so long that both the secretary and himself recovered during its progress, and he ended the dispute by requesting her to produce the saucepan in which the stew had been made, and satisfy herself and them by having it examined by the doctor. She readily agreed, and brought in a large copper pot, thick with verdigris, and it came out that the stew had been standing in it since the previous day. Their sickness was now explained, and they comprehended their recovery, for the doctor reported that the poison had supplied its antidote in the overdose.

The news of General Foy's advance drove the Count of Amaranthe across the Esla; but he resumed the blockade of Zamora as soon as he became acquainted with Sir Howard's plan for preserving his communications with the Gallician army. The two officers held a conference, and agreed in the importance of this measure; for there was a chance of capturing Zamora before General Foy learnt its danger. But Sir Howard recommended the greatest vigilance, as Foy might strike the Count by cutting off his retreat instead of marching forward. Thus he sought to guard the campaign at a moment when his mission had ceased, and he had actually received his recall, feeling the same interest in the cause of Spain, and the same zeal for its advancement.

But circumstances were occurring to subvert his arrangements, for General Castaños had handed over the Gallician army to General Cabrera, and he instantly changed his front, directing the retreat on the mountains, though the fall of Astorga had strengthened his position, and doubled his numbers. The news met Sir Howard on his way back, and he spurred so fast after the columns that he nearly rode into the ranks of the enemy, being stopped by a peasant, who told him they were in force at Labajesa. He turned into another road, and came up with the General in the village of Tornero. Murillo would have made a picture of their meeting. The hour was midnight. The Spanish General reined up at the head of his staff, as the English officer presented himself, covered with dust, and worn with his long ride. He adjured him to suspend the retreat, and take up a position to support the Count of Amaranthe, and preserve their communications. Cabrera replied that this could not be done without sacrificing his army, as he had no means of facing the French cavalry, which would appear in a few hours. But Sir Howard insisted that their movements showed they had no intention of advancing to Tornero in force, and that they would cut off the Portuguese corps when they heard what direction he was taking. Cabrera expressed the greatest deference for his opinion, but was unconvinced, and declined to halt.

" I will only ask you to remain here till morning," urged Sir Howard.

" I could not remain an hour," was the reply.

" Then I will remain alone."

The General rode forward, and Sir Howard kept on the spot, to the wonder of the soldiers, as they

hurried past, eyeing his familiar figure, thrown up
by the light from the inn. He could not but
think what they might have accomplished if they
had been properly led ; for the siege of Astorga had
shown him their quality, and he entertained the
highest opinion of the Spanish soldiers. " I must say
they are well deserving of being better commanded,"
he writes to the Earl of Liverpool [1] on this occasion. " They really possess all the qualities necessary to constitute good soldiers." But such thoughts
did not occupy him long ; for his mind now
wandered to the battalions of the enemy, and considered in what manner they would be employed
when Cabrera's movement became known. Nothing
could be ascertained till morning, but he had
formed an opinion, and it was to test its accuracy
that he incurred his present risk. He thought that
it might be imprudent to remain in the village,
and he established a bivouac about a mile away,
though not venturing to stay on one spot, and he kept
his horse ready saddled, that he might gallop off
on the first alarm. Thus he watched through the
night, and experienced no interruption, not a soul
appearing on the road. Some peasants came past in
the morning, and he then learnt that the French had
not occupied the village, though their patrols had
been seen on the other side, almost up to its entrance.
He now felt satisfied that he had penetrated their
designs, and that they had taken the direction he
anticipated.

[1] Despatch of Sir Howard Douglas to the Earl of Liverpool, August 26,
1812.

His perfect foresight on the occasion is suscept-
ible of proof; for General Foy visited England in
1817, and the Right Hon. William Wickham submitted to him a Minute from Sir Howard, detailing
what he conceived to have been his intentions in
the advance, with a request that he would state
how far it was correct. " L'officier qui a écrit
ceci a parfaitement deviné les intentions du Général
de Division Comte Foy pendant les opérations
du mois d'Août, 1812," wrote the General, and he
adds the details of his plan. The minute and the
commentary are given in the Appendix to this
volume, and form a worthy memorial of Sir Howard's
sagacity.

The fact of the French having taken the direction
of Tabra convinced him that their object was to seize
Carvajales, and this would place them between
Portugal and Zamora, cutting off the Count of
Amaranthe, which led him to hurry off his orderly
with a letter, begging him to be first at the point.
The Count acted with his usual energy, putting
his columns in motion as soon as he received the
despatch; and thus saved his army. An hour later
he would have been lost. The French cavalry overtook his rearguard near Constantina, and made a
furious charge, but his dispositions were so excellent that they captured only a few stragglers, and
he made good his retreat, after leading them a chase
by which they lost the opportunity of dashing at
Salamanca. For Sir Howard's report of their advance recalled Lord Wellington from Madrid, and
Marshal Clausel summoned Foy back to Valladolid

directly he heard of this movement. How different might have been the results if Sir Howard had accompanied the Gallician army in its retreat instead of passing the night at Tornero![1]

[1] Sir Howard was anxious to know whether the service he had rendered on this occasion was acknowledged by the Count of Amaranthe, and he made inquiries on the subject of his friend Sir Benjamin D'Urban, whose reply is dated Cintra, 10th October, 1815, and may furnish an extract:—"I wrote to the Count of Amaranthe to beg that if he had made such a report he would favour me with a copy of it, and that, if no such despatch had been made, he would send me a certificate of his having received important intelligence from you during the period in question. I enclose you his answer, which I think you will find satisfactory as an acknowledgment of most essential and valuable intelligence and service rendered by you."

CHAPTER XX.

Joins Lord Wellington.

Sir Howard's mind felt lightened after sending off his orderly to the Count of Amaranthe, and he was strolling down the village, when he heard the clatter of hoofs, and presently was startled by the appearance of two English Light Dragoons. He could hardly believe his eyes at first, but there was no doubting the blushing scarlet, or the English faces of the stalwart troopers. They recognised him as plainly and rode up in a canter, while he divided his admiration between their chargers and themselves.

"This is a strange encounter, Sergeant-Major," he said to the foremost. "Where are you from?"

"From General Anson at Tudela, sir," was the reply. "And I think you are Sir Howard Douglas?"

"Yes."

"I have brought you despatches from Lord Wellington, sir, which the General thought it right to send on."

"A dangerous service!" said Sir Howard, more astonished as he looked at the address on the despatch. "Is it possible you have come across the country by Valladolid?"

"Yes, sir. But I heard the enemy had come up

there, and that the Spaniards had retreated. I thought
it my duty to persevere in conveying the despatches;
so we made our way to Casta Contrigo, where we
heard you were here, and came across."

" You deserve great credit for your conduct: I
have very important intelligence for Lord Wellington,
and must send you on with it."

The letter was soon ready, and the two dragoons
were refreshed and at the door.

" Considering the importance of this despatch," said
Sir Howard, as he gave it to the Sergeant-Major, " I
should like you to proceed by the bank of the Esla
to Constantina, and then on to Salamanca."

The Sergeant-Major looked dubious. " Will you
be so good as to give me this order in writing, sir?"
he said, after a moment's hesitation.

" For what reason?" asked Sir Howard.

" Because I shouldn't take that way, if left to
myself, sir."

" Well, tell me how you managed in coming here."

" It was thought this would be a difficult service,
sir, and I was picked out to do it, with leave to choose
my companion. I chose this man, sir, and these
horses—because I knew they could be trusted; and I
settled in my own mind there'd be most danger in
blundering on too fast, while certainty would be better
than speed. I knew I should be safe with the people,
and that the French wouldn't: so I determined to keep
in sight of the French army."

" That was bold play."

" Yes, sir. But I knew their cavalry could only
chase me in a pretty large party; for a small one would

be cut up by the guerillas or peasantry; and the speed of a large party would be only the speed of their slowest horse, if they kept together and chased to a distance; so I could gallop round them with these mares half a dozen times in an hour." And he glanced with pride at the two chargers.

" Did they look after you?"

" Oh, yes, sir! I went on, and we soon fell in with them. They turned out a party of cavalry as I expected, and we gave them a good gallop. They turned, and we turned. I always drew off two or three miles at night, and went to some village or hamlet—generally to the priest, and told him what we were about. We got good treatment for ourselves and horses, and set off at daylight, sighted the French again, and let them give us a gallop. But they got to know our look after a few days, and then didn't give us much trouble."

" I'm sure I can't do better than leave such an excellent tactician to his own judgment," said Sir Howard.

" I'll carry the despatch in my own way, sir, as safely as if you'd put it in any post-office in England. That I warrant."

" I have full confidence in you. Now tell me your name."

" Blood, sir."

" And yours?" said Sir Howard to the private.

" Death," replied the soldier.

Sir Howard could not repress a smile at such a conjunction—Blood and Death! But he did not ask their names without a purpose, for he addressed a

P

report of their conduct to Lord Wellington, and suggested that it called for some mark of approbation. This procured them both a gratuity, and Lord Wellington offered to recommend the Sergeant-Major for a commission, but this he declined, on grounds creditable to his modesty and good sense, and which had weight with the Commander-in-Chief. But Sir Howard did not attach the same importance to his scruples; and he brought the case before his friend Earl Harcourt on his return to England, the Earl being Colonel of the 16th Dragoons, and interested him in the Sergeant-Major's favour. Mr. Blood was surprised to find himself gazetted to a Cornetcy in the regiment, and rose to the rank of Lieutenant, when he obtained the appointment of Riding-master, and subsequently held a more lucrative post. He never knew to what influence he owed his advancement, and may first hear of Sir Howard's intervention from these pages.

Sir Howard had no sooner parted with the two dragoons than he determined to cross the country himself, first to Villafranca to confer with General Castaños, and then to Salamanca, whence he intended to proceed to meet Lord Wellington. He had sent a despatch to General Castaños to complain of the retreat from Tornero, and also of the position in which he was placed by the conduct of General Santocildes, for this had interfered with the performance of his duties. Few could have succeeded in such functions under the obstacles he met, nor could he have prevailed himself, but for the co-operation of General Castaños and the good will of the Spanish army and people. These proved a great support, and rendered him equal

to every trial.   Opposition did not provoke him to
resentment, nor jealousy to ill-temper ; and he retained
his dignity under the slights of General Santocildes,
as under the shuffles of General Abadia.   They always
found him courteous and conciliatory, ready to leave
himself unconsidered, but inflexible on points of duty.
General Cabrera might retreat with the army, but he
would remain at his post—and he remained alone.
What a protest, and what an example !

His way to Villafranca lay across the Sierra de
Ochanis, a stupendous ridge, joining the mountains of
Asturia, and nearly their equal in height.   The
Spanish sierras impress the most careless, even after
we have seen the loftier chains of other lands, and
they inspired Sir Howard with a feeling of rapture.
Nothing could show more the innocence of his mind
than this appreciation of Nature, when he rode up
fresh from his bivouac, harassed with the anxieties of
his post and the toils of war.   His eye caught every
point of the scenery, the smallest as well as greatest,
and their interest was heightened by his coming to
every spot versed in its history and traditions.   To
hear him talk on these subjects was thus as instructive
as entertaining ; for his conversation gave impressions
that could not be obtained from books, and which remained on the memory, unconsciously opening glimpses
of his character, and the noblest of lessons.   There
was a modest suppression of himself in what he said,
and a recognition of others—often in the humblest
rank—and a Shakespearean blending of the poetic
and practical, that struck young and old.   The same
mind which treasured up the features of a landscape

and every legend and tradition, computed the dimensions of a bridge, caught the span of a river, noted the points of a fort or position, mastered the resources of a country, and even the nature of its soil. It thus taught that the steps to eminence are observation and industry, and that even genius must be content to climb by this road, and follow it with perseverance.

Nowhere could he see Nature in a more varied aspect than in the Sierra del Ochanis, which unites the sublime with the beautiful, and ranges them through manifold forms. The mountain shot up at his side till the peak disappeared in clouds, while the narrow bridle-path that led up the steep overhung a precipice, straight as a wall, and descending a fearful depth. The slightest trip would have thrown over horse and rider, yet he could not keep his eye from the plain below, which had no boundary but the sky, and spread a province as the prospect. The defile was piled with rocks, looking as though a touch would hurl them down, and sometimes almost forming a tunnel, so nearly did they meet overhead. And here a tree jutted out from the crags, in solitary prominence, and stark to its top, as if blasted by the same eruption that had cast up the rocks. Then the pass opened with a burst, showing the mountain region beyond, with its majestic peaks sweeping far out of sight, bare steeps, and slopes of the smoothest turf, ravines, torrents, and cascades, falling into a valley of perpetual verdure. Sir Howard dismounted to take in the scene, and imprint it on his memory. But even admiration of the beautiful did not carry him away from the useful, and his little pocket-book notes that he found a piece of iron-ore on the slope, and that the mountains are rich in sulphur.

The sierra was uninhabited, so he had to pass the night in bivouac; but he had now no apprehensions of the enemy, whose troopers could not penetrate the mountains, and he slept in security. Late in the evening of the 24th of August he reached Villa-franca.

General Castaños had disapproved of the retreat from Tornero, and called General Cabrera to the rear to justify the movement, the bad effect of which was now apparent. This satisfied Sir Howard, who bore no ill-will to Cabrera, but wished to make him aware that his duty imposed a responsibility which he would not be suffered to evade. It was important that he should receive such a lesson; for the time had come when the desultory warfare Sir Howard had organised must give way to operations depending on regular troops, and he could return to England with the conviction that he had put everything in train for this change. The service intrusted to him was thus completed. Henceforward the Gallician army would be under the eye of Lord Wellington, whose authority must bear down all obstructions, and he looked forward to the result with prophetic confidence.

His representations induced General Castaños to remove his head-quarters to Astorga, where they arrived together on the 27th, and found a sad picture of the misery brought on Spain by the invasion. Two of the suburbs of the town had been levelled with the ground to enable the French to put it in a state of

defence, and the number of inhabitants was reduced
from twelve hundred families to about two hundred.
The Spanish trenches tore up the ground beyond the
ramparts, and the interior presented nothing but
shattered walls, and buildings in the last stage of
ruin. The siege left more terrible relics in the works,
where the bodies of the slain lay unburied; and the
brutalising effect of war appeared in the insensibility
of the passers-by, even children showing indifference.
Sir Howard mentions the fact with horror, and it is a
proof of the innate goodness of his nature that it was
never blunted by such scenes. Indeed, they rather
made him more compassionate, and gave his sympathies a wider scope, enlisting them for every form of
suffering. He remembers the claims of humanity in
the midst of a scientific treatise, and pauses to lament
that Minié bullets will aggravate wounds by dragging
in tags of cloth, and that the horrors of naval combat
will be increased by the use of shells. Like the Great
Duke, he taught that war should be averted by almost
any sacrifice.

It is natural that such a character should honour
art; for art ministers to sensibility, and he looked
for its productions wherever he went with the eye of a
pure taste. Thus he snatched a few moments in this
ruined town, and his pocket-book records the result in
a note of his visit to the cathedral. The structure
had not escaped the havoc of the siege, and he marked
the traces in wall and column, and in shivered block
and cornice. But the interior showed little damage,
and the war might be forgotten in its silent aisles and
"dim religious light." It brought out some of the

best points of Spanish architecture, and was embellished with a beautiful altar, one of the finest efforts of Gaspar Bacera. The work comprised three storeys, and these rested successively on Doric, Corinthian, and Composite columns, the niches between being occupied by figures of saints, while those of the Five Virtues stood below. The statues were of marble, nobly chiselled ; and some fine low reliefs appeared in the background from the same hand.

Sir Howard left Astorga in the evening, and rode on to La Baneza, where he remained till two in the morning, and then resumed his journey. Five o'clock brought him to Zamora, but so fagged and jaded that he could go no further, and he was proceeding to one of the inns when his uniform caught the eye of the Marquis of Villagrodis as he stood at a window, and he hurried out to offer his hospitality. The servants heard his name, and it flew through the town, exciting the greatest enthusiasm—for every one knew the part he had taken in supporting the blockade which led to the withdrawal of the French garrison, General Foy perceiving that it must surrender on his retreat. The whole population assembled before the house, and called on him to appear, joining his name with that of Wellington ; and presently he was visited by the civil authorities, who invited him to an entertainment. He found it impossible to escape, for they waited to form his escort, and marched him through the town, while the people thronged round, cheering and shouting. The entertainment comprised a repast and concert, which occupied the rest of the day, and left him very exhausted. But a night's sleep restored his strength, and he was in the saddle by daybreak, making his way to Salamanca.

Here he found troops of friends, and took up his quarters with Marshal Beresford, than whom there could be no kinder host, and at whose table he passed a pleasant evening, discussing the campaign, and both hearing and telling good stories, which it is to be regretted that he forgot to insert in his note-book. He was early mounted in the morning, and his friend Colonel Hardinge conducted him over the field of battle, so fruitful of interest to his eye. Indeed, he never passed by these practical illustrations of the art of war; and his example is suggestive to young soldiers debarred from his experience of service; for such lessons are open to all, and what he could study with advantage must to them be full of instruction. Nor is it easy to appreciate the genius of the Great Captain till we have thus stood on one of his positions, and recalled his manœuvres on the spot where they were executed. Sir Howard's companion knew all the incidents of the combat, and related them in the clearest manner, with a soldier's pride and grasp. He often spoke of Colonel Hardinge's description of the battle, which he characterised as a perfect representation, bringing before him the whole scene. How must he have felt at the time the influence he had exercised over the action himself, in preventing Lord Wellington from being crushed by numbers!

He made a long ride from the field to Arivalo, where he met General Churton, who told him that Lord Wellington would arrive next day, and this determined him to await his coming. It was two in the afternoon before the Commander-in-Chief appeared. He met Sir Howard in the friendliest manner, invited him to dinner, and directed him to remain at head-quarters till further orders. He was to have another opportunity of displaying his abilities before he returned to England.

CHAPTER XXI.

At the Siege of Burgos.

Sir Howard marched with the army in the advance on Burgos, and learnt from his friend Colonel Gordon[1] that he would probably be kept at head-quarters till the movement was completed. But Lord Wellington did not make known his intentions, though they were in frequent communication, and he dined with him nearly every day. They were riding together on the morning of the 6th, when the enemy appeared in front, posted on some commanding heights near Valladolid. Lord Wellington made dispositions for attack, ordering up General Anson's brigade of cavalry, with the 6th Division as a support; and a dash at the French brought off some prisoners. The heads of the English columns came up in succession, and marched to their places on the ridge, where their Commander had taken ground, and Sir Howard expected a general action. To this he looked with the more satisfaction, as he considered a victory would restore Lord Wellington the advantages he conceived him to have lost by not following up the pursuit from Salamanca. But the opportunities of war are moments, and must be seized as they pass, for they neither linger nor return. No one better knew their value than the English Commander; and doubtless he was now aware of any slip he had made in that operation, though Sir

---

[1] Afterwards General Sir Willoughby Gordon, G.C.B.

Howard witnesses that he may have been influenced by considerations which did not transpire. He showed every desire to seize the present opening, but was prevented from attacking by the absence of the 9-pounder brigade; and it did not arrive till late in the day, when the time for action had passed. All waited impatiently for the morning, but only to meet disappointment; for the French withdrew from the position during the night, though they still occupied the city. Sir Howard rode forward with Lord Wellington to reconnoitre, and saw all that had occurred. An advanced party of the 12th entered the Campo Major, and drove before it the French pickets; while their army was seen retiring across the bridge, leaving a small rearguard in the Tree Walk. These made a rush at a smaller party of English sent to cut off their advanced men, and gave them a check, killing and wounding the foremost, and then retreated over the bridge, which was instantly blown up. The explosion shook the earth, and the fragments shot up as from a volcano, for a moment veiling the spot with smoke and dust. Sir Howard felt alarmed for Lord Wellington's safety, as he exposed himself in an unusual manner; but he turned aside after the destruction of the bridge, and they rode into the garden of the Scots' College, on the road to Calderon, where they obtained a view of the whole French army marching very close to the river on the opposite bank, and Sir Howard estimated their number at 17,000. They left the English in possession of Valladolid.[1]

---

[1] Napier describes the recovery of Valladolid very briefly, and his account is different. He merely says, "Clausel abandoned Valladolid on the night of the 6th, and, though closely followed by Ponsonby's cavalry, crossed the

The French Marshal covered his retreat by a series of movements which brought the English to Burgos; and hence he fell back upon Briviesca, in company with Caffarelli, who had joined him in time to reinforce the garrison. The appearance of Burgos greatly interested Sir Howard, and he rode forward to reconnoitre the works in the train of Lord Wellington. The castle occupied a steep hill in front of the city, and comprised a strong wall, with parapet and flanks, and the additional defence of two palisaded retrenchments, one within the other. The innermost enclosed the crown of the hill, surmounted by the castle keep, which was entrenched and casemated, and capped by a battery, named after the Emperor, and commanding all around. To the north stood a hill of almost equal height, sustaining a strong hornwork, not quite finished, but closed with palisades.

Sir Howard noted every point, and looked upon the place as of great strength in relation to Lord Wellington's means; but the other scientific officers conceived a different impression, and thought the means equal to the attack. His knowledge of their opinion made him doubt his own, as he entertained a high appreciation of their judgment, and he determined to satisfy himself more fully before he expressed dissent. He possessed an old plan of the castle, which he carefully studied, and then rode out in the twilight to steal a closer view. The town, the castle, and the open all lay still in the terrible suspense before battle, and the shades of

Pisuerga and destroyed the bridge of Berecal on that river."—Peninsular War, v. 259. Sir Howard's notes make no mention of the pursuit by cavalry, and affirm that the French held the town in the morning, as stated above.

evening looked like the gathering of doom.   He knew
how vigilant must be the watch at such a juncture,
and that ball and bullet would give no warning if he
became a mark.   But he threw fear to the winds,
adroitly stole within range, swept round the works,
and made some important observations.   There was a
flash from the ramparts, and the bullets whizzed past,
but he had gained his horse, sprang into the saddle,
and darted off.

What he had seen confirmed his estimate of the
place, and he resolved to impart his opinion to his
friend Colonel Robe, who commanded the Artillery,
and hence had a voice in the operations.   He found
him in conference with Colonel Burgoyne, the Commanding Engineer; and both officers seemed glad of
his appearance, for they invited him to remain, and
told him the measures they had concerted with Lord
Wellington.   But they represented these as defini-
tively settled, and expressed no doubt of their success;
so Sir Howard did not feel encouraged to speak out,
and reserved his opinion till Colonel Robe and himself
were left together.   He then stated his belief that the
proposed attack would fail, which startled his friend,
and he begged him to disclose his grounds for such
a conclusion.   He readily complied, and showed him
that the point marked for attack was the strongest
part of the place, defended by three enclosures;
whereas but one need be breached on the eastern
front; and here he proposed to make a lodgment in the
salient angle, and follow it up by running a mine from
the flank under the castle wall.   The directness of the
plan struck Colonel Robe, and he gave it his approval,
asserting that it was the only one that would succeed.

But he adverted to the difficulty of submitting to Lord Wellington a view so different from his own, and asked if he might mention it on Sir Howard's responsibility. Sir Howard did not object, but said that he must first unfold the plan to Colonel Burgoyne, as no step should be taken without his knowledge; and he went to him at once. All who know that officer will be sure that his communication was kindly received, and he thought that it made an impression, but he came away without eliciting an opinion.

Sir Howard mingled with the Staff next morning, and was chatting with another officer, when he was called to Lord Wellington, and found him in conversation with Colonel Robe. He looked grave, and Sir Howard saw that his objections to the intended operations had been mentioned.

"Well, Sir Howard, you have something to say about the siege?" he said.

" I think the place is stronger than we supposed, my Lord."

" Yes, by G——! But our way is to take the hornwork, and from there breach the wall, and then assault over the two advanced profiles."

" I would submit to your Lordship whether our means are equal to such an attack."

" I am not satisfied about our ammunition," replied Lord Wellington.

" The enemy's guns are 24-pounders, my Lord; and we have only three 18-pounders and five 24-pound howitzers. The 18-pounders will not breach the wall, and our fire must be overpowered unless your Lordship brings up some guns from the ships at Santander.'

" How would you do that ? "

" With draught-oxen as far as the mountains, and then drag them on by hand. We can employ the peasantry, and put a hundred men to a gun."

" It would take too long."

" I think the place may be captured with our present means from the eastern front, my Lord," returned Sir Howard; and he disclosed his plan, with his reasons for thinking it the most practicable. Lord Wellington made no remark. Possibly he saw the defects of his own plan, but it had been deliberately adopted, and he was not convinced that it ought to be abandoned.

The guns of the fortress had kept the English on the other side of the river up to this time, but they now effected a passage above the town, and drove in the French outposts. A force attacked the hornwork during the night, and it was carried, though with a fearful loss, its garrison breaking through the assailants, and making their way to the castle, which thus obtained a reinforcement of 500 men.

The captors of the hornwork established a lodgment in spite of the fire of the Napoleon battery, and began the construction of a first battery, and a musketry trench in its front. The men worked under a continuous shower of grape, shells, and cannon-balls, which grew more intense as they proceeded, fresh guns being directed on the spot, and inflicting a murderous loss. Sir Howard exposed himself in the hornwork to make further observations, and ascertained the weakness of the eastern front, so as to place it beyond doubt. He described what he had seen to Colonel Gordon, who reported it to Lord Wellington, and came back with an intimation that he would take an opportunity of hearing it from himself. Sir Howard was talking with Colonel Burgoyne next morning, when Lord Wellington sent for them both, and opened the subject. He mentioned the course intended to be followed, and then reverted to the plan of Sir Howard, requesting him to state it fully. Sir Howard explained it on the chart, and further represented that the eastern wall was in a ruinous condition, which marked it as the point for attack, and that the reduction of the place would be accelerated by a flank fire from heavy howitzers on the Mary battery. He refrained from pointing out what he considered insurmountable difficulties in the other plan in the presence of the Commanding Engineer, and these apparently escaped the notice of the Commander-in-Chief, for he finally gave it the preference. Sir Howard notes that Lord Wellington said " he approved of my plan if mining were to be used, and expressed himself handsomely to me."

The operations were carried on at such cost of life that Lord Wellington's faith in them became shaken, and he sent for Sir Howard again on the following day, when holding a consultation with Colonels Robe and Burgoyne. He then stated his intention of shaping the attack so as to turn the church. This was an entrenched building on one of the two crests of the hill, the other crest being occupied by the castle, which swept the position. Sir Howard expressed his belief that no advance would be made by the capture of the church, and that the success of such an attack was doubtful, though it must entail a great expenditure of blood, while nothing but the breaching of the castle would reduce the place. The capture of the church would even prove an embarrassment, the vantage being in the site; and this involved a strong occupation if it should be won, as the mere destruction of the works only imposed on the enemy the construction of others as soon as it was relinquished. He said the question to consider was, whether that point offered an opening for breaching the castle; and he gave his opinion that the operation would be difficult from there, if not impracticable, comparing the means of the besiegers with those of the besieged. His arguments elicited no observation from Colonel Robe or Colonel Burgoyne, but he so far swayed Lord Wellington that a battery was ordered to be erected on the eastern face; and his Lordship expressed his approval of the howitzer battery, requesting him to take Colonel Robe to the proper spot for its erection. They went there at once, and then separated, the Colonel returning to Lord Wellington, while Sir Howard passed into the trenches.

The plan of operations was now partially changed. The left battery was continued, and a sap pointed to an outwork on the western front, with the design of trying a mine communication with Colonel Jones. Sir Howard received a visit from Colonel Robe next morning, and learnt that he had been ordered to attend Lord Wellington to the spot they had marked the day before, and that he thought the howitzer battery would be erected there. But he had no faith in half-measures, and expected little from this step alone, considering that the whole weight of the attack should bear on the eastern front, and that every other method would fail. This he had frankly stated to Lord Wellington, and there was nothing to add; so he thought it undig-

nified to appear further.   "I keep out of his way," he
notes in his pocket-book, "that the professional men
may not accuse me of obtruding an opinion."

Nothing could be more becoming his position than
such a course, and the incident of the siege thus brings
out his character as forcibly as his talents.   He had
seen how the place was to be taken from the first, but
reserved his opinion till the two directing officers made
him acquainted with their designs, and only imparted
it for his friend to consider and apply.   It was Colonel
Robe who proposed to mention the plan as his, and he
willingly undertook the responsibility, though it put
him in opposition to Lord Wellington; but he saw the
propriety of first unfolding the plan to the Commanding Engineer, and apprising him of their intention.   Thus his delicacy and honesty equalled his
spirit; and we should be undecided which part of his
conduct to admire most if all were not consistent.

The time had now come to "keep out of the way,"
and it is significant of his great self-control that he
cast the situation aside, and threw himself into other
thoughts.   His notes present us with a sketch of
the castle's history dated on this very day, and he
describes the stand it made against Ferdinand and
Isabella in the siege of 1476.   They also tell us of a
visit he paid to the cathedral, under a volley from the
enemy, who fired at every one appearing in the avenue;
and he enumerates its attractions and rarities—the
noble altar, the picture by Michael Angelo, the tomb
of the Cid, and the banner that fell from heaven, still
showing the sign of the cross, though scarcely hanging
together; a proof that even heavenly textures are not
enduring.

How pleasant to find him again turning from the presence of war to the sanctuaries of art, and recalling history and tradition under the cannon's mouth! Yet he did not blind himself to what was passing, and it made him wish that he could withdraw; for he saw a catastrophe approaching when his presence might be embarrassing. The operations were carried on with vigour, but without success. The sap on the west was continued towards the wall, in connexion with a mine, and an approach advanced from battery No. 1, with an inclination round the face of the hill to a kind of parallel for musketry, designed to keep down the enemy's fire. The mine was sprung at one o'clock on the morning of the 29th of September, and effected a small breach, which was entered by a sergeant and four soldiers, composing the forlorn hope. But the storming party did not come up in support, having missed the breach in the darkness, and the men returned bleeding to the trenches. Here another attack was organized, but too late, the enemy having mustered in force, and next morning showed the breach scarped.

A despatch from Lord Liverpool reached Sir Howard at this crisis, and called upon him to return to England without delay, which was what he desired, and he rode off directly to inform Lord Wellington. He found him on the hill, watching an attempt made from battery No. 1 to reopen the breach, and directing the operation. The fire brought down a part of the wall, but it fell perpendicularly, rendering the breach more difficult, and Lord Wellington marked a site for another battery, to be erected during the night. This he ordered to be armed with the 18-

pounders, and directed on the same point, arranging to deliver the assault concurrently with the springing of another mine.

The battery was begun at sunset, and briskly completed, when the guns were placed and opened. But Sir Howard's anticipations of the result were literally fulfilled, for the 18-pounders made no impression on the breach, and the enemy's heavier guns overpowered their fire, while every shot and splinter came through. It became impossible to hold the battery, and Lord Wellington withdrew the men, though this had no effect on the enemy, who did not cease firing till he had destroyed the battery and disabled the guns, one being reft of a trunnion, and the others knocked off their carriages. It was seen that he had the exact range of the spot, and the Commander-in-Chief ordered the guns to be removed, and a battery to be erected at another point, a little to the left. Here a more solid work rose during the night, but only to entail the same doom, for the French brought their guns into a position equally commanding, and reduced it to ruin. The professional officers now held a consultation, and decided to remove the only serviceable 18-pounder to battery No. 1, and thence open again on the breach, seconding the attack by a mine.

Sir Howard did not remain to witness the result, but Lord Wellington invited him to a conference on his taking leave, and expressed his intention of obtaining some heavy guns from the squadron, as he had recommended. Sir Home Popham sent up a supply of ammunition, which arrived most opportunely, and he hurried off two 24-pounders as soon as he received the requisition. But this was three

weeks after Sir Howard had made the suggestion, and
the interval gave the French army a superiority of
force, allowing Caffarelli to effect a junction with
Souham.   They instantly advanced on Burgos with
forty-four thousand veteran troops, while the army of
Lord Wellington consisted of only thirty-three thousand, chiefly Spaniards and Portuguese, so that he
was obliged to fall back on the ridges of Olenos,
where he awaited attack.   Events intervened to prevent a battle, but the allies were compelled to retreat ;
and Napier tells us that their General resolved,
" though with a bitter pang, to raise the siege, after
five assaults, several sallies, and thirty-three days of
investment, during which the besiegers lost more than
two thousand men, and the besieged six hundred in
killed or wounded."   It was in this moment of disaster that Lord Wellington recalled the counsel given
by Sir Howard, and exclaimed to his officers, " Douglas was right : he was the only man who told me the
truth." [1]

[1] This anecdote of the great Duke was related to the author by General
Sir William Gomm, G.C.B.

CHAPTER XXII.

EMPLOYED AT HOME.

THE despatch which recalled Sir Howard to England explained the reason of that step, stating that, " in consequence of the repeated and earnest representations made by the Supreme Board of the Royal Military College in regard to the detriment which that establishment suffers from your absence, Lord Liverpool has found himself obliged to consent, although very reluctantly, to your recall from the service in which you are employed, and which you have executed to the perfect satisfaction of His Majesty's Government." [1]

Indeed, the service had been executed so well that nothing remained to be done; for the mere distribution of the supplies might be left to the ordinary channels. His tact, judgment, and resolution had carried him through a mission of unusual difficulty, and achieved results exceeding the hopes of his superiors. He devoted himself to the work so assiduously that his vigilance and industry proved as serviceable as his talents, though these were continually displayed; but neither talent nor zeal would have availed without his good temper. His suavity soothed resentments, and irritation subsided before his friendly manner and natural kindness, which showed itself at every turn.

---

[1] Despatch from the Minister for War to Sir Howard Douglas, in the 'Douglas Papers.'

He averted jealousy by seeking to advance the cause, not himself, being willing to leave the credit to others, if he attained the object; and it was impossible to be offended with suggestions urged in a way that made them seem half our own. Nor could they be resisted by argument, for they were based on information and forethought, and objections vanished before facts. His military knowledge gave the momentum, but this arose from the same habit; for he had trained himself for action by observation and study, and by recognising the value of things which others overlooked. His memoranda present nothing more curious than the odd bits of information he has jotted down, as if he read sermons in stones, and extracted a hint from everything he saw. Thus he exercised his perception, and brought himself to work by method, so that his instantaneous conclusions were deductions, never guesses. It is not difficult to understand how his measures were successful, when we see that they all rested on such a groundwork, that they were undertaken with determination, pursued with vigour, and carried over every obstacle and difficulty.

No man was ever more loved by his friends, and he met a warm welcome on his return to Farnham. We may be sure that Lady Douglas made a handsome report of his " boys," whom he had put on their good behaviour, and one who remembered his own boyhood did not inquire too curiously. Indeed, he looked with indulgence on little lapses whether in boys or men; and he had nothing worse to correct in his children. His leisure was devoted to imbuing them with the highest principles, and the reverence they entertain for his memory proves that it was not mis-

spent. But leisure he had now little, for he received
the appointment of Inspector-General of Education in
1813, while he retained that of Commandant of the
Senior College, and thus stamped his impress on every
officer of the day, both of the Royal and Indian armies.
Such a position brought him in contact with a number
of officials more jealous of their functions than General
Abadia, but very prone to interfere with his. An
instance may be mentioned from his experience at
Addiscombe, where he was conducting an examination
of the cadets, when he received a note from the Lieutenant-Governor requesting him to dismiss them for
parade. He read it with surprise, but made no remark
at the moment, laying it on the table till the cadet
under examination had finished his proposition in
mechanics. He then took it up again and read it a
second and third time, too prudent to act in a way to
commit either the Governor or himself. There was
not the least alteration in his manner as he turned to
the Professor of Mathematics and said, "The Lieutenant-Governor wishes the cadets to attend parade,
so we had better finish the examination for to-day."
Both the Professor and cadets heard the announcement
with wonder, the quick military instinct perceiving
the impropriety of the proceeding, and that the
Governor had overstepped his authority. But Sir
Howard knew that such a question could not be decided in the school-room, and was not one to set an
example of defying authority, or entering on an un-
seemly altercation. He complied with the Governor's
order, but immediately brought it before the Court of
Directors, with a request that the Public Examiner
should always have access to the College, without any

interference from the Lieutenant-Governor, and that he alone should be empowered to fix the lengths of the examinations, and originate alterations in the system of education. Nor did he make the application with any wish for a personal triumph, as he had received another appointment, and desired only to leave the way clear for his successor. This object he accomplished, as the regulations he proposed were adopted, and all ground for contention removed.

He exhibited the same moderation towards the professors, and could never be betrayed into an outbreak of temper, or a want of consideration. Once he was examining the Addiscombe cadets in fortification, and illustrated his observations by reference to one of the Indian sieges, when the Professor of Fortification exclaimed, "I beg your pardon, but I had it from my brother-in-law in the service, that the case was rather different from what you state." Such an interruption rather startled the cadets, but Sir Howard let it pass, and went on with the examination. He intended to settle with the Professor in a manner that would show him he was in error, but spare him humiliation; and he took him into a private room next morning and requested him to look at some official documents, which proved that he had stated the facts. "Even had I been wrong," he said, "it was neither considerate nor respectful to contradict me in that open manner during the examination. I hope that you will speak to me privately in future after the examination, if you have any remarks to make." The most sensitive could not murmur at a rebuke so gentle.[1]

---

[1] The author is indebted for these anecdotes to the Rev. Jonathan Cape, Professor of Mathematics at Addiscombe.

Sir Howard had not long returned from Spain when he received intelligence of the death of his cousin Charles, who had been his aide-de-camp in Gallicia, and was killed in action almost as they parted. He severely felt the loss; for their tie of kinship had been strengthened by their fellowship in danger, and his cousin's genial character. The remembrances he cherished are revealed in letters to his friends in the Peninsular army, begging them to gather for him what could be learnt of the Captain's last moments, making inquiries about his servant, and bespeaking their care of his dog, which he desires them to send home by any opportunity. Few officers of his rank would have thought of the servant at such a moment; but he recollects the poor soldier as a comrade, and excites an interest for him in officers as distinguished as himself. No answer arrived for months, when he received one from Colonel Frazer, and the letter has such a smack of the field, that the passage on this subject claims to be quoted :—

" I fear by my silence you may have given up all hope of seeing poor Charlie's dog. I had, in truth, very little myself, since, on sending to Major Rice of the 51st Regiment, to acquaint him that I had secured a passage for the poor creature, I learned that she had disappeared. However, Moore, poor Charlie's servant, luckily stumbled upon her with the 18th Light Dragoons, and a few days ago the lady was brought hither, and presented me with twelve puppies next day. I am glad to say a safe passage is secured for her through James Macleod, whose servants are taking home his horse, and will look well after poor " Bell," who was left in their charge the day before

yesterday.   Macleod sailed yesterday in the packet,
and will apprise you of the arrival at Woolwich of
the dog.   As you made inquiries about Moore, poor
Charlie's servant, I should add that the man is well,
and spoke feelingly of his master.   He was not, however, present when poor Charles fell."

The last shot fired by the French in this war struck
Sir Howard's friend Captain Herries,[1] and cost him a
limb.   The sad intelligence was communicated by
Colonel Gomm,[2] in a letter reflecting the opinions
prevalent in the army on the final operations of the
war :—

"MY DEAR SIR HOWARD,   "Biarritz, 24th April, 1814.

"Although I have been well aware how gratifying it would be to you to receive some accounts of
our poor friend Herries, in addition to the public
ones, I have delayed writing to you for some days
past, in the hope that the events taking place in all
other quarters would before now have obtained for
us a free communication from Bayonne; and that I
should have been able to have had an interview with
him before I wrote.   Our Governor, however, does
not yet consider himself authorised to desert the
Imperial cause.   Official communications are hourly
expected, both from the Government and from Soult,
which will no doubt point out his duty and his interest
in terms sufficiently unequivocal to bring him to a
decision: in the mean time, all hostilities are at an
end.

"I suppose you know the nature of Herries's

[1] Afterwards Lieut.-General Sir William Herries, K.C.H., C.B.
[2] Now General Sir William Gomm, G.C.B.

wound. He was with Sir John Hope in the morning the garrison made the sortie; his leg was broken by a grape-shot, and, as I feared, has since been amputated. The last accounts we have from the town state that he is doing well, and is well taken care of. Among many other circumstances attending this unlucky business (for it might have been prevented) that have given me great concern, there is nothing that has vexèd me half so much as this unfortunate blow upon poor Herries; for he is a young man that ought not to have been maimed so early in life, and by the last ball that the enemy has hurled at us; but I dare say he will bear it with much more temper than I do. It is a pity we did not think fit to communicate to the Governor the official intelligence we had received two days before of the entrance of the Allies into Paris, and all the circumstances attending it. It is to be supposed that this piece of justice (I think) towards the Governor, and of policy in our character of besiegers, would have prevented a loss of about eight hundred and fifty to ourselves, and something more to the French.

"The battle of Toulouse will have given a bright close to the career of Lord Wellington. It appears to have been one of the most hardly contested actions of the whole war. . . . . .

"Believe me, my dear Sir Howard,
"Ever most faithfully yours,

"WILLIAM GOMM."

Sir Howard had been anxious to obtain further war service, and pushed for employment in the Peninsula; but saw the war close without achieving his object.

The return of Napoleon from Elba gave him new hope, and he exerted his interest to be appointed to the army in Flanders, but with the same result, the ground being taken up by more powerful aspirants. But his meritorious services were recognised at the peace, and he was nominated a Companion of the Bath, and Knight of the Spanish Order of Charles III. He subsequently received the Peninsular medal and clasps ; and we are now to see how he worked his way to other and higher honours.

CHAPTER XXIII.

Becomes an Author and Inventor.

It has been shown that Sir Howard had noticed the little attention paid in the navy to gunnery, which he considered its right arm, and he mentioned the subject to some distinguished naval officers, pronouncing it a mine of danger. But the faith of English sailors in their profession was not to be shaken by a landsman, and he was reminded that they had swept the seas of every fleet, and had left no enemy the power to do harm. He contended that this was a reason for greater exertion, as weakness would resort to new modes of resistance, and must look for these in increased expertness. But his arguments made no converts; naval gunnery became more and more neglected; and all that he foresaw occurred. The war with America brought on the seas the very enemy apprehended—one who sought to balance superiority in force by a superior armament, which his sailors were trained to work. The English Admiralty measured him only by the number of his ships, and left him to be settled by a few old frigates, as badly armed as manned. The capture of these vessels by American cruisers gave naval confidence a shock, and it vibrated through the nation. But it was no surprise to Sir Howard, who had predicted the event, and found it arose in the manner he expected. The contest between the 'President' and the 'Little

Belt' made this apparent; for the guns of the American frigate crippled her English antagonist, and inflicted a loss of eleven killed and twenty-one wounded, while the fire of the 'Little Belt' killed only a boy on board the 'President,' and never struck her hull.[1] Such defeats left their cause unmistakable; and might have led to improvement, but that the impression they produced was effaced by later actions, in which the valour of English seamen covered all defects. The navy again seemed invincible, and things were allowed to remain in the old groove.

But Sir Howard's alarm was undiminished, and he determined to effect a change. He knew that such a purpose involved difficulty, and imposed years of labour, while it was more likely to bring him into bad odour than make him friends. Even a sailor might expect obstruction in breaking the calm of the service, and introducing a working system; and what opposition must not be excited by a soldier, who aroused the susceptibilities of a jealous profession at the same time that he discomposed the authorities! Evidently he must look for rough treatment on the one hand, and repulse on the other.

He prepared himself for the enterprise by laborious investigation, experiment, and study. It was like Stephenson mastering the structure of his engine by constantly pulling it to pieces and putting it together; for he used the same inductive method, and followed it with the same industry. He had little to learn of practical seamanship, but felt himself deficient in theory; and he applied himself to the

[1] James's 'Naval History,' vol. vi. p. 10.

study of spherical geometry, spherical trigonometry, and nautical astronomy, including all the theorems required for solving the laws of navigation, the projection of the sphere, the construction of maps, plane sailing, rhomb sailing, and great-circle sailing. Use made him so familiar with the sextant and the repeating circle that he began to think of simplifying their construction ; and this led him to invent his Improved Reflecting Circle and Semicircle for Land and Marine Surveying, which came into wide use, and were highly appreciated by scientific men. Their merit obtained his election to the Royal Society, the most gratifying recognition it could receive.

He proposed to carry out his naval reform by writing a treatise which should bring forward the whole subject, and both provide the navy with trained gunners, and prescribe their training. So he traced the science to its root, and showed it in all its developments, unfolding the theory and teaching the practice. He reviewed every description of naval ordnance, and their relative power and range, the effects of different kinds of shot, the use of sights, and the determination of distances, explaining the action of projectiles in vacuo and in their passage through the air, with their initial velocities, curve, and force ; denoting the effect of windage, length of gun, discharge, recoil, and preponderance. He treated of the process of loading, the amount of the charge, and the degree of penetration ; the disturbing influence of the waves, and the proper moment for firing. Shells were considered as fully as shot, and he even gave directions for their stowage, while a chapter was devoted to military rockets, and another to the treat-

ment of gunpowder.   Instructions were laid down for
going into action, for the attack of maritime fortresses,
and for boat and coast service.   The captain was told
in what way he should exercise his crew—the gunner
how he should point his gun—and the sailor how
he should dispose the charge, and avoid the recoil.
Lastly, every proposition was worked out by mathematical demonstrations, and sustained by the results
of experiments, or by examples of naval combats,
conveyed in the plainest language and diction.

This exposition of the science embraced a plan for
the enrolment of gunners and their systematic training,
which started with the dogma that nothing would be
attained by merely drilling a crew, as success in action
was not to be insured by the dexterity of a few
privates, but must depend on organisation, while this
would only be effective under the direction of experience.   Hence he recommended that the rising class
of officers should receive a course of theoretical
instruction at the Royal Naval College, and that
their knowledge of gunnery should be tested in the
examinations for promotion.   He provided for the
training of crews by suggesting the formation of
Depôts of Instruction, at which a certain number of
seamen should be taught the practice of gunnery,
in company with a proportion of officers, gunners, and
gunner's mates, and he laid down the principles that
ought to rule these establishments.   His scheme
included arrangements for retaining the trained seamen in the navy, which was to be done in a manner
that entailed little expense, but offered attractions to
sailors.

He did not meditate the publication of the treatise,

and presented it to the Lords of the Admiralty in
manuscript, his sole object being the elevation of the
service ; for he exulted in any connection with the
navy, and it was this that both sustained his efforts
and supplied their inspiration.   The treatise was
left to move by its own weight, as he made no
interest to get it considered, or obtain it undue favour.
Nor did he expect the Board to give it immediate
attention, and put everything aside for this purpose,
according to the wont of projectors and inventors.
But he had some of the leaven of an author in his
composition, and did suppose that he would be apprised
of its receipt.   It must be acknowledged that this was
unreasonable, but the treatise had cost him severe
labour, arduous investigation, and years of thought,
and he knew its value ; so he waited a few months
longer, and then wrote to complain of the omission to
Rear-Admiral Sir Graham Moore, one of the Naval
Lords.   His letter received a prompt reply :—

"MY DEAR SIR HOWARD,   "Admiralty, 19th April, 1818.

    "I think the receipt of your valuable papers on
a subject of great importance to the navy and to the
country ought certainly to have been acknowledged,
though I am not surprised that nothing has yet been
done upon them.   The subject has been long before
the Board (as they call it), though I do not believe
either of our two naval colleagues have yet read your
papers.   I will call their attention to them, and I am
sure they will feel, as I do, whether your ideas are
attempted to be put in practice or not, that much
praise is due to you for applying your genius and
science to the improvement of so essential a branch of

our profession. . . . . . Though I date this 'Admiralty,' it is really written from my house near Cobham, Surrey, to which I have made my escape for a couple of nights, and where it will be a real pleasure to me to see you when I can get a few weeks' leave from the Board.   I go back to-morrow.

"I am, my dear Sir Howard,

"Very truly yours,

"GRAHAM MOORE."

Sir Graham Moore exerted himself to get the treatise considered, and this is not the least of the services he rendered to the navy, which owes him so many.   But the question made little progress, and it cost as much strain to drag the treatise out of dock as to launch the 'Great Eastern.'   Three months later Sir Graham Moore writes to Sir Howard :—"I have given your Third Part to Croker, as he has the two other Parts, and is an advocate for something being adopted upon them.   I am ashamed of being able to do so little in forwarding your excellent plans for the improvement of the service."   Another letter from Sir Graham refers to a discussion on the subject at the Admiralty, in which Sir Howard had taken part :—"You had by far the best of the argument the other day, but I do not think that brings you nearer the mark you aim at.   I am glad you sent your papers to Sir George Cockburn.   He is in the situation in which Sir George Hope was, and has much more to say here than I have."

Still, Sir Graham did his best, and continually brought the subject forward.   But it is the fate of all improvements to meet delays, and be opposed by

difficulties and impediments. The trial is more painful
from the risk of forestalment, for the don may carry
off the prize, while the workman risks his life in
trying the lamp. Nearly was it so in Sir Howard's
case, for a carpet sailor snapped up the conclusions he
had gathered on board the ' Venerable,' under the
enemy's fire, and put them forward as his own. "Between you and I," writes Sir Graham Moore, " . . . .
has been here, with what he called a plan for the
improvement of naval gunnery, evidently taken from
the Second Part of your work; though he seemed
to be surprised when I told him that you had sent
to the Admiralty many months before a detailed plan
on the subject of establishing a corps of naval
gunners, to be composed of seamen. I do not think
you have any room for jealousy of . . . . robbing
you of the credit of any project that may be put in
practice."

But few besides Sir Graham Moore would have
spoken so frankly to one in the position of . . . . ,
and Sir Howard thought it time to give his treatise
to the printer. The desire to establish priority was
not his sole object; for he conceived that his scheme
might interest the public, and the authorities only
required an impulse to take it in hand. Indeed, they
had recognised its merits, but were restrained from
moving by considerations of expense. They now
gave their sanction to the publication, and the work
made its appearance in 1819, under the title of 'A
Treatise on Naval Gunnery.'

It had a different effect from what had been expected,
producing no impression on the public, but meeting a
cordial reception from the navy, and all ranks of the

service hailed it with approval. No jealousy was excited by the profession of its author, but rather appreciation, and the first officers in the navy wrote him complimentary letters, expressing wonder at his nautical knowledge, with a high sense of the service he had rendered the profession. " We are all indeed deeply indebted to an officer who takes such pains and bestows such an ability upon an object so requisite to the national honour," wrote Admiral Sir P. P. V. Brooke.

The 'Treatise on Gunnery' was followed by an 'Essay on Fortification,' combating the system of Carnot, and this drew forth a French work on the subject by Captain Augoyat, which is referred to in the following letter from the Duke of Wellington. The Duke's association of our heavy guns with the " earthen ramparts " of the Russians is curious, and has an air of prophecy, though the event did not come to himself, nor in his day, but fell to one of his lieutenants :—

"MY DEAR SIR,   "Tedderby, 19th Nov. 1821.

" I am very much obliged to you for the second copy which you have sent me of the work by a naval officer on Carnot. I received the first you sent me, and wrote to you to thank you for it. I gave it to General Thielmann, at Wherntey, and he is perusing it.

" I propose to follow up, next spring and summer, the experiments commenced this year in ricochet firing, with ordnance of the larger calibres. I expect that we shall bring it to such perfection as to be able to a certainty, even with reduced charges, to breach the walls which the Russians have constructed in front of, and detached from, their earthen ramparts, instead of the common revetment.   If we can succeed in this object, we shall completely destroy this new system of fortification.

" Ever, dear Sir, yours most faithfully,

" WELLINGTON."

Sir Howard's authorship made him less a literary man than a man of letters, since it did not address the public at large, but the military and scientific world ; yet it brought him the acquaintance of most of the distinguished writers of the day, and this circle included Robert Southey.   The following letter from the poet has an interest from bearing on his literary toils, showing the mode in which he collected materials for his ' History of the War:'—

"DEAR SIR HOWARD,   " Keswick, 15th March, 1819.

" I am very much obliged to you for your letter, which is full of interesting matter.   Before I notice it in detail, I must reply to your question.   With the Duke of Wellington himself I have had no direct communication as yet.   When next I am in London (which will be in the month of May) I shall seek it, and I have many means of access to him.   But many of his despatches and of his letters to Marquis Wellesley have been communicated to me, and I have the Marquis's permission (through his son-in-law, Mr. Lyttleton) to apply to him for any information where I am in doubt.

" In point of authorities, indeed, I have good reason
to believe that no similar work has ever been laid
before the world with higher claims.   I have made
large extracts from the papers of one public office ;
the others will be open to me.   Part of my business
in the South is to visit Sir Henry Bunbury, who was
my schoolfellow, and slept in the same room with me
at Westminster, and who has offered me the use of his
papers.   I shall have the same assistance from Mr.
Herries, with whom I have been acquainted some
twenty years.   I have had communications from Sir
Hew Dalrymple.   Lord Sheffield has supplied me
with information and documents respecting the operations of the army under Sir Henry Clinton.   I have
known Mr. Frere since his first appointment at Lisbon
in the year 1800, and I shall have all the assistance
which he can give me.   A great deal I have derived
from the private correspondence of intelligent officers.
The papers which the Committee in London for
managing the Portuguese subscription received from
the local authorities in Portugal are in my possession.   I have some communications of considerable
value from Spain.

"The fact which you state respecting Gallicia is
very curious, and explains what certainly appeared
one of the greatest oversights in the Spanish Government.   The details upon this subject will be very
important to me.

"Undoubtedly, Sir John Moore retreated in the
right direction, though surely not in the right manner.
Had Lisbon been abandoned, as in all likelihood it
would have been if he had moved thither and drawn
the enemy after him, it is very probable that the vile

spirit which was then so predominant in this country
would have borne down the Government, and that we
should have shrunk from the contest to our everlasting
disgrace.   Sir Robert Wilson's movement on Ciudad
Rodrigo at that critical time appears to me to have
been of great importance by imposing upon the
French.

"The affairs of Gallicia are those with which I am
least acquainted.   There was an apparent torpor in
that province after it had so nobly freed itself from
the French, which even the *provincialism* of the
Spaniards did not appear to explain.   While Romana
was there and in Asturia, I have procured information
of his movements from a Spanish officer in his army
(Colonel Stonor), who is now settled in England,
not as one of the Liberales.   But a long season of
inaction followed.   General Malega had the command
at one time : there were some things which induced
me to suspect his fidelity, and there was nothing in
his after conduct to diminish that suspicion.   But
upon such points it becomes me to be very cautious,
knowing how liable I must needs be to form an erroneous opinion, and how utterly unjustifiable it is ever
to advance an opinion which affects the character of
any man without the fullest information on the surest
grounds.   The defence of Astorga was one of those
things which I, who love the Spaniards, regarded with
wonder ; for I had been at Astorga, and seen its
ruinous walls.

"The guerilla part of this great drama is very
interesting.   I saw the younger Minas three years ago
in London, and obtained from him an account of the
commencement of his career.   I have also had a paper

respecting the guerillas which was drawn up by General
Alava for Lord Wellington.

"Did we not neglect for too long a time the coast
of Asturias and Biscay? and would it not have been
advantageous for us if we had occupied Santona?
On these and on any other points I shall receive the
opinions and information which you may have the
kindness to impart with the greatest respect and
attention.

 "I have the honour to be, dear Sir Howard,
  "Your obliged and obedient servant,

     "ROBERT SOUTHEY."

Sir Howard is again found in communication with
His Royal Highness the Duke of Kent at this period.
Twenty years had passed since his shipwreck, when
he appeared before His Royal Highness at Halifax,
in sailor's clothes, and received from him so much
kindness. He had now won a reputation as a man of
science, and the Duke of Kent consulted him as to the
merits of an invention for which its author sought his
patronage. His Royal Highness felt an interest in
every kind of merit, and this exposed him to impor-
tunities, as pretenders sought to float themselves by
his support. But his good nature did not mislead his
good sense; for the following letter shows that he
took counsel in his doubts, and it claims insertion, as
a testimony to the candour of Sir Howard :—

         "Kensington Palace,
"MY DEAR SIR HOWARD,   25th Nov. 1819.

 "I thank you for your obliging letter of the 23rd,
and for the candid opinion given as to the merits of

Mr. . . . . 's invention. After what you have said,
I shall of course let the subject rest, and leave that
gentleman to discover the real merits of his fancied
improvements.

"I thank you also for your endeavours to find for
me the old plan of Kensington Gardens; and although
we have failed in that object, I am equally obliged
by your ready attention to my wishes in furtherance
of it.

"If you will take advantage of any private con-
veyance for sending the models of Mr. . . . . 's
invention to the Palace, it will insure their arrival
quite soon enough.

"I remain, with sincere regard and esteem,
  "My dear Sir Howard, yours faithfully,

              "EDWARD."

All this time the Admiralty made no sign, and the
country never troubled itself about naval gunnery.
The season had not come for a movement, and Sir
Howard waited its arrival, satisfied with what he had
done. He was about to enter on a new chapter of his
life, and it will show him to us in a new character, as
a ruler, administrator, and statesman.

CHAPTER XXIV.

GOVERNOR OF NEW BRUNSWICK.

SIR HOWARD had now attained the rank of Major-General, and in 1824 was appointed Lieutenant-Governor of New Brunswick, and Major-General in command of the troops in that province, together with those in Nova Scotia, Cape Breton, Prince Edward Island, Newfoundland, and Bermuda. He embarked with his family in the frigate 'Samarang,' Captain Sir William Wiseman, Bart., and had a rough passage to Halifax, where he had landed thirty years before in a blue jacket and tarpaulin, but now came with decorations on his breast, and received almost royal honours. The vessels in the harbour were dressed with flags, officers in uniform waited his arrival on the beach, and cannon gave a salute as he left the ship. Little did those around dream what was passing through his mind in the midst of this pageant; for his thoughts had turned to the incidents of his first visit, and his heart swelled with gratitude to the Power which had given it this sequel. He used to say that the contrast struck him the more from his encountering on the beach a member of the Council whom he had met there in 1796 a subaltern in the Royal Fusiliers. This was the Honourable Justice Haliburton, the author of 'Sam Slick,' but Sir Howard mistook him for some one else at the moment, and asked him what had

become of little Haliburton of the Fusiliers. "Little
Haliburton!" said the humourist, thoughtfully. "Oh,
yes, I know ! He left the Fusiliers, sold out, turned
lawyer, got made a judge, came out to Halifax, and
here he is to meet the Governor:" when again he
stretched out his hand, which Sir Howard shook with
a hearty laugh.

Sir Howard inspected the troops in the province,
and then proceeded to St. John's, in the Gulf of
Fundy. Here he was received with every mark of
respect, and entered on the duties of his government.

The colony of New Brunswick dates its origin from
1764, when it was established by a body of New
Englanders, who settled at the mouth of the River St.
John, in what is now called the county of Sunbury.
The population received an addition in 1783 from an
influx of American Royalists, who abandoned their
homes in New York and Boston on the Declaration of
Independence, and came to live under English rule.
The numbers were further increased by emigration,
and Sir Howard found them amount to upwards of
74,000, of whom only 3227 claimed descent from the
New Englanders.

The Governor of a colony then held a different
position from at present, when he merely represents
the Sovereign, the government being vested in
Ministers nominated by a Parliament. Sir Howard
was associated with a Parliament, but responsible
to the Ministers at home, who formed their views
on his reports. The weal of a colony thus depended greatly on the Governor's abilities; and his
proved equal to the post. He came to a wilderness,

carried it through a terrible visitation, and left it a thriving province.

The New Brunswick of 1824 could boast of only five roads, and these were but roads by courtesy. Three led severally to St. John's, St. Andrew's, and Chatham, from the capital Fredericton; another ran in the direction of Quebec, and the fifth led to Halifax. They were constructed on the Roman plan of going up hill and down, and attracted little traffic, the colonists preferring to settle on the banks of the rivers, where they had the advantage of water communication. Sir Howard turned his first attention to this deficiency, and designed a road to connect Fredericton with the port of St. John's, by the Narapia river, pushing it forward with great rapidity; and the colonists were astonished to see a way opened that saved a third of the distance. It was so constructed that horses could trot the course without danger or distress, though it crossed a lofty ridge of slate. "In fact," writes a clergyman of New Brunswick[1] to the author of this work, "Telford or M'Adam could hardly have designed a better." Comfortable inns garnished the wayside, and insured the traveller good entertainment, whether he stopped at the sign of the "Government House," or that of the "Douglas Arms." The St. John's road was but the beginning of a system, and was soon followed by others, which opened up New Brunswick in every direction, while he contracted for the navigation of the St. John by a steamer, almost the first introduced in a British colony.

[1] The Rev. Edwin Jacob, D.D., of Mapledown, New Brunswick.

But it struck him that he could know little of the deficiencies of his government unless he visited its remotest parts, and he waited for neither roads nor steamers to carry him through. His old Indian habits made the task easy, and he penetrated forests and forced his way up streams to back settlements, hardly known by name, startling the inhabitants with a sight of the Governor. " I have received accounts of his visits to every part of the country," writes the Rev. Dr. Jacob to the author. " It has been especially observed to me, by persons likely to have taken particular notice of his peculiar habits, that Sir Howard showed himself determined to know men and things as they really were, and was accustomed to go in all directions, closely inspecting the abodes and occupations of the rich and the poor, and discovering a kind interest in the welfare of all classes."

His progresses brought him to perceive that the colonists were very backward in farming, and conducted its operations in the most primitive manner, whence he applied himself to promote a better system. He had not the advantage of personal experience, but he took counsel of the best agriculturists at home, and disseminated their suggestions. He also established agricultural societies, and obtained them the support of public grants, while he encouraged improvements by prizes, which he often distributed himself. He introduced a better arrangement in the construction of dwellings, affording more accommodation and domestic comfort, and he extended the same principle to churches and schools. These measures resulted in a general elevation of the popula-

tion.   Farmers multiplied their crops, and carried on
their work with superior implements, and the regene-
rating influence was apparent both in their stock and
seeds.   The remotest settler felt a stimulus to exertion, when any moment might bring the Governor into
his cabin, with a greeting for each of his household,
and an interest in all his proceedings.

CHAPTER XXV.

At the Great Fire.

The impulse Sir Howard had given the province met a sudden check in 1825. The season was advancing, and no rain had fallen for two months, which excited uneasiness for the harvest, and he visited some of the settlements to ascertain their prospects. An urgent letter recalled him to Fredericton, and he returned to find himself houseless, a fire having broken out at Government House on the 19th of September, and almost burnt it to the ground before it could be arrested. Happily it occurred in the daytime, and the courage and devotion of Lady Douglas nerved her to supply his place, which led to the preservation of the most valuable part of the effects; and the author is the more bound to mention this, as it secured him the materials for the present work; for nothing seemed more precious to Lady Douglas than the memorials of her husband's services.[1]

But his own misfortune was forgotten by Sir Howard in a calamity which fell on the community. The long drought continued, and October came in with midsummer sultriness, keeping the thermometer at 86° in the shade, and 126° in the sun. On the morning of the 7th he expressed his belief that a

[1] "By means of the fortitude, calm composure, and ready presence of mind of Lady Douglas, who remained until the last, his Excellency's papers, books, and most of the furniture were saved."—*New Brunswick Courier.*

large fire prevailed in the woods, as a breeze had
risen, and blew warm and parched, bringing in clouds
of smoke; but this was ascribed to the burning of
the brushwood by the lumberers. The explanation
did not allay his apprehensions, and he directed the
engines to be in readiness, and the military prepared
to assist, fearing that brands might be blown into
Fredericton. The wisdom of his precautions too soon
appeared; for the afternoon brought an alarm that fire
had broken out in the wood round the house of the
Hon. John Baillie, about a mile from the town; and he
ordered out the engines and troops, and galloped off
at their head, followed by nearly the whole population.

The air brought an odour of burning as they advanced, but they saw nothing of the fire except a
cloud of smoke, till a gust blew it aside and showed
the flaming trees. The house rose behind, and
appeared uninjured; nor had the trees caught beyond
a few yards, where a gap imposed a boundary. Sir
Howard directed the engines to play here and on the
house, though this presently seemed doomed, as the
trees began to fall and covered it with flakes of fire.
Indeed, it excited less interest than the wood, for
there the fate of the province was at stake, as a spark
winged across the gap might spread the fire to the
interior. Sir Howard watched both points, and so
posted the firemen that they got the mastery of the
flames, and less than an hour found the house preserved, and the fire extinguished.

All were rejoicing at the result, when danger presented itself in a new quarter, a messenger spurring
up to report a fire in Fredericton. Sir Howard
pushed on the engines to the spot, and ordered up the

troops at the double, while he hastened to be first himself; for the breeze had increased to a gale, and blew in a direction to imperil the town. The flames burst on his view as he galloped up, rising from the house and barn of Mr. Ring, which they had half consumed, and they now threatened a range of wooden houses beyond. The engines played on the nearest; but the gale blew about burning flakes, which rendered precaution futile; and smoke rose from two or three houses at once—then from a dozen; and a whole street was in flames. They spread like lightning, not from building to building, but in forks; and roofs lit up a dozen houses off as if they kindled spontaneously. A large area was one flame, crackling and crashing, as it shot over rafters, split walls, and brought down floors and beams, whirling smoke through the town till the whole seemed on fire. The torrents of water poured in had no effect; for the smoke and flame thickened where they fell, as if they supplied fuel, and house after house caught like tinder. But the engines worked on, the soldiers and population manning the pumps, and relieving each other, while parties kept back the crowd of women and children who watched their burning homes with frantic emotion. Nothing could be saved; for buildings caught at a distance where they appeared secure, and blazed in an instant, throwing out flames like arms, and dragging the next houses into the vortex. Night added its shadows to this scene; and some of the most respectable families of the town crouched destitute in the streets, reduced to beggary in a moment. All seemed lost; and all had been lost indeed, but for one man.

Sir Howard marked a point where he thought the fire might be arrested, as it was occupied by a brick building less in front of the wind, and here he concentrated a large force, and so saturated the adjacent houses with water, that flakes fell on them without igniting. How long this might have continued is doubtful; but the wind gradually veered further round and blew in the opposite direction, which turned the fire in upon itself, and a third of the town was a burning mass while the rest stood clear.

The deliverance was not understood at first, but the report spread, and families returned to their homes, carrying back their furniture which they had brought into the streets. Sir Howard remained at the angle, and urged the firemen to renewed exertion; for the wind grew more and more boisterous, and might shift any moment, when the flames would again be driven forward if not extinguished. The continuous stream of water began to abate their fury, or nothing remained to consume, for they now vanished in smoke, which rolled away from the town, and showed the sky above. Yet the air was so hot that it became difficult to breathe; a suffocating odour pervaded every quarter; and a belief arose that the fire smouldered somewhere, and would break out again. But imagination never dreamt of the conflagration at hand, the most stupendous ever witnessed by man.

A roar of thunder came from the forest, and a column of smoke shot up, followed by blaze on blaze, and then a burst of fire, like the eruption of a volcano. The flames fell in a shower, which the gale blew wide, hurling them about like darts; and here they might be seen on the tops of trees—there flaring in the branches—there running up or down the trunks, or from base and summit at once. The smoke blew back on the unkindled woods, making them darker than before—blacker than the blackest night; and the fire raged in the middle, imaging the mouth of hell. But this was only for a moment. Blazes gleamed at the sides, behind, in the depths of the woods, on the river's brink; trees of centuries' growth lit up in the midst of the darkness; fire rained from above, soared up from below, spread from the centre, and closed in from the distance. It burst in a hundred eruptions, mounting, declining, and mounting again, throwing up spouts, falling in showers or sheets, or glaring in mid-air. A thousand miles of forest had caught![1] The river was crimson with the reflection; the clouds took the form of flames; the very heavens seemed on fire.

The intense heat deranged the strata of the atmosphere; and the gale burst into a hurricane, tore through the town, wrenched up trees, and carried strong men off their feet. Horses broke from the fields, and galloped about in troops, snorting and neighing, their eyes starting from their heads and their manes on end, while the wind swelled the clatter of their hoofs to the rush of hosts. All occurred in an instant, and inspired a religious people with an impression akin to the spectacle—that it was the Day of Judgment. They threw themselves on their knees in the streets, or buried their faces to shut out the scene, as if they made the appeal foretold to the mountains and hills. And it did seem a burning

[1] The conflagration extended over six thousand square miles.

world, with the fire raging like a sea, in mountainous waves; the sky glowing like a furnace; the hurricane breaking in peals and crashes; and the scorched air flapping as with a million wings.

Sir Howard kept moving through the town, or paused only in the centre, where he had posted a reserve of the 52nd Regiment under Colonel M'Nair, and a body of firemen; while the remainder were stationed at different points, ready to operate on the first alarm. Only the greatest vigilance could preserve the remaining houses, and he went from post to post, giving directions and overlooking all. He was nobly supported by Colonel M'Nair and the other officers, as well as the gentlemen of the town, who formed parties to drive back the horses and patrol the streets.[1] This reassured the crowd, whose terrors calmed as they felt the presence of authority, and more as they saw the light of another day.

But now they began to realise their destitution, which horror had made them forget; and hundreds cried for bread. Sir Howard organised a system of temporary relief, and formed a committee to carry it out, but charity could do little in a case so desperate. Thriving men of yesterday had lost all they possessed; honoured families were beggars; and delicate women and children stood unsheltered before their ruined homes. It terrified him to think that they reflected a distress as wide as the province; for it could not be doubted that the fire had ravaged

---

[1] "The exertions at this critical period by all parties cannot be sufficiently applauded, aided and encouraged (as they were) by our active and indefatigable Governor, who throughout the melancholy scenes displayed the most anxious concern, and through whom wonders absolutely were effected."—*New Brunswick Courier*, October 10, 1825.

the interior, and left thousands without a roof. He considered that it must have destroyed the harvest, and that the navigation might close before they obtained supplies—so far did he look forward in a moment, and with courage to act on his forethought. He sent for an active merchant of the town, and ordered him to proceed to Quebec, and buy up food and clothing, furnishing him with bills on the Treasury, which he drew at his own risk. He then took measures for the relief of the misery in the town, calling a meeting of the inhabitants by proclamation; and this brought up the whole community—the rich and destitute together. He presided himself, and made a touching appeal to the more fortunate, while he set an example of liberality by subscribing 20*l.* from his own purse, and 200*l.* in the name of the King, appropriated from the casual revenue on his own responsibility. "Such conduct as his speaks volumes in his praise," says the 'New Brunswick Courier.' "It endears him to our hearts, and throws a moral splendour around his character, that the adventitious distinctions of birth, rank, and fortune cannot confer; and much as we admire his bravery as a soldier, his indefatigable endeavours to make himself acquainted with the real state of the province, and his profound political sagacity, we admire still more the distinguished efforts he has made in the cause of suffering humanity on this occasion." [1]

He did not confine his solicitations to the colonists, but addressed letters to the Governor-General of Canada, his friends in England, and the Colonial Secretary, claiming their succour; and his official

---

[1] New Brunswick Courier, October 10, 1825.

despatch stated the need so forcibly that the Government inserted it in the 'Gazette' to stimulate the public bounty.[1]   The result was a subscription of 40,000*l.* collected in England and the colonies, and the presentation of large supplies of food and clothing.

Several days elapsed before the fire subsided, and then it became masked by smoke which darkened the whole country.   But night proved that it had not burnt out: for showers of flame shot up at intervals, and trees stood glaring in the dark, while the mingled black and red of the sky seemed its embers overhead. Thus a week passed, when Sir Howard determined to penetrate the forest, and visit the different settlements.   A friend has described his parting with Lady Douglas and his daughters, whose pale faces betrayed their emotion, though they forbore to oppose his design, knowing that nothing would keep him from his duty.   But this was not understood by others, and the gentlemen of the town gathered round his rough country waggon at the door, and entreated him to wait a few days, pointing to the mountains of smoke, and declaring that he must be suffocated, if he escaped being burnt.   He thanked them for their good feeling, grasped their hands, and mounted the waggon.   It dashed off at a gallop, and wondering eyes followed it to the woods, where it disappeared in the smoke.

The devastation he met exceeded his worst fears; for the settlements he went to visit no longer existed. The fire seems to have burst in every quarter at once, for it broke out at Miramichi the same moment as at

---

[1] London Gazette, December 17, 1825.

Fredericton, though a hundred and fifty miles lay between. But here its aspect was even more dreadful, and its ravages more appalling, as Miramichi stood in the forest, completely girt round, except where escape was shut off by the river. Many were in bed when they heard the alarm ; many were first startled by the flames, or were suffocated in their sleep, leaving no vestige but charred bones. Others leaped from roof or window, and rushed into the forest, not knowing where they went, or took fire in the street, and blazed up like torches. A number succeeded in gaining the river, and threw themselves in boats or on planks, and pushed off from the bank, which the fire had almost reached, and where it presently raged as fiercely as in the town. One woman was aroused from sleep by the screams of her children whom she found in flames, and caught fire herself as she snatched up an infant and ran into the river, where mother and child perished together. Then came the hurricane, tearing up burning trees and whirling them aloft; lashing the river and channel into fury, and snapping the anchors of the ships, which flew before it like chaff, dashing on the rocks, and covering the waves with wreck. Blazing trees lighted on two large vessels, and they fired like mines, consuming on the water, which became so hot in the shallows that large salmon and other fish leaped on shore, and were afterwards found dead in heaps along the branches of the river. What can be said of such horrors, combining a conflagration of a thousand miles with storm and shipwreck, and surprising a solitary community at midnight? Happily, the greater number contrived to reach

Chatham by the river; but floating corpses showed
how many perished in the attempt, and nearly three
hundred lost their lives by fire or drowning.

A harrowing spectacle presented itself on the sub-
sidence of the flames.   Scarcely a house remained
standing;   not one uninjured;   and the road was
strewn with black heaps, which proved to be the
ashes of men and women.   One of these claims
mention as the remains of a woman who had so
disposed herself as to cover her infant while she
burnt to a cinder above, and the child was taken
from beneath alive — a witness to the sublimest instance of maternal devotion ever recorded.[1]   The
devastation struck the survivors with despair, and
they made no effort at retrieval, but wandered
about the ruins bewildered, or crouched down wherever they found shelter.   Suddenly there was a general movement; everybody hurried out — some without knowing why — and they hardly believed their
eyes as they looked up the forest, and saw Sir
Howard walking down, his waggon being blocked
by a fallen tree.   He had come a hundred and
fifty miles through the woods where the fire still
burnt, and received no injury, though he was often in
danger, and once all but suffocated.   Simultaneously
the whole crowd went forward, and every one uncovered as they met, receiving him with a silence
more eloquent than cheers.   But he spoke out; for
he knew what to say, and raised courage and hope in
their breasts, if he brought tears to no few eyes.   Soon
the axe and the hammer were at work; spades were

[1] This incident was communicated to the author by a lady of Sir Howard's
family, who was present at the fire.

throwing up the ground; men bustled about with loads on their backs; a vessel came round from St. John's with supplies; and the cloud began to pass from Miramichi, like the smoke from the forest. He remained through their trial, and shared its privations, while his presence alleviated its bitterness; and they followed him with blessings on his departure. He had distributed amongst them 1000 barrels of flour, 500 barrels of pork, and 1700*l.* worth of clothing, which he purchased on his own responsibility, though he was afterwards indemnified by the Government. Well and truly did Lord Sidmouth write to him :— "Happy was it for the province that such a person as yourself was on the spot. All its hopes of protection, relief, and redemption depended on the resources and energies of your judgment, fortitude, activity, and benevolence." He refers to the account Sir Howard had sent him of the fire in the following words:—" I was at a large dinner-party at Lord Stowell's, and your detailed communication had the effect of exciting all present to contribute and to promote the means of relief to the utmost of their power. In reflecting upon the ruin which surrounds you, I rejoice that it has been your lot to be the instrument of performing such duties as, I truly think, you, of all the men I have ever known, are the best calculated to discharge. The affectionate solicitude of every member of my family constantly attends you."

CHAPTER XXVI.

ON THE COAST.

THE duties of his government never diverted Sir Howard from those of his command. He inspected each division of the troops in turn, and made voyages to Halifax for this purpose, visiting every military post. He took the deepest interest in the soldiers, and was as anxious to promote their welfare as their efficiency. One of the measures he originated was SOLDIERS' SAVINGS BANKS, which worked so successfully that he thought it his duty to lay the result before the Horse Guards, and he made a report setting forth the effect produced on the character of the soldiers, particularly in checking desertion and drunkenness. He received a sharp reproof in reply, and was told that he had exceeded his authority in establishing the savings-banks, which he was ordered to suppress, but he afterwards had the satisfaction of seeing them introduced by the Government.

His voyages between St. John's and Halifax were attended with his usual fortune at sea, and his association with bad weather became a proverb, so that sailors began to look upon him as a sort of Jonah. The impression should have been just the reverse,' for proofs continually arose that he was not born to be drowned. He went to Halifax for a spring inspection in His Majesty's frigate 'Niemen,' Captain Wallace,[1] and intended to go from there to Prince Edward's Island, and then visit the military posts along the shore of New Brunswick. All went well till he left Charlotte Town, whence he passed along the coast to the Miramichi, and was entering the river in fine weather under the guidance of a pilot, when the ship struck. No bank appeared in the chart, but they found that the frigate had run on a ledge of rocks presenting such a slope that she did not stop till she had been carried high up. Her position was most critical, and excited as much alarm on shore as on board. Several large fishing-craft put off to her assistance, but the tide was falling, and the crew could do nothing but lighten the ship. This they effected in the promptest manner, the boats being got away, the water started and pumped out, the yards and topmasts struck, and the guns hoisted up and stowed in the fishing-craft. Every one waited for the rise of the tide, and then worked together, when the frigate was hauled off by an anchor laid out astern, and floated.

Sir Howard watched these operations with deep interest, and often expressed his admiration of the judgment displayed on the occasion by Captain Wallace, as well as the zeal of his officers, and the steadiness of the crew. The frigate was accompanied by the colonial brig 'Chibuctu,' which attended on the Governor, but he would not leave the 'Niemen' in her distress, and remained on board till a leak showed that she had sustained injury in her bottom and must go into dock.

---

[1] Afterwards Vice-Admiral Sir Provo Wallace, K.C.B.

The ' Niemen ' again brought him in peril in 1826.
The October of that year found him at Halifax in
company with Lady Douglas, and he proposed returning home by way of Hemapolis, to avoid exposing
her to the risk of a long sea passage so late in the
season, but Captain Wallace prevailed upon him to
break this arrangement and embark in the ' Niemen.'
They left Halifax with a fair wind, and the first day
passed very agreeably, promising a good passage.
But no such promise appeared next morning, when
they found themselves enveloped in a fog, such as only
that latitude presents.   The fogs of Newfoundland
surpass the imagination of Europeans, and that of
October, 1826, was one of the densest on record.   The
ship might be thought to be in the clouds, for above,
around, and beneath, nothing else could be seen, and it
was equally vain to look for the topmast or the waves.
Sailors describe such fogs as being " what you may
cut with a knife," but they defy cutting and must be
swallowed whole.   The atmosphere is one impervious
cloud, and so it remains for hours, for days, and for
weeks.   Now it is a bright white, as if day were struggling through ; now it becomes shaded, and now almost
night.   It is the same hue everywhere one moment,
and the next shows it with dark patches like shadows.
Then come the little openings called fog-gaps, so
familiar to seamen, and which raise delusive hopes
of a clear up, sometimes cutting through like a
vista, or a chasm between two precipitous cliffs, with
the sea clear in the midst, and filling up with fog
rolled in from the distance as you look.   Sometimes
the gaps take the form of galleries or caverns, as
steady as if hewn out of granite.   We seem to be in a

ghost-land, where nothing is real except the danger.
But the solemn time is night, when the fog is thickened
by darkness, and may be *felt*. You hear the waves
lashing the ship, and reflect that you are sailing you
know not whither, while imagination is haunted by
unknown arctic seas or hidden rocks, and the leads-
man goads it with his dismal chant as he gives out
the soundings.

The 'Niemen' felt her way alongshore by the deep-
sea lead, and kept between eighty and a hundred
fathoms, so working round Cape Canso, as they judged
from the reckoning, and entering the Bay of Fundy,
for the soundings began to mark deeper water. Thus
they went on for day upon day, and were now closing
a third week without having seen sun, moon, or stars,
or met a ship, or caught a glimpse of land. They
passed out of the deep water, and its gradual shallowing
led Sir Howard and the Captain to conceive that they
were approaching the coast of the United States,
which placed them in great danger, and their anxiety
was becoming intense when the fog suddenly cleared,
revealing a shore. An officer hurried off in a boat, and
ascertained the position of the ship, which was where
the Captain had supposed, but his report had hardly
been made when the fog returned, and shore, sea,
and sky again disappeared. A clear-up now seemed
hopeless, and nothing remained but to grope their way
to St. John's, an enterprise that the most faultless
seamanship could not divest of terrors. But Captain
Wallace never seemed more himself, and was perfectly
calm and collected, even when the reckoning marked
the offing of the port, a spot fraught with peril. Here
there was a sudden burst of moonlight: they saw the

masts and the waves, the dim outline of the cliffs, and
the opening harbour, and then the fog rolled up like
a curtain, and the shore appeared, like a scene in a
play. All danger seemed over; and they were swept
on by a fine leading wind, in spite of the falling tide.

Ten o'clock found them entering the Narrows,
where the breeze fell off, and the tide gathered increased force, rushing out with such violence that the
frigate could hardly bear up. It was now at flood,
and came on at the rate of six or seven knots, every
moment getting more power over the ship, as the wind
blew less home, and allowed her to be hustled towards
a shoal. The Captain thought to keep her in check
by letting go the starboard anchor, but it was impossible to give off a sufficient service of cable in time,
and she settled on the bank.

Lady Douglas might now see the advantage of
being in a well-manned ship, under a good Commander;
for there was no confusion or outcry as the frigate
struck, and all relied on the Captain, awaiting his
orders. Nor could the example of Sir Howard fail to
have an effect, and his calm bearing gave confidence
to others, as they knew that he understood the position
of the ship, and her chance of extrication. No attempt
to float her could be made by hauling, as the bank
was discovered to be very steep, with little water
on the port side, and a great depth to starboard;
and destruction must follow any haul upon the
anchor in a falling tide. Captain Wallace fired a gun
of distress to bring off help from the shore, but to
little purpose; for none arrived till the ladies had
been placed in a boat and sent away. Sir Howard
remained to share the fortune of the ship, and watched

the arrangements with his old interest.   Soon all
was ready, the starboard guns being hauled to port,
and all movable articles passed to the same quarter,
as the smallest list to starboard must heel the ship
over in deep water, when every one would perish;
for the sturdiest swimmer must yield to the rushing
tide.   The crisis arrived, and they stood between life
and death, but the frigate took the proper list to port,
and low water left her high and dry.   They were out
of danger, and the tide set her afloat.

The following day brought Captain Wallace to dine
with the Governor, and it came out that he had been
hearing tales about his Excellency which he did not
consider to his advantage; for he suddenly asked him
if he had not once been shipwrecked.   Sir Howard
replied by telling the story, and the Captain's face
became longer as he proceeded, though he made no
remark till the close.   He then observed that his
regard for him was very great, and he valued their
interchange of hospitality in port and ashore, but
should never like to take him to sea again; for he had
been twenty years afloat without mishap, except on
the two occasions when they had been together, and
he should now look upon his appearance in his ship as
a passenger as a very bad omen indeed.

CHAPTER XXVII.

Restores the Prosperity of the Colony.

Sir Howard's misadventures on the coast led him to more practical conclusions than those of his friend Captain Wallace. He had experienced its dangers, and sought to provide a remedy by the erection of lighthouses, beginning by a recommendation to the House of Assembly to place one on Point Escuminac, at the entrance of Miramichi Bay, and requesting a contribution towards the establishment of another at St. Paul's Island, at the southern entrance of the Gulf of St. Lawrence. Both these suggestions were adopted,[1] and he then procured the erection of lighthouses on the Ganet Rock, the Eastern Seal Island, East Quaddy Head, and Point Le Beau, in the Bay

---

[1] The following were the resolutions adopted on the subject in the sitting of the 6th March, 1826 :—

"Resolved unanimously, that an humble address be presented to his Excellency the Lieutenant-Governor, thanking his Excellency for the active measures he had taken to promote the establishment of a lighthouse on Saint Paul's Island; and whereas the erection of a lighthouse on Point Escuminac is recommended by his Excellency the Lieutenant-Governor, and would afford great security to vessels navigating those waters, from whence such light could be discerned,—

"Resolved, that an humble address be presented to his Excellency, praying that he would be pleased to cause plans and estimates of the proposed establishment to be prepared, and that he would take such other measures as he may deem most conducive to the furtherance of this very desirable object."—Resolutions of the House of Assembly, in the 'Douglas Papers.'

of Fundy. Thus his disasters probably led to the preservation of hundreds of lives.

But his energies were chiefly employed in retrieving the colony from the ruin caused by the fire, and he made surprising progress, giving expansion to every resource, and introducing regulations to extend the sale of lands and their cultivation, and to develop the customs, the exports, and the shipping. Nor is it least creditable to him that he started a fund for assisting a number of poor Irish emigrants who arrived in the midst of these changes, and addressed an appeal to the Colonial Secretary in their behalf. He carried out further improvements in the roads, and projected a canal for linking the Bay of Fundy with the water-communication of the Canadas, and so opening up a traffic which should embrace both the coast and the interior. He drew plans of the undertaking, and made an estimate of the expense, with a statement of his views and expectations, and submitted the whole to the Earl of Dalhousie, the Governor-General of Canada. The following letter shows that they obtained the approbation of that statesman :—

"MY DEAR SIR HOWARD,　　"Quebec, 14th May, 1827.

"I have had much satisfaction in the perusal of your proposed application to H. M.'s Government on the subject of the Bay Verti Canal. It would be useless, indeed, to offer any observations upon it, except such as may express my own individual opinions, which coincide entirely with yours, and I think it suffices merely to say so.

"A communication to establish a coasting-trade

with these provinces is to draw forth their natural resources in many ways yet unforeseen—impossible to foresee. One occupation for the lower orders produces another, creates industry, and multiplies the objects of it. On that view alone of our more immediate intercourse, I think it highly desirable, and deserving the attention of the Government, Imperial and Provincial.

"I have retained copy of your manuscript, and copy of Plan No. 5 with the line level of the canal . . . .

"My dear Sir Howard, faithfully yours,

"DALHOUSIE."

In nothing did Sir Howard more evince his zeal for the progress of the colony than in his efforts to promote education. Fredericton owes to him its college, which he expanded from a grammar-school, and then obtained for it a royal charter, conferring the privileges of an university. The project involved him in controversy, and imposed endless trouble, but he was not to be vanquished by obstacles. His first difficulty was to provide an endowment, and this he met by appropriations from the revenue arising from the sale of unoccupied lands, of which he possessed the disposal, and by inducing the House of Assembly to grant an equal sum. But the colonists remembered their "pilgrim fathers," and stipulated for the suppression of the Thirty-nine Articles and the admission of Dissenters. This aroused opposition, and the application for a charter was resisted by the Archbishop of Canterbury, while it had a local adversary in the Bishop of Nova Scotia, who not only opposed it on religious grounds, but because he favoured a rival scheme, which contemplated a college for the whole of British America in his own diocese.

No one could be less disposed than Sir Howard to disturb a barrier of the Church, but he also attached weight to the religious scruples of others, and the influence of associations.   He saw there must be a compromise, and framed one undeniably fair—opening the college to all, but reserving the direction to the clergy, and limiting the stipulation of the Assembly by exacting subscription for degrees of divinity.   Objections were more easily overcome in the colony than at home, where they could only be answered in letters, and it took reams of persuasion to gain over the Primate, and the same measure to convert the Bishop.   At last the charter was won, and the King gave his name to the college, commemorating its obligations to Sir Howard by appointing him its first chancellor.

He was installed in the office on the 1st of January, 1829, the day of the opening.[1]   The solemnity began with divine service, when the masters and students assembled in the hall, and were joined by the members of the Legislature and the Royal Council, who took possession of seats, leaving a space for the public.   All rose on the appearance of Sir Howard, and he advanced to his place amidst a burst of cheers, which were renewed when he announced that the institution had been established by the King, and that His Majesty conferred upon it the name of "King's College, New Brunswick."   He delivered an oration worthy of his office, and designed both to

---

[1] The ' British Colonist and New Brunswick Reporter.'

excite the emulation of the students and enlist the
liberality of the colonists, which he sought to stimulate by his own. "I shall leave with the College,"
he said, "I trust for ever, a token of my regard and
best wishes. It shall be prepared in a form and devoted to an object which I hope may prove an useful
incitement to virtue and learning; and at periodical
commemorations of the commencement it may serve
to remind you of the share which I have had in the
institutions and proceedings of a day which I shall
never forget." Thus modestly did he speak of his
donation of a gold medal as an annual prize. So late
as 1859 the Principal of the College bore testimony
that his promise to "never forget" had been fulfilled.
"This ever-watchful and indefatigable friend," said
Dr. Jacob, at the commemoration of that year, "has
persevered in his endeavours to maintain our existence and promote our prosperity. By a very recent
mail I have received the counsel of his experienced
wisdom, with the assurance of his yet unfailing
efforts for objects which, as long as life and light
remain, he will not cease to regard with unabated
solicitude :—

> "Then from his closing eyes thy form shall part,
> And the last pang shall tear thee from his heart."

In truth, neither time nor distance weakened his
attachments, nor lessened his interest in objects he
had taken up. His constancy is attested by his friendships, many of which extend over sixty years, and
have been preserved through separations of half a
life. The Atlantic did not divide him from his

friends in England, and he was in their minds as often, deepening their regard and making every letter that passed an interchange of confidence. This would forbid their publication if the grave had not closed over the writers, and events dispersed their secrets; so that they no longer claim to be suppressed.

His chief correspondents were His Royal Highness the Duke of Gloucester, Lord Sidmouth, and the Earl and Countess Harcourt. They send him the gossip of their different sets, and it is amusing to compare their sentiments as each comes into the confessional with thoughts begotten by the wish. The Duke of Gloucester holds by Mr. Canning, and augurs for him a long tenure of office: "Great changes have taken place in this country in the last few months. Happily for Great Britain and for the whole world we have now an administration in which there are many Whigs, composed of our ablest men, headed by our greatest statesman, and founded upon liberal and tolerant principles. Mr. Canning has certainly done more for England in the last three years than almost any Minister we have ever had. The nation and the House of Commons are, I conceive, very decidedly with the present Government, which will long remain in power."

But it is dangerous to prophesy smooth things. The letter of His Royal Highness is dated July, 1827, and the Ministry changed several times before the July following. Earl Harcourt writes to Sir Howard on the 4th of June, 1828,—"I have more than once intended to write to you upon the late extraordinary

situation of this country, which has, I think, had not
fewer than *three* or *four* different administrations in
the course of the last twelve months; but now has
one which is, I trust, likely to be more permanent—
thanks to the Duke of Wellington's firmness and
decision, which bids fair to carry us through all our
difficulties; as the new arrangement of offices, with
your friends Sir George Murray for the Colonial Department and Sir H. Hardinge for the War Office
have actually kissed hands. The disfranchisement of
the borough of East Retford, and the transfer of the
elective privilege to the neighbouring hundred, as
proposed by Peel but objected to by Huskisson, who
named Birmingham for the purpose, was the *osten-
sible* cause of the disagreement which produced the
resignation of the latter; but the real fact is that
Huskisson, who is a thorough intriguant, and who
has a powerful following in the House, is labouring
to overset His Grace's Government, which, notwithstanding all the disadvantages it labours under from
a very formidable opposition of talent and practice
in public speaking, will, it is thought, ultimately
prove successful."

Lady Harcourt does not feel so confident. She
looks at the political world with the minute perception of a woman, and seems to have a foreshadowing
of the convulsions about to shake Europe, and which
began with the Roman Catholic Relief Bill in England, soon followed by the French and Belgian Revo-
lutions, and the English Reform Bill. Her remembrance of the Church is equally characteristic, and
a late event gives an interest to the reference to

Dr. Sumner. Nor is there wanting a bit of scandal as a further mark of a lady's letter, and giving the moral of a painful story :—

"My dear Friend,   "St. Leonard's, 2nd Aug. 1828.

"Your letters of late have made us very anxious, and we feel more than usually uncertain respecting the health and situation of yourself and Lady Douglas and your family. . . . . The changes that take place here must be always against the interest of those abroad, and not advantageous at home. It is to be hoped that all will remain now as it is, but it depends on one life alone. Should anything happen to the present Premier [the Duke of Wellington], all will again break up. His health, however, I am happy to say, is better than it was. . . . . *There seems to be a general uncertainty respecting the fate of nations, as if some change was likely to take place.* In respect to the Church, Bishops have died, and London [Dr. Howley] goes to Canterbury—a popular measure; not so the translation of Bloomfield to London. But Dr. Sumner to Chester every one approves of. The Sumners have been a fortunate family. Dr. Sumner has been allowed to keep his Deanery of Durham with his Bishopric of Chester.

"Poor Lord Liverpool's health is as bad as ever, and there seems no prospect of his dissolution. Lord Grenville also is declining fast.

"About Sandhurst I can tell nothing but that Sir E. Paget is very popular, and something has happened respecting * * * * * *, about which we can get no

distinct information.   There has been some inquiry
respecting some pecuniary arrangements, which were
extremely trifling, yet he was somewhat to blame;
and it is said that his wife, who was a most amiable
woman, has died of the vexation it has caused her.
. . . . . I find it is perfectly true that the poor
woman died of a broken heart.   She said that
the mortification she experienced from the Court
of Inquiry was more than she could bear.   I was
told * * * * * * was a most pitiable object.   It was,
I believe, proved that he had made about thirty or
forty pounds a year by selling the boys' clothes
and trifling things.

" With my best love to your ladies, I am, my dear
friend, yours very affectionately,

                              " MARY HARCOURT."

The opinions of Lord Sidmouth may be omitted,
as they coincide with Earl Harcourt's; but one
of his letters contains a reference to two illustrious
characters who were highly esteemed by Sir Howard,
and the passage may be introduced here as bearing on the complications in which we were continually involved with the United States, one of
the most serious of which forms the subject of our
next chapter:—"It is probable that before you receive this letter you will have seen Lord Stowell's
recent judgment on the slave case.   On no occasion
has he been more powerful and convincing. . . . .
This judgment, I sincerely hope, will close his splendid
and eminently useful judicial career.   He met his
daughter and Mary Anne and myself yesterday at

Lord Powis's, and was well and cheerful; but he becomes very naturally more and more restless, and impatient for the society of his daughter, as his disposition and powers to engage as formerly in social intercourse diminish. Lord Eldon gives a very good account of himself."

CHAPTER XXVIII.

Disperses the American Filibusters.

Sir Howard's embroilment with the United States arose out of the Treaty of 1783, which left the colony with an uncertain boundary.   The interior of the country was then unknown, and England and America had divided their territories somewhat in the manner of Abraham and Lot; one power taking all that lay to the right of a point on the coast, and the other what spread to the left.   The interior boundary was to be marked by the highlands which should be found to divide the sources of the Connecticut and the St. Croix from the sources of the rivers which emptied themselves into the St. Lawrence; an arrangement which gave to America all the lands on the banks of her own rivers, and left to the British colonies the banks of the rivers known to reach the sea from their shores. The point of departure from the coast was the Bay of Passumaquaddy.

It might be imagined that such an arrangement left no ground for misunderstanding; but it afforded room and verge enough to the Americans, who made it a standing dispute.   Their pretensions grew in proportion as they were temperately met till they advanced their line 140 miles, and claimed the free navigation of the St. Lawrence, while they left the British colonies without a frontier.   The question became more and more serious, and a party in the States resolved to put it to the arbitrament of the sword if it were not adjusted in their own way.

Their design was known to Sir Howard, and he kept a watch on their proceedings, particularly in the State of Maine, where they were most active. Indeed, the mob there were for occupying the territory without waiting for its surrender; and the same feeling animated the Legislature, and even the head of the State. Governor Lincoln declared that Maine was entitled to fix her own boundary, and that she neither recognised the right of England to the disputed lands, nor the authority of the Federal Government to bind her by negotiations. Such an announcement increased the excitement of the population, for every one felt that he had a personal interest in the acquisition of a tract equal in extent to a kingdom, with a rich soil, watered by rivers, and possessing a harbour on the coast. They looked about for some pretext for occupation; and this was nearly afforded by some New Brunswickers, who made a dash down the St. John's River, and felled some timber in the disputed limits. But the same mail which reported their irruption brought news of their arrest, and the 'Gazette' announced that steps were taken for their prosecution. Sir Howard had declared that he would preserve the territory as it stood, and now showed that he intended it to be respected by the colonists no less than the Americans.

Such impartiality might satisfy the colonists, but found no favour with the people of Maine. They saw the land open before them, and knew no right so strong as possession, by which they could make it their own. The clamour became more furious; and

speeches were made in the Legislature pledging the
State to action, and teeming with abuse of England,
as if the meditated spoliation had been accomplished by
her in Maine, instead of being contemplated by Maine
at the expense of England.   Governor Lincoln called
out the militia, and marched it to the frontier, to
show that he was in earnest; and the leaders of
the movement arranged to take possession of the territory by filibusters, while the militia stood by.   It
was thought that Sir Howard would be too frightened to act; but they rather hoped that he might
be provoked to march up the troops, in which
case they would contrive to bring on a conflict, and
so give their proceedings a cover.   This design was
intrusted to a ruffian named Baker, worthy of his
employers; and he did not content himself with
violating the territory, but burst into a British settlement, which he declared to be a part of the United
States, and hoisted the American flag in token of
sovereignty.   Such an irruption struck the settlers
with amazement, but they knew where to seek protection, and sent a report of the occurrence to Sir Howard,
judging it better to remain passive themselves, that
they might not fetter his action.

The despatch of a messenger caused no alarm to
Baker, who warned his friends on the frontier, and
watched for the appearance of the English troops,
whom he expected to be hurried to the spot.   But
Sir Howard was not to be taken in a trap, and he
followed his own course without allowing for American magnificence.   He made such arrangements that
he could bring up all his force at a moment if the
militia crossed the border; but everything was done

so quietly that it did not strike even the soldiers themselves. While both parties awaited the issue the affair was settled by a constable, who suddenly entered the settlement, knocked down the flagstaff, bundled the American flag under his arm, and took Baker into custody, effecting the capture so adroitly that he was borne off in a waggon before it was understood.

The news of this insult startled the Union from its propriety. The indignation against England could not have been greater if the territory had been American and the invaders English, instead of the reverse being the case; and the most moderate admitted that the time had come for driving England from the continent and annexing her dominions. The State of Maine would accept no other terms, and her view seemed to be adopted by the Federal Government, as it advanced a body of troops to her aid.[1] But this commotion excited no stir in New Brunswick. Every one there went about his business as usual; no arrangements seemed to be making for defence; and not only did Sir Howard persist in keeping Baker in prison in spite of the warlike demonstrations, but he gave orders for bringing him to trial.

This contumely drove the people of Maine distracted, and the militia marched up and down on the frontier, and took up a threatening position—but kept on their own side. Indeed there was nothing to be done, for Sir Howard remained as quiet as if they did not exist. Governor Lincoln determined to force him out, and sent an envoy to Fredericton with a letter demanding Baker's release. But Sir Howard

[1] Letter of the Right Hon. C. Vaughan to Sir Howard Douglas.

saw his design, and refused the envoy an audience, though he was careful to abstain from offence, and instructed the Commanding Officer of the 81st Regiment to invite him to the mess, and pay him marked attention. But the American was not to be conciliated, and he spent the evening in warning the officers of the chastisement impending over England, and wondering at the Governor's infatuation. Nor would he take his dismissal, though Sir Howard despatched a reply to Governor Lincoln, stating that he was unable to enter into the subject in debate, as no communication was authorised between the two Governments except through the British Minister at Washington and the central authorities.

It had become so customary for England to submit to American encroachments that the attitude he held formed a topic for the whole continent, and excited a burst of enthusiasm in the British colonies. He was spoken of with pride and admiration, and none expressed these feelings more strongly than the Earl of Dalhousie, the Governor-General of Canada. " I beg you will offer his Excellency my best regards," he writes to Sir Howard's aide-de-camp, " and assure him that the steps he has taken regarding Baker, and his correspondence on that subject with the Governor of Maine, are in the highest degree gratifying to me. Nothing more firm, polite, and proper could have been done in these delicate and very important matters."[1] Sir Howard received a corresponding tribute from Mr. Vaughan, the British Minister at Washington. " I congratulate myself every day," he writes, " that at this moment of irritation we have such a person as

---

[1] Letter of the Earl of Dalhousie in the 'Douglas Papers.'

yourself Governor of New Brunswick. Your proceedings respecting the outrage of Baker and your discretion in avoiding any controversy with Lincoln please
me much." [1]

It became clear that nothing could be effected by
Governor Lincoln ; and a commissioner was despatched
to Fredericton by the Federal Government, furnished
with a letter of introduction from Mr. Vaughan.   But
Sir Howard was as inflexible to the one as the other ;
he persevered in the prosecution of Baker, who was
brought to trial before the Chief Justice, found guilty,
and sentenced to be fined.   And the fine was paid.

These proceedings had so enlisted public feeling
that they could not be disavowed by the Government,
and their success won it to approbation.   But it was
seen that such a question could no longer be left open
without danger, and the two powers agreed to an arbitration, referring it to the King of the Netherlands.
Sir Howard was called to Europe to assist in preparing the English case.

He was so endeared to the colonists that they
heard of this summons with dismay, and all classes
evinced their regret.   Much as he had been appreciated, it seemed that they never knew his value till
now, when they remembered his concern for their
interests, his zeal for their advancement, his wise
measures, and his good deeds.   He had been with
them in calamity, brought them through desolation
and ruin, and raised them to a point of prosperity
exceeding their fairest hopes.   They were now to see
him depart, without any assurance that he would
return, and felt it a common misfortune.

[1] Letter of the Right Hon. C. B. Vaughan in the ' Douglas Papers.'

Addresses were presented to him by the Council, the House of Assembly, the clergy, the merchants, the different corporations, the College, the various Friendly Societies, and every class of the community, expressing respect and attachment and fervent wishes for his welfare. Crowds waited in the way to give him a parting cheer; and many hovered round the ship in boats till the sails were spread to the breeze, and the vessel stood out of the harbour.

One of his last acts was to render a service to his aide-de-camp, whom he was to leave behind. He knew that he longed to obtain his company; and an opportunity presented itself to purchase, but he could not command the means. Sir Howard recommended him to see what could be done among his friends in Fredericton, and he would supply the deficiency. The amount was raised, but what sum he contributed is unknown, as the facts only transpire in the officer's letter of thanks, found amongst his papers, and endorsed by himself as " on a particular subject."

CHAPTER XXIX.

Predicts the Disruption of the United States.

The success of Sir Howard's policy towards the United States was grounded on observation and inquiry. From his post at Fredericton he kept his eye on the Union, taking note of every incident and popular movement, and considering whither they tended. He thus forecast public opinion before it took effect, and divined the influence it would exercise on the course of affairs. But he did not base his conclusions solely on the posture of parties. He viewed the States in all their relations, plummed the channels of their trade, and observed the divergence of their interests, marked the extent of their shipping, the condition and prospects of agriculture, the acts of the different Legislatures, and the range of the Central Government. He submitted to the Secretary of the Colonies a Report on these points in 1828, so prophetic of what has since occurred, that it forms one of the most remarkable State Papers ever written. Its object was to show there was a tendency in the States to create a manufacturing interest, which would ultimately lead to a prohibition of the manufactures of England; and that this policy was a necessity for the States, both on political and social grounds. He represents it as aiming to associate them by new ties, but goes on to show that it will fail in this object, and that England may look forward to a dissolution of the Union.

The paper opens with a reference to the restrictions then just imposed on the intercourse of the Americans with the British colonies, and remarks:—

" It is announced that the time has arrived when it becomes the duty of the Government of the United States to introduce such changes into the statistical policy of the Union, as may stimulate manufacturing industry to resolve itself into the establishment of numerous dense communities, in all suitable parts of the Union, to become the home manufacturers of those articles which have heretofore been imported from Europe, and principally from that country whose new measures of trade have so far closed external markets against the agricultural produce of the United States as to have rendered necessary this defensive system.   It is announced that this measure is moreover necessary to provide home consumers for those productions which can no longer be ensured external markets, as well from the recent restrictions as from the competition of British Colonial produce, which the Government of the United States gives to the British Ministry full credit for stimulating and favouring by all means in their power.

" The proposed alteration in the system of the United States is expressed in terms which show the dread which is entertained of revulsion and distress, from want of a vent for the prodigious quantities of surplus agricultural productions which the extending cultivation of waste lands is yielding in a high ratio; and as these waste lands lie chiefly in the vicinity of the frontier territory, lakes, and rivers of the British provinces, it concerns us much that we see distinctly in what practical shape the motives and modifications which I have noticed should be considered to affect our policy.   The well-known maxim is laid down with great truth, in an important state paper, that countries in which there is an undue predominance of agricultural population are the poorest, and their inhabitants the most distressed.   What room for reflection does not this observation, as applied to the United States, present! Anything, it is said, that may serve, therefore, to hold back the diffusion of a thin rural population from running too far and too long over a great surface of soil, can scarcely prove otherwise than salutary ; and in the present circumstances of the country the encouragement of manufactures by legislative measures will be a wholesome counterbalance, if not a check, to the extension of agriculture, which, according to the present terms upon which public lands are sold by the State Governments, and the natural tendency of a rapidly-increasing population to go on developing and engaging itself in the settlement and cultivation of vast and fertile tracts of land, that may be had at a very moderate rate, would otherwise get out of keeping with a wholesome statistical condition. To counteract and counterbalance this tendency, manufacturing industry, it is submitted, should be encouraged by such prohibitory duties as may be effectual to ensure success to the home manufacturer, even at the necessary sacrifice of cheapness to the individual purchaser. Though the establishment of manufactures, under the immediate protection of the laws, would at first raise the cost of the articles, and for a succession of years keep it up far beyond the price at which they are and might be imported, yet the forecast of the Government, looking rather to the future than to adapt its calculations to the existing hour, should not hesitate to embrace the protecting policy and found schemes of solid and durable advantage, even at the peril of temporary privation."

Sir Howard does not suppose that American statesmen reckon on creating a home demand for all the produce of the country. On the contrary, he considers they are looking for other markets, which can only be found by giving the inland States access to the sea, and hence the claim to the navigation of the St. Lawrence :—

"The Government appears to be fully sensible that these measures cannot be applied to absorb the vast quantities of produce raised in those portions of the States which front the British possessions, or which either join or communicate with the lakes and rivers of Canada ; and that, unless convenient outlets to the exterior can be ensured for disposing of these productions, the truth of the maxim which has been quoted with respect to the poverty and depression of extensive and thinly-dispersed agricultural populations, labouring under the want of a market, will apply with great force to the prodigiously extensive back settlements.   It is from a profound sense of this that we see the Government of the United States reagitating with sensitive pertinacity claims to the navigation of the Saint Lawrence, which, for other obvious reasons, becomes an object of great importance to them under the new aspects of affairs ; all of which are eminently calculated to manifest the great disadvantages to British policy, and to the well-being of these colonies, that would arise from making such a concession.

"A stand may be made by the United States to resist measures which might tend to make Quebec and Montreal entrepôts for dealing in articles the growth and production of the United States ; but the distress which such a rejection would ultimately occasion in the quarters I have indicated as demanding an outlet in some shape, would constrain the Government of the United States to continue to permit the export of those articles to the British provinces, and which would give to Great Britain the advantage of conveying them down the Saint Lawrence, in common with our own colonial productions, to supply the demand of our other colonies in the West."

Sir Howard reviews the relations maintained by the States to each other, and shows that they imply practical independence.   This opinion rests on a statement of facts, admitting no other inference, and proving that secession was already in germ.   The Federation is represented as solely a bond of convenience, which brings the States together, but imparts no cohesion, since each State claims exclusive sovereignty in its own limits. Any interference of the central government is resented, and the local governments look to the interest of their own State, not to the general good. Nothing can be more positive than the views expressed on this point. They were passed unnoticed by the statesmen of the day, but Sir Howard sees them big with import, and details them so forcibly, that his conclusions seem the natural issue. A league of States is seen to be guarding themselves from each other, with interests always clashing, and some right always in dispute. Such signs appear unmistakable after the event, but they were marked at the time by him alone. Others have dreamt of a collapse of the American Union, but no one but he has sketched its political horoscope, and foretold that it was hurrying to "a natural death."

His view claims to be given in his own words, though at the cost of a break in our narrative :—

"It is not the object of this paper to notice all the political effects which the intended measure of forcing an alteration in the statistical system of the United States must produce in dealing with, attempting to regulate, and to control, on principles so general, the rival interests of individual States, each endowed with sovereign powers and possessing separate legislatures, claiming the right to regulate their own internal affairs, territorial, statistical, and fiscal. Under all these heads remonstrances are making against the interference of the General Government with the jurisdiction of the 'Sovereign States,' within themselves severally ; and it is highly important to the objects of this paper that I should notice these very significant indications. This I shall do briefly, quoting and using, as much as is consistent with brevity, the resolutions entered into by some of the State legislatures, and the manner in which the questions are actually treated, in order that the deductions which it is my object to draw may be received by the Government as grounded upon no shallow or hypothetical premises.

"The State of Maine denies the right of the General Government to conduct the negociation pending between that Government and Great Britain respecting the disputed territory in this quarter, without the express consent of that State, and avows in the most solemn form her right and disposition to dispute and resist the authority of the General Government to ratify any decision which should go to deprive the State of Maine of the right which she considers she has to the disputed territory, without her express consent as a sovereign power.   Governor Lincoln, in his speech to the legislature of Maine, acquainted them that the executive of the Union has been considered as disposed to submit the question of the boundary of Maine, and with a perfectly friendly intent, but without regarding her as a party, to the umpirage of a foreign authority—a submission which in itself admits the possibility of an unjust and disastrous decision. That it has been considered due to the interest of this State (Maine) to advance a counter doctrine, namely, that a submission of its boundary to any umpire unknown to herself, and upon terms not confided to her consideration, will leave her at liberty to act upon the result, as to the country and herself, in the manner that may be dictated by just and patriotic inclinations.   That if the fifth article of the Treaty of Ghent has pledged the Federal authority beyond the limits which are contended to be the true demarcations of her powers, the delicacy of the case ought to have some influence upon the assertion of the rights of Maine, although an entire concession of those rights cannot be expected.

"But the Government of the State of Maine goes beyond the mere assertion of independence on this occasion, for, without the knowledge or consent of the General Government of the Union, Maine despatched an Envoy to this Government with powers to treat of a question actually pending in negociation between their General Government and that of Great Britain.   I reported to His Majesty's Secretary of State that

I had declined to recognise this Envoy, not from doubting
the powers or questioning the propriety of sending, but from
having no powers to receive, treat, or correspond with the
agent of any subordinate State.   Soon after the arrival of the
Envoy from Maine, an agent despatched by the General
Government, with letters of introduction to me from the
British Minister at Washington, presented himself, and was
immediately furnished with the fullest information respecting
the arrest of the American subject who had committed the
outrages (which I reported to His Majesty's Secretary of
State at the time) in an ancient British settlement in territory
in the actual possession of Great Britain.   It is sufficient for
my present purpose that I merely present to view the presence,
in the face of a foreign Government, of two Envoys, deputed
for the same purpose, under circumstances which on the one
hand amount to an actual exercise of independence upon the
gravest matter of state affairs, and on the other hand a denial
of such powers of sovereignty !

  " Near the other extremity of the Union again we perceived within the last year the Government of Georgia dis-
puting, and in martial array resisting, the authority of the
General Government to carry into effect the provisions of a
treaty with the Cherokee Indians, which, made and ratified
according to all the formalities of the constitution, had become
the supreme law of the land, and which we perceive the
General Government did not dare to enforce, in compliance
with the provisions of that treaty, over one of the constituent
States of the Union under whose sanction that contract had
been made, and with the decision of the congressional senate
which had ratified it; but actually proposed to purchase the
territory in dispute with the funds of the Union, thus attempting to accommodate the question by evading it and giving the
territory to the party to whom the treaty had awarded it; by
which evasion the Government of the United States has given
public and demonstrative proof of defect of constitutional
energy in its executive functions, and of moral weakness in
the centre of that Union.

  " But this question does not appear to be set at rest, although
Governor Troup, in whose administration these measures of

resistance were adopted, has been succeeded by another person.   By a resolution of a joint committee of the two branches of the legislature of Georgia (dated December 15, 1827), it appears that they consider the whole course of policy pursued by the United States not to have been in good faith towards Georgia, and that all the difficulties which now exist respecting the treaty of the Indian springs have resulted from acts and policy which it would be unjust and dishonourable in the Government of the United States to endeavour to screen themselves from by taking shelter behind the difficulties which these acts have created.

" The State of Georgia, as the resolution expresses, entertains for the General Government so high a regard, and is so solicitous to do no act that can disturb or tend to disturb the public tranquillity, that she will not attempt to enforce her rights by violence *until all other means of redress fail.*   That, to avoid such a catastrophe, Georgia makes this solemn, this final appeal to the President of the United States, that he take such steps, &c. &c.

" In the Senate of South Carolina we find it *Resolved,* within these two months, that the Constitution of the United States is a compact between separate and independent sovereignties, having legislatures to regulate their own internal affairs; and that all acts of the Congress known by the name of the Tariff Laws, by which manufactures are encouraged under the protection of imposts, are violations of the Constitution.   The Resolutions further deny that the Congress has power to construct roads and canals to the individual States, or to direct any other improvement or appropriation within those States.

" Governor Giles in his late message on opening the Legislature of the State of Virginia asserts that such a jurisdiction as that claimed by the Congress would annihilate the power of the State Governments, and expresses an exordium that not one State in the Union surrender this jurisdiction to the General Government.   He states that such an expectation is confirmed so far by corresponding Resolutions adopted by the State of Maine, which had been forwarded to him by the

Governor of that State; and he lays before the Legislature of Virginia a communication which he had received, containing a copy of the proceedings of the Legislature of Connecticut, which appear to sympathize with those of Virginia and Maine.

" The position taken upon this question is, that, if it shall be the determination of the Government of the United States to appropriate a part of its revenue to the internal improvements of individual States, in the construction of roads and canals, improving the navigation of rivers, and in promoting education, &c., that the funds designed for these objects ought to be distributed equitably among the several States, to be expended under the authority and discretion of their respective Legislatures. Then with respect to the tariff, it is expressly denied in this speech that Congress has power to regulate commerce *amongst* individuals within the limits of the several States. The Constitution expresses that Congress shall have power to regulate commerce with foreign nations *among* the several States,[1] but not *within* the several States; and that the exercise of the power claimed by the Congress to regulate absolutely the tariff of each State would be an usurpation of internal power which can only be exercised constitutionally by the local Legislatures; and that, whenever this constitutional jurisdiction of the respective States over *territory, persons,* and *things,* within themselves, shall cease to be so exercised exclusively, the Federal principle is for ever gone, and with it the sacred chart of American Liberty."

Sir Howard points to the dangers of the Slave question, which he considers at some length, predicting that any measure of emancipation will be linked with a scheme for colonization. This he characterizes as " a strange project," and declares that it cannot succeed. His observations so exactly foreshadow what is

[1] Section VIII. Article 4.

now in progress, that we need to reflect they were written thirty-four years ago :—

"Then, to these causes of disunion may be added the important, and perhaps most disturbing of all—*the Slave question.* Hopeless of leading the State Governments to any measure of abolition adopted separately, we perceive that the measure of forcing a general emancipation by manumission and COLONIZATION (a strange project!) under a general act of the Congress, is entertained, AND WILL SOME TIME OR OTHER BE ATTEMPTED. In the mean time its very agitation has powerfully affected individual interests, and those States in which slavery still exists manifest much discontent and ferment. Such a general measure adopted by the Congress would reach directly into, and menace the rights claimed by all the State Governments to regulate their own affairs, and would at once bring to issue the question of right and power on the part of the several States to regulate all that concerns *Persons* and *Things* within those States respectively—terms which Virginia and the other slave-holding States are continually using to warn the Government of THE STAND THEY MEAN TO MAKE against the manumission of these persons from slavery. To show the intensity of feeling and the vehemence of expression upon this subject, I shall quote a few sentences from the speech of an influential member of one of the slave-holding States, in some discussions which came on incidentally in Congress on the 7th of January last (1828)."

The passage quoted is a vehement protest against any interference by Congress in the internal affairs of a State, and particularly with slavery, the speaker declaring that his "countrymen will resist such encroachment with arms in their hands." Sir Howard considers that this crisis is approaching, and announces that it will develop itself by secession :—

"Here we may see the manner in which THE UNION WILL BE DISSOLVED—namely, THE SECESSION OF ANY STATE which, considering its interests, property, or jurisdiction menaced, may no longer choose to send deputies to Congress. This is a great defect in the bond of Union, which has not, perhaps, been very generally noticed, cloaked as it is under Article 1st, Section V. of the Constitution, which states, that, when there are not present of either House numbers sufficient to form a quorum to do business, a smaller number may be authorized for the purpose of forming one to compel the attendance of absent members. But this appears only to be authorized for the purpose of forming a quorum, and only extends over members actually sworn in, and who, being delegated to Congress by the States they represent, are sub-jected to whatever rules of proceeding and penalties each House may provide, with the concurrence of two-thirds of its members. But there is nothing obligatory upon the several 'Sovereign States' to *send* members to Congress, or to prevent those sent from being withdrawn. The 'Sovereign States' have never bound themselves to do either; so that the process of dissolution in this way is very simple, and the danger imminent of a separation being thus effected, whenever the interests of any particular State or States are touched by the Govern-ment, or brought into discussion in Congress, although those interests may be *outvoted by the preponderating influence of other States having different interests.* But the State or States which are to suffer will not, it is clear, send members to vote their own injury or ruin; and it may safely be pro-nounced, from what I have shown in this paper, that THIS IS THE MANNER IN WHICH THE AMERICAN UNION WILL COME TO A NATURAL DEATH."

The events we have witnessed could not be more clearly described, and the conflict they have opened seems the more horrible when we see that it is waged against natural laws at the base of society. The threat of the North to convert the American con-tinent into a desert must be realized before the South can be recovered, and then it will only bequeath the struggle to another generation. Sir Howard fore-shows that it will be met by the erection of a new Confederacy :—

"I have shown in this paper that the State Governments are beginning to resort to a practice (just alluded to) which is full of danger to the Union, namely, that of transmitting their views and the proceedings of their Legislatures to each other, whenever they are desirous of preparing a formidable opposition to any measures of the General Government which may be likely to interfere with any of those concerns which such States may be interested in opposing. The practice of corresponding with each other respecting grievances was very commonly resorted to by the people of the different Provinces before the Rebellion [against England], and was one of the most significant and alarming signs of the events that were coming on. They cannot be prevented from going any lengths in communicating with each other upon matters which concern their own individual interests and affairs, and out of this disposition and power may at any time be worked THE MOST POWERFUL COALITION AGAINST ANY GENERAL MEASURE affecting them in common; OR THEY MAY WITHDRAW FROM THE UNION ALTOGETHER, AND IF THEY PLEASE FORM ANOTHER COMPACT AMONG THEMSELVES."

CHAPTER XXX.

On a Mission to the Hague.

THE bark in which Sir Howard and his family sailed
for England was the 'Mutine' brig of war, one of a
class nicknamed " coffins," from their predilection for
foundering at sea.   The 'Mutine' did not go down
during the passage, but she went as near it as possible, sustaining both her own and Sir Howard's reputation.   The voyage was an unbroken gale, and the
brig was continually dipping, as if uncertain whether
to roll under water or turn over.   " I can only say,"
writes Sir Howard to a friend, " that in this tremendous winter passage of six weeks I never expected
to see England."

But the dangers were forgotten on landing when
he found himself in the midst of his friends, who hailed
his return with joy.   From none did he receive a kinder
welcome than the Duke of Wellington, though the
part he had taken in the boundary dispute made him
an object of interest to all the statesmen of the day,
and elevated him into a public character.   This was
recognised by the most dignified body in the realm,
the University of Oxford, which determined to confer
upon him the degree of D.C.L.; and he was invited to
receive the honour in person at the commemoration of
1829.   The spirit he had shown in the American

question excited the patriotism of the University, and
the theatre was crammed with the junior members,
who greeted his name with a burst of cheers. These
were renewed on his presentation by the Public
Orator, whose Latin oration may be thus rendered
in English :—

> " Most Illustrious Vice-Chancellor, and you, learned
>   Doctors,—

> " I present to you a distinguished man, adorned
> with many virtues and honours, belonging to military
> and civil affairs, as well as to literature,—HOWARD
> DOUGLAS, a Knight and Baronet, a worthy heir of the
> latter order from a renowned father, the former richly
> deserved from his own King and that of Spain ; a
> member of the Royal Society of London on account of
> the fame of his writings ; for many years the Governor
> of New Brunswick, followed by the admiration and
> favour of his country, and the reverence and love of
> the province : lastly, Chancellor of a College in that
> province, built under his care and direction, to which
> its patron, the King, gave his name and a University's
> privileges. Behold the man ! I now present him to
> you that he may be admitted to the degree of a
> Doctor of Civil Laws for the sake of honour."

Sir Howard received invitations from his numerous
friends to their country seats ; but none gave him such
pleasure as one from Sir Walter Scott, pressing him
to visit Abbotsford. Sir Walter's letter may be given
here, as everything from his pen commands interest,
and this beams with his hearty nature :—

                                        " Abbotsford, near Melrose,
" My dear Sir Howard,   21st July, 1829.

   " I have just received your most welcome letter,
and [write] to express my earnest wish and hope that,
as I have for the present no Edinburgh establishment,
you will, for the sake of auld lang syne, give me the
pleasure of seeing you here for as much time as you
can spare me.   There are some things worth looking
at, and we have surely old friends and old stories
enough to talk over.   We are just thirty-two miles
from Edinburgh.   Two or three public coaches pass
us within a mile, and I will take care to have a carriage
to meet you at Melrose Brigley End, if you prefer that
way of travelling.   Who can tell whether we may
ever, in such different paths of life, have so good an
opportunity of meeting ?

   " I see no danger of being absent from this place,
but you drop me a line if you [can] be with us, and
take it for granted you hardly come amiss.   Five
o'clock is our dinner-hour.   I have our poor little
[*illegible*] here.   He is in very indifferent health, but
no immediate danger is apprehended.   Always most
truly yours.   You mention your daughter.   I would
be most happy if she should be able to accompany you.

              " Always, my dear Sir Howard,
                        " Most truly yours,

                              " Walter Scott."

   The visit to Abbotsford led to Sir Howard's essay
on 'Naval Evolutions.'   In an after-dinner conversation Sir Walter Scott referred to the manœuvre of
breaking the line, and said that it was originated by

a Mr. Clerke, who had written a work on 'Naval
Tactics,' in which it was first mentioned.   Sir Howard
had heard of this claim before, and had collected all
the facts about the manœuvre, in case it should be
asserted in a manner that would require him to vindicate the credit of his father.   He thought this was
now done, and he wrote to town for the papers, stating
where they were to be found, and they came down to
him by post.   He happened to be alone with Sir
Walter when the packet was placed in his hand.
" Scott," he then said, " the other evening you ascribed
the invention of the manœuvre of breaking the line to
Mr. Clerke.   I must tell you the merit belongs wholly
to my father."

" Indeed ! " replied Sir Walter.   " Are you aware
that the Clerkes possess a copy of their father's work
with Rodney's notes in the margin, showing that it
was in his possession at the time of the battle ? "

" I know this has been said, but I must ask you
how the work could be in Rodney's hands at that time,
when it was not published till after his return to
England ? "

" It was not published, but fifty copies had been
struck off for private circulation, and one of these was
presented by the author to Rodney before he left
England."

" It is true that fifty copies had been struck off some
time before, and here is one of them.   Unfortunately
for the claim of Mr. Clerke, it does not contain the
manœuvre.   It is only after Rodney's return to England, when the manœuvre had been reported in the
newspapers, that it makes its appearance in Mr.
Clerke's work.   These letters prove that it occurred

to my father in the heat of the battle, as an inspiration
of the moment; and I shall be glad if you will satisfy
yourself on the point by looking over them some time
when you are at leisure."

" No time like the present," said Sir Walter, smiling ;
and he went through the case in Sir Howard's presence.
" You have removed all doubt on the matter from my
mind," he then said.   "This manœuvre was one of the
happiest ever introduced into naval warfare; and I
think your duty leaves you but one course to pursue
with those documents in your possession.   You must
lay them before the public." [1]

Sir Howard was of the same opinion, and ' Naval
Evolutions ' made its appearance in due course, though
not till he had entered into a correspondence with Sir
George Clerke, informing him that it was in prepara-
tion, and affording an opening for the withdrawal of
Mr. Clerke's pretensions. [2]

This did not interrupt him in assisting the Ministers
to prepare their case on the Boundary question ; and
his views were found to coincide with those of the
Duke of Wellington, who also examined the treaties
and drew up a memorandum on the subject, now first
printed from the autograph in the ' Douglas Papers.' [3]
But there were points not clear to the King of the
Netherlands, and Sir Howard volunteered to go to
the Hague and answer his inquiries.   His offer was
accepted, and he set out on this mission in May
1830.

A distinguished reception awaited him at the Dutch

[1] This conversation was related to the author by Sir Howard himself.
[2] Letters from Sir George Clerke to Sir Howard Douglas in the 'Douglas
Papers.'
[3] It will be found in the Appendix.

court, where his name was in high repute in consequence of his 'Naval Gunnery' having been translated by the Minister of Marine, though the King
needed no such credential in a companion in arms of
the Great Captain, under whom he had served the
Waterloo campaign. Sir Howard has preserved an
account of their first conversation, and it shows that
His Majesty desired to be thoroughly informed on the
subject of the arbitration, and to arrive at an impartial decision, while it is very characteristic of himself.[1]
The King began by inquiring how far the disputed
territory was settled by British subjects.

" There are about three thousand in Madawaska,
sire," replied Sir Howard. "The number settled in
other parts is not known."

" How many American citizens are settled there ? "

" None under a competent grant; but ten or
twelve reside there. Baker, of whom your Majesty
has heard and read so much, is one of these tres-
passers."

" How strange !" said the King, after some hesitation.
" We are now forty-seven years after the treaty, and
its limits not yet determined ; and at such a distance
of time such a question to be brought forward !"

" This is one of the many extraordinary features of
the case, sire. Such a boundary as is now claimed by
the United States was not contemplated at the time.
It was first mooted constructively, on some obscurities
in the letter of the treaty of 1783, at Ghent, but not
absolutely claimed till the census of 1820." Here Sir

---

[1] It is endorsed "Minute of a conversation which I had the honour of
having with H. M. the King of the Netherlands, on the subject of the
boundary, on Monday, the 13th May, 1830."

Howard paused, thinking it imprudent to say more
unless the King should invite him to speak out by
prolonging the conversation.   This he did, after a
moment's interval.

" You are now in the position, in some of the arguments, which was occupied by the French Commissioners during the discussions respecting the limits
between Canada and Nova Scotia," he said.   " You
appear to have the same interests."

"The settlement of the limits may involve provincial interests," replied Sir Howard, " but the case
to which your Majesty alludes has positively nothing
to do with that submitted for your Majesty's decision.
Those old boundaries were never settled."   And he
stated the case of the discussions of 1763, going on to
show that the treaty of 1783 was a distinct act, a
point important to establish, as the Americans sought
to occasion confusion by jumbling the negotiations
together.

"It is difficult to pronounce which view of this
matter is sound," replied the King, " the English or the
American ; and I fear I may give offence in deciding."

" Your Majesty's decision will be given in justice
and equity, according to the spirit and intention of the
treaty, the letter of which is, in one part, so obscure as
to have occasioned this submission to your Majesty for
the prevention of disputes."

" Yes.   The letter certainly is, as you say, obscure,
otherwise this reference had not been made.   If the
treaty had been clear and express, the limits would
long since have been settled."

" It is on this account, and to prevent further cavil,
that your Majesty is called upon to arbitrate," said

Sir Howard. And he proceeded to explain that Great Britain did not want territory, but security, which could not be obtained if the Americans were allowed to intersect the river St. John, or to class the Bay of Fundy rivers with the Atlantic rivers.

"Yes," said the King, "but this is a question of right."

"Great Britain firmly believes the right is on her side, sire," answered Sir Howard, "and your Majesty has full powers to settle the limits in any way your Majesty may deem consistent with the objects of an arbitration—even should it be by splitting the difference, as was proposed by Mr. Gallaton."[1]

"Did Mr. Gallaton propose that?" cried the King, eagerly.

"Yes, sire, and gave offence to the State of Maine by the admission this implied."

Sir Howard thought there was here an opportunity of contending for the right accruing from possession, and he pointed out what portion of the territory would thus fall to the United States, and what part to England, expressing his determination to uphold the English claim during the continuance of his rule in New Brunswick, unless it should be renounced; and for this he justified himself by an allusion to the King's motto.

"That territory has been placed in my charge, sire," he said, "and that, *par la grace de Dieu, je le maintiendrai.*"

"Good," replied the King, smiling; "that is our motto,—*Je maintiendrai!*"

"And it is our hope, sire."

"It is a difficult position for me," rejoined the King,

[1] One of the American Commissioners.

Y

good-humouredly; "but I hope to make my impartiality respected by my decision."

The decision was not satisfactory to England, and was rejected by the Americans, as it did not give all they demanded. This was eventually to be done by England herself, though only to encourage fresh claims, prolonging the dispute to the present day. But incidents now occurred that held it in abeyance for a time, and Sir Howard was called to attend to complications ·on the spot, arising out of the Belgian Revolution.

There never was such a testimony to the poet's doctrine that great events from trivial causes spring as this convulsion. Sir Howard writes to Sir George Murray from the Hague on the 4th of September, 1830 :—"There are many remote causes for what has recently occurred here, but the exciting cause was the late revolution in France, so far as it was insurrectionary. But the objects which the Belgians have in view are, in many respects, entirely different from those entertained by the French ; for high aristocratic and Roman Catholic influences are the sustaining powers of the Belgian confederacy, as it may now be called, and they have succeeded in giving a great special object to a movement which commenced *in the shape of a riot, occasioned by the performance of a certain opera*, and which might easily have been quelled, and all the subsequent disturbance prevented, if proper measures had been taken."

The ultimatum of the insurgents proposed to form Belgium into a separate state, in confederation with Holland, and governed by her Sovereign ; and Sir Howard learnt that the project was entertained by the King, conditionally on its acceptance by the

States General and the great Powers. "But," he writes to Sir George Murray, "should all this be smoothly done—*and I am sure it cannot and will not be so* [1]—there will come the details of execution." He sees no hope of an arrangement on these points, especially as respects the finances, the repartition of the national debt, and the surrender of the forts to Belgian troops. The last object he declares to be the aim of a French party, which is working to effect an entire separation, and so break down a barrier to France by the dissolution of the Netherlands monarchy. This is designed to be followed by the absorption of Belgium, and he describes the scheme as already laid. "Consider Lafayette," he writes, "his early career, his political impressions, his reception of and communication with persons who, in an evil hour, were prosecuted in this country, and, being banished, found a refuge in France!" Thus early does he warn the Government of the intrigues which led to the offer of the Belgian crown to the Duke de Nemours in the following year. "France herself might be applied to," he adds, in considering how the danger is to be met, "and France thus applied to, and thus engaged, the incorporation of the Belgian people will be headed back." But he declares that such a result cannot be averted, if England allows it to be seen that she will not intervene by force, however urgent the conjuncture.

On the 14th of November he writes to the same effect to Sir Robert Peel, and censures a notice of motion in the House of Commons, which pledged the

---

[1] The passage in italics is underlined in Sir Howard's letter.

country to this course. Sir Robert replies on the 7th of December—"You will have seen that Mr. Hobhouse abandoned, or at least postponed, his motion on the subject of Belgian affairs immediately on the notification of a change in the government of this country. If no such change had taken place, I think it doubtful whether he would have persevered in a motion so very inopportune, and in my opinion so very unwise, as a positive declaration against all interference on the part of England in the affairs of the Netherlands. Not to interfere is very different from a public notification to France while negotiations are pending that our mind is made up against interference."

So far Sir Howard's counsel was adopted, but the scheme for a mediation was not taken up so promptly, and the favourable moment escaped. The Belgians fell more and more under French influence, and gave the command of their troops to General Nyples, whose brother was a colonel in the French army, and who drew from France many of his officers. The military stores accumulated by the Dutch in the frontier fortresses had fallen into their hands, and supplied unlimited means, enabling them to equip 35,000 men, and bring into service 2542 pieces of artillery.[1] On the other hand, the loss paralysed the Dutch, who were left almost destitute, and now needed every resource, as General Nyples threatened to invade their ancient territory. Sir Howard indicated the danger to the British Government, and he received

[1] Report of Sir Howard Douglas to the Right Hon. Sir Charles Bagot, G.C.B., British Minister at the Hague.

orders to make a tour of the northern provinces, and report on their situation, that steps might be taken to insure their safety.[1]

He set out on this duty on the 30th of October, going first to Breda, thence proceeding to the cantonments of General Van Geeus, on the Antwerp road, and afterwards visiting Bois-le-Duc, Flushing, Batz, Wilhemstad, Bergen-op-Zoom, and the other strongholds. He found the Dutch troops animated by the noblest spirit, though the rank and file were imperfectly trained and equipped. "I cannot speak too strongly of the good spirit and intelligence of all the officers," he writes to Sir Charles Bagot. Some of the fortresses were in good order; others were in need of additional defences, or out of repair, and

---

[1] These instructions were embodied in the following letter from the British Minister at the Hague :—

"Sir,   "The Hague, October 30, 1830.

"The rapid progress which appears to be making by the rebel forces in the southern provinces of the kingdom, and the great probability which there seems to be that if the citadel of Antwerp should fall they may proceed to attack the line of fortresses which protects the ancient territory of Holland, make it very necessary that His Majesty's Government should obtain, if possible, the most exact information as to the state of defence in which these fortresses may now be, and the general means of resistance which the northern provinces may have it in their power to oppose to the insurgent forces in case they should attempt to invade this portion of the kingdom. . . . .

"I have now the honour to request that your Excellency will do me the good service of examining, with as little delay as possible, the whole of the military defences, extending from Grave to Bergen-op-Zoom and into the Scheldt, and of reporting to me, or, if your Excellency should think it more convenient, directly to His Majesty's Government, the condition in which they may be at the present moment.

"I have already acquainted His Netherland Majesty with my wish that your Excellency should be permitted to make this examination, and His Majesty has been graciously pleased to acquiesce in my proposal. . . . .

"I have the honour to be, &c.,

"Charles Bagot."

slenderly garrisoned. He mentioned what steps should be taken to make all secure, and suggested that the corps of General Van Geeus should keep the field, operating as a moveable column in North Brabant. General Van Geeus undertook to open a communication with General Chassé, who was in command of the citadel of Antwerp, as Sir Howard considered it important to learn the position of the garrison—the defensive measures for the northern provinces requiring time, which could only be secured by the maintenance of the citadel. But his information would not be complete unless he knew also the situation of affairs in the town, and such an object must be sought with great tact, or he might compromise the English Government. This he avoided by forwarding a message to the English Consul, requesting a conference at Lotto, within the Dutch territory; and he was soon visited by that functionary, who brought with him the Hanoverian Consul, and a gentleman who had just left General Chassé. The General sent a cheerful account of his situation, engaging to hold the fortress so long as there should be no frost, but foreseeing that his position would then become critical. On the other hand, the Consuls described the town as in a ferment, and compared it to a volcano which might burst forth any moment, though General Chassé threatened to lay it in ruins on any demonstration of hostility. Batteries had been erected by the insurgents at commanding points on the river, and fire-ships were preparing to drive down the Dutch fleet, the destruction of which would deal Holland "a mortal blow," while the attempt would expose Antwerp to a bombardment.

It was of the highest moment to prevent both consequences, and this Sir Howard proposed to do by withdrawing the fleet, which now gave no support to General Chassé, as he had victualled the citadel for two months, and trusted his water defences to gunboats. Sir Howard represented that the gunboats could also be used for keeping up a blockade, which would hold the population in check, and yet involve no risk, as the gunboats could run up and down in the shallow channel, but the ships must pass close to the batteries.[1]

Throughout this tour Sir Howard moved about in the strictest privacy, but no precaution could avert recognition, and his movements were even noticed in the London newspapers. "Notwithstanding every possible circumspection on my part," he writes to Sir C. Bagot, "not to give publicity to my proceedings, my visits, my inspections of the works, my confidential reception by the general officers, and my person being known, have given rise to many surmises. But whilst I have neither said nor done anything to compromise, it has afforded me much satisfaction to observe that my appearance has had a good effect. It has shown a solicitude for the safety of the Dutch frontier; it has had a sustaining effect on the morale of the Dutch people and the Dutch troops; and has operated on the other side to deter attack."

Such was the impression created on our oldest ally by the appearance of an English officer on her frontier in a time of national danger. His suggestions to the Government were appreciated, and proved of great

---

[1] Letters of Sir Howard Douglas to Sir Charles Bagot, dated 1st, 2nd, 4th, 6th, 12th, and 16th November, 1830.

service, while they obtained the approbation of his
own Sovereign, signified to him by Lord Palmerston,
then Secretary for Foreign Affairs. The expectations
he had formed of the Dutch troops were fulfilled in
the event; and how General Chassé redeemed his
promise to make the citadel of Antwerp the citadel
of Holland, is a world-known story. Sir Howard's
exposure of French intrigues proved equally useful;
for the resolution of Lord Palmerston compelled the
Duke de Nemours to decline the Crown, and thus
saved Belgium, which must have been absorbed by
France in 1848, if the convulsions of that year had
found it ruled by a French prince.

CHAPTER XXXI.

Defeats the Government.

FROM the moment of the expedition to Algiers, the
French Government seemed uneasy as to its relations
with England, and hence took measures for strength-
ening its navy. One of its first steps was to introduce Sir Howard's scheme for an organization of
gunners, as detailed in his treatise on Naval Gunnery;
and the Institute rewarded Marshal Vaillant for his
translation of the work by electing him one of its
members. The activity displayed at Brest and Toulon
did not attract notice in England, where the navy
was engaging no attention, and the public thought
little of the French armaments till the appearance of
a pamphlet on the state of the navy, purporting to be
by an "Old Flag Officer." This created a panic; its
statements were the general theme of conversation;
and the nation trembled for its naval supremacy.
Several leaders on the subject appeared in the *Times*,[1]
and attention was called to the "Flag Officer's"
strictures on our naval gunnery, and his advocacy
of the scheme of Sir Howard Douglas, which
the *Times* warmly commended. Sir Howard was
at the Hague when the pamphlet reached his hands,
and there heard of the sensation it had produced,
and the prominence it gave to his plan. The advo-

---

[1] *Times* of 17th, 20th, and 24th May, 1830.

cacy appeared to him so strong, that he feared it might be imputed to himself, or at least to his inspiration, and this he hastened to disclaim. "Understanding that the author is not yet known," he wrote to Lord Melville, the First Lord of the Admiralty, "I think it necessary to assure your Lordship that I am utterly ignorant from whom the publication proceeds. However I may concur in some of the opinions advanced, and which, indeed, are founded upon my work, yet that is not the way in which it would become me to approach your Lordship." [1]

His consideration for the authorities was the more praiseworthy as he had obtained so little of their attention, and they were now set to work by the pamphlet, not by his representations. The credit of giving this fillip to their movements must be assigned to Admiral Sir W. Bowles, who has long been known as the author of the pamphlet, and could not have rendered a greater service to his profession. A beginning was made with the plan before Sir Howard left Holland, as he had the satisfaction of hearing from Sir S. J. Pechell, one of the Lords of the Admiralty. "The 'Old Flag Officer' has done what even you could not effect," writes that officer, "though not to the extent that either of us could wish, but within these few days an order has been given to establish a gunnery-school on board the 'Excellent' at Portsmouth." The order would appear to have been slowly carried out, for a year passed before the work made any progress, and it is not till November, 1831, that Sir S. Pechell

---

[1] In the same letter to Lord Melville, Sir Howard refers to "other communications" he had addressed to his Lordship, and adds, "which I hope have been received," implying that they had never been acknowledged.

writes about it in good spirits : " We are now likely to do something more. Sir James Graham has approved of the plan, and has appointed the 'Excellent' for this service, and I am sure you will not refuse me your assistance in drawing up a prospectus for our future sea-gunners."

Thus Sir Howard saw his system launched, after he had patiently waited fourteen years, during which time his labours were left unnoticed and his letters unanswered, though he could never be provoked to complain. The system has fulfilled all that he hoped, resting the supremacy of our navy on the surest bottom by supplying it with the most expert gunners. In after years he might feel proud that he had rendered this service to his country, and perhaps the more so as it was not only left without reward, but even without thanks.

The establishment of the 'Excellent' was first placed under Commander George Smith, but it acquired its repute under the next director, Captain Chads, and this has been extended by its present chief, Captain Hewlett. Never did it assume greater importance than now, when artillery is making such developments, and naval warfare is revolutionised by the introduction of armour-ships. Happily it has had the counsel of Sir Howard up to the last moment, and nothing can be more complete than his programme of drill for the Armstrong gun, which appears in the latest edition of his treatise.

It was now necessary that he should return to New Brunswick, and he was preparing for his departure, when the Government proposed a new arrangement of the timber duties, giving an advantage to produce

from the Baltic by abolishing the protection afforded
to colonial timber, which had to meet greater cost of
transport.   He considered such a measure unjust, and
entreated Lord Goderich to recede, declaring the
change would ruin New Brunswick, and be very
injurious to the sister colonies.   But his representations produced no effect, though backed by a report
on the condition of the colonies, and a statement of
their imports from the United Kingdom and the West
Indies, which were shown to depend on the continuance of the duties.   The question seemed so linked
with his position, that he thought himself called upon
to urge it by every means, and even appeal to the
public if he could not persuade the Government.   He
had deemed such a course unbecoming in the case of
his gunnery movement, for that had a reference to
himself; but here was a question no way personal,
but in which he represented interests confided to his
care by the Government itself.   Those interests would
be looking to him as their advocate on the spot, and
he considered them as important to the mother country
as the colonies.   Hence he must speak out, and he
could only do so by following the example of the
" Old Flag Officer," and publishing a pamphlet.   Such
productions are now little heeded, but they obtained
readers in a day when they strengthened or unseated
a minister, and made bishops.   An opposition pamphlet
could bring no advantage to Sir Howard.   On the
contrary, it exacted from him the sacrifice of the post
he held, and even his hopes of further employment,
as far as concerned the existing Government.   It is
impossible that such considerations should have been
overlooked by one who was not rich, and was weighted

with a young family; but they could not stay his
hand. He drew up a careful exposition of the question, much like the one he had laid before the Government, stating everything in a temperate way, and
basing his arguments on facts and figures. He maintained that the colonies had a claim to favour, as our
largest customers; the returns proving that they took
three-fourths more per person of British goods than the
people of the United States, who stood next on the
list. He pointed to the employment they afforded
to British shipping and sailors, which had embraced
400,000 tons and 25,000 seamen in 1828, being
one-fifth of the whole foreign trade of the kingdom.
And he contended that the good effect of a fostering
system was apparent in the expansion of the provinces,
which had increased their population 113 per cent.
between 1806 and 1825, while the numbers in New
England had only increased 37 per cent. in the same
time. But it must not be supposed that he argued
for restrictions on trade. Quite the reverse: he was
for giving trade every latitude, but this latitude was
to be reciprocal, and he proposed to yield a preference to the produce of the colonies in return for
their preference of the manufactures of England. His
principles are now adopted by the chiefs of free-trade
themselves, and we may see them embodied in the
late commercial treaties with France and Belgium.

The pamphlet combated the notion that the colonies
are an encumbrance, and do not repay our outlay,
adducing proof of their advantage both to our revenue
and power. A detail of the arguments would be out
of place here, but they claim the attention of statesmen now that the question of abandoning the colonies

has been revived. Only one who had lived in a colony could present the subject in a form so striking; and all who have had this experience will give the same testimony.

The sheets were sent to press, and Sir Howard received a stitched copy, which he instantly took to the Colonial Office, and presented to Lord Goderich.

" I have published this pamphlet against the repeal of the timber duties, my Lord," he said, "and I beg to present your Lordship with the first copy.   And here, my Lord," he added, producing a letter, "is my resignation of the government of New Brunswick."

" I am sorry for that, Sir Howard," replied the Minister : " I have no feeling about the timber duties, but you know we are all for free-trade."

" I am not for free-trade, my Lord," said Sir Howard : "I am for fair trade." [1]

To this creed he adhered to the last, living to see it generally accepted.   He was "not for free-trade," yet no one could speak more kindly of its founder, from whom he differed on almost every question. "We don't agree with Cobden," he once said to the author of this work, "but he is a great man, and no one stands higher with the masses.   I had a curious proof of this lately in the country.   I was passing a very fine house, where there was a van of furniture at the door, which some men were unloading.   I asked them whose it was, and they answered, 'Richard Cobden's.'   I walked in, as the door stood open, and asked some men who were fixing up blinds at the windows the same question.   The answer was the same—'Richard Cobden's.'   A name so familiar in

[1] This anecdote was related to the author by General Sir Hew Ross, G.C.B.

the common mouth seemed a title, and such a title Cobden needn't care to change." His words recurred to his biographer when the newspapers announced that Mr. Cobden had refused a baronetcy.

The pamphlet made an impression. It formed the subject of articles in all the newspapers; and a leader in the *Times* described its author as "the stanch friend and able advocate of the interests of our North American colonies," complimenting him on "the frank and manly manner" in which he stood forward in their cause.[1] His facts gave weight to his arguments, and excited a sensation in the commercial cities, where the pamphlet was in every hand. A corresponding effect was produced on the House of Commons, where the Opposition determined on resistance; and the second reading led to a warm debate, mainly turning on the statements made by Sir Howard. It became evident that the measure was in danger; and the division resulted in its rejection, a shout from the Opposition announcing the defeat of the Government.

The news flew across the Atlantic, and caused the greatest joy in the North American provinces, though the victory was thought dearly purchased by Sir Howard's resignation. "The very unwelcome tidings," writes the President of New Brunswick[2] from Fredericton, on the 20th of April, "that you had felt yourself so circumstanced in your exertions in the cause of the colonial interests as to determine on the great sacrifice of resigning your government, must long continue a subject of deep regret to this province. A day or two since we received the gratifying news

---

[1] *Times* of February 25, 1831.   [2] The Hon. William Black.

that your able and indefatigable efforts have been crowned with complete success. Your pamphlet is by all here considered one of your happiest productions."

The colonists displayed their satisfaction at the result by bonfires and by enthusiastic gratitude to Sir Howard, holding public meetings to express their sense of his services, which it was decided to recognise by a testimonial, to be subscribed for by every parish in New Brunswick. The result was a noble service of plate, presented to him in England, together with an address and letters of thanks from the provincial Chambers of Commerce—a spontaneous and general tribute of respect, which he always remembered with pride.

CHAPTER XXXII.

Lord High Commissioner of the Ionian Islands.

The pamphlet excluded Sir Howard from employment for four years, though the authorities recognised his merits, and he stood equally high as a soldier and administrator. His cause was taken up by the King, who wished him to be given a command in India, but Lord Hill returned what Sir Howard deemed an unfavourable answer. A letter he received from Sir Herbert Taylor represents His Majesty as taking a more hopeful view.[1] "The King agrees with me in considering it [the answer of Lord Hill] by no means so unsatisfactory or so unencouraging as it would seem to appear to you; Lord Hill appears to His Majesty to have said more upon this occasion than he usually does." But Sir Howard's interpretation proved correct, as the move led to nothing, and he remained unemployed. Still his time was not lost to the country, for he occupied himself in attending artillery experiments and bringing out improved editions of his 'Naval Gunnery' and 'Military Bridges.' The King paid a tribute to his worth in a public address at the Royal Military College at Sandhurst, in June, 1834, and eulogised his services and literary productions, describing him as "an officer of first-rate ability and scientific attainments." His

---

[1] The letter is dated Windsor Castle, August 3, 1832.

z

Majesty remarked that "his high talents and zeal in the service of his country were hereditary;" and added in a pointed manner and with great emphasis, that "to his own knowledge the distinguished merits of Sir Howard's father—Sir Charles Douglas, to whom the naval service of the country was greatly indebted —had not met their commensurate reward, merely owing to party spirit, of which he was the victim."

Such an allusion from the Sovereign might be expected to produce an effect; but no employment was found for Sir Howard till 1835, when he was appointed Lord High Commissioner of the Ionian Islands, at that moment a most unenviable post.

The Republic of the Seven Islands comprises a group on the coast of Greece, in a situation that gives them an importance exceeding their size, as the largest of the cluster locks both the Adriatic and Levant. Such a fastness should be held by a nation with a strong grip, but whose traditions guarantee that the vantage it gives will not be abused; and the Congress of Vienna vested the protectorate in Great Britain, as a power answering these conditions. The islands are not to be coveted for themselves, as they afford no room for colonization, and are a source of expense instead of profit; while the population embraces an impoverished gentry, who think it their interest to be disaffected. Thus a field presents itself for foreign intrigue; and this was not overlooked when the feeling which ruled the Congress of Vienna subsided, and the position of England in the Mediterranean was seen to be an obstacle to aggressive designs. But England could not resign such a post to a strong power, and it would be wrested from a weak one; so that she has been obliged to maintain the protectorate for the common security. The situation is changed by late events, and arrangements are now proposed for its termination.

Corfu did not escape the political agitation of the time, and a cry had been raised for a new constitution, which received encouragement from a proclamation by Sir Howard's predecessor, Lord Nugent. The expectations thus raised were damped by his appointment, and he immediately became an object of attack, the agitators denouncing him as a violent Tory, opposed to progress, and a sworn enemy to concession. An opposition was organised against him before he arrived; and it was determined to resist him from the first, and make his government impracticable.

It did not take Sir Howard long to perceive how he stood, but he kept his own counsel, and acquainted himself with the views of parties and the state of popular opinion, from which he drew up a statement for the British Government as to what he thought necessary to reform. This was done within a few days of his arrival at Corfu, but threatened to be useless, for it had scarcely been completed when news came of the fall of the Ministry, placing the Government of England in the hands of the Whigs.

The change threw the Ionians into ecstasy. It was not doubted that Sir Howard would be recalled, and he entertained this opinion himself. But his mere recall would not satisfy the anti-English party, and they resolved to give it the appearance of a concession to themselves, which would make it an humiliation. Accordingly they accused him of overstepping his authority, and embodied the charge in a memorial to Lord Glenelg, the new Secretary for the Colonies, representing him as a despot, who trampled on every right and class. The memorial was despatched to England by the same mail that carried his programme, and its statements were then made public, there being no doubt that they must work their effect before he could furnish a refutation.

Sir Howard was not one to sit down under imputations, but these could only become important from being entertained by the Government, and he left them unnoticed for the moment, waiting to be apprised of their reception. Nor did he look for more than strict justice, having determined to resign his post, as he hardly expected a Whig Minister would afford him that support without which it was impossible to meet the Legislative Assembly.[1] But he resolved to maintain his authority while it remained in his hands, and became more resolute as his assailants became more violent. They found consolation in anticipating the effect of their machinations in England, and exulted at the prospect of his recall, naming the very hour when it would arrive. At last the packet steamed into the harbour and landed her mails, and the news spread through Corfu and through the Mediterranean. It was a surprise to every one, for the memorials of the agitators were returned unanswered, Sir Howard was confirmed in his post,[2] and the new

---

[1] "My first impulse, seeing these difficulties, was to resign."—Letter of Sir Howard Douglas to Lord John Russell.

[2] The author was up the Mediterranean when the news arrived, and remembers the impression it produced, though he was only a boy at the time. A feeling prevailed that Sir Howard triumphed through his interest, but the following letter will show that he received no favour:—

"My dear Sir Howard,   "Downing Street, 14th April, 1835.

"The intelligence will doubtless have reached you of the dissolution

Minister adopted his programme, and supported it with all his authority.

For a moment the opposition was checked, but influences were at work to keep it together, and proved successful. Sir Howard traced the action of Russia and Greece, or rather of Greece under Russian direction, and saw its object. The first indication of these troubles comes from the letters addressed to him by Sir Edmund Lyons, the British Minister at Athens, and he hears of a panic at the Greek Court, caused by an intimation from the lady of the Russian Ambassador that three Turks in Corfu had sworn to assassinate the King. Sir Edmund Lyons does not apprehend much danger, but he tells Sir Howard that the Greek Prime Minister is of a different opinion, and entreats that he will take measures of precaution. These were hardly necessary, as the assassins existed only in the imagination of the lady, who used them to further Russian intrigues. The King fell more under Russian influence, and Sir Edmund Lyons announces that a post at Court has been given to

of Sir Robert Peel's administration; and if you have had the means of observing the course of proceedings in the House of Commons, as reported in the public papers during the last fortnight, you will not have been surprised at this result. Our resignation was tendered to the King last Wednesday, and we only hold our offices until our successors shall be appointed.

"I will not indulge in any speculations affecting our future prospects either at home or abroad, but sincerely hope that whoever may succeed me in this department will feel it to be his duty not to disturb you in the Ionian Islands. I have established no precedent for such a practice since I have been here, and your appointment had the additional recommendation of being in conformity with the Report of the Committee of the House of Commons. . . . . .

"Believe me, my dear Sir Howard,

"Very truly yours,

"ABERDEEN."

Count Bulzo, an Ionian agitator, and one of the partisans of the Czar.   But Sir Howard continued to show his goodwill, and rendered the Greek Government some important services, for which he received the King's thanks.[1]   He availed himself of this opening to obtain several immunities for the Ionians, arranging that their vessels were to be admitted into Greek ports on the same footing as those of Greece, in return for a like privilege, and that no fees were to be charged on their passports.   He also made overtures for establishing reciprocity of trade, and negotiated a convention for the transmission of letters between the islands and Greece, and another for the regulation of quarantine.[2]

He was very solicitous for the material advancement of the islands; and this he sought to promote by the construction of roads and the removal of impediments on commerce, at the same time initiating several improvements.   The means for such projects were limited, as Lord Nugent had endeavoured to propitiate the Ionians by abolishing the Customs-duties, which deprived the revenue of 150,000l. a year,[3] and it now fell short of the expenditure.   But he procured funds for a poorhouse and lunatic asylum, and for the improvement of prisons, as well as a large sum for purposes of public instruction.   The town of Corfu had long suffered from a scarcity of water, and he looked round for a source of supply, which he found on a neighbouring height, where it had been unheeded before; and here he constructed a reservoir, employed

[1] Despatch from Sir Edmund Lyons to Sir Howard Douglas, October 18, 1835.

[2] Despatches of Sir Edmund Lyons to Sir Howard Douglas.

[3] Letter of Sir Howard Douglas to Lord John Russell.

soldiers to lay down pipes, and brought water to the town in an abundant stream.

About this time Her Royal Highness the Duchess of Gloucester addressed to him the following letter, which gives a glimpse of the affectionate relations maintained between the members of the Royal family, and possesses an historic value, from the allusion made to the character of Her Majesty in her youth :—

"My dear Sir Howard,   "April the 15th [no year].

"I trouble you with this letter by the Rev. William Greville, who was for some years curate at Egham, and has made himself respected and beloved by everybody round that neighbourhood. Sir William Fremantle, and Lady Anne, and Mr. C. Smith have begged me, as well as many other of the neighbours, to recommend him strongly to your notice and that of Lady Douglas. Any kindness or attention you can pay to him or Mrs. Greville I shall feel obliged to you for.

"I venture to send by this family a dress for each of your daughters, the last of our new manufacturing that has appeared, which I hope they will kindly accept as a mark of my affection and regard; and I also send to Lady Douglas an album, which I trust she will fill with her daughters' drawings; and a ring, which she will *love* for my sake. I trust this may find you all in good health and enjoying the fine climate you are in. I have to thank you for some very entertaining prints which Mr. Buckhouse sent me. Every proof of your kind recollection is gratifying to me. I am vain enough to believe you will rejoice to hear that my health keeps improving, and I have passed a good winter, and hope to venture to go out a little in the world. I appeared for an hour at three most splendid parties the Duchess of Kent gave during the time her nephew, the Prince of Portugal, was in England, on his way to Lisbon, and did not suffer from the exertion. I have become a subscriber to the Ancient Concerts, but have not been there yet. I determined not to go to any place before I paid my respects at the Drawing-room; and next Thursday I propose to make my first appearance there for the last five years. Of course I shall not attempt to stay longer than I am equal to, as the King and Queen have given me leave to go away when I feel fatigued. Gloucester House is now most comfortable, and I am quite settled in my new apartments, and the whole house looks clean. I have had two little parties and some very good music, which answered particularly well; and my friends encouraged me so, and appeared to like it so much, that I intend giving another the day the King and Queen dine at Gloucester House. Bagshot Park is to be put under repair. Being a Crown house, the King has kindly ordered the Office of Works to go down and see what is required, which will make it impossible for me to be there this summer. Should my health continue as good as it is now, I have some idea of using this opportunity to take a trip, and make my brother the Duke of Cambridge a visit at Hanover. . . . . The King, thank God, keeps well, and avoids all the anxieties of the times he can. In the painful state of politics and parties it is a mercy he keeps so well. The great prosperity of the country keeps this Government in. How long it will last,

God knows; but I believe that the longer they remain in, the *more mischief they will do.* . . . .

"All my sisters are well. My brother Augustus is about to undergo the operation for his eyes, and we have every hope of success, as Alexander assures us he never saw eyes look more in *health.* My niece Victoria is a kind, pleasing, and interesting, promising young person, full of good and right feelings.

"I think by this time you must be quite tired of myself and my family concerns, but I am sure you will be glad to have these few particulars from me. I hope this volume [1] will bring me as long an one from some of *you*, and that you may be able to give a good account of all those dear to you. Offer my love to Lady Douglas and your daughters, and my kind regards to Percy, and believe me

" Yours sincerely,

" MARY."

The elements of discord existing in Corfu attracted the notice of the Pope, and the Roman Catholic party in England, now exercising great influence, under O'Connell. They had formed a design of apportioning the British empire in Roman Catholic sees, and decided to begin with the colonies, where the proceeding was not likely to excite alarm, and where success would give a warrant for action in England. There seemed no spot so favourable for a commencement as the Ionian Islands. It might be objected that a

---

[1] The term "volume" is applied to the letter, which is of great length, but the portions relating to Her Royal Highness's private affairs are suppressed.

Bishop there would be without a flock, as there were few Roman Catholics; but this was rather an advantage, for the British Government and the Lord High Commissioner would jump at the introduction of a counterpoise to the Greek Church, which drew the Ionians towards Russia; and the recognition of a Bishop in Corfu involved recognition in every other dependency. Such was the prospect opened in October, 1838, when the 'Catholic Magazine' announced the erection of an Ionian see, and its bestowal on the Right Reverend Dr. Hynes. "These are gratifying circumstances for the Ionians," remarked the Editor, " in the difficult position in which the Catholic religion is placed amongst them, and they have reason to be grateful to his Holiness for selecting a divine to preside over them who had gained the distinguished notice of the Holy See, obtained the merited confidence of the British Government, and secured the love and veneration of those whom he formerly guided on the road 'that leadeth to eternal life.' We have no doubt that Lord Glenelg and Her Majesty's Ministers will, besides their liberality and sense of justice, be actuated by a desire to secure the affectionate loyalty of that part of the population whose difference of religion secures it a barrier to Russian intrigue, and strengthens their hold of those islands, which, though small, may become of the greatest importance, should the forebodings of great political convulsions in the East be realised."

The paragraph is obscurely worded; but it does not hide the bait, and none could look more tempting. Nor is the British Government to be discouraged that the Roman Catholic fold in the islands is "small," but rather consider what it "may become," and rest the English dominion on its "affectionate loyalty."

Sir Howard little dreamt of the ally who was coming to his aid—so little, that he expected to see one of his opponents, when a page announced "the Bishop of Corfu." How was he startled to behold a stranger, robed in the canonicals of the Roman Catholic Church!

The Bishop delivered his credentials in the shape of a letter to Sir Howard from Lord Glenelg, the Colonial Minister; another from the Sacred College of the Propaganda; and a third from his friend Major-General Sir Charles Napier,[1] all of which were read with attention.

"You seem not to be aware that there is already a Bishop in Corfu?" remarked Sir Howard.

Dr. Hynes intimated that he was a Catholic Bishop appointed by the Pope.

"I know of but one Bishop here, sir," replied Sir Howard, "and no other could be recognised."

Dr. Hynes remonstrated, and pointed out the importance to England of the Roman Catholic interest in the islands; but Sir Howard could not be persuaded that the British Government was not strong enough to hold its ground without this bulwark. The prelate appealed to the letter of the Minister of the Colonies; but was shown that this was no recognition, nor could such be given without the sanction of the Ionian senate. He declared he would assume his functions, and abide the consequences; but met a firmness surpassing his own, and learnt that he would not be

---

[1] "Minuto d'una conversazione che ebbe Sua Excellenza col Dr. Hynes," in the 'Douglas Papers.'

permitted to remain in the island. He denied that he could be expelled, and warned the Lord High Commissioner that his conduct must be answered in England.

"I have only to say," was the reply, "that you will be removed by the police, if you are not gone within twenty-four hours!"

Dr. Hynes threw down his defiance, but seems to have been better counselled; for he took his departure from Corfu within the time. So ended the papal aggression in the Ionian Islands, and it might never have been attempted in England if it had met the same front in our other dependencies.

The dismissal of the Roman Bishop gratified the clergy, but nothing could appease the anti-English party; and they continued their agitation, giving the Lord High Commissioner no respite. They even established an agency in England, and the Colonial Office was beset with his assailants, who went to prefer their complaints in person, while a memorial was forwarded from Mr. Dandolo, accusing him of infringing the constitution, and praying for his recall. But Lord Glenelg declared that such a memorial could not be received while the constitution existed, as this provided that all communications to the Government must be transmitted through the Lord High Commissioner. The weight of this support and his own energy carried his measures through the Assembly: he won the adhesion of the senate, and terminated the session in triumph. Nor was he unappreciated by the people, and an attack made upon him in a Greek journal was repelled by an Ionian, whose sentiments are reflected in the following paragraph, quoted in the

'Morning Chronicle' at the time from 'Galignani's Messenger:'—

"The 'Soter,' of Athens, having published not long since an article complaining of the manner in which the administration of the Ionian Islands was conducted, and asserting that the tribunals were overawed by the Government, and that the police exercised a most oppressive control over the inhabitants, prying into the secrecy of their domestic relations, and destroying all social confidence, a reply to this article has been sent to that journal from a resident of Corfu. The writer, after observing that it is by no means the duty of an honest and impartial editor of a public journal to provoke turbulent individuals to write against the Government, declares that the accusation of the 'Soter' is based on a totally false view of the actual condition of the Ionian Islands. He observes that the administration of Sir Howard Douglas is justly popular throughout all the islands; that their material prosperity is rapidly on the increase, as is proved by the circulation of capital, the alterations going on in the towns, and the ameliorations introduced into the agricultural districts; while, as far as the moral and political condition of the islands is concerned, they enjoy much greater liberty than many other European states; that perfect freedom of discussion is allowed; that the functions of the police are in reality confined only to the furtherance of justice and the preservation of liberty; that the tribunals are totally uninfluenced by the government; and the perfect freedom of the press will in all probability be speedily established. This reply the 'Soter' inserts in one of its recent numbers."

CHAPTER XXXIII.

At the Great Earthquake of Zante.

It is pleasant to find proofs of Sir Howard's goodness of heart in the midst of so much vexation. To what extent it was practised cannot be told; for some of his kindnesses come as a surprise on his own family, and his papers show that it never slept. One instance may be recorded here. An officer in England found that he must be prepared to pay a large sum by a certain day, or he would be ruined, and he wrote in despair to Sir Howard, revealing his situation and the circumstances. Sir Howard mentioned the importance of procuring the money to three or four of the officer's friends in Corfu, and proposed that they should club together and make it up. This was done, and the amount transmitted to England, eliciting the following acknowledgment :—"I cannot express to you, my dear Sir Howard, how grateful I feel for what you have so kindly and so readily done for me; nor do I feel less so for the kind co-operation of my good friends who surround you. I will confess I was most dreadfully alarmed when I saw the perfectly unforeseen order come out, and felt the most intense agony of mind, passing miserable days and sleepless nights. May the time not be distant when I may have it in my power to return, with most heartfelt thanks, what

you, my dear Sir Howard, and those others to whom
I owe my present peace of mind, have so kindly
advanced to me."

Distress or suffering never pleaded to him in vain,
nor was any appeal needed if they came under his
notice; for he carried his succour unasked.   Thus
we have seen him relieving the poor soldiers in the
Spanish hospitals, riding miles to visit a wounded
Frenchman, and sharing his own little comforts among
the sick at Walcheren.   He now exerted his influence
to curb the despotism established in Greece, and put
a stop to its atrocities, the nature of which may be
conjectured from the following extract from a letter
addressed to him by Sir Edmund Lyons:[1]—"The
women whose persons had been lacerated by the cats
which were placed in their drawers presented themselves to the King; but His Majesty says the end
justifies the means.   *Now what was the end proposed?*
To torture these women into accusing the Minister's
political opponents!"   Immediately on receipt of
this letter, Sir Howard inserted an article in the
'Corfu Gazette,' describing the outrage and holding
up the Greek Government to the execration of Europe.
He made the strongest representations to the King
himself, and his attitude and proceedings caused such
alarm, that his Majesty deemed it prudent to recede,
at least in appearance.   "I cannot sufficiently express
my sense of the importance I attach to your valuable
support," writes Sir Edmund Lyons, after this success.
But the King had become his enemy, and henceforward
favoured every movement against his authority, and

[1] Dated January 12, 1839.

maligned him to every Englishman of influence who visited Athens.

Yet a time came when his rule extorted homage even from the Court of Greece. Most of his adversaries made him the same reparation, and for the same reason—that his motives were disinterested and sprang from a sense of duty. He had no warmer friends, in later years, than some of his Corfu opponents, who had gone to lengths in their hostility which it is better not to review; and others were his admirers in secret, without being admitted to his friendship. One instance may be mentioned: his administration had secured to the islands new channels of trade, involving extensive transactions, which led to an occasional pressure for money; and great inconvenience arose for want of the proper facilities. Advances could only be obtained from usurers, at rates varying from twenty to forty per cent.; and the extortions of these money-lenders became a hindrance to trade, as well as a scandal. It attracted the notice of Sir Howard, and he suggested to some of the chief merchants the propriety of establishing a bank on the joint-stock principle, which would be open to all. He could not aid the undertaking with money, as he considered persons in authority debarred from engaging in speculations; but the necessary funds were provided, and he then brought the project before the Legislature. Here it met an unexpected opponent in the Treasurer-General, Mr. Woodhouse, who looked upon it as calculated to lessen his importance, and threw every obstacle in its way. His conduct was the more culpable, as Sir Howard had just recom-

mended him to the Colonial Secretary for the second
class of the Order of St. Michael and St. George,[1]
though he had before provoked his displeasure.   As
an English functionary he gave dignity to the opposition, and it seemed impossible the measure could
pass.   But the discussion brought out the objects it
contemplated, and it was now espoused by the public,
who obliged the faction to give way, and the project
received the sanction of the Assembly, in spite of the
Treasurer-General.   It proved a great public benefit,
and Mr. Woodhouse marked his respect for Sir Howard
on his departure from Corfu by buying his horse, which
he declared should never be saddled again.

It was impossible to keep up a bad feeling against
Sir Howard; for he gave it no provocation, meeting hostility with conciliation and forbearance.   He
resented an affront, but he forgave an injury, and
no one acted less under the influence of anger.   An
incident of this period may be cited as an example
of his self-command and generosity.   A member of
his staff was so affected by the climate as to be
unable to perform his duties, which were of a confidential nature, and could not be intrusted to a
deputy, so that they fell on Sir Howard himself.   But
the labour was not his whole burden; for the state of
the gentleman's health made him fretful, and the Lord
High Commissioner had not only to do his work, but

---

[1] This recommendation is revealed in Lord Glenelg's reply, dated London,
January 28, 1839, and which says :—" I have not answered your despatch,
marked 'separate' of the 9th of October last, because I have felt much
difficulty regarding the advance of Mr. Woodhouse to the Commandership
of the O. of St. M. and St. George.   I am quite ready to do justice to the
merits and services of that gentleman; but I question the expediency of
conferring that dignity on the officer holding the rank of Treasurer.   It is
with sincere concern that I feel myself obliged to differ from you."

to bear with his temper. Thus things continued for
a couple of years, when the doctors reported that a
longer residence in Corfu would shorten his life, and
might affect his reason. Sir Howard then gave him
leave of absence, and sent him to England with
despatches, at the same time making a strong appeal
for him to the Colonial Secretary. "I venture," he
writes, "my earnest recommendation, suggested by
the greatest regard for him and his family, that your
Lordship will do what you can to get him removed
to a better situation in a better climate. From the
effects of bodily ill-health and great depression of
spirits and great languor, and from the very embarrassed state of his pecuniary affairs, I forebode serious
consequences to my poor friend, if we cannot rescue
him by a more suitable, more healthy, and more pro-
fitable employment."

The mention of the gentleman as his "poor friend"
instances his unaffected character. This showed itself
continually, and sometimes in a way to excite a smile,
linking his wisdom with the simplicity and ingenuous-
ness of a child. One of his local improvements was
the construction of a cemetery, for which he had difficulty in obtaining funds, as there were doubts whether
it could be made to pay. "Well, Sir Howard,"
cried a friend, who met him out riding, "how do
you get on with the cemetery?" "Oh, capitally,"
was the reply; "we have half-a-dozen burials every
day."

A letter from Sir Edmund Lyons acquaints him
with an incident in his family which caused a noise
up the Mediterranean at the time, and agitated
fashionable circles in England. Indeed, it still has

an interest, and might be made the subject of a novel;
for it opens a wide field for the imagination in its
association of romance with love.   Chance brought to
the British embassy at Athens the young Lord Fitz-
alan, heir to the oldest dukedom of England.   There
he was seized with a fever, and received the tenderest
attention from Sir Edmund Lyons and his household,
which led to the restoration of his health, but at the
cost of his heart.   As soon as his strength allowed, he
flew to England, and asked his father's permission to
seek the hand of Miss Lyons.[1]   Sanction was readily
given, and here we obtain a glimpse of the sequel:—

" My dear Sir Howard,   " Athens, 15th March, 1839.

    "I am sure you will be glad to hear that we
have received very delightful letters from Lord Fitz-
alan's family.   Lord Surrey writes to me, and Lady
Surrey writes to my wife and to my daughter.   They
differ, however, with their son upon one point—*he*
would come to Athens—*they* engage us to come to
England, for many reasons which they give ; such as
the register of the marriage ; but above all, that the
Duke of Norfolk may have the happiness of witnessing
the marriage of his grandson, the heir to all the
honours of his ancient house.   Lord Surrey contem-
plates the possibility of my not being able to quit my
post, and in that case urges me to send the ladies, as
he is of opinion that, when once such matters are
decided upon, the sooner they are fully accomplished
the better.   This, my dear Sir Howard, is irresistible ;
so Lady Lyons and my daughters will start from

---

[1] The present Duchess of Norfolk.

Ancona next month, probably by the Austrian steamer of the 12th, and they will be under the protection of Mr. Griffith, the secretary of this mission, who is going on leave. It is a great sacrifice of private feeling to public duty that I am making; but make it I must, and my son, who has just been attached to this mission in the most flattering manner to me, will remain with me.

"Pray present me to the ladies, and believe me, my dear Sir Howard,

"Yours most faithfully,

"EDMUND LYONS."

A high position claims the practice of hospitality, and few carried this duty further than Sir Howard, bearing in mind his limited means and the demands he had to meet. His dinners, and parties, and balls are talked of in Corfu to this day, and not their least attraction was the warm friendliness of the host and hostess. He was not a lover of state, and made no display, but he kept up the dignity of his position, and the palace gave a welcome to all comers. Its saloons formed a common centre for English and Ionians, and the Lord High Commissioner mingled in the same spirit with each, smoothing down antipathies, and setting an example of good fellowship. He never forgot that he was an author, and surrounded himself with whatever the islands possessed of literary talent, while Lady Douglas showed the same favour to artists, merit being a passport to both. Nor were their invitations confined to the inhabitants of Corfu and the English functionaries and garrison. They constantly entertained persons who brought letters of introduction from friends in England, as well as many of the English nobility, royal princes, and even crowned heads, as they passed to and fro in the Mediterranean.   The visitors in 1839 were unusually numerous, and included His Royal Highness Prince George of Cambridge, who visited Corfu on his way to Greece.   From that country His Royal Highness addressed to the Lord High Commissioner the following letter, giving an account of his proceedings :—

"MY DEAR SIR HOWARD,   "Athens, 6th June, 1839.

"I take advantage of to-day's post to write to you a few lines to tell you of our safe arrival at Athens, after a very prosperous journey, and which, thanks to your kind assistance, was made as comfortably and as easily as possible. We stopped at Santa Maura and Samos, and I can assure you that nothing could exceed the attention and kindness of both Colonel Sutherland and Captain Fitzgerald, as well as of the Regent of Cephalonia. We were tolerably fortunate in our excavations at Samos, and I have taken the liberty of sending you some of the things we found. Nothing could exceed the attention of Captain Gavalzo, whom we found an exceedingly amusing man ; and I cannot thank you sufficiently for your kindness in letting me have one of the Ionian steamers, by which means I was enabled to see so much more than I otherwise should have done. I also must beg leave to thank you once more for your hospitality and kindness in allowing me to remain in your very agreeable house, and for the trouble

you took in making my stay at Corfu in every respect
delightful and interesting. We shall go on to Constantinople on Saturday evening by the Austrian
steamer. I am here at the house of Sir Edmund
Lyons, whom I find a delightful person, and to whom
I feel greatly indebted. Of Athens I have as yet
seen but little, with the exception of the Acropolis,
with which I am quite delighted. May I request you
to present my best compliments to Lady and Miss
Douglas and to the officers of your staff; and believe
me ever, my dear Sir Howard,

"Your most sincere friend,

"George."

The young Prince had not passed Sir Howard unnoted, and he reported to the Duke of Cambridge that
he saw in him high qualities such as he has since displayed. This grasp of character at a glance was one
of his gifts, and rarely missed—though his glance was
open and trusting, never covert. He invited frank-
ness by being frank himself, and had no trick of the
eye to surprise or disturb. The Duke of Cambridge
received a testimony to his son with pride from such
an authority, and this feeling pervades his reply :—

"Cambridge House,
13th July, 1839.

"My dear Sir Howard,

"I have many thanks to return you for your
kind letter, and to assure you that I feel very grateful
for the attention you have shown to my son during
his stay at Corfu. He is delighted with all he has
seen there, and he feels deeply your kindness to him.

Nothing can be more satisfying to my feelings than the opinion you give of dear George, and I trust he will continue by his future conduct to prove that he is worthy of being the grandson of George the Third.

" Believe me, my dear Sir Howard,

" Yours most sincerely,

" ADOLPHUS."

The year was not to close without calling Sir Howard to other duties, which brought out his best qualities, nobly displaying his character. It is re- markable how his career placed him in situations open to such actions, as it embraced the range of human catastrophes; for he experienced the perils of battle, storm, shipwreck, and famine; faced pes- tilence at Walcheren, revolt in Belgium, and fire in New Brunswick; and now destiny made him a witness of earthquake. He could have had no fore- boding as he entered the harbour of Zante in the Ionian steamer, and saw flags fly up to bid him wel- come, while the sun beamed on an unrippled sea, looking like a mirror. Every one exclaimed at the prospect, so familiar, but which had never appeared so lovely. But this calm veiled a dislocation of Nature, and the exclamations were interrupted by a sudden concussion, which threw all on board from their feet. Sir Howard thought the steamer had run on a rock, but a cry of " *terra-mota* " from the crew gave another explanation, and realised the convulsion to every mind.

The sea was raging in an instant; the clouds seemed to have been shaken from heaven, and girt

the shore ; and the air rang with a terrible cry.   Sir
Howard swept the land with his glass, and saw that
the seeming clouds were volumes of dust thrown up
by the cliffs, which heaved like waves.   Houses were
lying in heaps, and people were running to and fro
distracted.   He had come to the island to inspect the
garrison, and preparations had been made to receive
him in state ; but this he now forbade, and landed
without delay.   He sent one of his staff to the castle
to look after the troops, selecting for this service
Colonel Dawkins, the Assistant Quartermaster-General,
and made for the town himself, in company with his
aides-de-camp, Captain Best and Lieutenant Forbes.
The scene that met his eye blended horror with desolation.   The air was dark with dust ; walls gaped in
seams ; houses leaned over, so that a breath would
throw them down, and nothing remained of others but
shapeless ruins or piles of rubbish.   But more harrowing than this spectacle was the wail of human
terror.   It rose from every quarter, and might daunt
the stoutest heart.   But Sir Howard had not come to
think of himself : he was there to rescue others ; and
this was soon felt.   A man rushed up with a cry, as
he caught sight of his well-known face.

"Ah, Excellency ! you are here to help us ? " he
exclaimed.

"As far as I can," replied Sir Howard.

The earth shook as he spoke ; the houses rocked,
and a huge coping-stone fell over, and crushed the
man to death at his side.

The panic was now appalling.   Every one rushed
into the streets—the men white with fear, and women
and children screaming, crowding together, or running

they knew not where. The ground seemed alive,
yawning under the foot, or rising to its step ; the
houses rocked and fell ; rolling thunder beneath was
answered by crash on crash above ; and the scene
lacked no element of horror. But one man moved
through it undismayed. His voice was heard amidst
the din, calming and reassuring ; his example gave
courage, and his presence inspired hope. He directed
the people to the spots where they would be in least
danger, and took measures to extricate the inmates of
fallen houses and remove the dead—sending for the
troops to assist. All the operations were carried on
under his own eye, and he went from point to point
during their progress, and remained on the spot
through the night. Such a night! The darkness
enveloped heaven and earth, hiding the usually clear
sky and every object beneath, except where the
torches of the soldiers and working parties threw up a
glare, or when the lightning burst in a vivid flash.
The people were lying in the streets, but started
up with shrieks at every shock, which now made the
earth heave, now came like a quiver—at one moment
with crashing thunder, at another amidst the silence
of the grave. Morning brought reports from every
quarter announcing the same destruction, and Sir
Howard learnt that scarcely a house in the island
remained standing.

The work he undertook tasked all his powers, and
was not to be despatched in a day, though he pushed
it rapidly forward—constructing temporary barracks
for the troops, who were left without a roof, and then
providing shelter for the inhabitants, so that all might
be under cover before winter. For this he drew on

the public stores, and obtained supplies from Corfu, where his appeal for help met a prompt response. He became his own almoner and architect, and made a tour of the island, visiting every village and almost every house, and comforting as much by his words as his succour. Indeed, Zante would have been deserted but for his presence; for the earthquake did not cease, though it diminished, and such terror prevailed that many feared to lie down at night, lest the island should be engulfed before morning. The shocks occurred every hour, and extended over a fortnight, till they numbered upwards of six hundred, and it seemed that the convulsion would never end. But the most timid rallied at sight of the Lord High Commissioner, always calm and resolute, and sure to be found at the point of danger. They became influenced by his example, and he swayed the population as one man, so that he was able to act with extraordinary vigour and effect. Nor did he leave the island till the shocks had ceased and he had brought his work to a completion.

Services so signal could not pass unnoted, and they were reported to the General Commanding in Chief, whose approbation was conveyed to the Lord High Commissioner by Lord Fitzroy Somerset in the following terms :—" I have to express his Lordship's sense of the great exertions made by yourself, and by those acting under your judicious direction and authority, in affording the most effectual relief to the sufferers the circumstances of this unforeseen calamity would admit of, and equally in providing cover and temporary accommodation for the troops when their barracks were rendered uninhabitable. The General

Commanding in Chief further commanded me to observe that it was, in his opinion, fortunate that the
inspection of the 38th Regiment had so opportunely
brought you to the island, where your personal direction and authority have been exerted with so much
advantage to the public service."

CHAPTER XXXIV.

Effects a Coup d'État.

THOUGH taking a wide range, Sir Howard's hospitalities had a limit : the doors of the palace were shut against such of the English functionaries and residents as had formed loose connexions. To have extended the same rule to the Ionians would have been to proclaim an interdict, and hence he was more rigorous with the English, by whose example he hoped to put the prevailing corruption to shame. He had conceived the design of raising the Ionians to the English level—as near as might be ; and proposed to base their regeneration on a scheme of general education and a new system of laws. The difficulty of such a work may be understood from the character given of them by Sir Thomas Maitland, than whom no one knew them better :—" To a British mind," he writes, " the feelings of the people of these countries are equally repugnant and revolting, and it does require a positive experience and knowledge of their character to be able to make up one's mind to the belief that people exist with principles so degrading and feelings so debased. . . . . They are much fonder of Russian than of British liberty, and they would prefer any Government, however corrupt and tyrannical, to the only one Great Britain can ever wish to give them—one that would tend to their

general happiness, prosperity, and security.   I doubt
much, to say the truth, whether the character most
dreaded and most detested in these countries is not
that of an honest and upright man."

Sir Thomas Maitland's description is corroborated
by a French traveller, M. Lacour, who visited Zante
in 1832, and notices the islanders in an account of
his travels published two years later :—" Aussi à nous
Français confient-ils qu'ils détestent souverainement
les Anglais, et Zante serait en notre pouvoir ; qu'ils
adresseraient aux Russes les mêmes vœux et les
mêmes plaintes.   Le Grec est l'homme le plus vain,
le plus ingrat, le plus léger de tous les hommes.   Le
Zantiote sous ce rapport est plus que Grec ; il porte
ses vices de lâcheté, de perfidie, et de fanatisme a
l'extrême."

The French opinion of the Greeks will not be
raised by their tender of the Crown to Prince Alfred,
but this has shown them in a better light in England,
and corroborates the testimony they received from
Sir Howard—that their vices are caused by their
rulers, and show a redeeming margin.   He was not
for leaving this barbarism unchecked in the case of
the Ionians, but sought to effect a reformation.   The
principles he kept in view are unfolded in a despatch
to the Colonial Secretary, on the 25th of April,
1839 :—

" A sense of national dignity, and all the high
and noble sympathies which so peculiarly distin-
guish our country, unite in requiring us to show that
we are not actuated solely by selfish motives in retaining possession of these islands, and that we recognise the moral obligation that rests with us, above all

others, to dispense the blessings of internal improvements, education, and civilisation which Great Britain has it so much in her power to confer, and which may realise to these people, and exhibit to adjoining nations, the peculiar advantages which accrue to all who have the happiness to be connected with our great nation. . . . . .

"As the right of initiation, the power of control, and the responsibility of execution, rest in so high a degree with the protecting country, so the obligation is the more binding, the duty the more sacred, for that country to exercise vigilance and activity in pressing forward discreetly and rationally all measures tending to improve the moral and political condition of these States, to bring the people to that point which may admit of such modifications and changes in their constitution as should be consequent upon and cannot safely precede an improved state of society. . . . .

"But this sacred duty will be but indifferently discharged, and these splendid prospects but imperfectly realised, if, whilst establishing firmly our military possession of these islands, we do not evince a still greater solicitude to secure ourselves as firmly in the affections and confidence of the people by devoting ourselves to the internal improvement of the country, and by treating the people in all respects with as much favour as we show to the interests of the inhabitants of our other possessions. But truth and a strong sense of duty compel me to declare that the internal state of the country, the moral and physical state of the people, have not been benefited by British connexion so far as to protect us hereafter from the reproach of having attended less to their interests than our own."

It might seem there could be no opposition to a ruler so alive to his duties, and so sensible of what had been left undone. But this was a character the Ionians did not want. They saw in him an enemy of abuses and a promoter of economy, while they were all looking for a job or sinecure. He aimed at the public good, and they at their private advantage, raving about their country, but offering to sell it for a mess of potage. They could not understand benevolent designs framed to elevate a wretched community, and everything Sir Howard proposed with such a view appeared to them a deception and snare. He had urged the Colonial Secretary to remit the tribute of 35,000l. paid by the islands towards the military expenses, and represented that a fund would thus accrue for internal improvements; but he did not allow the fact of his having made an application to transpire, fearing that it might be rejected, as proved to be the result. The same reserve was not practised in England, and the secret oozed out, whence it might be expected that the Ionians overwhelmed him with gratitude. But the effect was very different. The Cavalier Mustoxidi accused him of seeking the remission of the tribute by stealth, in order to get it into his own hands, and thus secure the means of covering appropriations from the revenue applied to his private use ![1]

---

[1] Lord John Russell thus speaks of this charge in a despatch to Sir Howard Douglas of the 4th of June, 1840:—"I can only therefore reprobate conduct so unworthy of respect, and assure you of the continued confidence of the Queen whom you have the honour to serve."

But the Lord High Commissioner could not be turned from his policy by slander. He rather looked on the Ionians with pity,[1] and ascribed their vices to ignorance and "centuries of misgovernment,"[2] maintaining that it should be the aim of England to put them in a way of distinguishing between good and evil. He had no respect for what he described to the Colonial Secretary as "paper constitutions," and declared that any such change in the islands would render government impossible;[3] but he looked forward to a time when the Ionians might be intrusted with self-government, if it were preceded by the diffusion of education. He now framed a measure with this object, and laid it before the Legislature, recommending it in the strongest manner. But his initiation of the project made the opposition more bitter, and they resisted it at every stage, while they raised a tempest among the people by representing it as a blow at their religion. Such a form of opposition seemed insurmountable, as it leagued faction with fanaticism, and arrayed against the measure all the power of the Church. But Sir Howard knew when to advance and

---

[1] "They are a good-natured people, but it never enters into their heads that any Government should act on the simple dictates of common sense and impartiality."—Letter from Sir Howard Douglas to Lord John Russell.

[2] Despatch of the 25th April, 1839.

[3] In the despatch of the 25th of April he says :—" But no change other than that for improving the judicial organization and administration can in my opinion be safely made for many years ; and if by prematurely altering in principle the law by which the elective franchise is at present regulated, granting perfect freedom of the press or other essential changes before the people shall have acquired just views of their real interests, and be in a little fitter condition than at present to be intrusted with a more unlimited management of their own affairs, *such concessions would infallibly prove a deathblow to the supremacy of British influence, and plunge these States into anarchy and confusion.*" How completely have these words been verified !

when to recede, and thought it better to gain imperfect education than none at all; so he permitted the introduction of a clause establishing an ecclesiastical censorship on the printing of school-books, which conciliated the clergy, and the measure was carried.[1]

His next aim was to establish a code of laws which should effect for the islands what Napoleon accomplished for France, and what baffled Lord Macaulay in India. Such a work exacted study and inquiry; for he must shape his notions by the jurisprudence of the Levant and the traditions of the people; and for this he prepared himself by mastering the statutes of Greece, which he obtained through Sir Edmund Lyons.[2] His check on the prevailing corruption was a new law of marriage and divorce, which raised the social position of women, and might be called the breath of the code. But here the anti-English faction pretended to see a new attack on the Church; the outcry was encouraged by the Patriarch of Constantinople at the instigation of Russia; and the faction again enlisted the priests, whose denunciations lashed the populace into frenzy.

Sir Howard used every means to allay the excitement, and prove their apprehensions groundless. His friends in the Senate made statements in explanation, and articles appeared in the public journals detailing the points at issue, and revealing their bearings. It was shown that a revision of the laws was demanded by public morals, and that the new code rested on the dictates of nature, and possessed the advantage of simplicity. There could be no interference with religious

---

[1] Despatch of the 25th April, 1839.
[2] Letter from Sir Edmund Lyons, 28th January, 1839.

dogmas, as they were not brought into question, the regulations as to marriage and divorce being similar to what existed in Greece, where they had the sanction of the Greek clergy. But the opposition could not be persuaded, being only actuated by malice; and Sir Howard saw that he must exert his authority or forego improvement. He reported the situation to Lord John Russell, who had succeeded to the Colonial Department, and begged that he might be left to act as he should judge best in the crisis. Lord John expressed confidence in his judgment, but recommended conciliation, and suggested that the Assembly should have one more trial. The Lord High Commissioner understood the duty of concession, and practised it to the utmost; but he knew that it must be backed by decision, and that occasions occurred when it would be out of place. In what way could he conciliate the faction? By relinquishing his projects for the elevation of the population, the retrieval of the finances, and the increase of trade and production? Such was the aim of the measures they resisted, but not because they deemed them objectionable: it was only to create obstruction. Hence nothing would be gained by a change of policy, as this was not the object sought, though made a pretext. The purpose was to stir up sedition and a cry need never be wanting. Indeed the agitators did not conceal that they desired the termination of the English protectorate, and could be satisfied by nothing less; for that alone would give them the direction of affairs and possession of the revenue. It was this they had in view, whether clamouring for reform or ranting about religion, and they taught the people to look upon it as the cure for their ills, all of which they

laid to British connexion. They knew that Sir Howard
aimed at improvements, but his good intentions es-
tranged them the more; for whatever tended to win
the people raised an obstacle to their schemes. Their
policy was to nurse discontent and foment disorder,
and several members of the Assembly bound themselves by oath to resist ameliorations.[1] How could
such opponents be conciliated? Conciliation they
did not understand, except as a proof of weakness,
and they now formed the opinion that Sir Howard
was either held in check by the Ministry, or had
come to the end of his devices. Their language
grew more violent, and the sittings of the Assembly
became so stormy that he was twice obliged to resort
to prorogation. Their subtlety caught a perception
of his situation, but misinterpreted his attitude, mea-
suring him by its own standard; and he was derided
for his fears, while they taunted him with his perplexity, exulting at having placed him in a dead-lock.
The leaders held meetings at the house of Count
Bulgari, and agreed on a bolder course of action,
which commenced on the reopening of Parliament.[2]
Their scheme was to obtain the control of the civil
government, by withholding the allowance to the Lord
High Commissioner guaranteed by the Constitution;
and a motion for this object was brought forward by
Mr. Dondi. Sir Howard received an intimation that
no change would be made in his own case if he
allowed the measure to pass, and he replied to such
an insult in a manner little expected. He had wrung

---

[1] Copy of Instructions by Sir Howard Douglas to the Cavalier Viletta,
President of the Assembly, in the 'Douglas Papers.'
[2] Letter to Lord John Russell.

from Lord John Russell the mandate from the Queen empowering him to act, and instantly made his appearance in the House and dissolved the Parliament.

The faction now learnt that he had lost none of his energy, and were thrown into confusion, while the friends of English rule were reassured. Congratulations poured in upon him from every quarter, and he received letters of approbation from Her Majesty's Ambassadors at Vienna and Constantinople, the British Minister at Athens, the Consul-General in Egypt, the British Admiral, and other important functionaries, the tone of whose sentiments may be gathered from those of Sir Edmund Lyons:—" Your moral courage in punishing by dissolution the *soi-disant* Liberal, but real Russian party, has had an effect the benefit of which will, in my opinion, be felt for years to come in Greece as well as in the Islands." [1]

But the agitators were not resting on the Parliament alone. They thought the moment favourable for an insurrection, and had called in the aid of Count George Capo d'Istria, an intriguing Greek, and employed him to set it in motion. The Count drew up a plan of revolt, aiming to unite the islands with Greece under the protection of Russia, and combining the political with a religious movement, which was to extend to all the countries professing the Greek faith. A communication was opened with the Patriarch of Constantinople, and met an eager response, securing the adhesion of the clergy, who kept up the excitement, and preached a crusade against the protectorate. The conspirators met by stealth,

---

[1] Letter to Sir Howard Douglas, January 9, 1840.

under an oath of secresy, and took their measures with the greatest dexterity. They arranged the quarters where each should act, and concerted a rising in Greece which was to have in view the same objects. But they were reckoning on blindness in the Lord High Commissioner, and he was watching their movements and waiting till they were unmasked. At the proper moment the police were at the door : they burst into the room, seized all who were present, and secured the evidence of their papers.

CHAPTER XXXV.

It is worthy of note that Sir Howard cannot be charged with a single severity. The defamers of his government never adduced an instance of his overstepping the law, though he came down on his adversaries at every turn with resistless energy. His administration was a continued struggle, but without a stain; and we hear of no hangings, scourgings, or imprisonments, but of unceasing lenity. He was not accused of rigour even in the memorials that denounced him to the Colonial-office, indictments proved to be without a particle of truth, and framed by persons who acknowledged themselves his debtors. His inclination to mercy was so well known, that Sir Edmund Lyons promised pardon to one of the d'Istria conspirators, without deeming it necessary to learn his intentions. " Doctor Mavrojammi," he writes to Sir Howard, " has sent to me to say that he sees his error, and deeply laments having been led into it. I said that, if he really were repentant, it must appear in his conduct, and that you were the last person to shut the door for ever against a political sinner." [1] Indeed, the Lord High Commissioner might have brought the conspirators to the gallows with the evidence he possessed of their guilt; but he regarded them as no worse than

---

[1] Letter from Sir Edmund Lyons, June 24, 1840.

their countrymen in general, and granted them bail as soon as they had been examined.

He looked with a different eye upon their instigators, and especially the chief mover, the Patriarch of Constantinople. The Ionians he could watch, but how was he to guard against the intrigues of Russia and Greece, carried on by a foreign pontiff who ruled the Ionian Church? The problem cost him anxious meditation. He saw a mode of solution, but it involved so bold a measure, that he hesitated to set it in motion until he should have felt his way. What he contemplated was the deposition of the Patriarch, and the establishment of the independence of the Ionian Church, which might be wrested from the Patriarch's successor, by making assent a condition of his promotion. This would cut off a fruitful source of intrigue, while it would be a salutary display of England's power. But he must first establish the Patriarch's guilt in a manner that could not be disputed; and the proofs in his hands might be held inconclusive; so he determined to open his designs to Sir Edmund Lyons, and engage him to obtain evidence.

He had apprised Sir Edmund of the conspiracy, and requested him to procure the seizure of Capo d'Istria's papers at his house in Athens; and he now sent Captain Douglas [1] to explain to him what he projected. But the Greek Government had no intention of giving up papers so charged with secrets, and postponed their search till they could be put beyond

---

[1] His son, now Major-General Sir R. Percy Douglas, Bart., Lieutenant-Governor of Jersey.

reach. Capo d'Istria was warned of their intention,
while the King professed a warm regard for Sir
Howard, and pronounced the defeat of the conspiracy
a service to himself.[1] Nor was such an assertion
unwarranted; for the plot contemplated his assassina-
tion, though his own duplicity prevented the point
being established. His effort to screen the Patriarch
did not obtain the same success, for a letter was found
proving that he had received an agent from the conspirators, and Sir Howard brought to light a pastoral
he had addressed to the lower classes, inciting them to
revolt.[2]

The fact of this complicity came to be understood,
and it is a testimony to Sir Howard's wisdom that
the step he meditated was recommended to Captain
Douglas by Mr. Tricoupi, the leader of the Greek
Liberals, and declared by him the only remedy.[3] Sir
Howard now communicated with Lord Ponsonby,
the British Ambassador at Constantinople, and found
him well-disposed. Fortunately the foreign affairs of
England were then directed by a Minister of great
experience, and he saw the question in the same light,

[1] " The King said many complimentary things of you, acknowledges the
great kindness and attention you have always shown him and the Queen,
expressed a wish to have the advantage of seeing you, and begged me to
thank you for the steps you had taken in this affair."—Letter from Sir
Edmund Lyons, 9th January, 1840.

[2] " I have the honour to forward your Lordship a translated copy of a
pamphlet written by his Holiness and transmitted by his emissaries to
Zante for circulation among the ignorant classes."—Letter of Sir Howard
Douglas to Lord Ponsonby.

[3] " I told Mr. Tricoupi that this important and indispensable measure
had occupied much of your attention, and that you were only waiting for a
more convenient and safer opportunity of doing this, if possible."—Letter
from Captain Douglas, dated Athens, 23rd January, 1840.

and caught at the opportunity of effecting an object which would both administer a check to Russia, and shut the door against future intrigues. Lord Palmerston enlisted the support of France and Austria in the project, convincing those powers that the Patriarch was a Russian tool, and that their interests in the Levant were identical with those of England in relation to Russian designs, which penetrated all the countries embraced by the Greek Church.[1] Marshal Soult declared to Lord Granville that Lord Palmerston's views were his own, and that the Ambassador of France should be instructed to aid the English Ambassador in carrying out their common policy.[2]

All being ready, the impulse was given to the Porte, and the blow struck. The 'Corfu Gazette' announced to the Ionians that the Patriarch of Constantinople had been deposed. Sir Howard had baffled the Pope, but it required him to move three of the great powers to overthrow the Patriarch. The Ionians were as impressed by his vigour as by the display of England's influence, and the incident told wherever it was reported. " It has confounded the Russian party here," writes Sir Edmund Lyons from Athens.[3] And Sir Robert Stopford writes from Malta, " I heartily congratulate you on the success of your energetic measure in putting down that hydra of faction, fomented in

---

[1] "I see that Lord Palmerston invited the Courts of Vienna and Paris to assist in endeavouring to depose the Patriarch."—Letter from Sir Edmund Lyons to Sir Howard Douglas, March 28, 1840.

[2] Copy of a letter from Lord Granville to Sir Edmund Lyons, in the ' Douglas Papers.'

[3] Letter to Sir Howard Douglas, March 28, 1840.

every quarter by Russian intrigue to the detriment of British interests." [1]

But the faction was not "put down," though it was checked. The men composing it knew the measure of English forbearance, and the latitude it permitted, and their audacity revived as danger lessened. The lenity of the Lord High Commissioner then became an affront; for it proclaimed their insignificance, and challenged their resentment. None were more bitter against him than the brothers Caravalla, the elder of whom he had brought into the Legislature, and the first use he made of his elevation was to turn against his patron, because he could not bestow upon him the post of Protonedics of Zante. The orphan children of another of the brothers had been left destitute, and he maintained them for five years at his own expense, paying for their education, and keeping them in their own sphere of life. Yet their uncle was not ashamed to wear on his breast Russian and Greek decorations, the reward of his abuse of their benefactor. Mr. Andrea * * * * had likewise been brought forward by Sir Howard, who made him a member of the Primary Council, and only incurred his enmity for not creating him a senator. Mr. Dandolo had been treated by Sir Howard with the greatest kindness, as he acknowledged himself, and was also alienated by the refusal of promotion, after he had sought it with threats. The Lord High Commissioner had shown the same good feeling to Dr. * * * *, raising him to the grade of senator, and bringing his brother-in-law into

---

[1] Letter from Admiral Sir Robert Stopford to Sir Howard Douglas, March 6, 1840.

Parliament at his request. But he became a rabid Oppositionist because he could not be appointed Regent of Zante. The Cavalier * * * * was found by Sir Howard in poverty and obscurity. He took him by the hand, introduced him into the Legislature, and then recommended him for a Commandership of St. Michael and St. George; but he could not satisfy the ambition he had awakened, and the Cavalier joined the Opposition. D * * * * was another of those who owed him his place in the Legislature, and was a constant visitor at the palace, till he learnt that an action brought against him for peculation raised an obstacle to his promotion, when he went the way of the others. The Count Bulgari had twice been nominated President of the Senate, the highest post in the State, and lived in the closest intimacy with Sir Howard, the two families being inseparable; but the Lord High Commissioner thought it unjust to give him such a post a third time, and bestowed it on the next in rotation, offering the Count the Regency of Corfu. All the claims of friendship were then renounced; all the remembrances of an unbounded hospitality forgotten; and the Count threw his weight into the Opposition.

The faction was emboldened by a change in the attitude of France, arising out of the movements of Mehemet Ali, and counted on a rupture between that power and England. The armaments in the French ports gave a sanction to this opinion, and we know that it had real grounds, though the danger was averted by the firmness of Lord Palmerston.[1] Something like the Ionian impression infected

[1] Guizot's Embassy to the Court of St. James's.

the British Admiral, and he confided his uneasiness to Sir Howard,[1] who appears to have taken alarm some time before, for one morning he set the engineers to knock down the land fronts of the fortifications, and thus made Corfu defensible by a naval power.[2]

This unexpected measure drove the Opposition frantic ; for they saw that the small English garrison was now equal to the duties, and possession secured, leaving no hope of a change. They denounced Sir Howard in the most opprobrious language, and declared that he had violated the stipulations of the Treaty of Vienna, which guaranteed the maintenance of the fortifications. They sent a mission to England to represent his conduct in the most odious light, and even applied to the great powers to terminate the English protectorate, which they declared to be voided by this breach of the compact. Such an appeal might have occasioned a complication at another time, though the treaty afforded it no warrant ; but it now fell to the ground, as the powers were intent on the quarrel between Turkey and Egypt, and too much occupied in watching each other to heed the Ionians. We shall see that the machinations of the faction were not so unsuccessful in England.

---

[1] "From the open declarations made by. the French that they propose having a squadron of fifteen sail of the line, including three first-rates, in the Archipelago this spring and summer, it is to be hoped that the Government at home is fully and satisfactorily apprised of their pacific intentions." —Letter from Sir Robert Stopford to Sir Howard Douglas, March 6, 1840.

[2] Letter to Lord John Russell, February, 1840.

CHAPTER XXXVI.

Establishes the Douglas Code, and receives the Tribute of a Public Monument.

SIR HOWARD had not dissolved the Parliament a moment too soon; for hardly was the step taken when Lord John Russell forbade the dissolution, and again enjoined conciliation.   Such a relapse took Sir Howard by surprise.   He knew that some Ionians were intriguing in England, but they were persons of such infamy that he could not expect their statements would be received by a Minister of the Crown, much less that they should outweigh his own, and deprive him of the support due to the Queen's representative. Hence he felt annoyed at Lord John's vacillation, but not discouraged; for events were justifying the course he had adopted, and proving it the best.   His vigour had taken a form that won the multitude, while it brought the faction into contempt, and the Government had never been so strong.   He was once more popular, and was received with cheers whenever he appeared in public, so that he looked for an accession of support at the coming elections.   And his anticipations were realised, for everything passed off with effect, and the constituencies returned the Government candidates by large majorities.[1]

[1] "The measures completely disconcerted and defeated the faction, enabled me at once to restore perfect tranquillity, and so entirely put down all excitement, that the general elections were carried on in all the

The Parliament assembled in the best temper, and
instantly entered on the public business, which it
had been customary to impede by motions of ad-
journment, or throw over altogether, in order to
place the Administration in a dead-lock.   There was
no contention or dissension, and the Ionians were
astonished by a Legislature engaged in legislation,
and acting in harmony with the Government. Several
useful measures were introduced and passed both
Houses, receiving the assent of the Lord High Commissioner.   But the interest centred on Sir Howard's
system of laws, which drew out a number of speakers
and incurred some criticism, but gained adherents at
every step, and finally overcame all opposition.   It
passed almost unaltered, and the Legislative Assembly
voted an address to the Queen, which they directed
their President to present in person and obtain Her
Majesty's ratification of the code.

The care and labour bestowed on the work appeared
more clearly in debate, yet was only in accord with the
tenor of Sir Howard's administration, which had raised
the islands from penury to affluence, secured them
new channels of trade, endowed them with public
works and useful institutions, and carried them through
a political crisis of the gravest nature.   The establishment of a new jurisprudence seemed but the crowning
of the column with a capital, but made the work more
prominent and his merit more conspicuous.   The
official regulations limited his government to six years,
which he had nearly completed ; and speeches were

islands in the most orderly manner, the electors attending for the exercise
of their rights in greater numbers than on any former occasion."—Despatch
of Sir Howard Douglas to Lord John Russell.

made extolling his administration, and looking to its close as a public misfortune. It was then determined to introduce a paragraph in the address to the Queen setting forth the benefits he had conferred on the States, and praying her Majesty to prolong his term. At the same time the Legislature awarded him the highest honour in its gift, by decreeing him a statue, which was voted by acclamation.

The President of the Senate informed him of the resolutions, and they caused him the deepest emotion; for such a tribute did more than symbolize success—it rendered homage to his motives. Any recognition of his usefulness gave him pleasure, but this affected him the more, because it expressed attachment, and so touched his heart. Yet he shrank from a reward his modesty deemed excessive, and obtained the suppression of the paragraph in the address, while he declined the statue. At the same time he exerted his influence to procure a good reception for the code from the Government. It was conveyed to England by the Cavalier Viletta, the President of the Assembly, and he recommended that the opportunity should be taken to invest him with the Order of St. Michael and St. George on his presentation to her Majesty, which would give dignity to the Order by the personal interposition of the Queen, and exalt the Legislature in the same degree.

The approaching termination of his government had not been overlooked by Lord John Russell, and he wrote to assure him that " neither his reputation nor interests should run any hazard from anything he was likely to do with respect to it; " nor can there be a doubt that he spoke sincerely. But the Government was actuated by a conciliatory spirit, and thought to win the Ionian agitators by concession, which was pressed upon it by adherents in the House at a time when it could not dispense with support. The situation is described to Sir Howard in a letter from Sir Henry Hardinge. "The Government is low in reputation, and we all think cannot exist much longer. Peel is very well and very able; Stanley[1] unrivalled and vigorous, and ready for any course of action; the Duke sadly changed, but his intellect as clear as ever." Such was the opposition to be faced, and so shaken the means of resistance. The loss of a single vote might overthrow the Government—indeed, a few months later carried a motion of want of confidence by one vote—and hence the Ionian difficulty suggested to Lord John Russell incompatible objects: he sought to uphold Sir Howard, while he conciliated his traducers, receiving complaints against him from Dandolo, Mustoxidi, and others, and meeting them with soft answers, at the same time that he defended him against attacks in the House. "With regard to the motion," writes Sir Henry Hardinge, " it was so wretched an affair, and Peel supported you so effectually in the House (although briefly reported), that I am confident it would have answered no good object if I had taken part in the debate. I hear that the Government express themselves highly satisfied with your administration, and I may, with great truth, most cordially congratulate you on the ability and success of your measures."

It is due to Lord John Russell to say that he pronounced the same opinion, and avowed it in the

---

[1] The present Earl of Derby.

House, as will be seen by the following letter from Sir Robert Peel :—

"MY DEAR SIR HOWARD,   "Whitehall, June 29th.

"I have no doubt (although the proceedings were very imperfectly reported in the newspapers) that you will have received full accounts of the discussion in the House of Commons on the motion respecting the Ionian Islands. It was half-past eleven at night when brought on, in a very thin House, and a speech almost inaudible, and which appeared to make no impression on those who, from being in the immediate neighbourhood, had the advantage of hearing it.

"The previous publication by the Government of the correspondence with you on the main subjects under discussion had greatly contributed to deprive the motion of the interest it might otherwise have excited, inasmuch as it had produced a general impression that there was no ground for parliamentary interference, none for questioning any part of your conduct, and that the whole question had better be left, and could safely be left, in the hands of the Crown and the local authorities acting under your general superintendence.

"Not a word was said reflecting on you personally, and I had scarcely a fair opportunity, though I did not neglect to do so, of bearing my testimony to your character and public services, and of explaining the grounds on which a former Government had appointed you to this charge of the Ionian Islands.

2 c

" The conduct of Lord John Russell was in every respect fair and satisfactory, and the impression of the House as favourable as you could wish.

" Believe me, my dear Sir Howard,

" Very faithfully yours,

" Robert Peel."

But Lord John clung to the notion of conciliation, and continued to receive memorials from the agitators, who now turned on the Cavalier Viletta; and their aspersions so influenced the Minister that he delayed presenting him to the Queen. It is true he acted with the best motives, as he believed the charges must have some ground, and the baseness of their framers did not enter his imagination. But the effect was to give them encouragement, and the faction again raised its head in Corfu, where Sir Howard was attacked in a pamphlet which charged him with aiming at the subversion of the Greek Church, and pilfering from the revenue, though it had increased 40,000l. a year under his management. How different might have been the result if Lord John had acted with the same energy as Lord Palmerston, when he ranged three of the great powers behind the Lord High Commissioner and procured the deposition of the Patriarch !

Sir Howard felt so mortified at his situation, that it became insupportable. " I am perfectly certain, my Lord, that there was nothing intentionally unjust or unmindful in this," he writes to Lord John Russell, in February, 1841, " and I will also add the like of everything else I venture to complain of; but the effects were nevertheless as if it had been otherwise, and unfortunate, untoward circumstances, expressions, and discrepancies have so greatly pained and paralyzed me, as have determined me instantly to withdraw from these States."

He mentioned his approaching departure in an address to the Senate on the 8th of the following month, and excited a general feeling of sorrow. "Your Excellency has alluded," said the President, "in terms that sensibly affect us, to the approaching close of your distinguished administration. You will, however, be ever present to us in the numerous works of general utility which you leave in this country—the lasting monuments of your indefatigable exertions for the solid welfare of the Ionian people. These will ever keep alive in our hearts the feeling of gratitude, as sincere and profound as it is inextinguishable."

The same sentiment animated the Legislative Assembly; and its President was directed to address Sir Howard the following letter:—

" My Lord,—

" One part of your Excellency's speech contains the announcement that your public relations with these States are drawing to a close : this information is painful to us and to the people whom we represent ; for we never can forget how greatly you have exerted yourself to promote all those institutions that render nations prosperous, and give them full enjoyment of an advanced civilization, and how, on every occasion, you have shown yourself the beneficent father of these people.

" Accept, my Lord, our most sincere thanks both for the wisdom of your administration, and for the regard you have expressed for us. Your Excellency will reap great satisfaction from the consciousness of having to the utmost seconded in this country the beneficent views of the gracious Sovereign that protects us; and we must seek consolation in the assurance you make us feel, that you will ever have at heart the welfare of the Ionian people. Our prayers for your happiness and for that of your family will attend you everywhere, and the remembrance of you will ever be most pleasing to our minds."

It was again determined to commemorate Sir Howard's administration by a national monument, and the Senate passed the following resolutions by acclamation :—

"UNITED STATES OF THE IONIAN ISLANDS.

"Corfu, March 24, 1841.

" Resolution of the Senate.

" The Senate, desirous of making some public demonstration of gratitude to Sir Howard Douglas, Lord High Commissioner of the Protecting Sovereign in these States, for the real benefits which, by his unremitting care, have been procured to them during the course of his distinguished administration, have resolved :—

" Art. 1. That a bust in marble of his Excellency be made at the public expense, and placed in the hall of the Senate.

" Art. 2. That in each of the islands of these States
an obelisk be raised, the sides bearing analogous
inscriptions and emblems.

" Art. 3. The competent officers of the Government are charged to carry the above resolution into
effect.

" P. Petrizzopulo.

" T. J. Gisborne,
" <i>Sec. to the Senate for the Gen. Dep.</i>"

A copy of the resolutions was forwarded to Sir
Howard by the President, who thus notified the vote
of the Senate :—

" Excellency,—

" The Senate, duly appreciating the general feeling
of gratitude with which your Excellency's distinguished
administration throughout has inspired the Ionian
people, have resolved to perpetuate the remembrance
of the peculiar claims your Excellency has acquired to
universal respect and esteem.

" And in order that your Excellency's name, associated with our truly grateful recollections, may be
handed down to our latest posterity, the Senate have
voted the resolution which I have the honour to trans-
mit, accompanied by the relative <i>procès verbal</i>.

" Happy in being the channel of communicating to
your Excellency the wishes of the Senate in this respect,
I seize this opportunity, as one of the happiest moments
of my life, to express also my own heartfelt gratitude
for the deep and unwearied interest your Excellency

has ever taken in the prosperity of these States through the whole course of our official relations.

" I have the honour to be,

" P. Petrizzopulo."

Sir Howard did not feel warranted in declining such a tribute a second time, and perhaps the less so as it refuted his traducers by the voice of their country. Nor was the testimony confined to himself; for the ladies of Corfu determined to present a token to Lady Douglas; and this made its appearance at the palace in the shape of a costly gold vase, which an irresistible deputation begged her to accept. Such were the terms on which the Ionian States parted with one English Governor—the only Governor who ever won their affection; and there can be no nobler memorial than the inscription they have placed on the obelisk erected to him at Corfu, and which may be thus rendered from the Italian and Greek :—

" Howard Douglas,

Cavalier and General,

High Commissioner,

Benefactor of the Ionian Islands.

The Benefits common to all: comprising extension of the University Studies; the founding of the Ionian Colleges; the completion of the Preliminary Schools; the establishment of the Ionian Bank, and of Savings Banks; the Codification and Revision of the Laws;

the construction and completion of the Public Roads, including the Strada Marina, from which great utility is derived, not only to the inhabitants of the city, but also to the suburbs ; the construction of the Cemeteries of the Oriental Orthodox Church, and also of the Latin Church ; the founding of the House for the Poor, and the Asylum for Lunatics; the Restoration of the Hospitals and Prisons ; the conception and completion of the Aqueduct built by F. Adam ; the erection of the Exchange for Merchants, of which he became the Patron ; the Increase of Communication between the City and the Country ; the Draining of the Lake ; and the improvement and construction of Bridges.

The Community of Corfu have raised this in Eternal Remembrance, in 1843."

CHAPTER XXXVII.

Returned to Parliament for Liverpool.

A vacancy occurred in the representation of Liverpool soon after Sir Howard's return to England, and he accepted an invitation to become a candidate in the Conservative interest. The other side advanced Mr. Morris, and called on the second commercial city of the kingdom to decide between Protection and Free-trade. This was the question of the moment, though not the only issue ; for all the doctrines of our two parties were brought out in the struggle, and its progress was watched by the whole country.

The day of nomination set Liverpool in commotion, and every avenue to the hustings was blocked with Montagues and Capulets, though they confined their feud to jibes and sarcasms, and the usual party cries. Sir Howard delivered a temperate speech and stated his opinions, as they were set forth in his life, and are recorded in this volume. But the uproar was great, each party being determined to shut up the other, and it cannot be affirmed that he made many converts. The same greetings saluted Mr. Morris, and caused such a strain on his voice that he became hoarse, and was brought to a stop in the middle of his harangue. Some one touched his arm at this juncture, and he was surprised to find it was Sir Howard, who had

made his way across the hustings, and offered him a
lozenge. This relieved his hoarseness, and enabled
him to finish his address, which obtained him the
nomination ; but the poll resulted in the return of Sir
Howard.

Twenty years later Sir Howard was walking in the
country, and passed the entrance to a noble domain,
which attracted him to enter—for the gate was open,
and he could never resist a beautiful prospect. The
owner stepped out of a side-walk as he stood there,
glanced at him, and instantly raised his hat. " I
believe I have the pleasure of addressing Sir Howard
Douglas ? " he said. The answer removed all doubt ;
and he added, " You don't remember giving me a
lozenge on the hustings, when I opposed you at
Liverpool ? " They shook hands, and had a pleasant
chat ; for it was his fortune to leave impressions of
kindness where others shed only bitterness.

He was introduced to the House of Commons by
two of his political friends, and went to a vacant place
on the Conservative benches where he found a warm
welcome. " It is curious, Sir Howard, that you should
have taken that seat," remarked an old member, " for
it was successively occupied by two of your prede-
cessors from Liverpool, Canning and Huskisson." He
was so sensitive as to feel disturbed by this information, fearing it might be thought that he knew
the associations of the seat, and had selected it pur-
posely, so he rose to take another, but his neighbours
persuaded him to remain. He never pretended to be
an orator, like those eminent statesmen ; but his speeches
were impressive from their simplicity, the knowledge

they showed of the subject, and the manner in which they were delivered, obtaining the ear of the House from the first. He was a steady supporter of Conservative principles, but in a constitutional sense, advocating progress, while he resisted innovation. Nor would he bind himself to a Minister's car, to be dragged wherever it drove, and he refused to follow Sir Robert Peel in throwing open the colonies to the United States, his doctrine being that such concessions should be reciprocal and not all on one side; and he let him know that they could not receive his support. Sir Robert replied to him in a kindred spirit:—

" MY DEAR SIR HOWARD,   "Whitehall, 6th May, 1842.

" I am much obliged for the communication with which you have favoured me.

" The question is one on which I must not seek to impose any restrictions on you, in respect to the opinions which you may think it right to express in Parliament. I consider it necessary to diminish the cost of production in the West Indian colonies, in order to give them the means of competing, now that slavery has been abolished, with other countries in which it continues to exist. Our commercial intercourse with the United States is not on a satisfactory footing. Notwithstanding our immense imports of cotton, our exports to the United States far exceed our direct imports, and there is great difficulty in making remittances for the balance. The extension of intercourse, direct or colonial, with the United States has advantages preponderating on the whole, in

my opinion, over the partial evils which it may en-
gender.

> " Believe me very faithfully yours,
>
> " Robert Peel."

Sir Howard joined mastery of facts with fluency of
speech, and this gave him power in debate, as he did
not come down to the House with a set oration, but
stood to answer the previous speakers, whatever their
arguments or statements.   An example may be cited
from his speech in the debate on the state of Ireland,
in February, 1844, which elicited the cheers of the
House by its instantaneous refutation of an unfounded
assertion :—" Notwithstanding what is said by the
hon. Member for Waterford, that the taxation of
Ireland is one-fifth that of England,—and what the
hon. Member for Kilkenny says, that it is as three to
four,—the fact is, that the taxation of Ireland is not
one-tenth of that of England and Wales, and about
four-fifths of that of Scotland.   Thus, Ireland, with a
population of about 8,200,000 is taxed to the amount
of 4,000,000*l.*, whilst England and Wales with a
population of 16,000,000 are taxed to the amount of
42,485,000*l.* ; and   Scotland, with a population of
4,600,000, is taxed to the amount of 5,000,000*l.*   At
the time of the Union the Irish debt was 23,000,000*l.*
He spoke in round numbers ; that of Great Britain was
451,000,000*l.*   The Irish debt has only increased from
23,000,000*l.* to 34,000,000*l.*, whilst the debt charged
to Great Britain has increased from 451,000,000*l.* to
740,000,000*l.*   The charge for interest is, for Ireland,

1,183,845*l*,; and for Great Britain, 27,357,330*l*. It was settled, at the Union, that for the space of twenty years the contributions of Great Britain and Ireland, respectively, towards the expenditure of the United Kingdom, should be in the proportion of fifteen-seventeenths, and two-seventeenths; and that after that period, the expenditure, other than the charges for interest of debt to which either is liable, should be in such proportion as to the united Parliament may seem fit. According to this, the budget of 1801 was, for the expenditure of the United Kingdom 42,197,000*l*., of which 4,324,000*l*. was for Ireland. It thus appeared that, in all these respects, Ireland has been treated with the greatest liberality, and that all the financial stipulations and engagements made at the time of the Union have been most faithfully carried out."

He indignantly repelled a threat that Ireland would turn against England, if invaded by a hostile force. "But in the name of the soldiers and the gentry of Ireland he protested against the supposition that, under any circumstances whatever, they would join in rebellion. He had heard with admiration the sentiment of an hon. Gentleman who said, ' Whatever may be our difference at home, if an enemy dare invade us, it would be the most certain means of uniting us as one man.' Indeed he could oppose historical proof against any aspersion that foreign invasion would be seconded or supported in Ireland. He was old enough to remember the cases of Bantry Bay and Killala. A French force of ten ships of the line and seven frigates, after suffering something from stress of weather, arrived in that Bay with 20,000 troops on board, in expectation of assistance and co-operation from the people. But the very French officers who first went on shore to reconnoitre, and prepare for landing the troops, were made prisoners by the peasantry, and the fleet returned to France without striking a blow. At Killala a force landed, invited by certain rebel agents. But they were not supported by the people; they were joined by only a few hundred unarmed peasantry. They were met by a force consisting chiefly of Irish militia, and taken prisoners, execrating those who had deluded them to come over by representations of the great support they would receive."

He received a cordial invitation from Sir Robert Peel to join him in the country:—"I wish I could hope for an opportunity of seeing you at Drayton Manor. The period for my departure for London is fast approaching, and I could hardly calculate upon now finding you disengaged. Baron Brunnow and Lord Aberdeen are coming here on Tuesday the 23rd for three or four days; and if you should be at liberty at the time, it will give Lady Peel and me great pleasure if you will join the party. You will be in time for dinner by the two o'clock train from Euston Square."

Sir Howard maintained an independent attitude towards the Premier in his day of power; but he clung to him in his decline, and joined Sir John Yarde Buller in rallying round him the Conservative party on the occasion of his being outvoted on the sugar question. The meeting was held at the Carlton Club, on the 17th of June, 1844, and passed the following resolution :—

"That this Meeting has heard with deep regret the rumour of an intended resignation on the part of Her Majesty's Ministers, a step which, in their opinion, would be fraught with the most disastrous consequences to the best interests of the country; and, while they reserve to themselves the full exercise of an independent judgment upon all measures submitted to the consideration of Parliament, they take this opportunity of expressing a grateful sense of the services which have been rendered to the empire by Her Majesty's Ministers, an anxious desire for their continued maintenance in power, and a firm determination to afford them a general and cordial support."

Sir John Yarde Buller communicated the result in the following letter:—

" MY DEAR SIR HOWARD,   "Spring Gardens, 10, New Street, 19th June, 1844.

"I send you a copy of the letter I received yesterday evening from Sir Robert Peel in answer to the address we presented to him, and I likewise send a copy to Lord Ingestrie,[1] to whom I spoke concerning the mode in which we should make the letter known to those gentlemen who joined in the address; and we thought the best plan was for each of us to have a copy to show to those we are acquainted with, and thus give the letter sufficient publicity.

"I am yours truly,

"J. B. Y. BULLER."

---

[1] The present Earl of Shrewsbury and Talbot.

"My dear Sir John,   "Whitehall, 12th June, 1844.

"I availed myself of the earliest opportunity of communicating to my colleagues in the service of Her Majesty the address which you were deputed to present to me yesterday. On their part and my own I return to you, and to the gentlemen who were parties to that address, our grateful acknowledgments for the gratifying terms in which they express their sense of the services rendered by us in the conduct of public affairs, and for the assurance which they give (reserving the right of judgment in respect to particular measures) of a cordial disposition to place confidence in and give support to the Government. We are fully sensible of the value of these declarations, and most anxious to retain the esteem of that powerful and most honourable party to which we have been deeply indebted, on many trying occasions, for zealous support.

"I am, my dear Sir John,
"Most faithfully yours,
"Robert Peel."

The address is a foreshadowing of the rupture between the party and its leader, and swells with the import, mingling doubt and perplexity with the impress of attachment, and distrust of the future with assurance from the past. The curious may speculate whether Sir Robert would have regained his old position if he had lived over the tide of events; but we may think this was impossible when his personal friends already "reserve to themselves the full exercise of an independent judgment upon all measures submitted to the consideration of Parliament."

Sir Howard took especial interest in questions connected with the army and navy, or those with which he had been concerned in his official career, and which he might be said to represent still, as they had their roots in Liverpool. He was always at his post in discussions on the estimates, the shipping interest, and the relations of trade, and gave several overthrows to Mr. Hume, generally referring to him as "the great economist, the Member for Montrose." He insisted on the importance of maintaining a proper naval force, and was the first to suggest the formation of a naval reserve, though he lived to see the credit appropriated by others. The Admiralty seem to have flattered him with hopes that his suggestion would be adopted in 1847, and then broke faith; for he speaks of it in a desponding tone in the debate on the navy estimates in that year:—" I must express great regret and disappointment that no vote is taken for a purpose which I think of the first importance, and even indispensable to the safety of the State in these times, and which I cannot doubt the Committee would have received by acclamation, and the country would learn with general approbation—I mean a vote to provide, in some form or other, for a reserve of seamen to be organized and kept always ready to form fighting crews, for a moderately extended establishment in case of any emergency or combination; thus to insure, that in the event of any aggression upon us, any sudden breach of the peace, the first operations might be telling and triumphant. The material of our navy is in the most efficient condition. We could commission in a day twenty or thirty sail of the line, and innumerable smaller vessels. Our armament is the most perfect in the world ; our ships and fleets commanded by excellent, and in many cases experienced officers ; and those vessels might gradually be manned by abundance of British seamen, trained to the sea by our commercial marine. But where are the men to man those ships for the first emergency of a war ? "

He reminded the House that England existed by her naval supremacy, and called attention to the development given to the ports and armaments of France, quoting the latest appropriations :—" These amount to no less than 126,560,900 francs—about 4,800,000l. sterling. To Cherbourg, 15,500,000 francs ; to L'Orient, 8,000,000 francs ; to Rochefort, 3,000,000 francs ; to Toulon, 14,300,000 francs ; to Havre, 25,880,000 francs. Never has any nation made such stupendous exertions—such successful efforts—in creating, or at least recreating, a naval power of the first order as France since 1815. Her commerce had been destroyed, her commercial marine ruined, her naval power destroyed ; but, guided by a lofty policy, sacrificing nothing to her *docteurs économiques*, she has restored her commerce, fostered her maritime resources, and reconstructed a formidable naval power. Not in the days of Rodney and De Grasse, Hughes and Suffren, was the navy of France more powerful than it is now. No British statesman, of whatever party, can or ought to be unmindful of this. No British House of Commons, however economical in other respects, should affect to disregard this. Distant may the period be when these tremendous powers are

2 D

to be called into activity! but whilst we are determined to commit no act of aggression, let us not fail to
provide effectually the best means of preserving peace,
namely, to be well prepared for war ; and that, if any
act of aggression, any pregnant ambition be attempted
against us, we may always be in a condition to make
the first blow of a war the most effectual, and so herald
a course of successes as signal as those which distinguished the commencement of the late war, and terminated with an ever-memorable naval victory."

The debate on the vote of thanks for the battle of
Ferozepoor called on him to vindicate his friend Sir
Henry Hardinge, who was thought to have encroached
on the functions of Sir Hugh Gough, the Commander-
in-Chief, and his speech drew from the Governor-
General the following letter, written on the ladies'
plan of reserving the pith for the postscript :—

" My dear Douglas,   " Simla, 5th May, 1846.

    " I thank you for the very friendly and decisive
manner in which you defended me when the vote of
thanks came before the House.

    " I have been in a strange position, where the line
of demarcation between my powers and the professional rights of a Commander-in-Chief are not easy
to be defined ; but there is one unerring rule, to be
determined to act with cordiality where the interests
of the general public are concerned ; and Sir Hugh
Gough and myself have always kept on the best of
terms.

    " I will not speak to you of my policy at Lahore

until it is fairly launched before the House, and there it will I hope be scrutinized by friend and foe, for I have nothing to conceal.

"In sixty days we have fought four battles, occupied Lahore, disbanded the mutinous Sikh army, and sent to Calcutta 256 pieces of very fine large artillery, curtailed the Sikh State by about one-third of its territories, established a new dynasty in the hills under our protection as a counterpoise against the Sikhs, and, having effectually crushed them as a warlike power, we are now protecting them by a British garrison at Lahore, affording them every co-operation to re-establish a government.

"After years of military anarchy it is not to be expected that a military people will suddenly turn their swords into ploughshares. If they do, so much the better. If they do not, the annexation of the country will be easier hereafter. In March last it was impossible. I had only 15,000 infantry at Lahore. I have left 9000, and have no fears of a Cabool disaster.

"My sons are absent on a tour to Cashmeer, and I am hard at my work trying to keep down the mass of arrears of the last four months.

"I am gratified to have the approbation of my former master at High Wycombe. My very best regards to Lady Douglas.

"Ever yours very sincerely,

"H. HARDINGE.

"At the assault of the Sikh entrenched camp at Sobraon we should have been repulsed if we had not persisted in using thirty-six pieces of heavy artillery to bombard the camp for two hours before the infantry attack began.

" When I went down and saw the two field officers of Engineers and Artillery, they decidedly told me that, as the enemy had only field guns in their camp, their heavy guns being in battery on the other side of the river, that our heavy guns and mortars could reach well into their camp, whilst their 6-pounders would not reach our open batteries.

" Having been opposed to the plan of an attack by infantry alone, I sent these officers to the Commander-in-Chief, with the member of the Military Board (an Ordnance Department officer), Colonel Benson, to say that, as they were of opinion that the enemy must be shelled out of his camp by such a proceeding, that I recommended the attack. I was so very lame I could scarcely move, and in the doctor's hands. Gough came to me, and it was agreed when these guns arrived in two days to make the attack.

" The next day the Artillery and Engineer field officers declared the proposed attack to be impracticable, that their men in open battery would be cut to pieces. This they reported to the Commander-in-Chief. He came to me and agreed that an attack by infantry alone would be too expensive, although he thought he could carry it. The attack, therefore, was given up ; but I desired him to require the *written* opinion of these officers why they had changed their opinion. I got into my carriage and returned to Feroz-poor to expedite the bridge by which we were to pass the river.

" In conversation with Major Abbott of the En-

gineers, I told him what had passed, and he and I
both agreed that the heavy ordnance could in open
battery remain at a distance out of shot of field guns,
and yet fire into the enemy's camp. I wrote to Gough
recommending him to assemble the officers of these
professional departments, and stated what I had explained in 'a letter which I sent by Major Abbott.
This letter was read to the officers. They *again*
changed their opinion, and agreed they would make
their thirty-six heavy guns very effective, and we
agreed to make the attack.

" The guns began at daylight. We could not see,
from the haziness of the morning, what was the effect
produced at 1200 yards, but we saw they all went
into the camp. *Only two* of our artillerymen were
even wounded.

" We moved the infantry column forward. It got
in, and, not being strong enough to fight against 35,000
men, who turned their light guns upon them, our right
of the attacking column was driven out after they had
got in. The second divisions of Gilbert and Smith
were ordered simultaneously to assault the works in
front. *They were both repulsed.* But the attacking
column, that is, the right of that division, animated by
the advance of one division in the first instance, returned into the entrenchments and took the enemy's
batteries in reverse, whilst the two divisions again
attacked and got in. Then the slaughter of the Sikhs
in crossing the ford was very great.

" But we always expected that our left, when it
got in, would be greatly exposed to the enemy's
heavy guns 600 yards on the other side of the river,

having a plunging fire into their own camp. Our astonishment was great that they did not fire, for we felt it was the worst part of the affair we had in hand.

" Subsequently the Sikh General, and Colonel Mouten, a French officer, explained that, when the bombardment was going on, the Sikhs in the camp were so discouraged, our artillery having dismounted some of their guns and killed their men, whilst it was evident their shot could not and did not reach us, that they sent to their batteries on the other side and took away all their artillerymen to reinforce the camp batteries, took up two of the boats of the bridge, and told their men there was no retreat.

" By this piece of good fortune we suffered a less severe loss than we otherwise should have done ; and in confidence I will say that, if the thirty-six heavy guns had not been brought to bear, we should have been repulsed, for they did much execution and produced the effect of causing their heavy batteries to be of no avail. Our captains of troops and batteries are good."

Sir Howard exerted himself to obtain a better position for the army surgeons, and brought their claims before the House, representing the devotion he had seen them exhibit, and the dangers they incurred in the field. His efforts opened to them the honours of the Bath, from which they had been excluded, and they determined to show their gratitude to him by a testimonial. A Committee was formed, and started a subscription which reached a large sum, but the project came to his knowledge, and he begged that it might be dropped.   The promoters reluctantly yielded, and confined the movement to an address, which he received with pride and emotion, valuing it more than gifts—so highminded was he in every relation.

CHAPTER XXXVIII.

On the Retired List.

Sir Howard retired from Parliament in 1847, when he was in his seventy-second year, and ceased to engage in political affairs. But his public spirit was undiminished, and showed itself in his readiness to aid the Government on military questions, whenever they arose, hardly a commission being formed without his counsel. The Duke of Wellington treated his opinion with great respect, and almost his last speech in the House of Lords upheld him on an artillery question, declaring that he "quite agreed with his gallant friend Sir Howard Douglas." One incident of their intercourse reached the author and may be mentioned here. Sir Howard had observed the decline in military education, and addressed a report on the subject to the Duke, who made no reply for nearly a year, and he began to think that the report had been laid aside and forgotten, when it came back to him, with a letter from the Duke, stating that he had read it through, and calling attention to his notes in the margin. The report affirmed that the outbreak of war would find us with a deficiency of trained officers, and this occurred as he foresaw, which led Lord Panmure to despatch a commission to the military schools of France, Austria, and Prussia, to ascertain their modes of administration, with a view to introducing an efficient system in

England. But the labours of the commission might
have been spared, for it only discovered that the con-
tinental schools were founded on regulations we had
rescinded and which had been established by Sir
Howard at Sandhurst forty years before. He attended
the funeral of the Duke in 1852, and took a deep
interest in Wellington College, the memorial erected
to him by the national subscription originated by
the Hon. Colonel Talbot. He also supported the
Cambridge Asylum, of which he became President,
and other charities and institutions.

He employed his leisure in watching the development of artillery, mastering the bearings of steam,
and making experiments in mechanics. The result
appeared in new editions of his ' Naval Gunnery,'
issued in 1850 and 1855, and in a work on 'Naval
Warfare with Steam.' The fourth edition of 'Naval
Gunnery' afforded him an opening for remarks on the
Russian war, reviewing the naval movements in the
Baltic and Black Seas, as well as the operations on
shore. He had been consulted by Lord Aberdeen
about the expedition to the Crimea, and stated his
opinion that the season was too advanced for such an
enterprise, and the army too unprovided, whence it
could not be attempted without disaster. He ex
pressed the same views to Lord Derby, Lord Lans-
downe, and other statesmen both of the Conservative
and Liberal parties. He dwelt on the great importance of equipment in war ; and it is curious to find
Lord Fitzroy Somerset writing to him on this subject ten years before, and foreseeing the expense that
will arise, but not that equipment will be considered
unnecessary. " This country is not easy to move in

matters of expense, whatever party may hold the reins
of Government," Lord Fitzroy observes, dating the
letter in 1844 on November 5, the day on which we
commemorate the battle of Inkerman; " and this it
is that renders our outlay so enormous on the first
breaking out of a war." The force which landed in the
Crimea wanted all the requisites for service, being only
a moveable column; and Sir Howard asserts that " all
the establishments which are indispensable to enable
an army to take the field had to be restored and
reorganised." He described the siege of Sebastopol as
" a desperate and dangerous operation," and considered
that " the most advantageous point of attack was the
north side; there the ground is most elevated, and the
large octagonal work on its summit is the citadel and
the key of the place." It was objected to his view
that he did not know the place from personal observation, but this only shows his quickness of perception;
for Lord Raglan formed a similar impression, and
requested Marshal St. Arnaud to attack the fort on
reaching the Belbek from the Alma. The fort is
described as " taking in reverse all the water batteries
on that side," in a report by Major-General Macintosh,
drawn up on the outbreak of the war, and transmitted
to the authorities through Colonel Airey, the Military
Secretary;[1] and the General adds that " it is not a
strong work, and that its capture would be the most
effectual preliminary to an attack on the town and
harbour." This was the opinion of Lord Raglan, but

---

[1] 'United Service Magazine,' November, 1859. General Macintosh's
' Military Tour' (London, 1854) points out that " Fort Severnaya, or
Constantine, is an important point, but not strong, and ought to be cap-
tured as a preliminary step in attacking Sevastopol."

the fort stood in front of the French, and the usages
of war vested them with the attack.   The enemy had
given the work an air of strength by fronting the
northern scarp with a thin wall,[1] such as the Duke of
Wellington describes to Sir Howard in his letter (p. 233
ante), but which Marshal St. Arnaud appears to have
taken for a revetment,[2] for he refused to countenance
the operation, declaring that it required heavy guns.
Lord Raglan had seen the Duke of Wellington reduce
fortresses in the Peninsula with 12-pounders, and believed the place might be carried by a rush, but the
Marshal's obstinacy closed the way, and he resorted to
his celebrated flank march to the south side, as "a
matter of necessity"—in Sir Howard's opinion.   But
he did not know how far his views were shared by
Lord Raglan; and the facts are now published for
the first time.   His review pointed out the difficulties
opened on the south side, and they were fully estimated by Lord Raglan, who knew that he had nothing
to depend upon but a dash.   He proposed an immediate attack—the very course he has been censured
for not adopting; and it is now established that both
the Severnaya and the Malakoff must have fallen if
his views had been adopted.[3]

Sir Howard sustained a great affliction in 1854
in the death of a grandson bearing his name.   It
would seem there was to be but one Howard in the
family, for he had lost a son of the name in 1820,
after a short service in the navy.   Death had since

---

[1] 'A Voice Within Sevastopol.'

[2] A revetment is never less than three feet thick at the top, and ten feet
at the base.

[3] It may be right to state that Sir John Burgoyne was not in favour of
a *coup de main*, as the author learnt from his own lips the morning after
his return from the Crimea.

carried off his eldest son, Colonel Charles Douglas, his
second son, Captain James Douglas, his daughter
Sarah Mary Harcourt, and his daughter Mary, wife of
Captain Murray Gartshore.

Mrs. Gartshore has left an impression in many
a circle, where she is remembered as uniting her
father's genius with her mother's beauty, and these
with their winning qualities. Her form was so faultless that she was called an animated statue; and her
gifts so varied that she was both a composer and musi-
cian, a novellist and poet. Nor did Sir Howard feel
less pride in his son James, who promised to be one of
those men who shed such lustre on our rule in India,
but fell in action in the midst of his career. We
gather his history from a tablet erected by his brother
officers in the church of Meerut, and which may aid
us to imagine how his father felt the blow :—

Sacred

To the memory of

JAMES DUNDAS DOUGLAS,

Late Captain in the 53rd Regiment Native Infantry,
Assistant Adjutant-General
In Afghanistan,
And a few days prior to his decease,
In appreciation of his high talents and services
In that country,
Appointed Deputy Military Secretary
To Government,
Who was killed in action near Pesh Bolak
On the 25th February, 1841, aged 41.
An adequate tribute
To the merits of this amiable and talented officer
It would be vain attempting
To express within the limits of this Tablet,
Which is erected
As an earnest though simple token
Of the undying attachment of Friends
By whom his memory is deeply revered.

A bereavement of more than sons and daughters overtook Sir Howard in 1856, when he was plunged in grief by the death of Lady Douglas, the mother of his children and the companion of fifty-seven years. The shock prostrated him for a time, but his brave spirit rallied, and showed its sorrow in a manner indicative of his character, and blending fortitude with pathos, for he took her room as his study, and always kept her portrait on the table. She had expressed a wish to lie near her daughter, Mrs. Gartshore ; and her remains were conveyed to Boldre, near Lymington, where that lady was interred. Boldre thus became the family burialplace, and we shall see others follow to that last bourne.

Mr. Gladstone wished to be informed of the military value of Corfu, on his appointment to a mission to the Ionian Islands in 1858 ; and Government referred the question to Sir Howard. He made a report on the subject to the Minister for War, opposing the surrender of the Protectorate, but this was under a different posture of affairs. The following letter implies that he was consulted about it by the present Government in 1861, and replied by mentioning his report. The glance thrown at the Turkish succession gives the letter interest :—

"MY DEAR SIR HOWARD,   "Wilton, Salisbury,
                                        4th April, 1861.

"I believe that the question with the Ionian Islands is not one of good or bad government, but of nationality; and, if Greece had been decently governed, it would by this time have been powerful enough (at the expense of its Turkish neighbour) to take over and hold the islands, of which the Protectorate was forced upon us.

" I will look up the document you allude to when I return to town, and will communicate it to my colleague.

"Pray believe me yours sincerely,

"S. HERBERT."

The year 1858 brought forth ' Naval Warfare with Steam,' which aimed to introduce a system of tactics applicable to the conditions arising from the use of steam by ships of war.   It was easy to see that these must be different from the old evolutions, and opened dangers to our supremacy, but no one attempted to grapple the subject and frame a principle of action. This is what Sir Howard wished to indicate, and he followed his purpose with his usual persistance, furnishing a programme of manœuvres adapted to every conjuncture.[1]   He lays down the doctrine that naval actions with steam must be conducted with as much strategy as battles on shore, since fleets will no longer be subject to atmospheric conditions, but be moveable at will; and the time may not be distant when their commanders may again be styled "Generals at Sea." The publication is too professional to be dwelt upon

[1] The work is thus described by Commander Ward, of the United States Navy :—" So recent is the introduction of steam into the navies of the world, that no maritime battle and but little experience of any kind is afforded from which to draw examples and illustrations ; but the language has been graced and naval science enriched by Sir Howard Douglas in this work, to which the reader is referred as to a mine of professional knowledge. As a landsman, Sir Howard treats subjects which especially appertain to the sea with remarkable clearness and accuracy."—*Manual of Naval Tactics.*

here, except to say that it announced an improvement in the screw propeller, which he had successfully worked out, though now in his eighty-second year. The defect of the screw is its excessive vibration, caused by the revulsion of the water in its frame, and involving a loss of speed and lapse of steerage way, which amounts to a deflection of two and a half points. Sir Howard considered whether the shake might not be lessened, so as to add to the power and reduce the deflection; and he thought the object might be attained by a curvature, cutting off the leading corners. He made experiments with a curved blade, and found that the vibration had greatly diminished; while the screw obtained power in the same ratio, the speed being increased, and the steerage corrected. At the same time he provided against fouling, by forming the edges of the blade of hard metal, which would cut through any rope or spar coming in their way, though such a hitch seemed impossible, as two knife-blades projected from the trunk surrounding the screw, and severed every obstacle in front. He entered a specification at the Patent Office, to secure the credit of the invention, and then threw it open to the world, publishing this licence in 'Naval Warfare with Steam,' with a full description of the improvement.

Its merit was first tested by the Admiralty, and Sir Howard heard of the experiments with satisfaction, particularly as they had been intrusted to a competent officer, Captain Gordon, of Her Majesty's ship 'Doris.' But he thought it strange that he had received no intimation that his invention was under trial, and the silence of the Admiralty surprised him the more, when rumour announced it a success. He thought it right to ascertain what had been done, and wrote to the Admiral Superintendent at Portsmouth for information, which he obtained in the following note from Captain Gordon :—

"Dear Admiral Bowles,

"H.M.S. 'Asia,'
23rd June, 1859.

"I cannot return Sir Howard Douglas's note without remarking how very gratifying it must be to that talented officer to observe how *correct* his views were as to the necessity of removing the leading corners of the screw propellers, by which the steerage of the ship is much improved, and the vibration diminished.

"Believe me yours faithfully,

"G. J. Gordon."

Sir Howard now complained to the Admiralty of the treatment he had received, and was informed that he had no claim to the invention, as it had been brought to light by the experiments of the 'Fairy' in 1853, though never utilized. The Admiralty thus affirmed that it had fitted vessel on vessel with defective screws, while able to provide superior ones, and treated a great improvement as non-existent. But this position they found untenable when they were put to the proof, and an article in the *Times* asked, "How can any inventor look for success at the Admiralty when even Sir Howard Douglas, with all his claims upon the consideration of the authorities, cannot get them to acknowledge gracefully that the

improvement they get for nothing is an important
one, and is his?"   A new claimant was put forward
in Mr. Griffiths, who had introduced an improved
propeller, adopted by the Admiralty, and which he
declared embodied the discovery.   It was a sufficient refutation of this assertion that Sir Howard
had applied to the three principal engineers of the
kingdom for their opinion of his invention, and they
all gave an unfavourable verdict, but made no reference to the Griffiths propeller, which was fabricated
at their works, so that any resemblance must have
struck them directly.   Indeed, the principle of the
two constructions was entirely different.   Mr. Griffiths'
specification runs thus :—" I claim the making of
propeller-blades narrower or tapered towards their
outside extremities, in contradistinction to the form
hitherto adopted of increasing the width of that part
of the blade."   Sir Howard's specification retains the
" form hitherto adopted," which Mr. Griffiths abandons,
and cuts off the leading corners.   But it must here
speak for itself :—" My invention of improvements in
screw propellers consists, first, in a modification of the
form of the blades, so that the advance or leading
edges of the propeller-blades shall receive less shock
in cutting through the water, and therefore produce a
more equable action of the propeller, which will result
in less tremulous motion in the stern of the ship when
under weigh, and also steady and equalise the propelling force.   For this purpose I form the advance
edge of the propeller-blades of a convex curved form,
in such manner that the curve of this edge of the
blade at the extreme end or periphery will be in the
rear (as regards its position in the screw) of the inner

2 E

termination of the curve or that next the centre; the curve is such that it produces an easy cleaving action in the water. By this form of the advance edges of the blades a further advantage results, which is this, that any spars, rope, or wreck with which the screw blades may come in contact are thrown off in a radial direction, or have a tendency to be so acted on; the propeller therefore assists to clear or effectually clears itself from any wreck or material with which it is liable to come in contact. By forming the advance edges as described, as they enter and leave the opening in the dead wood of the ship, the transition is gradual, and therefore will not induce shakes or tremulous motion, so perceptible in all vessels propelled by screws by reason of the right line edges thereof striking the disturbed water throughout their whole length, and the violent reactions of such water in propelling, the water in the dead wood being in a comparatively quiescent state and inoperative as regards propulsion. I also form these advance edges of the blades of screw propellers of steel or other suitable metal so sharpened or serrated like a saw that they will sever any unyielding obstacle with which they may come in contact in the manner of a circular saw."

Mr. Griffiths' letter to the *Times* determined Sir Howard to vindicate his claim, and he took counsel of his friend Lord Lyndhurst, who recommended him to submit the facts to Mr. Carpmael, of Southampton Buildings, and he obtained from that authority the following opinion :—

" I have very carefully examined into the claim made by General Sir Howard Douglas, in regard to his being the first to devise the screw propeller-blade of the particular form shown and described at page 61 of his work on 'Naval Warfare with Steam.' This propeller-blade consists in a modification of the Admiralty screw propeller, each blade of which was formerly made of about one-sixth of a helix or complete screw, with the forward or leading edge, and also the after edge, perpendicular to the shaft; consequently such a blade increased in width the further it proceeded from the axis, and was widest at its outermost edge or periphery.

"Sir Howard Douglas, as I understand his claim, alters this propeller-blade in respect to its leading or forward edge only, and he does so by removing parts of such forward edge, so that, in place of its being a straight line, he makes it into a convex curved line, and he leaves the after edge of the blade as heretofore.

"If the above be the correct expression of Sir Howard Douglas's claim, I am clearly of opinion that he was the first to devise and publish that particular form of screw propeller; and I am further of opinion that, whatever be the advantages which may arise from the use of that propeller-blade, to Sir Howard Douglas will be due the merit of having originated it.

"I am intimately acquainted with Mr. Griffiths' screw propeller-blades, and I can only imagine that that gentleman, when he wrote the letter to the *Times* newspaper on the 30th August last, was uninformed of the precise nature of Sir Howard Douglas's claim, or he would not have fallen into the error of supposing that Sir Howard Douglas claimed his (Mr. Griffiths') previous invention. It is of the

2 E 2

essence of Mr. Griffiths' invention, and of his patent, that screw propeller-blades should become '*narrower or tapered towards their outside extremities, in contra-distinction to the form hitherto adopted of increasing the width of that part of the blade.*' Now, Sir Howard Douglas's propeller-blade does go on increasing in width as it proceeds outwards from the axis, and it is widest at the periphery, consequently his blade is the reverse of that invented by Mr. Griffiths.

"I would further state that the giving a convex curved form to the forward or leading edge of a screw propeller was not new either to Sir Howard Douglas or to Mr. Griffiths, Lowe and others having used and published descriptions of screw propeller-blades with curved forward or leading edges; but these propellers differed in other respects both from those of Mr. Griffiths and also from those of Sir Howard Douglas.

"WILLIAM CARPMAEL.

"24, *Southampton Buildings, 27th September,* 1859."

This opinion satisfied Sir Howard, and he communicated it to Mr. Griffiths, who could not impeach its fairness. Indeed, he admitted that he had "nothing to complain of in Mr. Carpmael's opinion," [1] but maintained that he was acquainted with the advantages of the curved blade years before, though he had not made it available. Such assertions carry no weight, and Sir Howard has established the right of any one to use his propeller without interference from Mr. Griffiths. "You may with the most perfect propriety

[1] Letter from Mr. Griffiths to Sir Howard Douglas, in the 'Douglas Papers.'

go on making and maintaining your claim to the particular form of screw propeller as if you had received no letter from Mr. Griffiths," writes Mr. Carpmael to Sir Howard, in reference to this letter. "He cannot take any proceedings at law against you for so doing." Yet the nation continues to pay a royalty for Mr. Griffiths' propeller, when it has here a better one without charge.[1]

[1] Messrs. Maudslay altered their opinion of the Douglas principle on witnessing the trials of the 'Ariadne,' the results of which they communicated to Sir Howard. These showed an increase of speed in his form of blade, though not to a great extent, but were decisive in the correction of the vibration which causes the deflection in steerage, and is such a strain on the ship :—" The 'Ariadne' having been originally built for engines of greater power, the screw aperture was one foot larger fore and aft than in any of the other vessels fitted with engines of the same power, which was much in favour of less agitation, and the stern was not nearly so much shaken by the action of the propeller as in other vessels ; and to this we may add that on the last trial, *when the forward corners were cut off, it was agreed by all that it was still more reduced;* in fact, that THERE WAS NO AGITATION PERCEPTIBLE. We have the honour to be, &c., MAUDSLAY, SONS, and FIELD."

CHAPTER XXXIX.

Pronounces against Armour Ships.

THE great interest Sir Howard took in naval gunnery led him to consider whether ships might increase their means of defence, as well as their powers of attack ; and he was prepared to decide the question when Sir Robert Peel consulted him as to the expediency of building iron vessels of war in 1848. He declared that iron ships would not be invulnerable, and recommended Government to forego the pursuit of an impossibility, and turn its attention to the development of artillery, which might be carried to an indefinite extent, and given irresistible penetration. His arguments prevailed, and the notion was dropped for a time, but revived as a movement when the Emperor Napoleon launched the 'Gloire,' the public being brought to believe that squadrons could be as effectively protected by armour as the knights of old, who fought battle after battle without drawing blood. Sir Howard showed the fallacy of this view, but conceded that we must take up the armour to the same extent as the French. " Although we would not have initiated such a system," he observes, "yet so long as our neighbours the French persist in building iron-cased ships, we *must* do so likewise, and *that* in a manner to keep well ahead of anything the French or any other power may do for aggressive purposes. I think, therefore, the country is much indebted to Sir

John Pakington for having had the moral courage and
the administrative enterprise to effect these objects,
and *that* on a scale adequate to satisfy all the require-
ments which such vessels demand, and which cannot
be attained by vessels of the displacement of the
' Gloire.' [1]

But he pointed out that we must not consider iron
ships the same thing as iron-cased ships; for the latter
are " less vulnerable by being so protected than ships
that are not so covered," though " they are not invulnerable to the penetrations and impacts of heavy
solid shot," and iron ships are still less so.   Sir John
Pakington differed from him on this point.   " I quite
agree with you that ships formed of iron and iron-
sided ships are very different questions," he writes on
the 28th of February.   " I confess my own present
impression to be that ships formed of iron will make
the *best* ironsided ships, but this is a question open to
much discussion."   The discussion was settled by the
demolition of Mr. Scott Russell's iron target by the
Armstrong 300-pounder, while the shot of the same
gun stuck in the wood backing of the target representing the ' Warrior.'   Sir Howard forecast the result
exactly as it happened, though he did not live to see
it.   " I consider the ' Warrior ' and the other vessels
now being built of timber combined with iron to
belong to the category of iron-cased ships; for
although the only timber used in the formation of the
' Warrior ' consists of two layers of wood, 8 and 10
inches thick respectively, placed behind the plates, yet
it must be observed that, *but for the timber* by which
the plates are backed up, *the side of the ship would not*

[1] 'Observations by Sir Howard Douglas, read before the Institute of
Naval Architects, Feb. 28, 1861.'

be shot-proof." [1] He repeats the opinion in another
paragraph. "In reply, therefore, to the question which
forms the title of Mr. Scott Russell's pamphlet—'Iron
or Wood? of which shall our Fleets be formed?'—
*I confidently reply, Of neither singly, but by a combination
of both* to constitute that new description of vessel for
special purposes in which the French have taken the
lead, but which lead we must take out of their hands
by constructing iron-cased ships, which like theirs
should be formed of timber, that is, on wooden bottoms
having iron-cased sides; the number and strength of
these vessels to be extended according as the circumstances of the case and the perfect security of the
country may demand." [2]

He thus foretold the degree of impenetrability that
would pertain to iron-cased ships, and gave a qualified
assent to their construction—not as being on a right
principle, but because they were a necessity, required
for "special purposes." He considered that there was
no worse material for ships' hulls than iron, except
steel; and his observations trace its weakness to every
point. "The bottom of a well-built copper-bottomed
timber ship scarcely ever wears out," he tells us, "but
will at least wear out three tops. In iron ships it is
the reverse. One top will wear out three bottoms."
The dockyard authorities have just reached the same
discovery. The 'Defence' was found to have made
her bottom as foul in a short cruise, as that of a timber
vessel from the coast of Africa after five years' service.
It was coated with rushes three feet long, jammed in
a layer of mollusks. A few weeks converted the
bottom of the 'Resistance' into a geological formation,
the mollusks hanging in accretions as large as a

---

[1] 'Observations before the Institute of Naval Architects,' &c.   [2] Ibid.

child's head, and the grass adhering so tenaciously that it carried away the grain of the iron when chipped off by adzes.

It is contended that the American civil war has decided the question between wood and iron, by proving the superiority of the latter; but the facts point the other way, for all the successes have fallén to wood. Wooden gunboats forced the obstructions at New Orleans and captured the city; and the Federal wooden flotilla remained half an hour under the Confederate batteries, while clearing the obstructions of the Mississippi, and afterwards destroyed the Confederate flotilla of iron-clads. On the other hand, the vaunted 'Monitor' and her consorts were unable to pass Fort Darling on the James River, and have not achieved a single triumph. Much has been made of the onslaught of the 'Merrimac' on the 'Congress' and 'Cumberland,' as if it had been undreamt of, and settled wood for ever. But Sir Howard proposed an experiment imaging what happened. "Steam-ram ships, as proposed by Admiral Sartorius, endowed with great power of speed," he says, "would undoubtedly be of great use in preventing a landing." And he adds that he "would, therefore, submit that this project should be tried on a real service scale— by running a floating battery, well strengthened at the bow, and covered with iron, direct at the broadside of a line-of-battle hulk, brought down to her load water-line by being sufficiently loaded."[1] Here we see the line-of-battle hulk placed in the very position of the 'Congress' and 'Cumberland,' when the 'Merrimac' ran on; while the 'Merrimac' was a

---

[1] 'The Defence of England,' by Sir Howard Douglas, in his work on Fortification, 1859.

floating battery, "covered with iron and well strengthened at the bow," on the principle laid down by Sir Howard. He commanded more attention in America than his own country, and the Confederates put his suggestion to practical use.

The 'Monitor' claimed the merit of driving off the 'Merrimac,' but it afterwards transpired that the shock of collision had dislocated her machinery, and that her withdrawal was owing to this cause, not the fire of the 'Monitor.' Sir Howard states that he "has great misgivings as to the destructive effects which so enormous a shock as running butt at a large ship would produce upon the ram. Exclusive of the effects that such collision might produce upon the ram-ship, by the fouling of the screw amongst the floating wreck of the vessel so run into, there remains one important, and perhaps vital evil, which has not hitherto been considered. It is, that the vis-viva of an engine weighing, with its appurtenances, 800 or 1000 tons—carried forward in a ship moving at the rate of, it is said, fourteen or fifteen knots per hour—being sudddenly arrested by the stoppage of the ram when the collision takes place, would cause a shock so enormous that, in the recoil, any ordinary fastenings by which the engine is attached to the ship must be torn asunder, and the whole of the internal machinery dislocated." Sir George Sartorius affirms that derangement might be prevented by solidity of construction ; and the author will not presume to throw a doubt on this assertion, coming from such an authority. The ram principle has proved a success to a certain extent, and Sir George Sartorius must be credited with its revival, but it has not overstepped the limit assigned to it by Sir Howard, who tells us that rams "should not attempt to charge line-of-battle ships, but should, as they might, charge through, and overrun, one after another, any number of comparatively light transports, each having, perhaps, 1500 or 2000 troops on board, and a considerable number of these very formidable monsters should be provided accordingly." [1]   Such results are more important than running down line-of-battle ships, and Sir George Sartorius has rendered a great service to the country in furnishing it with this means of defence.

The 'Monitor' did not come out of the contest unscathed, and it is difficult to see how she proves the case of iron against wood.   The 'Merrimac' fired but two or three shot—we know not of what weight nor with what charges, but one split a block of iron 9¼ inches thick at the foot of the 'Monitor's' turret, another dinted her side, and one that struck the turret blinded her captain, while the concussion knocked down her engineer and another man inside, whence they were carried below insensible.   Blood dropped from the eyes and nostrils of the crew as they fought their guns; and the disabled and sinking 'Merrimac' was allowed to retire, without an attempt at pursuit. Neither 'Merrimac' nor 'Monitor' ever renewed the battle, though they had frequent opportunities; the 'Merrimac' was ultimately destroyed to save her from capture, and 'Merrimac No. 2' was settled by the wooden gunboat 'Echo,' which sent a shot through her iron sides, and left her to be blown up.   The 'Monitor' has since foundered at sea, while in tow of the 'Rhode Island,' and realised one of the casualties foreseen by Sir Howard, and which he based on the facts that "timber, when immersed in water, loses as

---

[1] 'The Defence of England,' &c.

much of its weight as is equal to that of the water dis-
placed by it, and it floats. But the excess of the
weight of a cubic foot of iron over an equal volume of
salt water is 6180 oz., and with this force it sinks."
And he instances the case of the iron ship 'Connaught,'
which "sprung a leak, and sank in deep water, the
origin of the leak being therefore unattainable with
certainty." [*Postscript*, foot-note in pp. 6, 7.]

It may be urged that experience has not led the
Americans to relinquish ironclads, but we must remember that the press there is in the pay of con-
tractors, and this persistence will be explained. Nor
should it be forgotten that their naval operations
have been restricted to the sphere which Sir Howard
appropriated to ironclads—namely, service in still
water,—and that the sea value of ironsides has yet to
be tested. Or does not the coast voyage of the 'Monitor' set the question at rest?

Sir Howard foresaw that ironsides would possess
two qualities fatal to sea-going men-of-war—difficulty of
rising to the water, and excessive rolling. The bows
of the 'Warrior' are not iron-clad, and she might be
expected to show no want of buoyancy, but the weight
of her sides throws a strain for'ard, and she is found
to labour heavily in a rough sea. It is curious that
her crew describe her as an "awful roller"—using
the very words by which Sir Howard prefigured her
character; and her behaviour is a poor augury for the
ships with iron-clad bows which we are constructing
in such a hurry. She is said to have attained a speed
of thirteen and fourteen knots under full steam, but
the 'Defence' has never exceeded eleven, and requires
eight minutes to perform a circle. Speed is an important quality in a man-of-war, but a more essential

one is handiness, and steadiness is equally valuable.
" The roll of a ship," says Sir Howard, " is a matter
of the very greatest importance in naval gunnery, and
I have made it the subject of elaborate consideration
under all the circumstances of the case, namely, the
lee roll or the weather roll, whether to fire with the
rising motion or the falling motion of the side, whether
to fire when the ship is on the top of the wave, or the
trough of the sea; the gunner considers the roll of
the ship, so far as it effects gunnery, to be seriously or
' awfully' great when, irrespective of gunnery, it is
not immoderate.   There is no comparison to be made
between the roll of the ' Great Eastern,' carrying no
armament, with that of the ' Ariadne' under different
circumstances, but overweighted as all that class of
vessels is with heavy armament."

Official experiments have proved that a ship cannot
be rendered invulnerable by any armour that she can
carry, though it is alleged that this may be indefi-
nitely thickened by obtaining a larger displacement.
It is true that vessels may be built of the size of
the ' Great Eastern,' which might allow a six-inch
armour-coat, but the ' Great Eastern' has not inspired
confidence in magnitude, and there might be less
reason to admire ' Great Easterns' in armour.   The
experiments rather lead to Sir Howard's doctrine—
that our future fleets must look to the weight of their
ordnance, not of their armour.   The law now is that
ships cannot carry heavier guns than five tons, and
this is laid down as if it could not be altered.   Heavier
guns certainly present two difficulties—the topweight
they would throw on the deck, and the scope of their
recoil.   But the Americans have removed the latter

objection by firing a 410-pounder on board a gunboat, proving that it can be done with safety, and we have but to deal with the former. The author of this work projected a mode of transport which has received the approval of several distinguished naval officers, and it is given in a note below as not irrelevant here.[1] For a greater weight of ordnance is incompatible with iron-sided ships, and we must choose between armour and armament.

It is one of the favourite arguments for ironsides that they will keep out shells though they are vulnerable to shot, but the experiments at Shoeburyness have made this pretension doubtful. In point of fact, they are no longer shell-proof when they are penetrated by shot; for every such shot becomes a shell of the most destructive kind, scattering splinters of the iron in every direction, while it would only strike ahead in a wooden vessel. Sir Howard traced the

---

[1] The author's scheme proposes wooden frigates, of very solid construction, carrying four 48-pounders and two 400-pounders. The 48-pounders are to be on the orlop deck for ordinary service : the 400-pounders will be carried below on a turntable and platform, one gun for'ard and one aft ; but will be raised to the deck for service, the platform being ringed round six pillars of iron, one in each corner of the hatchway, and one midway on each side. It will be lifted to the deck by machinery worked from the engine-room. Beams of iron will then be slid from the deck, fore and aft, through the corner pillars into the centre pillars, where their lips will lock each other ; and two lipped beams of iron will be slid from *beneath* the deck on each side, and lock in the centre with a bolt through the platform, the bolt having a worm at the point for a nut. Thus the 400-pounder, carriage, and slide will rest on a bed as firm as the ship, and may be pointed to starboard or larboard, or over the bows or stern, by a whirl of the turntable, avoiding the derangement caused by pivots. The weight of the 400-pounder, carriage, slide, platform, and turntable, is estimated at 12 tons, which will be the weight of the 600-pounder constructing by Sir William Armstrong. There could be no difficulty in lifting and lowering this by a piston-apparatus, or even by a capstan, which easily raises a line-of-battle ship's anchor from the bottom of the sea, a weight of five tons, apart from the heavy cable.

effect in an experiment with a Whitworth 68-pounder against an iron and wood target, when the shot made a hole 13½ inches by 21 inches, "the shot and plate breaking up into very small pieces, spreading about the main deck to the extent of 22 feet, and making marks on the opposite side to the depth of half an inch, which sufficiently indicates the destructive effects that would be produced on the crew in real service."[1]   The shot from the Armstrong 300-pounder against the 'Warrior' target produced the same results on a larger scale.[2]   The experiments with the Whitworth 68-pounder caused the gun to burst.

Sir Howard's stand against the iron clamour exposed him to the taunts of Mr. Scott Russell[3] and other theorists, and drew down upon him an anonymous letter, warning him to "take care of what he was about."   Surely more consideration might have been shown to a veteran of eighty-five winters, devoting his last hours to the service of his country, and who had a better right to speak on this question than any of his assailants.   These men would do well to study the concluding paragraph of his observations to the Institute of Naval Architects.   "I will not follow Mr. Scott Russell in the plunge which he takes to dive into the future of the British navy; not from any dread on my part that the naval power of England can ever be destroyed by open force, single or coalesced, if right be done; but from the apprehension that a power which has withstood a world in arms, defeated maritime coalitions of the most formid-

---

[1] 'Naval Gunnery,' p. 400, fifth edition.
[2] Letter from Sir W. G. Armstrong to the *Times.*
[3] 'The Fleet of the Future.'

able description, and which formed the only obstacle that stood in the way between the ambition of Napoleon I. and universal conquest, might possibly thus be tampered with by a speculative philosophy, which would prescribe to our descendants the mode and means of warfare for a remote future, and even provide them with armour and armament. Britons will not degenerate; we should be thankful for the past, careful of the present, *and leave the future to our sons.*"

The following letter is written in a spirit akin to his own :—

"My dear Sir Howard,

"Wilton House, Salisbury,
12th October, 1860.

"I am an old friend of the editor of the *Saturday Review*, and read the articles you mention with great interest, without, however, having an idea as to their author. I thought many of the suggestions they contained were admirable. But I do not think we are yet in a position to judge of the success or failure of 'La Gloire' or any other iron-plated ships. Experience alone can prove which will be the most valuable in time of war, and in the mean time we must go on with our experiments, and earn success at the last, even through failures.

"Ever yours most truly,

"Sidney Herbert.

"I ought to have added that I think a full discussion and ventilation of the subject must do good."

CHAPTER XL.

Last Days.

Sir Howard published a new edition of his work on 'Fortification' in 1859, and brought it down to the present day, reviewing the new systems, and introducing a plan for the naval, military, and littoral defence of England. He again urged the formation of a Naval Reserve, and recommended a better organization of the militia and the erection of works for the protection of the arsenals and dockyards. The necessity of these measures had been seen by Lord Palmerston, and the two first were soon carried out, while a Commission was formed to report on the sites for fortifications. It included the most distinguished scientific officers in the country, and Government requested Sir Howard to become its President. His great age rendered this difficult, as the duty involved journeys round the country and examinations of localities in all weathers; and he requested to be excused if the public service permitted. The reply of the Minister for War assigned him a more important duty, but one not imposing personal exertion :—

"My dear Sir Howard,   "War Office.
                                    1st August, 1859.

"I returned to town this morning and found your letter.

2 F

"I find we have on hand other work which must be referred to some central authorities of experience and capacity to arrange and decide upon. This would not be confined to the one subject of fortifications, but would require an intimate knowledge of military topography and a general view of how the country could best be defended.

"It appears to me that if you would give your services to the Government in this matter they would be even more valuable than on the Fortifications Commission, where the subject is narrow and the range of knowledge required far less. You would not in this case be exposed to any risk to health by moving about and examining ground, nor, if you found yourself incapable of such exertion, would you have any misgiving as to the manner in which you were discharging the duties you had undertaken. Hoping that you will be able without risk or hesitation to accept this latter proposal, the details of which I will forward to you in a few days, I will act on your official letter as regards the Fortifications Commission.

"Believe me, my dear Sir Howard,

"Very sincerely yours,

"SIDNEY HERBERT."

No testimony is needed to Sir Howard's attainments, but nothing could more strongly mark them than the relations thus maintained with him by successive Governments, while his character stood so high that no one suspected him of blinking his principles. "You could not, I think, do otherwise than

accept the arduous duty which the Government seek
to impose upon you," writes Lord Derby.   " The proposition is equally honourable to you and creditable
to them ; and if an inquiry so extensive is to be insti-
tuted on a subject of such vital importance, I rejoice
that the country will have the advantage of having
it presided over by one so thoroughly conversant
with every branch of it.   I only hope the inevitable
labour attending it may not overtask your physical
strength." [1]

We see a kind warning here, but his strength was
to be tasked in harder measure, and by a trial not
to be averted.   He had gone to Folkestone with his
daughter Helen, his only companion since the death
of Lady Douglas, and they appeared to derive benefit
from the change, though Miss Douglas did not gain
strength.   But her spirits were good, and she accompanied him in his afternoon strolls, and one day seemed
so well that he left her to prolong her walk with her
friend Miss Ross, returning home alone.   She joined
him at dinner, and they spent the evening together,
when Miss Douglas retired quite cheerful.   They
were never to meet again, for she was found dead in
her bed in the morning.

Her maid alarmed the household, and one of the
servants ran for Mr. Bateman, the well-known sur-
geon of Folkestone, while the others gathered at Sir
Howard's door.   But there they felt the difficulty of
speaking, and came to a stand.   He was reading his
prayers at the moment, but heard them whispering,

[1] Letter from the Earl of Derby to Sir Howard Douglas, Nov. 27,
1859.

2 F 2

and went to the door; for it struck him that something had happened to Miss Douglas, as he afterwards told the author. Their looks confirmed his fears, and he instantly asked for his daughter. No one ventured to speak. "Is she dead?" he exclaimed. The truth could not be concealed, and he fell on the floor insensible.

But he shook off the weight, or rather rose beneath it, bearing it like a giant. He was now joined by Mr. Bateman, and they found Miss Douglas with her head reclining on her arm, her face wearing a placid expression, so that she might be thought to have died without pain, and this soothed her father. "No one can tell what a loss she is to me," he said to Mr. Bateman; "she has devoted herself to me. But I must do what is to be done. She will sleep beside her mother, where I shall soon join them." He went to his dressing-case, and took out a paper. "This is the address of the undertaker," he continued, "for I have thought of these things beforehand, and I had prepared everything in case of my own death. Perhaps you will kindly order him to come, and telegraph for my son Frederick."[1]

His wishes were attended to, and Mr. Bateman returned in the evening, and did not leave him till he retired. He was joined by his children as soon as they heard of their loss; and even they were surprised at his fortitude, often as they had seen it displayed. He watched the coffin to the hearse, and could hardly be dissuaded from attending the funeral, though now bordering on his eighty-fifth year. But he gave way,

---

[1] The Rev. W. F. Douglas, Rector of Scrayingham, near York.

and was satisfied with assembling the household, and
asking them to join him in prayer. They knelt down,
and Mr. Bateman writes that "he offered up an
extempore prayer, which touched the hearts of all by
its pathetic eloquence." The same spirit pervades the
following letter, which he addressed to the author of
this work on the occasion; and rarely have so many
emotions been expressed in so few words, or a character so mirrored by its own reflection.

"MY DEAR FULLOM,   "Folkestone, 15th October, 1859.

"I shall have a great deal to write to you about
in a few days, D.V. At present I reply to your kind
inquiries that I have been supported wonderfully by
the mercy of Almighty God through this sudden and
awful bereavement of the only remaining daughter,[1]
and the only child domesticated with me, and that I
begin to feel as if I should be spared to do for some
time my duty to th se that remain, and perhaps to be
useful to my country.

"I do not feel that my intellectual or mental
faculties are impaired nor my public spirit dead, and
even think it is increasing.

                    "Yours ever truly,

                        "HOWARD DOUGLAS."

These were not mere words; for "to do his duty
and be useful" had been the aim of his life, and was

---

[1] Sir Howard means "the only remaining daughter" under his roof.
This was afterwards shared by his surviving daughter, Mrs. Dawkins, who
was not living with him at the time.

now his consolation. The narrowing of his family ties threw him on his " public spirit," and this carried him 'through so much work that he thought it had " increased "—as if that could be ! But those who loved him saw the strain, and feared that it would prove too great.

Government now requested his advice as to the action they should take on the Fortification Report. " It is not yet signed, and still subject to correction," writes Mr. Sidney Herbert: "I send it therefore in the strictest confidence. You are so familiar with the subject that it will not take you a long time to come to an opinion on the principle of its various proposals. Your opinion will be most valuable to me and the Government, who have now immediately to decide what course they will take on this report."

The Minister was right in thinking that the task would " not take him a long time," for he received his opinion within three days, and Sir Howard learnt that it had been adopted by Government:—

" My dear Sir Howard,   "49, Belgrave Square,
                                        31st January, 1860.

" I am very much obliged to you for your Draft Observations on the Report of the Fortification Commission, which I have read with the greatest interest and attention. I do not think it can be in a better form than that in which it now stands, namely, a Confidential Minute on the Report; neither would I shorten in any way matter at once so pregnant and so

valuable.   I return the original as you wish, but
without in any way giving up my copyright.

"Pray believe me, with renewed thanks,

"Very sincerely yours,

"SIDNEY HERBERT."

The next letter has a sad interest, and seems to
come fitly here, though the date is a year later:—

"MY DEAR SIR HOWARD,   "Belgrave Square,
                               7th January, 1861.

"If anything could soften to me the pain of the
step I have been compelled to take, it would be the
warm expression of sympathy and regret which that
step has called forth from old and valued friends like
yourself.   It has been a terrible struggle to me; but
I had no alternative.   I have never recovered the last
session; and my doctor came to the conclusion that
the only chance for prolonging my life was to give up
my seat in the House of Commons: I can only hope
that I may thereby gain an increase of health and
strength to enable me the better to discharge the
duties of my office.

"Pray believe me, with renewed thanks for your
kind letter,

"Yours very sincerely,

"SIDNEY HERBERT."

Sir Howard presented a copy of the new edition
of 'Naval Gunnery' to His Royal Highness Prince
Alfred, through Her Majesty and the Prince Consort,

who set a high value on his productions. The volume was appropriately bound, and he wrote in it the following inscription, than which nothing could be more suitable :—

To His Royal Highness
PRINCE ALFRED,
Of H. M.'s Ship St. George,
One of the foremost hopes of future glory
To the Royal Navy,
This Volume
Is respectfully and affectionately presented
by
A Veteran of fourscore years and five,

Howard Douglas.

" Nil Claudiæ non proficient manus
Quas et benigno numine Jupiter
Defendit, et curæ sagaces
Expediunt per acuta belli."—*Horace.*

The motto may be thus rendered :—

[There is] nothing [which] the Claudian hosts will not accomplish,
Which both Jupiter with a favourable providence
Defends, and wise care
Brings through the perils of war.

Her Majesty and the Prince Consort looked at the volume with much interest, and gave orders that it should be forwarded to Prince Alfred by the first Admiralty bag.[1]   It reached His Royal Highness in a few weeks in the West Indies, and drew from him the annexed letter, which the author found put up by itself in Sir Howard's pocket-book.

[1] Letter from Major-General Grey to Sir Howard Douglas.

"H.M.S. 'St. George,' Port Royal,
6th April, 1861.

" Dear Sir Howard Douglas,

" Accept my best thanks for your kindness in
sending me a copy of your new work on ' Naval
Gunnery,' which I received by the mail to-day, and
which I shall study with much interest. Although I
have been only a short time in the navy, I have been
able to recognise how much it is indebted to you, and
I can wish you no greater satisfaction than that this
edition may have the same success as the first.

" I remain yours truly,

" Alfred."

Sir Howard enjoyed excellent health up to Miss
Douglas's death. All his teeth were sound; he walked
three or four miles a day, and obtained eight hours'
sleep at night. But that event gave his system a shock,
and the controversy about armour-ships wore it more,
showing his friends a marked change. His sleep was
less regular and composed, and he frequently recited
the lines of our great poet :—

> " O sleep, O gentle sleep,
> Nature's soft nurse, how have I frighted thee,
> That thou no more wilt weigh my eyelids down,
> And steep my senses in forgetfulness ?
> Wilt thou, upon the high and giddy mast,
> Seal up the shipboy's eyes, and rock his brains .
> In cradle of the rude imperious surge,
> And in the visitation of the winds,
> Who take the ruffian billows by the top,
> Curling their monstrous heads and hanging them
> With deaf'ning clamours in the slippery clouds,
> That, with the hurly, death itself awakes ? "

But he hid his sorrows, appearing calm and cheerful, though his manner was subdued, and his conversation less animated. His vivacity revived at times, particularly when he spoke of Scotland, the theme he liked best, or when he recalled his early life in America, and described the pathless forests, the villages of wigwams, or the falls of Niagara, reciting the lines of Thomson :—

> " Smooth to the shelving brink a copious flood
> Rolls fair and placid ; where collected all
> In one impetuous torrent, down the steep
> It thundering shoots, and shakes the country round.
> At first, an azure sheet, it rushes broad ;
> Then whitening by degrees, as from it falls,
> And from the loud-resounding rocks below
> Dash'd in a cloud of foam, it sends aloft
> A hoary mist, and forms a ceaseless shower.
> Nor can the tortured wave here find repose,
> But, raging still amid the shaggy rocks,
> Now flashes o'er the scatter'd fragments, now
> Aslant the hollow channel rapid darts ;
> And, falling fast from gradual slope to slope,
> With wild infracted course, and lessen'd roar,
> It gains a safer bed, and steals, at last,
> Along the mazes of the quiet vale."

He derived little benefit from the Folkestone breezes on his last visit, though enjoying his walks on the promenade, which he pronounced the noblest platform in Europe. Its attractions were just to his taste, for he could here see the coast of France, against which he had raised such bulwarks,—watch the yachts and shipping in the harbour and channel,—and glance round at the military strollers. Shorncliffe camp was within reach, as well as the Musketry School at Hythe, in which he took great interest, highly appreciating General Hay. He supported the Volunteer movement, and aided in its organization, addressing a letter of advice to the National Rifle Association through his friend General Hay, and receiving an acknowledgment in his election as an honorary member.   " I have most carefully considered the contents of your valuable letter," writes General Hay, " and am proud to feel that my views in regard to the training of the Volunteers have always harmonized with those expressed by you."   So well did he keep abreast with the age.

He showed the same interest in the movements at the camp, and attended any display, though not always to commend.   He particularly censured a sham fight, representing an attack on an enemy who had landed in the bay near Hythe.   The troops were marched down, and skirmishers thrown out on the beach, when the whole body fell back on the heights, holding them to cover their retreat.   " What an absurd proceeding ! " remarked Sir Howard to Mr. Bateman, who was by his side.   " The movement ought to have been exactly reversed.   They should have brought down every man and gun as quickly as possible, if the enemy had landed, and attacked him and driven him into the sea.   There would be some sense in that."

Sir Howard looked a soldier to the last, retaining his erect bearing, and walking with a firm step, though cautiously, and with looks bent on the ground. His sight had begun to fail, and cataracts were forming on both his eyes, but he did not submit them to medical treatment.   " They will last my time," he remarked to the author.   He contrived to write by never raising his pen, forming the letters by habit, and all were plain to one acquainted with his hand.

A career of three score years and ten seems to have left his character much what it first appeared, with all its elements of dash, vigour, enterprise, aptitude, and perception, its habits of industry, its generous instincts, and its warm sympathies. Neither heart nor mind showed the wear of life, and he is the same at eighty-five as seventeen, inspiring the Volunteers at Hythe as he inspired them at Tynemouth, and exercising the inventive genius which scared the rats in improving the screw propeller. The hand that caught up the child in the shipwreck obeyed the same impulse still, and Mr. Bateman saw him walking up the street at Folkestone with a loaded basket, which he had taken from a poor little girl. "My dear, give that to me," he said, as he saw her bending under the weight; "I am better able to carry it than you." The words were reported by a lady, who heard them in passing, as the General of eighty-five and the poor child of five walked away together.

One of his most marked qualities was courage, for he shrank from nothing. An instance of this was witnessed by two of his sons. They were fishing in the Farnham mill-stream, when they heard an outcry, and saw a man pursuing the miller, while his wife screamed for help. The miller escaped, and the man went back and stood watching the house. "What is the matter?" asked Sir Howard of the woman, who remained terror-struck at the door. "That man is a lunatic, sir," she replied, "and has got a carving-knife, with which he has sworn to kill my husband." He went up to the man, who kept his hand in his breast, holding the knife. "Give me that knife," he said sternly. The man drew it out, grasped the blade, and presented him the handle. Sir Howard threw it to the woman, and remained by the poor fellow till he was secured.

Another of his prominent traits was benevolence, which in him became a principle, not confining itself to persons, but seeking to benefit communities. His correspondence shows that he was always exerting his interest for some one—usually people who had no other friend ; and the author has entered his room as these applicants withdrew, yet never heard their errand, though possessing his unlimited confidence. But what were such acts compared with the good he effected in office, by the influence of his position and the exercise of his talents ! There are many careers more dazzling, but few have been more useful.

Nothing attests his worth more than his friendships, which were formed for life. General Forbes was as much his friend at eighty-five as when he dragged him out of the sea in the shipwreck, and now mourns his loss. " I rejoice to find that you are writing the Life of my lamented friend Sir Howard Douglas," writes Sir Frederic Smith to the author. " I knew him from my childhood, and a more amiable, noble-hearted, gallant, talented, and devoted soldier has seldom existed." " And I can bear witness," writes Sir William Gomm, " with many, many more, to the unsullied purity of his mind and whole course of life, the warmth and tenderness of his affections, and, combined with his rare proficiency in severe science, the childlike freshness of nature and feeling which Mr. Gladstone so happily instances in the character of the lamented Prince Consort—animating him and abiding with him to the last of his days."

The time had come when this life was to be laid down—laid down in sorrow, but in calmness, with a pious trust in his Redeemer, and still thinking of his fellow-men. A stranger solicited his opinion of an apparatus he had invented for steering, and he began to answer the letter with the hand of death upon him. " It is my duty," he replied to entreaties to refrain. But he could not finish.

" There was no appearance of disease," writes Mr. Bateman to the author. " Even his teeth were perfect, and, if he could have been induced to take the repose which he had so well earned, his life would in all probability have been prolonged for many years." The kind doctor warned him against such toil. " Of what consequence is it whether I live a year or two more or less?" he replied. " I never was idle, and it is misery to me to be so. I have served my Queen and country, not unprofitably I hope, and it is the wish of my heart to die in harness."

But his resistance to armour-ships bore him down: his arguments met unbelief, or elicited taunts, and ceased to influence the public. He discovered the barrenness of fame after a life of success, and the harass and toil hastened his end. His thoughts turned to a better existence, for which he had prepared, and he always bade his family " good night " with a tender look, as if they should never meet again—for he remembered the fate of his father and daughter. But it was to fall otherwise with him. His children surrounded him at the last, and he passed away in their presence, in possession of his faculties, and assured of resurrection. Armour-ships proved vulnerable a few weeks later, leading to their renouncement by Mr. Fairbairn before the British Association; and it is remarkable that a letter arrived as Sir Howard expired, announcing his spontaneous election as an Associate of the Institute of Naval Architects, where his opinions had been most strongly opposed.

Yet he knew that he was right. "All that I have said about armour-ships will prove correct," he remarked, twenty-four hours before his death. "How little do they know of the undeveloped power of artillery!"

His services had won him the honours of the Bath, of which he was a Knight Commander in the Military Division and a Grand Cross in the Civil, wearing both decorations by the authority of the Prince Consort. He was also a Grand Cross of the Order of St. Michael and St. George; and Lord Palmerston offered him the Grand Cross of the Military Division of the Bath shortly before his death, but this he declined, alleging that he was "too old for such vanities." On the 9th of November, 1861, earthly distinctions ceased for him, and

> "He gave his honours to the world again,
> His blessed part to Heaven, and died in peace."

APPENDIX.

Opinion of the Duke of Wellington *on the Boundary Treaties.*

The difference of opinion between Great Britain and the United States respecting the true course and position of the St. Croix River appears important in the discussion of the question respecting the boundary in the following views.

The second article of the treaty says, "From the north-west angle of Nova Scotia, viz., that angle which is formed by a line drawn due north from the source of the St. Croix River to the Highlands," &c.

The conclusion to be drawn from the perusal of this article is that the position of the river St. Croix must have been known to both parties when the treaty was concluded; and it must be supposed to have been the intention of both to fix the north-west angle of Nova Scotia upon a point in the Highlands due north of that position. This point had before been fixed, by the Commissioners of the United States, at the source of the St. John's River.

It appears, however, from subsequent transactions, that the real St. Croix River and the position of its real source were not known till the year 1794.

The British Commissioners considered the Penobscot to be the St. Croix. The river designated by that name in the treaty was at length fixed upon by Commissioners appointed under the article of the treaty of 1794.

Even if the position of the source of the St. Croix had been accurately known at the moment that the treaty of peace was concluded in the year 1783, the north-west angle of Nova Scotia as described in the second article remained to be found. That point depended on the Highlands described on

2 G

which the due north line from the source of the St. Croix should strike those Highlands.   But in the article as framed every-thing was to be discovered—the St. Croix River, its course, its source ; the due north line from that source, and the point at which that due north line should touch the Highlands.

It is very important that the arbitrator who shall decide the difference which has arisen under the treaty of Ghent should understand exactly what passed respecting the St. Croix River and its source; and seeing how little was known of that important point at the time the article was drawn, should seek for the intentions of the parties from other sources of information besides the words of the article itself.

We should attend to the original instructions of the Com-missioners of the United States in 1779; to the admission which they contain that the north-west angle of Nova Scotia was to be found at the source of the river St. John; to the geographical features of the country; and to the distinction which clearly exists between the term *sea* and the term *Atlantic Ocean*, and between those parts of the sea called respectively Atlantic Ocean, Bay of Fundy, Bay of Chaleurs, and Gulf of St. Lawrence, in the diplomatic act referred for his arbitration.   It is quite clear that neither party knew what was the real source of the St. Croix River.   Is it not probable, considering the source of the negociation of the definitive treaty, that both parties considered it to be placed further to the westward than it has been found to be ?   In that case the due north line from that point would have struck the Highlands not far from the source of the river St. John.

Translation of one of the Addresses presented to SIR HOWARD
DOUGLAS *by the Chiefs of the Spanish Alarms.*

To BARON DOUGLAS.

" SIR,
> "Sn. Esteban deribas del Sil,
> 4th April, 1812.

" When I was anxiously expecting to see you, Sir, in
this province of Orense, in order to have the honour of paying
you my respects as the most beneficent representative of the
British Nation, and to present to you my Company of Alarm
(in which although you would not find military men for
parade, yet you would meet with a few brave Mountain
Tirailleurs, good Spaniards, lovers of their religion, their
country, and their King, which they have proved at the time
of the first invasion of the enemy, and are ready to do it
again, if again he dared to invade us, if the Nation would
assist us with such articles as are necessary to render this
point inaccessible), my heart was overwhelmed with grief to
learn that you had returned to Corunna, and the motives you
had for taking that step; my grief was increased when I
announced to my companions your return, as I saw that it
filled them with the same sentiments, to see their hopes
frustrated, and thus deprived of the aid and protection they
expected to receive from you, Sir. They expressed their
sorrow to me in these very words: 'Why, Sir, should we
molest ourselves with exercising and sacrificing our families
and properties when we see that fortune is so very adverse to
us? If till now after so many sacrifices we have not been
able to advance a step, what shall we do now without them?
And what can we do without arms, without ammunition, and
without hopes that the generous nation who assisted us will
furnish us?' These and other such plaints which they expressed to me, filled my breast with sighs, and I could not
help exposing the whole to you, adding, that if the represen-
tatives of the Spanish Nation do not take a leading part with
regard to the opposition of the military in the organisation of
the Alarms and their armament, this same Alarm will

2 G 2

become a monstrosity and its enthusiasm be turned into a lamentable terror.

" I have sworn with them to defend these points at the cost of my life; for this purpose we need arms of every description; my means and faculties are already sacrificed for the benefit of the country; I supplicate you, Sir, in the name of the whole, that you will assist us with those necessary articles, and may the Almighty preserve you many years, &c.

" (Signed)   Br. José Rozal."

Sir Howard Douglas *and* General Foy.

The following paper was drawn up by Sir Howard on the operations of General Foy in 1812, and submitted to him on his visiting England in 1817 by the Right Hon. W. Wickham :—

" After the retreat of the Galician army before General Foy, from Valladolid and Tordebaton, in August, 1812, to Benavente and La Bañeza, it was an object of extreme solicitude to me, in the then critical state of the campaign, to ascertain in time what General Foy would attempt when he should hear of the fall of Astorga; being persuaded, from his character, that he would attempt some important blow.

" On Friday night, the 21st of August, I was in a small village near the Bañeza, and remained the next day near that place, after the Spanish Division had retired from Castrocontrigo and Torneros. Having ascertained General Baron Foy's march to be in the direction of Tabra, I imagined the following to be his aim. That he would march rapidly upon Carvajales; by gaining which point before the Portuguese Division then before Zamora, he would certainly have captured that division; and as Toro as well as Zamora was in possession of the French, I suspected that, should General Foy succeed in his well-arranged plan against the Portuguese, that he would then attempt a *coup de main* upon Salamanca. Lord Wellington was then at Madrid with the

bulk of his force, and one division was at Cuillar. Salamanca
was left with a very weak garrison, and the trophies of the
victory, and was the chief entrepôt on the line of communication with Portugal.

"Apprehending this, I sent instant information to the Conde
de Amaranthe, and entreated him to raise the blockade of
Zamora, cross the Esla, and get through Carvajales as soon as
possible, for that Baron Foy would certainly attempt to anti-
cipate him upon that point.

"I should very much like to know if I was right on the
whole case, and how near the Baron was to succeed in the
part he *did execute* against the Portuguese Division.

"*Farnham, March 25th,* 1817."

General Foy appended to these observations the following
remarks :—

"L'officier qui a écrit ceci a parfaitement deviné les intentions du Général de Division Comte Foy pendant les opérations du mois d'Août, 1812.

"L'Empereur Napoléon attachoit la plus haute importance
à la conservation d'Astorga. Cette place n'avoit des vivres
que jusqu'au 10 Août, tout au plus.

"Aussitôt qu'on eut acquis dans l'armée Française la certi-
tude du mouvement de Lord Wellington sur Madrid, on
résolut de se porter en avant, et de délivrer les garnisons laissées
précédemment à Toro, Zamora, et Astorga. Le Général
Clauzel commandoit l'armée par intérim, comme plus ancien
Général de Division. Le Général Foy fut chargé de détache-
ment, comme dans le second.

"Le Général Foy proposa au Général Clauzel de partir de
Valencia pour Astorga. Celui-ci, ne croyant pas que la place
fut très-pressé, mit de la lenteur dans les ordres. Le Général
Foy ne put partir de Valladolid avec deux divisions d'infanterie, et quinze ou seize autres chevaux, que le 17 Août, à
cinq heures du soir.

"Le Général Foy, passant à peu de distance de Toro, appella
à lui la garnison de Toro, qui n'avoit été bloqué que par des

guerrillas Espagnoles, et continua sa marche sur Astorga. Il eut le 19 sur l'Ezla, près Benavente, un engagement avec l'arrière-garde de l'armée de Galice, qu'il fut impossible d'arrêter. Le 20, à trois heures après midi, en entrant à la Bañeza, il apprit qu'Astorga s'étoit rendu la veille, et que le Général Castaños* se retiroit en hâte sur le chemin de Villafranca.

" Dès lors l'opération principale étoit manquée. Le Général Foy voulut que son mouvement ne fut pas inutile. Il savait que la division de Milice Portugaise du Comte Amaranto était devant Zamora, faisant un simulacre de siège; il voulut l'enlever. A cet effet il se dirigea de la Bañeza sur Miranda du Douro. Il étoit impossible qu'une pareille marche restât secrète, dans la disposition unanime des habitants contre l'armée Française. Le Général Foy arriva à Tabra le 23, dans l'après-midi. Il apprit là que les Portugais n'avoient pas encore évacué Carvajalis.

" Dès l'entrée de la nuit du 23 au 24, le Général Foy se mit en route dans la direction de Miranda du Douro. Les troupes étoient horriblement fatiguées, et la pointe du jour le 24 l'avant-garde de cavalerie Française aperçut l'arrière-garde des Portugais, qui se retiroient en grande hâte sur Constantin. La cavalerie Française étoit mal commandée, et ne fit pas ce qu'elle devoit et pouvait faire. L'infanterie étoit à deux lieues en arrière. Le Général Foy courut avec trente ou quarante chevaux sur la colonne de Selviera, et l'attaquoit à l'entrée du Portugal, dans un pays difficile. Elle étoit assez serrée pour exiger qu'on tirât contre elle quelques coups de fusil. On ne pourroit pas courir à l'entamer avec trente ou quarante chevaux fatigués. Le Général Foy fut obligé de se contenter de quelques prisonniers faits à dehors de la colonne.

" Le Général Foy arriva le 25 à Zamora, avec le projet de se porter à Salamanque, où étoient les hôpitaux, les bagages de l'armée Anglaise, et plusieurs officiers généraux, parmi lesquels le Maréchal Beresford. Il se proposoit de marcher en deux colonnes, l'une dirigée sur Salamanque, l'autre sur [blank]. C'est avec cette dernière qu'auroit été la plus

---

¹ Castaños, instead of being with the army, was at Villafranca.

grande partie de la cavalerie.   Les dispositions étoient faites pour cette opération ; le succès étoit infaillible ; mais on eut dans ce moment des avis secrets de Madrid, desquels il résultoit que Lord Wellington alloit partir avec son armée de cette capitale pour se porter à Valladolid, et peut-être même en droiture à Burgos.   Le Général Clauzel prescrivit au Général Foy de se rapprocher de l'armée.   Les avis reçus de Madrid étoient fondés.   Lord Wellington arriva à Arevolo trois ou quatre jours après que le Général Foy étoit arrivé à Tordesillas."

THE END.

LONDON : PRINTED BY W. CLOWES AND SONS, STAMFORD STREET,
AND CHARING CROSS.